Also by Chet Williamson
published by Tor Books

Lowland Rider

Chet Williamson

Ash Wednesday

TOR
HORROR

A TOM DOHERTY ASSOCIATES BOOK
NEW YORK

This is a work of fiction. All the characters and events portrayed in this book are fictitious, and any resemblance to real people or events is purely coincidental.

ASH WEDNESDAY

A TOR Book
Published by Tom Doherty Associates, Inc.
49 West 24 Street
New York, NY 10010

Cover art by Lee MacLeod

ISBN: 0-812-52720-8   Can. ISBN: 0-812-52721-6

Library of Congress Catalog Card Number: 86-50957

First edition: February 1987
First mass market printing: April 1989

Printed in the United States of America

0 9 8 7 6 5 4 3 2 1

TO MY MOTHER AND FATHER

The plots of God are perfect.
The Universe is a Plot of God.
—Edgar Allan Poe, Eureka

PROLOGUE:

A Resident of Merridale

For the whole town, I suddenly realised, was something other than I so far saw it. The real activities and interests of the people were elsewhere and otherwise than appeared. Their true lives lay somewhere out of sight behind the scenes. Their busy-ness was but the outward semblance that masked their actual purposes. They bought and sold, and ate and drank, and walked about the streets, yet all the while the main stream of their existence lay somewhere beyond my ken, underground, in secret places.

—Algernon Blackwood, "Ancient Sorceries"

The dogs saw it first.

It was very early on a Friday morning, a few hours before sunrise, when they noticed the glow. The first to start barking were Sim Peters's two foxhounds, lying together on top of their doghouse in Sim's backyard. Mitzi's nostrils flared at the glow, even though she could sense no strange scent. Her low growl woke Mike beside her, who, at the sight of the lights, immediately sent up a shrill baying. A few backyards away the Smiths' Great Dane took up the cry, and soon all three were yelping. As the animals looked from the hill down into the shallow depression that had given Merridale its name, they saw more and more dim pools of light take form below, man-shaped nebulae that gleamed darkly, in muted contrast to the bright streetlamps that poured specks of diffused whiteness across the town in the early-morning mist.

That the images were those of naked and unmoving human beings meant nothing to the dogs. All that Mike and Mitzi and Jocko knew, as Rex and Spike and Butch and King and every other dog in Merridale just as quickly learned, was that they were alien, something that did not belong, and that

3

barking at them might frighten them away, or draw the masters out to chase them off or ask what they wanted in the dogs' dominions.

So the dogs barked, and one by one they woke one another, from street to street, house to house, until all of Merridale resounded with their ragged voices.

And slowly the people of Merridale woke, and rose, and discovered.

Marty Sanders sat bolt upright in his bed, a sheen of terror-sweat covering his body, making his cotton pajamas stick to his hairless back like flour paste. He'd had the dream again. Over six months now and still that damned dream of that damned night. Dotty stirred in the bed beside him and cleared her throat in the darkness. He could make out the large lumpish shape of her in the cool blue glow of the clock-radio numerals.

"Marty?" she slurred sleepily. "Y'okay?"

"Yeah. Yeah, sure," he told his wife, who grunted noncommittally.

But he wasn't okay, and wondered if he ever would be again. He flopped back onto his pillow and looked up at the black ceiling, his tired mouth open in a grimace of self-loathing. He ran his fingers through his damp thinning hair and finally dried his forehead with a tissue. He felt sick.

When he remembered what he had done, how he had done it, he always felt sick. Even though no one would ever know, would ever grasp him by the arm and drag him away to pay for what he'd done, he still felt sick.

One time. One time in thirty years of marriage he had cheated and look how it had ended. It had seemed so *safe*— Dotty out of town visiting her mother in Lauderdale for two weeks, his running into Sheila Sommers outside the 7-Eleven, her teasing him, talking about last summer at the pool and asking him if he had liked her bathing suit, and then asking where his wife was, and when he told her, her saying how lonely he must be in that big house all by himself and wouldn't a little company be nice and no one would know.

Something had happened then that had totally surprised

4

him. Thirty years of husbandly fidelity, fifty years of moral training had slipped off of him like a robe off a whore's shoulders, and he said yes. A little company *would* be nice.

Even now, he could scarcely believe he had done it, but he had. They went back to his house. The outside lights were off, and they were out too far for streetlights, so the chance of being spotted by his neighbors was unlikely. Once inside, they had a drink and talked—he about his business, she about her two failed marriages—and finally she just said, "Well, it's about time, isn't it?" and started to undress right there in the living room. By the time everything was off, they were in the bedroom and he was half undressed too. Then they did it, right there on the bed in which he and Dotty had slept for years, and goddamn if it hadn't been *good*. If *he* hadn't been good. But then she started teasing him. And right away he knew how stupid he'd been. He hadn't remembered, with her pressing up against him in the car on the way over, how she'd busted up Larry Drebbins's marriage with her big mouth, but now it came back to him all too clearly.

"Did ya like that?"

"Bet you haven't had it that good for a long time."

"Does your wife do it like that?"

"Wouldn't she die if she knew about us?"

"Maybe we oughta call her in Florida . . ."

And with each remark from the strange naked woman stretching and moving like a cat in heat beside him, his stomach tightened more and more and the memory of what had just occurred grew tasteless, then bitter. He realized that he had no idea what Sheila *would* do, but it might be something crazy. After all, wasn't she crazy enough to pick up married men outside the 7-Eleven?

"C'mon, let's call her."

He laughed, trying to reassure himself that she was joking.

She laughed too, but then looked at him half seriously. "What's the number?"

He laughed again, less jovially. "You're crazy."

"Maybe. What's the number?" He didn't say anything. "I'll find it," she said, rising from the bed. He followed her through the house until she found the personal directory by the kitchen phone. He could only stand and watch her, his own nakedness forgotten, as she flipped through it. "Here we go. Mom." She moved back into the bedroom then. "More comfy in here, huh, Marty?" When she picked up the phone was when he stopped her, grabbing her hand.

"Are you crazy?" he said, and then she said something horrible and laughed at him, and he got mad, so mad that he pushed her.

To stop her. Just to stop her.

The next thing he knew she was lying there and her eyes were open but she wasn't moving, and when he looked, there was this *thing* on her head like a lump, a knot. There wasn't even any blood. Just this *knot* on her head, and he couldn't remember if she'd hit the sharp corner of the headboard or the bedside table or *what*, and there was just this *lump* and her not moving or even *blinking*, and he knew, he knew even as upset as he was, that *live* people *blink*.

He was so scared he cried. Just cried and cried until he couldn't anymore. So he blew his nose into a wad of Kleenex from the bedside table and thought about what to do next. He considered calling the police, but talked himself out of it. All that would mean would be that they'd take him away. And even if they freed him, everybody would know. Dotty would know, Pastor Craven would know, Tom Markley—hell, the whole damn *town*. And it wouldn't bring her back, would it? It wasn't like he was a *criminal*, was it? What had he done? Self-preservation, that was it—she would have destroyed him. And his punishment wouldn't bring her back. Nothing would bring her back.

Back to tell the truth.

Once he made his choice, the emotion seemed to fade, at least for the moment, and analysis took over. She lived in an apartment house two blocks away from the town square, had probably walked to the 7-Eleven, and he was fairly sure that no one had seen him with her. If he could get her back to her building . . .

Everything slipped into place then, and he made himself wait until three in the morning, when all of Merridale was sleeping. He dressed Sheila slowly and awkwardly, nearly

6

panicking over his inability to fit her into her panty hose without twisting the legs. But after twenty minutes of back-breaking effort, she was dressed presentably enough that Martin Sanders felt confident that it would appear she had dressed herself. He took the scotch bottle from which she'd been drinking and splashed a bit on the front of her sweater and over her chin. Just enough, he thought. Don't overdo it. She drank, but she wasn't a drunk. And that's why, isn't it? That's why she fell—she wasn't used to it.

He was unable to pick her up, so he dragged her outside to his car and put her into the trunk on top of a blanket. On the way to her building he didn't pass a single car. It all went perfectly then—hauling her out, dragging her up the dimly lit stairway to her apartment, opening her door with her keys in *her* hand (fingerprints), turning on her lights, leaving the door open, and finally lifting her erect and letting her fall down the rubber-treaded concrete stairs. That was the worst. He was barely able to let her go, but he closed his eyes and forced himself to shove her slightly out so that she flopped loosely down the whole long flight, like a boneless rag doll, to strike her head with a dull *crack* at the bottom.

He ran then, ran down the steps, leaping fleetly over her, making himself slow down just a hair as he passed the sole streetlight on the way to his car parked in a shadowed corner. Then home. Home to a nightmare of stuffing soiled sheets in the washing machine, looking for long ash-blond hairs on the back of the couch, the upholstered headboard, everywhere, everywhere she'd stood, sat, lain.

The nightmare hadn't stopped there. It had continued even when the sheets were dry, the few hairs were found and flushed away, the glasses were washed and rinsed. It plagued him when the lights were out, when his eyes were closed, when dreams shredded his waking veil of forgetfulness.

The passage of months had not helped, nor did the total and unexpected success of his pulpish plot. Accidental death had been the ruling, had made him at least physically free. But he was still chained by the nightmares, and now he lay there, replaying them involuntarily on the dark ceiling. The pressure of his bladder temporarily took his mind off them and onto his tiring prostate. He rose and padded into the bathroom.

He had just finished when the dogs began to bark. Damn mutts, he thought. Four in the morning . . . never sleep now. He had just hit the flush lever when he heard Dotty scream.

The sound froze him, and the first thought that entered his mind was insane, irrational, and totally correct. *She knows*. He shivered, and thought again, *She knows*.

As he entered the bedroom, the blue glow was brighter than the clock radio had ever been, bright enough for him to see his wife huddled on the floor in the corner, staring and screaming at the slightly transparent corpse of Sheila Sommers lying on the bed in the same position in which she had died. Her eyes were still open and, like her entire accusing body, shone with a pale blue light.

Up to that moment, Martin Sanders had never thought that a man could scream more loudly than a woman.

Brad

A transgression, a crime, entering a man's existence, eats it up like a malignant growth, consumes it like a fever.

—Joseph Conrad, *Nostromo*

CHAPTER
1

Merridale had had its last sleep for a time. It seemed a village made for sleep, designed for a permanent, contented somnolence. From Interstate 79 it was already said to look like a town of the dead. But this image followed the actual event, the result of journalistic second-guessing, one of a slew of rapidly devised images for a poetry-hungry public.

For only in the poetry of image, metaphor, even parable, could the phenomenon of Merridale be dealt with by the ignorant, which included the entire human race in terms of truly understanding what had happened and how. *Why* was beyond even the wisest and greatest of the mystical. Poetry triumphed because prose was too stark, too frighteningly clear in the pictures it drew. So Merridale, from afar, was "a town of the dead, nestled among the hills of Pennsylvania like a curled and sleeping giant."

But Merridale had not been as the press later described it. Instead, it had been a bustling little village of 8,000 inhabitants that showed few signs of growth, but fewer still of deterioration. As it did not welcome strangers, neither did it shun them. But one had to have a *reason* to live there, either

11

ancestral or occupational. No one, thought the townspeople, should live in Merridale who did not either work there or grow up there or have a job nearby, nearby generally defined as within a fifteen-mile radius of the town. It was a town where people worked hard, went to church, seldom cheated on their mates, drank moderately, took only prescribed drugs, and nursed their frustrations without giving them reign. It was strongly Republican, overwhelmingly Protestant, universally white. It was no different from half a hundred other towns in the area—no better or worse, no more tolerant or bigoted.

Merridale sat at the base of a glacial ridge. From the town below, the ridge, denuded of trees and pocked with small ranch houses, looked like the spine of some great beast lying facedown just beneath the earth's surface, arching its back as it had for years in an effort to break through the rocky soil and free itself. This stark mound was called the mount, and the town at the bottom, the dale, though why the trappers who had settled the area in the early eighteenth century had called it merry was a secret lost in time.

Like the legs of Ozymandias, the spine above Merridale was the only break in the surrounding landscape for many miles. A rolling hill lay on the other side of the town, but its height was only half that of the ridge, although it enabled the town to be described as lying in a quiet valley, the only valley for as far as the eye could see. All about was the unrelieved flatness of farms, broken by occasional towns and cities, the largest of which was Lansford, fifteen miles southeast, to which a good portion of Merridale residents drove daily to work, or boarded the first or second Amtrak train of the day, depending on whether their collars were blue or white, whether they bore paper bags or briefcases.

The farms were everywhere, rich with the bounty of dark soil. Unlike the withering earth of the plains states, leached out by chemicals and weakened by corporate interests that strove to make the land produce as much in as short a time as possible, most of the farms were still in private hands, many run by members of Amish or Mennonite sects who farmed the way their fathers and grandfathers had before them, caring for the land with a near-religious devotion, almost worshiping it, as further removed ancestors had adored the sun and rain that nurtured that same soil.

Because of the farms, Merridale could easily have been self-supporting had the need arisen. There were hogs, sheep, a few stringy herd of beef cattle, as well as all the vegetation necessary to life, even tobacco, which grew in great fields of flat green. Dozens of chicken farms and egg ranches completed the menu. But Merridale was not and never would be self-sufficient. It was too much a part of its county, its state, its country, to become a separate unit, though before too long county, state, and country alike would wish it out of existence.

The thought of his town and its people was far from Bradley Meyers's mind when the dogs woke him from a sound sleep. All he knew was that he was mad. It generally took hours for him to drift into a repose as solid as the one that had just been shattered, and his first response was rage. The alarm clock read just past four, and he knew any sleep he could grab until he had to get up at six would be ragged, unsatisfying, pierced with consciousness. He muttered a curse and kicked his feet out over the side of the bed. The covers slipped off Christine's shoulders and he pulled them back up over her roughly, wishing that he could sleep through anything, as she did.

. He threw on his terry-cloth bathrobe and stepped into the hall, listening for a second at Wally's door to the thick asthmatic snores that told him the boy was sleeping. Brad sighed and ran his fingers through his long, straggly hair. Might as well make coffee, he thought glumly. Those dogs aren't gonna shut up. He went into the bathroom, drained the remainder of the previous night's beer, and was rinsing night fuzz from his mouth when the sirens started up. It was weird, he thought. It was usually sirens first, *then* the dogs, not the other way around. If there were a fire, it might be nearby. Maybe he could even see it from a window. That would be one way to pass the hours until dawn.

He saw the man in his living room out of the corner of his eye as he was walking to the kitchen. He wasn't sure what

13

he'd expected to see when he turned and looked. Someone with a gun, perhaps, or a knife, someone wearing a look of surprise tinged with aggressiveness, someone who would hiss a warning not to move or he'll shoot. What he did not expect to see was an old naked black man standing half in and half out of the sofa, as though it were quicksand into which he was sinking.

His mind thought, Jesus, but his voice could not even whisper it. Fright had clogged his throat, thickened his lungs, and he could only stand and stare at the softly gleaming figure who looked not at him but at some unnamed spot a few feet to Brad's left. The man was terribly emaciated, and Brad fancied he could see the outline of the backbone pressing against the diaphragm. The arms and thighs were like sticks, and the neck that supported the grizzled head was not much thicker. That head was capped with a gray-white patch of hair and mapped with wrinkles. The genitals were shrunken into insignificance.

The sirens wailed, the dogs howled, and Bradley Meyers stood shaking, waiting for something to happen, for the man to turn, to disappear, to move toward him holding out a pencil-fingered hand. But the man did *not* move, not at all, not even to sway like a leaf in the breeze. He only stood, his lower legs and feet lost in the worn-out sofa, looking languidly at that spot until Brad turned and looked too, trying to keep half an eye on the withered figure.

There was nothing there, just the wall with the big red, black, and white Nazi flag Brad had had there for years. Could he be looking at that?

What the hell does it matter what he's looking at! Brad thought savagely, turning back to the wispy figure. He tried to speak, cleared his throat, tried again. "Hey," he said softly. "What . . . Are you for real?"

There was no answer, no tremor of understanding in the old man's countenance.

"What *are* you?"

Still no answer. Just the old man standing there, shining weakly, and as Brad's eyes became adjusted to the poor light, he thought he could see the opposite wall through the

14

man's body. *A ghost*, he thought with numbing certainty. *A ghost*.

"Chris," he called, but the bedsprings did not squeak, she was not coming. "Chris!" he barked, and he heard an answering moan from the bedroom. "Come here!" His words did not banish the thing. It still stood silently, as if it too were waiting for Christine.

"What is it?" she called, her speech sleep-dulled.

"Just . . . come *here*." He heard her bare feet on the floor, the rustle of her robe as it left the hook, her footfalls down the hall, a deep yawn in which irritation was evident.

"Jeez, Brad, it's four in the—"

"Shut up. Look at that. Do you see that?"

Behind him, she drew in breath for a scream that never left her. She stood, breath locked, over an abyss that reached up with dark hands to catch her, unable to scream, to breathe, to move. Brad turned and saw her chained features, her mouth like a great black "O" in the blackness around her, and knew that she saw it too. Finally her breath blew out in a whistling whimper that held such terror and helplessness that he put his arms around her, blocking her view of the old man.

But she gazed straight into his chest as though she saw it still, then closed her eyes as the first paroxysm of fear shivered out of her. "Oh, migod, migod, migod," she whispered in a rapid litany. "Who is it, who is it?"

And because he did not know he said nothing.

"Who *is* it!" she grated, clawing at his arm. "What's he want? Who *is* he?"

"Let *go*," he said, pushing her away to where she could see the old man once more. She whimpered again, transfixed by the sight, unable to turn her eyes away. Outside the sirens screamed. "It's a ghost," he said over their wail. "What else? It's a ghost."

"Nooo . . ."

"Look at it! You can see *through* it." Bradley Meyers felt a strange excitement interwoven with his fear, pushing it down on the loom of his emotions until it faded into the background like a neutral color in a field of vivid red, leaving

15

only that intense *interest*, an overpowering need to *know*. He had seen too much of life to be scared for long by the semblance of death. Now he felt the adrenaline surge within him, and all he could think was "What is it? What is it?"—concerned only with the knowing, not with fear. He moved toward it slowly, with a healthy respect for the unknown, his tongue licking his dry lips.

"Brad . . . don't—"

"Shut up," he hissed. She knew better than to disobey, but the room seemed filled with her hoarse panting. Brad shuffled closer, until he was only a few feet away, then reached out a hand. But something he could not name stopped him from touching the man, and instead he moved to the side, grasping the arm of the couch, which he slowly slid toward himself.

The couch moved easily enough, its worn casters creaking as they rolled over the carpet. But the old man's body did not move, and soon his lower legs and most of his feet were revealed. It seemed to Brad that the bottom half inch of flesh sank into and became part of the carpet.

"Brad . . ." He looked at Christine. Her face was pinched and she was shaking, tears running down her cheeks.

"Go back in the bedroom."

"Oh, Brad . . ."

"Go *on*." She slowly backed away toward the hall. When she could no longer see the old man, she turned and ran to the bedroom, slamming the door behind her, her frenzied sobs still clearly audible in the living room.

Bradley Meyers swallowed and cleared a piece of phlegm from his throat. Then he walked in front of the old man so that he stood directly before his gaze, staring into the blue-lustered eyes. He felt nothing, no suggestion of being looked inside of, no psychic tingle. It was merely like looking into the eyes of a particularly well-rendered statue. He stepped out of the line of its gaze then, and walked closer to it. It stood, seemingly relaxed, arms hanging loosely at its sides, not noticing that he approached. Now only a foot away, Brad steeled himself as he did when he was a child taking his first plunge off the high board, and tried to touch the old man's arm.

At first he thought that perhaps he *was* afraid, that though his conscious mind wanted to touch whatever was there, his terrified subconscious would not permit it, keeping his fingers from coming into contact with the blue-black skin. But then he realized with a start that he *was* touching it, or touching the space it filled. His fingertips seemed to be *inside* the old man's flesh, although he could still see them, dim and hazy, like phantom fingers. He withdrew them quickly, then carefully put them back again. In, out, in, out, making contact without feeling or sensation. There was not a trace of coldness, wetness, warmth, *anything*.

"You really *are* a ghost," he said in awe. But the black man did not confirm or deny Brad's statement. He only stood, unaware of the young man touching him, looking patiently at the spot on Brad's Nazi flag.

"Brad!" Christine's cry came from their bedroom. It was high and fluttery as if the madness that had been stalking her had at last taken hold, and Brad turned from the apparition and ran down the hall, hoping that the black man would still be there when he returned.

When he opened the bedroom door, Christine was standing at the window, the curtain drawn back. She was looking out onto Market Street below. "What's wrong?" he asked curtly. She only shook her head in short birdlike jerks, unable to turn away from the window. "What *is* it?" He went to her, jostled her aside, and looked out.

The street was filled with ghosts. Blue shapes stood, sat, reclined, all of them gleaming dimly like dozens of broken neon signs. Some were half in, half out of parked cars, just as the black man had been partially encased by the sofa. Across the street in the parking lot where a transient hotel had stood until the late fifties, vertical rows of naked blue bodies, men and women alike, hung stationary in the air. One of them, laden with fat, was in a half crouch, as if in the process of falling. His right arm was up, elbow out, in the position of holding something unseen to his throat, which gaped with a wound from which a gout of dark liquid hung

17

suspended. Brad could see the thick ropiness of the man's severed windpipe.

Near him a young woman lay on her side in midair, her belly bloated with pregnancy. Her hands were jammed between her legs, her eyes were closed, her mouth open in an unheard howl. Most of the apparitions were older, but many were young and middle-aged, and there were more than a few children. Brad noticed one boy no older than ten lying in the doorway to the Murphy Apartments across the street. Only the top half of his body was visible through the door, but Brad could see that he was lying facedown like a bearskin rug, arms out in front of him, his chin resting on the rough sidewalk, his head cocked awkwardly. The pale blue glowing eyes looked up toward the window where Brad stood with Christine whining and shivering beside him, and something in the eyes froze Brad for a second, as though they were speaking to him, trying to make him remember something long forgotten.

"Brad . . ." Christine whimpered.

"*Shh!*"

"Brad, let's *go!*"

"Shut *up!*" he snarled, turning to her, furious at her for invading his thoughts just as he almost had it, just as he'd nearly remembered.

But she would not be quiet. She shook her head back and forth, her eyes darting to the window and away again. "No," she said. "We gotta get out—we gotta leave—"

"Leave? Leave what?"

"Leave this place, leave this . . . this . . . this *town!* We gotta get *away!*"

"For the last time, Chris, *shut up*. We're not going anywhere, so just shut the fuck up. Get back in bed and pull the covers over your head, or go hide in the closet, but don't you open your goddamn mouth *again!*" He shoved her to punctuate his order, and her body rocked back so that she fell weeping to the floor, from which she crawled up onto the bed and under the covers, pulling them over her head.

Now, Brad thought. Now who . . .

"Whassamatter?"

18

He turned, his teeth grinding together in anger, to see Wally standing in the doorway, his outgrown Fred Flintstone pajamas leaving his round tummy bare and vulnerable. "Go back to bed."

"I heard Mommy—"

"Go back to *bed!*" Brad shouted, crossing the small room in a bound and pushing the boy across the hallway and against the opposite wall. Wally's lip quivered, but he did not cry, only picked himself up and padded head down back into his room. Christine whimpered loudly under the covers, as if the blow had hurt her as well as her son, but she said nothing. Brad looked out the window at the boy half on the sidewalk, half hidden by the door, and let the sirens drown out her cries.

He struggled, trying to remember, to recall so long ago, so many years, the summers past, the town park, rubber horse-shoes and snowcones, *and now he was starting to get it,* trading baseball cards and drinking Double Cola and riding down those steep dirt paths over the bank on their bikes with devil's head decals and pinwheel spinners and *box hockey,* oh, Christ yes, the kid who *always* beat everybody at box hockey, and he could see long ago the knuckles covered with Band-Aids and the same hands outstretched *now* on the side-walk with those scabs and cuts and bruises and (Andy) that shock of wheat-colored hair (Andy Koser) and the ears that stuck out too far . . .

Andy Koser.

CHAPTER
2

"Oh, no . . . oh, no . . . oh, what a shame, May." Mrs. Meyers seemed glued to the phone. Her head was shaking back and forth, and Brad knew it was something bad. Probably nothing that touched them or their family because Mom wasn't crying, but something bad just the same. His appetite was swiftly disappearing the longer his mother clucked, and he dabbed at the stiffening Maypo with a spoon, building a small dam to hold the milk from the center. He hoped she would hang up before he had to go to school so he could find out what the news was, but she showed no signs of putting down the phone, and his Hopalong Cassidy wristwatch told him he'd have to leave now if he wanted to meet Al Withers on the corner of Orange and Spruce.

"Mom . . ." he said softly, standing up.

She heard and raised a hand to tell him to wait, still enrapt by what Mrs. Nolt was telling her.

"I gotta go, Mom."

She tightened her face and gave him one of her pruney looks. "Brad's got to go, May," she said into the phone. "Call you right back, 'kay? . . . Uh-huh. Bye-bye." She

21

hung up with a reluctant sigh. "Okay, hon. Got your lunch?" He held up his lunch pail and she nodded approvingly. "Eat all the celery now, okay? And the apple."

"What was wrong, Mom?"

"Oh, on the phone? Well . . ." She looked away—at the sink filled with breakfast dishes, then at his half-eaten Maypo. "Oh, you didn't finish your cereal. . . ."

"What was it? Something I shouldn't know about?"

She squared her shoulders as if about to tackle a particularly rotten job, like cleaning the oven. "No. No reason why you shouldn't. Do you know the Koser boy?"

"Andy?"

"Is he the one close to your age?"

"Uh-huh."

"Well, he had an accident. You know the Murphy Apartments?"

Brad nodded. He and his cousin had gone to Andy's one time last summer to trade for a Richie Ashburn card.

"Well, there's a steep stairway up to the second floor where the Kosers live, and . . . Andy fell down it."

"He fell down the *stairs?*"

"Uh-huh."

"Was he hurt?"

His mother's face wrinkled up again and she nodded shortly. "Yeah, hon. Real bad. He's, uh . . . Andy's dead."

"Dead?"

"Uh-huh."

"From . . . just from fallin' down the *stairs?*"

She nodded. "Mrs. Nolt said he broke his neck. Died very fast. I don't think he suffered at all."

Brad swallowed hard. The Maypo was dancing and churning in his stomach. "When was it?"

"Last night after supper. Mrs. Nolt found out because Mr. Nolt is on the ambulance crew. Seems Andy was going out to play baseball down at the park and he just tripped or something."

Brad bit the inside of his lip. He didn't think he was going to cry, but he didn't know what else the feeling that was boiling up inside him could be. "Maybe . . . uh . . . maybe

22

his bat," he suggested in an effort to seem detached, adult.

"His bat?"

"Maybe he tripped on it."

"Oh. Well, yes, maybe he did." His mother bent and kissed him on the cheek. "You'd better run now if you're not going to be late." She seemed uncomfortable, as she did whenever his father told a joke that had anything to do with s-e-x. "If you want, we could talk some more about this tonight. Or with your father when he gets home." She smiled wanly. "Go on now. Watch the street corners."

He was a little late, but Al Withers was waiting for him anyway. "Ya hear about Andy Koser?" was the first thing he said.

"Yeah," Brad answered. "Mrs. Nolt called my mom."

"Mine too. Bet she musta started around six this morning. Bet *everybody* knows." They walked for a while without speaking. "Boy," Al said at last, "it's really weird, isn't it?"

"Yeah."

"You ever know anybody else that died?"

"My grandma. But she was pretty old." Brad had been six at the time, three years before. His maternal grandmother had gotten lung cancer after smoking a pack of Luckies a day since her twenties. Her husband, a retired railroad man, had had to quit years before, after a bout with TB. Brad thought his grandfather's house smelled a lot better now.

"All my grandparents are still alive," said Al with a trace of pride. Then his smug smile turned into a frown. "I wonder what happened."

"You mean how he fell?"

"Naw, I mean after. You know, did he go to heaven or what?"

"I guess so. He was kind of a good guy."

"You believe in heaven?" Al asked.

Brad didn't answer right away. "Yeah, I guess."

"Me too. I guess."

"I don't think my dad does. He doesn't go to church or anything. And when I ask him about God and all, he just says he doesn't have much time to think about that."

"He an *atheist?*" Al's eyes got big.

"No!" Brad replied. "I didn't say that. He just doesn't *think* about it much." He spotted a bottle cap on the sidewalk and they shuffle-kicked it back and forth for a while until Al missed and it went into the gutter. "I wonder if he *did* go to heaven," Brad said.

"Sure. What would God send a little kid to hell for? Cheatin' at box hockey?"

"Andy didn't cheat—he was just good."

"You're not supposed to block the puck with your knuckles."

"Ah, you're just too scared of getting hurt to do it."

"So are you," Al shot back, and it was true. Brad had always admired the nonchalant way Andy Koser had taken the sharp raps of the rough wooden puck on his knuckles without complaint. He'd once asked Andy if it didn't hurt. Andy'd grinned and said, "Sure, but if you wanta win, you gotta get your knuckles stung." Brad didn't think winning was worth that.

"I wonder," mused Al, "how he . . . uh . . . how he looks. You know?"

Brad nodded.

"I mean, how long before he . . . before bodies start to rot?"

"Pretty fast."

"Yeah, I guess. You think he'll have those white worms— what are they?"

"Maggots?"

"Yeah, that's them. Like in that Edgar Allan Poe movie. You think he'll have them?"

"Dunno," said Brad. "Probably not. I don't think you get them when you're embalmed."

"They got tighter coffins today too, huh?"

"Oh, yeah." They walked on. Brad didn't know what was in Al's head, but in his own there were things he hoped he could forget about before he went to bed that night. Things like losing his balance and falling, the same kind of feeling as when the Comet at Dobbs's Park went over the first ridge, dropping the coaster down that long chute so that you seemed

24

to fall forever. But there you never hit bottom—there the pavement never came up smack against your head. To kill you.

Kill you. Brad tried to imagine what being dead was like, but couldn't. He could only think of it as a long sleep from which you'd never wake up. In his heart he really couldn't conceive of heaven, of a place with clouds and harps and wings and white robes and everybody flying around and singing all day about how great God was. It just didn't seem right. He tried, but he just couldn't make himself believe it. Then *that* worried him, because in the back of his mind he *did* believe in hell. Or at least in punishment. Now he tried to picture Andy Koser in heaven and found the spectacle ludicrous. Andy Koser, with his turned-up nose and those Dumbo ears that stuck out way past the limits of his butch cut, sitting on a cloud with King David and Moses and George Washington, and all of them singing hymns. . . . If they didn't have box hockey and baseball cards in heaven, Andy was going to be pretty bored. "You think," he asked Al, "they got baseball cards in heaven?"

"You nuts?" Al answered, giving him a funny look. "C'mon, we better run. Gettin' late."

They ran, and made it to school on time. Mrs. Wrigley, the principal, told their class about Andy being killed, and added that any children who wanted to donate money toward a "floral memory" could leave it with their teacher. Some of the girls cried, and so did one or two of the boys, though they bit their lips and jammed their fists in their eyes to stop themselves. Scott Jones, who knew Andy better than most of them in fourth grade, snapped the pencil he was holding in two when he heard Mrs. Wrigley's announcement, then looked at it stupidly as though wondering why he'd done it.

The day went as slowly as any before, and Brad thought and thought about Andy, about his grandmother, about death. At home that night neither his mother nor his father mentioned the subject, although when his father tucked him in he asked if there was anything bothering Brad, anything he wanted to talk about. Brad told him there wasn't, so his father said good-night and left the boy alone.

25

He lay there in his bed in the dark, listening to his parents' footsteps as they went back downstairs, the low hum of their voices talking softly so that he could make out only the inflections, not the words themselves, then silence, broken in a minute by the muffled roar of the TV set, of dimly heard lines and the audience's laughter.

He lay there listening to himself breathing, putting his hand on his heart to feel the low but distinct pounding beneath his flesh and bone. Andy's heart isn't pounding, he thought. Andy's heart isn't doing anything.

He put his hand at his side and stared up at the black ceiling, frighteningly aware of the rise and fall of his chest under the bedclothes, going up and down, up and down, unlike Andy's chest that was now so still, and would never rise or fall again. And then thoughts came that had never come before—questions, concerns:

What makes me breathe?

What if I forget?

What if I fall asleep and I forget to breathe? Would I wake up or would I just die in my sleep?

What if my heart stops beating and I was asleep? How would I know to get it started again?

He lay there, afraid to go to sleep, afraid to trust his heart and lungs to keep working without his conscious supervision. And as he lay wondering and worrying, he started to think about swallowing his tongue when he slept and choking on it, of turning his head in a dream so that his nose pressed against the pillow, smothering him, of half a dozen other ways that death could come upon him in the night, quietly, unexpectedly. He had never been afraid before tonight, had never asked for a night-light or used the feeble excuses most children do to avoid being taken from their parents' side and thrust into the *Night*, the *Dark*, where the shadows wait. But now he was afraid to sleep, afraid even to close his eyes.

He lay there.

He lay there listening to the cars pass outside, listening to the TV below, listening as his parents finally climbed the stairs, ran the water in the bathroom, walked down the short hall to their own room, clicked the light switch so that the bright crack under his door died, drowned in darkness. The whole house was dark now, and soon the house would be asleep.

It was not until he heard his father snoring that he started to worry about his parents. They were older than he was, closer to Grandma's age, and he remembered Mel Rickert's dad dying last year of a heart attack in his sleep. He felt suddenly chilled, listening to his father's rumbling snores. He should listen for *him* too—stay awake to make sure *he* was all right. And his mother as well.

He slipped out of bed and opened his door, then stepped across the hall and went into his parents' room. His father's snores were louder now, but he could not hear his mother breathing. He tiptoed to her side and leaned down over her. It was too dark to see her covers rise and fall, but he heard a soft hissing and knew she was all right, she was alive.

He knelt by her side then, and finally lay down next to the big double bed, his head against the thinning carpet. It was hard beneath him, and he was glad, because he knew the discomfort would keep him awake. So he lay listening to their breaths, listening for his own, until sleep finally claimed him just before midnight.

His mother's cry woke him the next morning. "Brad!" she said. "Honey? What are you doing?"

"Whazzat?" His father's voice, phlegmy and thick.

Brad groaned as he moved, feeling as though all his muscles had been tied in knots. "I . . . uh . . . I got lonely."

"Lonely?" She giggled, not understanding.

"F'pete's sake," his father said. "You been there all night?"

Brad shrugged. "I dunno. I . . . I woke up . . . had a bad dream. I didn't . . . I didn't want to wake you up."

"Oh, boy." His father sat on the side of the bed and stretched. "Well, you got another hour before you have to get up for school, so why not sleep in a bed, huh? Come on."

"I'll make breakfast," his mother said, and disappeared.

Brad's father ruffled his hair and walked him back to his room. "Whatcher pillow on the floor for?" he asked.

27

"Guess I knocked it down while I was dreamin'."

"Rough dream?" He put the pillow back on the bed. Brad lay back against it.

"Uh-huh."

"Anything to do with . . . what happened the other day?"

"Huh?"

"With your friend Andy?"

Brad looked away from his father's face and down at the paisley pattern of his tentlike pajamas. "Yeah," he whispered. Then he started to cry.

"Hey, hey, what's the matter?" His father held him against his thick chest.

"I . . . I don't wanta die, Dad!" He was barely able to get the words out.

"Aw, aw, c'mon, sport," said his father, holding him clumsily. "Don't cry now, you're not gonna die . . . least-ways not for a long, long time. C'mon, hey, don't be a baby."

"I don't wanta die at *all*. And I don't want *you* to die neither. Or Mom."

"Everybody dies, Brad. But you won't die for a long time. Not for years and years."

"What about you?"

"Me neither."

"How d'ya *know?*" he wailed.

"Hey, I just *know*, okay? Trust me. I'm not gonna die for a long time."

"Andy Koser didn't think he was gonna die either. But he *did!*"

His father frowned. "Sometimes things like that happen. But not often. Not often enough to worry about. So just forget it."

"I *can't!*"

"Look," his father said, "nobody knows when they're gonna die, so it don't do you any good to worry about it. So just forget it." He stood up. "I gotta get dressed, I'll be late." Leaning down, he patted Brad's shoulder. "Don't worry," he said, and left.

Brad had never felt more alone. He sat up in bed and

waited for his alarm clock to go off. When it did, he dressed, ate breakfast silently, his mother puttering too busily around him, and went to school.

He slept little the following few days, but when he discovered that a week had gone by without any deaths by suffocation, he gradually forgot his fears, and even became less careful on stairs until eventually he reverted back to his old self.

Almost.

CHAPTER
3

"Andy Koser," Brad whispered in awe.

"What?" Christine's voice was muffled by the bedclothes over her head. "*What* did you *say?*" She was near hysteria.

"Come here," he said. She didn't move. "I said come *here.*"

"No . . . Why?"

"I want you to see something." He crossed to the bed.

"No . . ." She was crying when he pulled the covers off of her. "Please, Brad, *please*, don't *make* me!"

He dug a hand into her armpit and hauled her from the bed. She staggered, but remained erect, and he dragged her to the window.

"No," she blubbered, starting to thrash about in an effort to break his hold. "Nooo . . ."

He smacked her across the cheek with his open hand, his fingers stinging from the contact. "Shut up," he said quietly, without malice. "I want you to see something."

"Why do I have to?" The fear was leaving her now. The blow that had reddened her cheek had brought anger in its

31

place. "I don't have to do what you say! I don't"—she gasped for breath—"don't *wanta* see out there!"

He smiled a smile edged with promises, grim with threats. "I really want you to, Chris," he said. "I want you to do this for me."

In the light of his tone, her anger slipped fearfully away, leaving only the red marks where his fingers had met flesh. Her lip quivered, and she looked at him like a beaten dog that would take the throat out of its master if it thought it could. "You . . . bastard," she said weakly.

"Will you do this for me, please?" His smile faded. "You will, won't you." There was no longer even the hint of a question.

"You bastard," she mouthed, but he could not hear the words.

"Look down there."

She turned her head toward the window. Her face trembled as though made of jelly, and she clamped her eyes shut. "*Look*," he said. "Open your goddamned eyes."

She did. Her head shook with the effort not to turn away, and he saw the veins in her neck press against the slightly chubby flesh above. Another few pounds, he thought, and she would have wattles. "You see that boy?" he asked her, unable to take his eyes off her face. "That's Andy Koser. I knew him when I was a kid. He's been dead twenty-five years."

She looked at him, disbelief in her glare. "Are you . . ." she began, then turned back to the window. Brad put his arm around her shoulders, and she shivered at his touch.

"Recognize anybody?" he said. "Any familiar faces for *you* out there?"

"What . . . are they, Brad?"

He shook his head and gave a short barking laugh. "How do I know?"

"Oh, G—" She brought a hand to her mouth.

"*What?*"

"There," she breathed, pointing to a worn green bench that sat under a streetlight. There was something on the bench that had once been human. But now the body from the

32

sternum down looked like raw, oozing meat. Trunk and legs were indistinguishable from one another. The head and face, however, were untouched, and gleamed, as did the lower chaos of mortality, with the same cold blue light the other figures radiated.

"Oh, Jesus," said Brad, a plunging sadness in his tone. Tears welled up in his eyes, and his jaw tightened and trembled as he gritted his teeth, trying to force back the crying.

"You know him?" Christine asked in awe.

"Yeah," he managed to get out. "Yeah. You do too. It's Rorrie."

CHAPTER
4

"Aw fuck, B. J., you really *like* that shit?"

"Yeah. Yeah, Rorrie, I think I'm gonna like it. I mean, it's a nice campus, and I liked school, so what the hell."

"I thought you'da had enough of school." Rorrie Weidman put his hands behind his head and sank lower onto the bright red bench. He took off his aviator sunglasses and let the warm rays bake his eyelids. "*I'm* ready to *do* something, you know?"

Brad snorted. "Like what?"

"I don't know." Rorrie shrugged. "Maybe Dad's garage for a while, maybe I'll just bum around the country, maybe—"

"Maybe the Army."

"Huh?"

"Man, are you nuts? You'll be drafted for sure if you don't go to school. Hell, Rorrie, you're smart enough. You could get into State *easy*. They take kids with some really low boards—*mine* were shitty."

"Yeah, but I'd need a scholarship. I don't have the bread."

"You could get one."

"Bull*shit*. I'm not an orphan or a nigger."

"Don't say that, man."

"What, 'orphan'?"

"You know what I mean."

" 'Nigger'? That bother you? Hey, lighten up, B. J. I'm just foolin' around."

They sat for a while, watching the cars go by on Market Street, calling an occasional greeting to a friend, pulling in their legs when an adult walked past. Rorrie lit a cigarette. "What would you do," Brad said, unwrapping a stick of gum, "if you *did* get drafted?"

"I dunno. I guess I'd go. What about you?"

Brad shook his head. "I don't have anything against those people."

"That's got nothin' to do with it."

"It's got a lot to do with it," Brad answered.

"Crap. You been listening to too much folk-rock. You think they asked our dads in World War Two whether or not they had anything against Germans? 'Mr. Weidman, Mr. Meyers, you do hate Germans, don't you?' Hell, we *are* Germans. Our grandparents, great-grandparents anyway. I bet ninety percent of the people in Merridale got German blood."

"World War Two was different from Vietnam."

"My ass." Rorrie spat into the street. "You're dumb enough to get drafted, you go where they tell you and fight who they tell you to. Anyway, it doesn't matter. They're not gonna draft me."

"Why not?"

"I got a funny little toe on my left foot."

Brad laughed.

"No shit! I *do!*"

"Your little toe?" Brad was still chuckling.

"Okay, laugh. You think it's funny, go ahead and laugh. They don't take you if your feet are fucked up, because you can't *march*, dummy." Rorrie pulled off his left sneaker and propped his foot yoga-style on his thigh. "Lookit that."

Brad looked. The smallest toe curled under the fourth one so that the toenail was only partially visible. "Didn't keep you from playing football," Brad said, realizing that he was actually jealous of Rorrie's curly toe.

"Doesn't matter." He slipped the sneaker back on. "You ever check *your* toes?"

"There's nothing wrong with my toes."

"Too bad," Rorrie said, grinding out his Marlboro on the sidewalk.

As it turned out, there wasn't enough wrong with Rorrie's toes either. That August, while Brad was working at the A&P to make enough for his living expenses at Penn State, Rorrie Weidman was called for a pre-induction physical, which he easily passed. The examiners dismissed the turned-under toe, laughing gruffly and saying that Army boots would straighten it out. Rorrie was not even permitted to come home, but had to call his parents from Fort Indiantown Gap and tell them to bring the personal things he would need. He started basic training four days later. Through the remainder of August Brad always felt a twinge as he drove his Chevy past the bench by Western Auto and saw it empty, or occupied by kids other than Rorrie. That had been *Rorrie's* bench for the past three summers. He'd sat on it when he'd finished the workday at his father's garage during the week, wearing his greasy mechanic's jumpsuit, in the evenings with a work shirt and cuffed jeans, on bright steaming Saturdays in a tank top and cutoffs. It was Rorrie's bench, although he was more than willing to share it, especially with his friends and with older people, like Eddie Karl. Rorrie and Eddie would sit for hours on a Saturday afternoon or Friday night, talking, smoking, watching cars, Eddie telling Rorrie (and Brad, when he was there) about old days and old friends, none of whom had ever died in Eddie's mind.

But through the rest of August the bench, though often occupied, seemed strangely empty. Rorrie's presence was gone.

In September Brad went off to State. He found his freshman year difficult, not because of the course material but rather because of the hundred distractions he had never had to overcome when he lived at home. Loud roommates, Saturday night dances, football games (he tried out for the team with no luck), the letters he'd write every two or three days to Bonnie back in Merridale, the dates he had when he was able to forget about her—all these resulted in a 1.68 grade point average his first semester. Instead of trying to correct that semester's flaws, his studies became even more secondary in the spring. He joined the campus civil rights group, one of the two established (and feuding) antiwar organizations, and auditioned for and got a small speaking part in an off-campus production of *Lysistrata*. In June he learned his average had dropped another half point and found himself on probation for his sophomore year, even though he had not actually failed a course.

During that freshman year he received two pieces of correspondence from Rorrie Weidman. The first was a postcard that his parents brought up to campus one Saturday afternoon in October. It was postmarked Fort Bragg, and was dated three weeks previously. It read:

> B. J.—Greetings from beautiful Fort Bragg. The Army food isn't all that bad, and we get to hear a lot of rock. May be heading over to the big V in a month or two, so wish me luck. I'll see you in two years (I hope). Give Bonnie a squeeze for me—not too many ladies here.
>
> Rorrie

Brad hadn't answered. He'd intended to, and had stuck the postcard to the wall above his desk with a piece of Plasti-Tak. The color photo of a row of recruits in front of green-gray barracks under an impossibly blue sky hung there for two months before he finally took it down when he went home for Christmas vacation. He intended to answer it over the holidays, but used it as a bookmark in a library book and so lost it.

He received the letter in April. It had an APO postmark.

> B. J.—Don't come here. Stay in school. Work at it. Don't lose your deferment. It's bad. It's really *bad*.

38

That was all. Rorrie had underlined "bad" three times.

That night, after getting back to his dorm at 1:00 A.M. after an antiwar candlelight vigil, he wrote a letter to Rorrie, telling him to hang in there, see it through, not to give up hope, and every other comforting and inane cliché he could think of. At the end, he told him to desert if it got too bad. He mailed it the next morning and received no reply.

That summer he worked at the A&P again for $1.85 an hour. His parents had naturally been concerned about his grades, and he felt an unspoken need on their part for him to play the dutiful son. So he took Bonnie out only on Friday and Saturday nights, and spent the other evenings at home watching the Phillies on TV with his father, and reading Abbie Hoffman, Mao, and Che Guevara in bed late at night. He read over a dozen volumes before he decided that he found politics dull and communism heartless. He filled the rest of the summer with William Goldman novels, Grove Press Victoriana (he was one hundred pages into *My Secret Life* before he got bored), and Doc Savage paperbacks, which he devoured like popcorn.

He also managed to lose his (and Bonnie's) virginity on a blanket in the middle of a Sunday afternoon. There was a small clearing a half mile into the woods in back of the town park. They'd gone there before to make out, a process that consisted of French kissing, hand exploration, and dry-humping that had up to that time produced no more than a lasting erection and dime-sized stains in Brad's underpants that he hoped his mother wouldn't notice on laundry day.

But this time more happened. Bonnie knew that Brad had been dating at State, though *she* had chosen to "stay faithful," as she put it rather accusingly. So when she opened her legs a little wider than usual, and actually unzipped his fly to touch him, he knew why. It was to keep him, as if sex would lock them to each other not only temporarily but permanently. Although he thought he might love Bonnie, there was no way he could reciprocate the unthinking devotion with which she tried to claim him.

But he wanted her, and so he made love to her in the clearing, trying to be slow and careful with her, while she moaned in a combination of feigned pleasure and actual discomfort. When it was done, he told her that he loved her, not from any sense of true emotion, but from duty, and he held her as she cried.

Her period came the next week, so the length of their mutual worry was brief, although Brad suspected that Bonnie would have preferred being pregnant. She disliked her line job at Allied Pressing, but told him that she was saving the money for them. Brad had never asked Bonnie to marry him. It was simply assumed that it would happen. They had dated steadily since tenth grade, and when Brad had told her that he wanted to go out at State, she cried but agreed that it would be best, "to prove our love. If we get through this, that means we can get through anything." Brad didn't see it that way. The girls he'd dated at State had shown little interest in him, and he in them. The dates had been mostly pairings of convenience, and a few French kisses after some beers was the closest he'd come to any physical involvement.

But to Bonnie the threat was all too real, and he could easily tell that her sexual surrender was only a calculated ploy to hang onto him for as long as she could.

It was two weeks after her period started that he had his conversation with Eddie Karl. Brad and Bonnie hadn't made love since that afternoon, or even talked about it except for her telling him not to worry, because she wasn't pregnant. He did take the precaution, however, of buying a twin pack of Prince prophylactics from the machine in the rest room of Ruhl's Sunoco and slipping one of them into his wallet, where he was achingly aware of its presence, wondering what his mother would think if he were killed in an accident and she found it while going through his things.

He was thinking about that and about Bonnie Allen, and wondering if he could make love to her that night, when Eddie Karl sat down beside him on the bench in front of the bank. "You just get off work?" Eddie asked in his raspy voice.

Brad nodded, annoyed at having his thoughts interrupted, but unable to show that annoyance. Eddie was too benign, too friendly to spurn. Even if Brad *had* said something

40

smartass, he doubted if Eddie would have paid it any mind. "How's it going, Eddie?"

"Good, good." He nodded his grizzled head. "I like Saturdays. Nothin' like a nice warm Saturday. Everybody's out, everybody's around." He rapped his cane on the sidewalk as if for emphasis. "Saw Coot Brierly over at the drugstore."

"Yeah? How's Coot?"

Coot Brierly had died several years before Brad Meyers was born. It was a fancy of Eddie Karl's, accepted by the town, that he often saw the friends of his youth, though youth and friends had long since passed away. When people were exposed to Eddie's delusion for the first time, they found it strange and a little frightening. But Eddie's manner was so sincere and his words so ingenuous that after a while it was difficult to disbelieve him, so his delusion, at least in Eddie's presence, became shared by the community, and when a person would see an acquaintance parting from Eddie's company on the street, he would be likely to ask who he and Eddie saw today. A knowing smile would be shared, and heads shaken in wry understanding laced with a kindly pity.

"Coot's good," Eddie said, and tried to spit into the street, barely making the curb. "Shit. Used to be I could spit in a skeeter's asshole at fifty yards. Gettin' old, Jim."

"Brad," he corrected.

"Yup. Brad. Jane and Oscar's boy."

Brad chuckled and nodded.

"There, y'see. Ain't *that* old. Slip on a name now 'n' then, so what? People's important, not names." He pulled a mangled pack of Pall Malls out of a pants pocket and shoved one of the twisted white tubes between his thin lips. "Got a match?"

"Sorry."

" 'S'okay." Eddie dug into the other pocket and finally extricated a barnburner. "Yer pal Rorrie's always got matches."

"Rorrie smokes. I don't smoke."

"Y'oughta." The match flared into life like a small gre-

41

nade. "Then I wouldn't have to dig for matches." He lit the Pall Mall and tossed the match toward the gutter. It landed on the sidewalk. "I seen him today."

"Who?"

"Rorrie." Eddie hissed out a bit of tobacco from his mouth. This time he didn't even attempt distance.

"Rorrie?" Brad straightened. "Where, Eddie?"

"His dad's garage."

"Jesus," Brad said. "Is he back, then?"

"Back from where?"

"From Vietnam, Eddie. You know, he went to Vietnam?"

Eddie frowned and shook his head. "He didn't go to no Vietnam. That boy's too smart for that. Christ, a person could get hisself killed over there. Get blowed up by a mine—all sorts of things."

Under the late-afternoon sun, Brad felt suddenly cold, and his hand on the back of the bench started to tremble.

"Good boy, Rorrie. Never be an old fart like me, I'll say *that* for 'im."

Brad stood up, his legs rubbery. He cleared his throat. "I'll see you later, Eddie. Gotta go . . . do something." Eddie waved a spidery hand in a gesture of dismissal, and Brad walked away, thinking, *Not Rorrie, oh, Jesus, please no, not Rorrie*, but not knowing, not sure. He knew who would know.

Merridale had one newsstand. When you went in the front door, the magazines, comics, and paperbacks were on the left, roughly arranged by size. *Time*, comic books, and *Sports Illustrated* shared the same wooden rack, while *Reader's Digest*, *Analog*, and *Alfred Hitchcock's Mystery Magazine* rubbed spines in the digest bin. To the right was a long glass counter, behind and on top of which were gum, candy bars, shoelaces, pocketknives, combs, and piles of the *Merridale Messenger* and the *Lansford Courier*, a small stack of the *Philadelphia Inquirer*, and three or four copies of the *New York Times*. Behind the counter on a small stool sat Marie Snyder, a *True Confessions* ensconced permanently in her lap, although no one had ever seen her eyes on it longer than a few seconds. The minute any customer—man, woman, or child—entered the store, the head would go up on the stalk of a neck, the glasses would drop as if of their own volition off the beaky nose onto the flat bosom, and the pale birdlike eyes would transfix the visitor while the mouth would split in a harshly lipsticked smile. The ears, contrary to legend, did not perk and flare at the mention of rumors, but if they could have, they would.

Rumors were Marie Snyder's stock in trade, and actual *news* interested her only on the local level. She knew who had been born, who had died, who had conceived, and who had attempted conception. Her newsstand was the hub of every story true or false to come into or out of Merridale. If anyone would know about Rorrie Weidman, Marie Snyder would.

She smiled at Brad as he entered the tiny store, her thin fingers brushing invisible lint from the front of her shapeless, patterned dress. "Afternoon, Bradley," she said in surprisingly soft, flutelike tones. "Help you with anything?"

"Uh, not really, Miss Snyder. I was just wondering . . ." He was afraid to ask, but the fear of not knowing was worse. "I was talking to Eddie Karl, and he said something kind of funny about Rorrie Weidman, and I thought maybe . . ."

He stopped. At the mention of Rorrie's name, her lips had closed and stretched taut like two thick rubber bands. They were deep dark red, the color of fresh liver, and the illusory look of stern regret upon them was hard for Brad to bear. "You haven't heard?" she said, shaking her head. Brad thought her eyes shone with excitement, with the urge to bear bad news, and he remembered a scene from some Greek play he'd read in Lit II of killing the messenger of bad tidings, and imagined Marie Snyder at the point of a sword, wondering if that would erase her carelessly concealed delight.

"Heard what?" he asked calmly, suddenly angry with himself for coming to her, for now his reaction would be grist for her mill. He decided to show no emotion, to speak only noncommittal words.

"Poor Roland." Her head still shook, and she gave three *tsk-tsks* in rapid succession, like a hen pecking corn. "I just

43

heard around two o'clock. From his aunt, Molly Weidman. You know her, I'm sure. Very tall woman."

She was doing it on purpose, he knew, baiting him, playing him like a fish, or a nightclub comic telling a long story whose only point is to ultimately make fools out of his audience. But Brad would not be treated that way. He would not. "Was he killed?" he asked coldly.

Marie Snyder's head stopped shaking in the middle of a right-hand sweep so that it seemed locked in a cocked position. She eyed him appraisingly, as though this were a new and different audience she was not used to. "Why, yes," she said with the hint of a smile. "Yes, he was."

Brad nodded shortly.

"I understand he stepped on one of those whatchamacallits— a *mine*, I think. At least he didn't suffer. They're shipping the body back quick as they can." Brad moved toward the door, and Marie speeded up, anxious to get in as much as she could before she lost him. "Of course, they won't have a viewing or anything; he was too messed up for that, and that hot weather too, well . . ." The screen door squeaked, then banged shut on its spring, leaving Marie Snyder talking to an empty store.

". . . that wouldn't help much either." She frowned again, and turned back to *True Confessions*.

Brad walked numbly up the street, knowing that he should start home, that his mother would soon have supper on the table. But he couldn't. And yet he didn't want to be alone. So he went back to the bench next to Western Auto. Eddie Karl was still there, talking softly to friends unseen, and Brad sat next to him. Eddie nodded a greeting, stopped talking, and went back to watching cars.

Brad watched too for a while, then turned to face the old man. "Eddie?"

"Mmm?"

"Next time you see Rorrie . . . say hi for me, will you?"

Eddie Karl smiled, nodded, and spat. This time he made the street, and his smile broadened. "Not that old yet," he said.

*   *   *

44

Rorrie Weidman's body came back in October, when Brad was away at State. The burial was held on a Wednesday, so there would have been no way for Brad to have attended, even if he'd known. As it was, he didn't find out until two weeks later, from an out-of-date *Messenger* his mother sent him, and he gave it little thought. A dull, nearly forgotten regret had replaced the sorrow and disbelief he'd first felt, and his mind was primarily concerned with (a) keeping Bonnie while at the same time building up his relationship with Louisa Brewer, who'd let him fuck her on their first date inside a walk-in closet in a friend's apartment, (b) battling to keep his grades from slipping even further, and (c) whether or not to cut down on some of his campus activities. The leaders of the antiwar group he'd joined as a freshman were still strident and even more demanding than before, *requiring* his presence at a rally, a sit-in, a demonstration, on evenings before tests for which he should have been rabidly studying.

Finally, the draft lottery solved his problems once and for all.

There must have been a hundred of them packed into the small lounge, each jockeying for a view of the screen on which their fates would be decided. Brad sat toward the back of the room with his roommate, not caring that the screen was blocked by assorted long-haired and short-cropped heads. When it was time, he could hear the numbers, hear the dates. He didn't really want to see as well.

"Okay! Shut up! They're doin' it!" came a voice from up front, and a flat silence fell over the room like a sheet. The first date was read in a clear treble from the tinny speaker that had been turned to maximum volume. Everyone looked around, at friends, at strangers, but no one spoke, laughed, moaned. The Angel had flown past without swinging the sickle.

The second date rattled out, and, amazingly, no one reacted. Free again.

At the reading of the third date, a neatly bearded boy near the front twisted his head as though he'd received a blow and gave a deep throaty grunt. He stood up, his face red, shrugging off the hands, unused to touching, that sought to com-

45

fort him, and stalked out of the lounge. First blood had been drawn.

Strangely enough, everyone suddenly seemed more at ease. Their birth dates might be called, but at least they would not be the first, and Brad thought it was like death in a way, and whispered to his roommate, "It's like we're all gonna die sooner or later, but who wants to go first, y'know?"

His roommate chuckled, then held a finger to his lips. The next date was already being read. Brad heard only the tail end: ". . . ary 14."

"What?" he said in alarm.

"February 14, now shut up," came a voice, and murmurs of agreement followed.

After the fifth date was called, his roommate looked at him with a question in his eyes. Brad nodded. "Number four," he whispered. "Got me." He sat there silently as the rest of the 366 dates were drawn. Then the room emptied of students, all of them talking, some in a fast-paced tone of relief, others in a quiet monotone. Still others instructed friends how to fail the physical: "Drink some ink"; "Put sugar in the piss jar"; "Say you're a fag." One boy was crying silently. No one made fun of him. The last words Brad heard before he walked out alone into the night were, "Shit, they even got *Jesus.*"

Sitting on a bench in the grove just like the bench he and Rorrie Weidman used to sit on, he thought about Rorrie long and hard. Desert, he'd told Rorrie, get the hell out if you can't take it. He wondered if he could give himself the same advice. He knew in his heart he couldn't make it, even if a miracle struck and he didn't have to go to Vietnam. But the only alternative was Canada, and that frightened him. To be an outcast from his country, maybe forever, was a concept that he had never before confronted head-on. It would mean separation from everything and everyone he knew and loved. *And he could never come back.*

If he *did* go to 'Nam, though, if he did, it would be two years of the Army, no more than a year in 'Nam, probably. He could stay alive for a year—he wouldn't be in combat all the time—he'd just be *careful*. That was Rorrie's problem.

46

He was fast, casual, quick to do crazy things, take stupid dares. He'd probably walked into that mine on *purpose*, for God's sake.

Brad shook his head and stood up. He wished he could buy booze at nineteen, and then he considered crashing someone's pad and drinking *their* booze. But instead, he went back to his dorm. His roommate, whose number was 287, was studying when he came in. "You okay?" he asked Brad.

"Yeah."

"What you gonna do?"

"Go."

"Shit . . . man, it's all such shit."

In a few weeks Brad got the notice to report for his physical, which he passed. He went home, said good-bye to his parents and to Bonnie, who told him she'd be faithful and cautioned him to be careful. When he replied that he'd stay out of the way of bullets, she clarified her admonition by having it include a sexual warning as well. He decided bitterly that he would fuck the first gook whore who made him an offer.

He didn't get the chance for quite a while. Basic training was a two-month nightmare of close bodies, filthy talk, and a series of near-fights that gave him constant bouts of diarrhea, which the Army doctors treated with large doses of Kaopectate. He went to Vietnam in March 1970 and came back thirteen months later not only alive, but untouched. He had not suffered so much as a scratch from the time of his arrival in the country to the time of his departure. He came back to the United States and to Merridale with an athlete's body—lean, rock-hard, cable-muscled, over which was stretched a tanned surface of smooth, unblemished skin. But if his mind could have shown a human form, it would have been shriveled, diseased, filled with the decay of a month-old corpse.

It was April when he returned. Buds were slightly greening the trees, and his mother's daffodils were just starting to open, laying a slash of yellow across the base of their house. He entered his room as if it were a stranger's. He had forgotten the boy who had lived there, could not remember his reasons for putting up the posters of rock stars, the

47

wrinkled map of Middle-earth. Only the poster of Doc Savage touched a note of response: the torn shirt, bunched muscles, face wrinkled with something more than age. This he did not touch, but the others he took down, rolled up, and put into the closet, tossing into the wastecan the nearly dry balls of Plasti-Tak that had held them to the walls.

His mother was finishing the supper dishes, so he went onto the back porch, where his father was sitting reading the paper. He put it down when Brad came out the door, and they smiled at each other, sitting side by side on the glider and listening to the clatter of Melmac, the soft liquid sound of rinsing, the metallic rattle of silverware hitting the drying rack. Brad laughed low in his throat. "Jesus, what a pretty sound."

His father nodded. "Don't let Mom hear you say that," he said with a grin.

"Yeah, sure." He dug out a pack of Winstons from his pocket and lit one.

"When did you start that?" his father asked.

"Smoking? In 'Nam." He exhaled slowly, watching the smoke turn a small space of evening air gray, souring for a moment the scent of honeysuckle drifting up from the back fence.

"Not too good for you, is it?" His father had never smoked.

Brad shrugged. "I never thought about that. It didn't matter much. Maybe I'll quit."

The father looked at his son's profile in the dying light. The face had changed, he thought. There was a depth in the eyes that had not been there before, the sense of having looked over the edge of a great abyss and having teetered on its edge, and the knowledge that one could balance there for a very long time without falling. The mouth was different too. It seemed larger, the lips thick and full, almost sensuous if the line of the mouth had not been so straight and firm, as though a knife edged in coal dust had scored across the petals of a rose.

"Was it . . ." His father paused. "Was it very bad? Over there?"

The full mouth twisted up on the side away from the older man so that all he saw was a crooked frown. Then Brad chuckled, and there was true humor in the sound, but he said nothing.

"I . . . uh . . . I remember the World War. In Italy," his father went on. "There were a lot of things then I wished I'd never seen. I was about your age too. War's a . . . a terrible thing."

Brad, silent, kept smoking, smiling.

"You see much action?" his father asked. Brad made a nearly imperceptible move that might have been a nod. "Well, I know . . . I know what you must have gone through. I—"

"Uh-unh." The sound floated out on gray smoke.

"What?"

"You don't know." It was said without rancor, merely as a statement of fact, to set the record straight.

"Well, uh"—his father laughed uncomfortably—"I think I do. I mean, I was in combat—"

"No." Brad looked at his father and smiled strangely, so that just his two top front teeth showed, like a rabbit's. "You really don't know, Dad. And no horror stories could make me think you do." The smile faded. "There was a master sergeant. Fifty years old. And he fragged himself. Just took a grenade, and pulled the pin, and held it up to his head like he was talking on the telephone. He did it because of something he saw. Something I . . . saw too. And twenty-five years before he'd been one of the first inside when they liberated Dachau." He smiled again. "So don't tell me you know. You don't know."

The storm door opened and Brad's mother came out onto the porch. She bent over Brad and kissed his hair. "It's so good to have you back, honey. What are you boys talking about?" She sat between them on the glider.

"I was just noticing your tulips, Mom. They really came out early this year."

"I'm just glad we had some flowers for your homecoming." She folded her hands in her lap. "Do they have many flowers in Vietnam?"

Brad laughed. "Oh, yeah, Mom, big ones. Bright orange.

And white." He put an arm around her and hugged her closely. "So big you'd swear they fill the whole sky. But they don't last long," he said, looking upward to where the stars were just beginning to appear, like far-off flares of some impossibly foreign war. "They die real fast." His voice was barely a whisper.

No one said anything for a long time, and Brad seemed not to notice his mother's shoulders stiffen as she wondered in a dim, dull, unimaginative way if her son had really come home.

The next day was a Saturday, and he picked up Bonnie in his father's car just before noon. She was out the door of her parents' home even before he'd pulled the emergency brake, and threw herself into his arms as he left the car. "Hey"—he laughed—"take it easy, okay?"

"Oh, Brad, thank God you're home, you don't know how much I've missed you, I prayed every night that you'd . . . ." And so it went until he stilled her mouth with a kiss. He felt relief at the sudden quiet rather than any passion she might have aroused in him. They went into the house then, and he said hello in a remote and disinterested way to her parents. Afterward they drove out to the park and shared the picnic lunch Bonnie had packed. It was warm for April, and Brad was in shirtsleeves, and Bonnie, in a loose open blouse with a halter underneath. Throughout the lunch she seemed in a state of perpetual excitement, and after they'd eaten, she nearly dragged him the half mile back to the small clearing in the woods, where she pulled him to her and asked him to make love to her.

"I'm on the pill now," she said. "I knew you were coming home and I wanted it to be so good for you, so I went on the pill."

"That was nice of you," he said, giving a small laugh that startled her.

"What's wrong?" she asked.

"Why? Something seem wrong?"

"You just seem . . . funny."

"Funny," he repeated. He looked down at her for a moment before he asked, "Do you still love me?"

"Oh, yes," she said, making her eyes as soulful as she knew how.

"And you want me to make love to you?"

"Yes."

"And you want us to get married?"

"Yes. I do. I want that . . . so much."

"Okay, then." He sat down next to her, but he didn't touch her. "I'm going to tell you some things. And if after I tell you you still want what you want now, then I'll want it too. All right?"

Terror ran through her. She fully expected to hear of every sexual escapade Brad had had in Vietnam, of teenaged whores and older mama sans, or whatever they called them, trained in how to please men in a hundred different sick ways, ways that she could never hope to compete with. She made herself smile and nod just the same, and sat up and listened as he spoke.

But his words were not of sex and whores and strange diseases. Rather, to her surprise, he spoke of jungles and narrow caves, of grim things done in the middle of the night, couched in words and concepts she did not understand. Yet he painted scenes for her that parts of her mind could dimly comprehend—scenes of blood and fire, agony and death, glimpses of Brad, khaki-clad, tinted with red, eyes gleaming in orgasmic fear, doing *things* that she could not dream of anyone doing, not in *real* life, not in life as it was and had always been lived in Merridale. These were other dreams, the dark dreams, the dreams that would sometimes come to her unbidden in night's black heart, the same kind of things of which Brad spoke now, trying to gnaw their way into her sleep; but she would not let them, for they were *filthy*, worse than the worst things the whores of Saigon could ever bring themselves to do. And those dreams would turn from her and fade back to where they came from, and she would awaken from her effort and lie there sweating, thanking God that she had escaped from that confrontation with shadow.

And now Brad was saying, wasn't he, that those dreams had been real, that he had *lived* them.

It couldn't be. That was all. It couldn't be. And the words

51

struck her and moved, not through her, but around her, like a stream parting to either side of a great rock, to be deflected, divided, weakened. If she heard now, it did not matter.

Brad finished. His face was solemn but not shaken by his tale of horrors. His cheeks were still ruddy, his hands steady. He looked at her coldly, appraisingly, and she smiled.

"But were you faithful?" she asked. "Were you true to me?"

He laughed as though he could not believe what she said, laughed and embraced her. "Oh, yes." He chuckled. " 'I have been faithful to thee, Cynara! In my fashion!' "

She did not ask who Cynara was, though she wondered about it.

They decided to get married in June. When, in a moment of doubt, she asked him *why* he wanted to marry her, he told her that he needed her. Not loved, not wanted, but needed, and he did. He longed for normality, stability, even mediocrity. He wanted to drown himself in dullness. Though his parents suggested returning to college under the GI Bill, he told them that he had had enough of college. "I already learned too much," he said. "It's not easy to learn things." His father didn't know what he meant, but did not press him for an explanation. Since his return from the service, it was difficult to talk to Brad. He would speak readily of inconsequential things—baseball, television, movies—but on more serious matters, such as politics, he seemed to have no opinions at all, and of his own past and future he would say nothing. When his father or mother broached such subjects to him, he simply would not respond, or would walk out of the room without speaking.

The week after he'd returned home he told them at the dinner table that he'd gotten a job that day at the Universal Shoe plant. They had not even known he was applying. "What kind of job, Brad?" his father asked.

Brad put down his knife and fork. "I stand in front of a machine. I push a button, and two metal plates come together in front of me. Hot liquid plastic pours into a mold, and in twenty seconds the plates come apart. There in front of me are two plastic soles and heels. I put them in a box, rip out what's left in the feed tube, and push the button again.''

"A . . . machine operator," his father ventured.

"That's right. It's a job I think I'm going to like very much." He picked up his knife and fork and turned his attention back to his meat loaf, not saying a word for the rest of the meal.

Brad started working at Universal three days later, and with his first paycheck he made a security deposit on an apartment in the Shady Dell complex, a cluster of twelve newly built pseudocolonial buildings on the outskirts of town, each housing eight families. The rent for the one-bedroom unit was $175 a month, a third of what he took home from Universal.

The wedding took place in the second week of June, a justice of the peace presiding, and only the parents of the bride and groom in attendance. Bonnie was disappointed but uncomplaining. That fall, when she delightedly discovered she was pregnant, she quit her job at Allied Pressing after Brad assured her they could manage on his salary alone. Frank Donald Meyers was born the following May, a healthy eight-pound boy who resembled Bonnie far more than he did Brad. Brad began to work double shifts whenever he could to pay for the extra expenses the baby incurred. The extra work paid off in another way, for in early 1974 he was made assistant foreman. Mr. Rider, Universal's owner, liked the no-nonsense way in which Bradley Meyers handled himself. While the other workers seemed to use any excuse to indulge in horseplay, Brad was serious-minded, refusing to join in the pranks, choosing instead to keep working.

Bonnie became pregnant again in late 1974, and Linda Marie followed Frank the next summer. The apartment quickly became cramped, and Brad made a fifteen-percent down payment on a six-year-old house on Sundale Road, a middle-income development. He had had no trouble saving the $5,000, as he spent money on nothing but his family. He had quit smoking, did not drink, had no hobbies and no apparent vices. No longer did he go hunting with his father, as he often had before he was drafted. He came home, played with

53

Frank until it was the boy's bedtime, then sat in front of the television until 11:00, when he would switch it off. He never watched the news, and he seldom laughed at any of the sitcoms. When he talked to Bonnie, it was about trivial things, and when he made love to her, he was curiously detached, almost clinical. She was not and had never been a bright girl, but slowly it began to dawn on her that something was wrong with the marriage. Yet she was incapable of dealing with abstractions, and so could not solve or even define the problems. Brad did not beat her, as some of her friends were beaten by their husbands. He seldom lost his temper, never came home drunk or spent money foolishly. It was just that sometimes, after a late night feeding, when she slipped back into bed beside Brad, she thought she was next to a stranger. And sometimes then, in the middle of the night, she would almost but not quite remember what he had told her that day in the clearing. But just as she was about to think of it, to really remember what he had said, she would fall asleep, or think about something she would have to do the next day, or worry if she was pregnant again, and the memory would slide into the dark.

She continued to be unaware of the condition of her marriage, even for a long time after Brad began to change. The first few incidents she dismissed as random flares of temper, things that she could have prevented. One morning just after six o'clock, she was fixing breakfast when Brad walked into the kitchen in his underwear. "Where are my socks?"

"Um . . . in the dryer, honey. I'm sorry, I forgot to take them out," she babbled, moving to the basement steps. "I'll get them right away, I just hope they're not damp." She ran down the steps and opened the dryer. The socks and the other clothes were not merely damp, they were soaked. "Oh, God, Brad, I'm sorry," she called up the stairs. "Honey, they're still wet. But there's one pair left in your drawer, I think. . . ."

"They have holes in them." She looked up the stairs. He was standing at the top, looking vaguely threatening even in his near-nudity.

"Well, hon, couldn't you just wear them today, and I'll—"

"Fuck!" He spat out the word so gutturally that it was

almost unintelligible, and slammed the cellar door on her.

Her first thought was gratitude that the children were still sleeping; her second was a flash of concern that Brad might have awakened them. Not until these primarily maternal reactions were gone did she think of Brad's response at having to wear socks with holes in them as irrational overkill, and then only for an instant. He had a *right* to get angry, she told herself. He did so much for all three of them and expected so little in return. It was the least she could do to make sure his clothes were clean and dry, the house was picked up, the kids were quiet when he wanted to sleep late on weekend mornings.

Brief outbursts of rage followed, randomly at first, then in a continuous pattern, and it seemed as if the most insignificant affronts received the most intense reactions. The inability to find a bottle opener in the kitchen, when all he had to do was ask Bonnie, drove him into a barely suppressed fury. A missing section of newspaper resulted in the paper being torn into shreds and scattered around the room. When Bonnie reused the coffee grounds because they'd run out, Brad took one sip and hurled the pot into the sink, where the glass shattered, nearly spraying Frankie and the baby with the steaming liquid. He seemed to come to his senses then, and while Bonnie held the baby to stop its crying, Brad put an arm around Frankie, who started to shy away from him in fright. A look of great sadness came over Brad, and he straightened up, watching the boy go to his mother's arms.

"Take the kids in the living room," he said softly. "I'll clean this up." He did, and didn't speak of it again, never saying that he was sorry.

Before long the invisible gate that had kept his temper from touching the children had opened, and though he did not strike them, Bonnie giving the spankings when they'd been earned, his words cut and tore them more than a heavy ring-fingered hand could ever have done.

The Christmas of 1976 Frankie received from Brad's parents a battery-operated police car. The top of the car was rounded, and underneath was a plastic flap that was forced out during the motor's cycle, making the car flip over completely as it rolled along. On the day after Christmas the flap got stuck halfway, unable to flip the car or to let the wheels keep moving it. "Daddy," Frankie whined, "my car don't work."

"Doesn't," Bonnie corrected.

"*Doesn't* work."

"Let me see." Brad took the car and opened the battery case underneath. The batteries were alkaline, put in the day before, and the contact points were all right.

"It's stuck there, Daddy. That thing's stuck."

"I *see* that, just shut up a minute."

Bonnie could see the anger rising. "Honey," she said to Brad, "maybe your dad could take it back where they—"

"Just let me *look* at it for a minute, for Christ's sake!"

Frankie turned and looked at his mother, uncertain of what to do. When he looked back, Brad had his fingers in the small hole between flap and underbody, his teeth gritted with the effort to grasp a small metal spring that had somehow become twisted. "Daddy, don't break it!"

"Do you want me to *fix* it or *don't* you?" Brad snarled, and the boy quailed.

"Y-yeah . . ."

"Okay, then, *here!*" He grabbed the plastic flap in one hand and snapped it off like a dead twig. The boy's face melted, butterlike, trembling with weeping, staring unbelievingly at his broken toy. "It'll run *now*," said Brad defensively. "It won't flip, but it'll *run!* Goddamn Hong Kong crap anyway. *Here*"—he thrust the car into Frankie's hands— "and don't ask me to fix your shit again." He stalked into the kitchen, and Bonnie heard the refrigerator door open, the metallic rattle of the nearly depleted six-pack, the door slam, and the pop and hiss of a ring tab being pulled.

She hadn't really been aware of when the drinking had started in earnest. One Friday he'd come home from work a little high—he'd stopped at the Anchor with a few of his friends, since one of them was getting married that weekend— and she'd thought nothing of it. She'd seen her own father far worse every weekend when she'd lived at home. That next week he brought home a six-pack, and on the weekend, a

56

case. Then slowly he began to drink more and more beer. At first a case had lasted two weeks, then a week and a half, and now he would drink four or five bottles in a single night, more on weekends. Instead of relaxing him, it seemed to Bonnie to make him more irritable, more impossible to talk to.

Now Frankie's crying brought her back to the present, and she hugged the boy, looking sadly at Linda's wide puzzled eyes staring up from the floor where she played with her pop-beads. Bonnie didn't mind it when he got mad at her—she was a big girl, she could take it—but the kids were something else. She had to try to talk to him. Now, before he got too many more beers inside him.

"Honey," she said to Frankie, whose cries had shrunk to soft, high-pitched sniveling, "you take Linda Marie to your room, okay?"

"You mad at me too?" the boy asked.

"No, hon, I'm not mad at you. I just want to talk to Daddy, that's all." The boy took his sister's hand and led her down the short hall to the room they shared, while Bonnie walked into the kitchen.

Brad looked at her from under glowering brows. "Well?" he said with a surly cockiness that set her teeth on edge.

"I don't want to fight," she said.

"Who does?" He took a deep swig from the can. "What *do* you want?"

"I . . . I just want to know why you picked on Frankie like that."

He belched. "Scuse me. And excuse me for picking on Frankie. God forbid I should ever harm the little darlings."

"*Stop* it."

"Did I *hit* him?" he flared. "Do I *ever* hit him? Or *you?* Or Linda?"

"No, but—"

"I never lay a *hand* on you!"

"But your temper!"

"*Fuck* my temper. So I got a temper, so what?"

"So what?" she asked astounded. "So you're getting impossible to live with is what."

57

"Then get the hell out." He turned away from her, as if ashamed of what he'd just said, and sat down.

"You mean that?" she said quietly.

His head shook almost imperceptibly. "No. No, I don't mean it." The voice was calm, his anger gone. She stepped behind his chair and put her hands on his shoulders. "I'm sorry," he said. "I don't know what happens sometimes. I just . . . I just blow up, you know?"

"I know."

"I don't mean to. And I'd never want you to leave. I need you, Bonnie."

"I know that too." She sighed. "If you'd just try to keep your temper, keep control of yourself—"

"I will."

"The littlest things get you going, Brad, it's scary—"

"I will, I promise. I'll really try."

She thought she heard his voice break, and when she looked, his eyes were wet with tears. She left him alone then, having forgotten how to be tender.

That night he didn't drink any more beer. Instead, he played with Frankie and Linda and read them bedtime stories. Later, when the children were asleep, he and Bonnie made love for the first time in several weeks, and she had one of her intense but infrequent orgasms. They fell asleep exhausted, holding each other, and sometime in the middle of the night, after comfort had placed them on their appointed sides of the bed, Brad had his first bad dream.

He did not normally dream, at least not so that he would remember when he awoke. But the dream he had that night was so real, so crystalline, that it seemed for months afterward that it had actually happened. *Déjà vu* was not a primary factor, for although memory was a part of what formed the deep scenario, it was only a small part. The dream was born of wishes as well, and desires and fears and possibilities.

It began as a sexual encounter. The girl was young, younger than Bonnie. Her skin was smooth as a child's, her body fully formed, and though she seemed anxious and willing for each variation he imposed upon her, still there was a hesitancy, as though all this were new, done to please him, as though she feared his displeasure. At the last he was in her mouth, pounding away as savagely as at the true coin of a vagina, hardier, made to accommodate power, built to accept the force of seed. And as his pleasure and intensity grew until he was within a wisp of coming, she drew back from him and turned into darkness, a monolithic blackness that engulfed him only momentarily, then brightened to become a green vastness of overhanging limbs lit by orange flame. He looked down at himself. He was still naked, his erection failing, shrinking before the mystery of his situation. Then suddenly he knew.

Flames lit the whole sky in a canopy of fire, and he began to notice the bodies around him. Most of them lay facedown, and he could see the black hair charred even blacker, and he knelt beside one and touched it. As he had expected, the hair turned to powder in his hand, exposing blackened skin the texture of moldy oranges that parted like scum on pudding as his fingers pressed down on it.

He felt horror in the dream, but felt too that he had known what his hands would encounter, that he was somehow meant to press and probe at these burned, dead things, and though he knew there was no reason, though he knew that sane minds would recoil in revulsion at what he did, he touched the bodies scattered about him, rigid fingers piercing flaking skin, hands sinking into hollow stomachs, drumhead-thin barriers of flesh parting like tissue paper at his caress.

I'm bathing in it. I'm washing. Why am I doing this? How will I be clean?

He could not answer himself. He could only move from corpse to corpse, now walking, now crawling, anointing his hands over and over again, a supplicant washing in the blood of the lambs.

Here were two together, a father and son perhaps, the man lying face upward, charred coal-eyes staring out of blackness through blackness into blackness, lips that smiled and kissed now only twin red-black sponges crisped and curled, brow that wrinkled in concern or smoothed with joy now fissured in basaltic ridges, once-living lava hardened by the passage of fire. It was a face sculpted in a furnace.

59

What he had worn for clothes was forgotten, no more than a thin layer, clumped in spots, that clung to his body like a second skin. His fingers were black twigs.

The boy lay across him facedown, small head pressed into the man's stomach. His bare arms and legs were smooth and light brown, not black, and Brad knew that fire had not touched him. But something else had, for where his head lay on the father's stomach was a great puddle of blood that ran over the edges of the man's rib cage like water over a birdbath onto the dark ground below.

There had been no sound in the dream to this point, only the thin, high keening that comes at times of absolute silence, heard by the brain and not the ear. But now there was something else—a wet bubbling, slow and methodical, like the gurglings of a pot carefully tended. He looked down again where the boy's head nestled in the cavity of his father's bowels, and saw fat bubbles explode on either side. *Drowning. Drowning in blood.* He bent down to lift the boy out of the red pool, and his limbs moved slowly, as through a thick jelly. But as his fingers finally touched the yellow-brown shoulders, the head came up of its own accord and turned toward him, the almond eyes glowing, the cheeks and mouth crimson with gore. The nostrils were pulsing rhythmically like an animal's, and between the teeth Brad could see, just disappearing down the bobbing throat, a morsel of what the boy had been feeding on.

Eating the dead.

The terror started low in him, at the knees, and moved up with the force of a riptide, and suddenly the boy's eyes were his, and he was looking up at himself, no longer naked, but clothed in khaki. He ignored his own horrified expression and felt a growl form deep in his throat. In another second he had sunk his head into the open wound of the man beneath him, blowing air out through his nose like a diver, and, despite the mind that shrieked at him to stop, began to tear and gnaw with strong white teeth at the slick, gleaming viscera within the bloody cavern. The bubbling increased in volume, rising in pitch, until he realized that what he heard was his own strangled voice trying to shout himself awake.

60

He came to consciousness with a start and a sob, striking his head against the headboard in his haste to pull himself erect, as though remaining prone would throw him back into the nightmare.

Bonnie awoke immediately. He could hear the panic in her voice. "Brad? Brad!"

He couldn't speak at first, couldn't answer. He tasted the salty sting of blood in his mouth.

"Brad? What's wrong?"

"Nothing," he was finally able to say. "I'm all right."

"Bad dream?"

"Uh-huh." He let her put an arm around him and pull him down beside her, but he would not go back to sleep. He was too scared. After Bonnie fell asleep he went into the kitchen and opened a beer. It relaxed him, so he had another. And another. After the third, he thought he could sleep, and he did, dreamlessly.

From that night on he would not go to bed without having at least thirty-six ounces of beer in his stomach, and sometimes more. He never had the nightmare again that vividly, but traces of it would creep into his mind when sleep took him, making him awaken with a start.

The temper returned as quickly as it had fled, and Bonnie began looking for excuses to be away from home with the kids on weekends. Left alone, Brad drank harder, and Sunday nights were often times of mental savagery in the Meyers home, Bonnie and the children returning to find Brad drunk and sullen, with perhaps two or three friends from Universal in nearly as nasty a mood. One night Brad suggested that they "pull a train" on Bonnie. She hadn't known what he meant until later, but luckily the others were not so drunk as not to be embarrassed by Brad's offer. The party broke up early that night.

Brad was not always difficult to live with. At times he was kind and loving. Holidays seemed to bring out his better nature, and he loved going trick or treating with Frankie and Linda Marie, cutting out paper turkeys and Pilgrims to decorate the house at Thanksgiving, trimming the tree, always a live one, and setting up his old Lionel O gauge in the basement at Christmas. There were times when things he would do or say would wrench her heart, and she would find herself wishing that he would *never* be kind, would always be an unmitigated son of a bitch so that she would not be forced to love him. But when she saw him bending over Frankie's bed, tucking the covers around his fragile shoulders, whispering "I love you, pal" and meaning it, when he pushed the light brown curls back from Linda Marie's sweating forehead on summer nights and blew gently on the girl's face to cool her, kissing her softly before he left the room, when she saw these things, she weakened, and hugged him, and decided to wait a little longer, give him another chance to make up for his last outburst, not leave him. Not just yet.

So she hung on for the children's sake, and her own, and Brad's. She tolerated the drunkenness, the shouts, the cruelties. At first she even tolerated it when he pushed her, then one night actually slapped her face. But there was always a point, she told herself, beyond which he would not go. She knew he would not hit the children. And he never did. No matter how irrationally outraged he would become at Frankie or Linda Marie, he never struck them. Instead, some other object received the blow—a table at which he sat, a magazine he held, a can he had just emptied, or perhaps Bonnie herself.

She could not, however, put up with it permanently. Life with Brad hardened her, annealed her in the furnace until his moments of tenderness meant less to her and his times of brutality meant more and more. At one time she had worried about what he would do if she left him, but eventually she was past caring. Being murdered, she told herself, might even be preferable to the life she had with him.

In 1979, three years after his fits of rage began, Bonnie Meyers filed for divorce on grounds of mental cruelty. She did not tell him she was leaving, not because she was frightened of his reaction, but because she felt he did not deserve to be told. She took Frankie out of school and the three of them went to Allentown to stay with Bonnie's aunt until Brad could hear of and react to the desertion. She'd left him a note explaining things as well as she could, and the attorney she'd hired called Brad the next day at noon. He'd been sleeping, and had seemed calm and reasonable, the attorney told Bonnie. "In fact," the attorney said, "he told me he was surprised you hadn't walked out a long time ago."

Brad's mother called him, finally breaking her self-imposed lack of intervention in her son's affairs, to ask him if he didn't think the marriage was worth saving. "It's dead," he told her. "You can't save the dead."

Arrangements were made. Bonnie got the house, the children, and child support, while Brad got visitation rights, the only thing he had specifically asked for. He had not even hired an attorney. Taking his personal effects and what furniture and kitchen things Bonnie felt inclined to share, he rented a small two-bedroom apartment on Market Street for $150 a month. He drank less after the separation, for his weekends were spent working at the 7-Eleven down the street. Along with his job at Universal, his work totaled fifty-two hours a week and as many as seventy-six if he got some extra days at double shift. Often he went home, drank a few beers, and fell into bed, getting up in seven or eight hours to go back to work again. With this schedule, he was able to handle the child-support, mortgage, and rent payments, and save a considerable amount as well, since he seldom had time to spend anything. Slowly he began to put the money into the furnishing of his apartment, buying a water bed one month to replace the single mattress on the floor, a Pioneer stereo system the next, with hundred-watt speakers, on which he played a mixture of rock and classical that had the third-floor tenant, old and half deaf as he was, pounding on the floor, and a four-seater padded bar the next month, on whose shelves he placed no liquor, but only bottles of Heineken. The Nazi flags were almost an afterthought.

One afternoon at a local flea market he was struck by the bright red, black, and white banner strung up behind a table of military memorabilia, and thought how good it would look on that large bare spot on the living-room wall. Then came German World War II posters, a large black and white shot of Hitler at Nuremberg, helmets, crossed sabers.

One Saturday night when a drinking buddy saw Brad's apartment for the first time, he asked him bluntly, "What the hell are you, Meyers? A Nazi?"

Brad smiled. "No. I hate Nazis. I like their uniforms."

"What about that picture of Hitler?"

"I like his moustache."

"And that big flag?"

"I like red, white, and black, and I couldn't find an Egyptian flag, all right?"

The man laughed. "Christ, Meyers, you're so fuckin' weird. . . . Got another a' those beers?"

Brad opened two more bottles. "Let's drink a toast," he said, his words only slightly slurred.

"Fine with me. What to?"

Brad jutted out his lower lip and thought a moment. Then he looked out the window at the empty green bench across the street by Western Auto. "To Rorrie Weidman," he said, raising his bottle.

"Who?"

"A gentleman and scholar and bench sitter with a prodigious appetite for living, but now, alas, without a life to live."

The man shrugged. "Your beer," he said, raising his own bottle in the toast. "Rorrie . . . what's his name . . ."

"Yeah," said Brad, his eyes on the bench in the pool of lamplight. "Rorrie what's his name."

CHAPTER
5

"Rorrie?" Christine said. "Rorrie *who?*"

"Rorrie Weidman," Brad whispered.

Christine's voice was sharp, panic-hued. "The one who *died?*"

Brad nodded, and Christine shuddered again, as though a wave of arctic cold had just swept the room. He pushed past her, heading for the bedroom. "Don't *leave* me!" she squealed, pattering after him.

"Mommy"—Wally's small voice leaked out from behind his bedroom door—"what's happenin'? Mommy, I'm scared, there's funny things outside."

But Christine's own fear was too great to share with another, and she gave his door a harsh rap as she passed it. "Shut up! Oh, just shut up, Wally!" She was inches behind Brad when he entered their bedroom, bumping into his back when he stopped suddenly at the clothes tree and began to pull on jeans and a work shirt. "What are you *doing?*" she said. "What are you getting dressed for?"

"Going outside." He tugged on a tattered pair of Adidas.

"Outside? *Why?*"

"I've got to see something."

"You're not gonna leave me in here with that *thing?*" she wailed, grasping at his shirtfront.

"Then come with me." He pulled away and started for the hall.

"*No!*"

"Then go to hell," he threw back as he half ran for the apartment door, slowing only to note that the black man in the living room was still there.

"*Brad!*" Christine cried, but as she reached the end of the hall, she heard the apartment door slam shut. He was gone, and to follow him now would mean having to go alone past the thing in the living room.

Suddenly she became aware of her son's muffled sobbing, but it was the desire for companionship rather than the maternal instinct that made her enter his room, say, "Wally, Mommy's here," and crawl beneath the sheets of the narrow single bed with the quivering boy.

Even Brad, for all his reckless speed, was shaking before he stepped out onto the pavement in front of his building. He paused at the bottom of the stairs, looking out through the streaked window at the streets and sidewalks of Merridale. The sirens had finally quieted, but the dogs were still sending up a raucous cacophony. Beneath their howls he could hear voices of men and women, shouts, cries, screams. Lights in other apartments on Market Street flickered on and off in a warped harmony. He thought it seemed like hell on earth, with the souls of the damned encased in blue fire.

He took a deep breath and stepped outside. The screams were louder here, the blue lights brighter, and at first he nearly turned around and went back upstairs. But then he remembered that he'd been through worse, and kept moving. All around him the cerulean lights gleamed, each one a huge candle made by a corpse, for death was stamped on every face, molded in the curve of each naked body. Like the old man in Brad's apartment, like the sprawled form of Andy Koser frozen on the sidewalk, not one moved, and the light breeze that poured through the funnel of the street did not stir a single hair of the dead.

As far as he could see, Brad was the only living creature on the street. Now and then a door would open, a head would peer out, but it would be quickly withdrawn, as though pulled back inside by an unseen hand. He began to cross the street, thinking as he did that everyone was really very foolish to be screaming and yelling, to be afraid. After all, what could the dead do? They weren't moving, were not even speaking, and as he thought this, he heard, above the cries of dogs and humans, a laugh that stopped him halfway across the street, and he wondered if it had all been a trap designed to bring a victim out among them, and if now they would begin to move, to gravitate toward him with out-stretched hands and hungry, grinning mouths.

The laugh faded and became words. "They all thought I was *nuts!*" Brad turned and saw Eddie Karl standing ten yards away. Eddie laughed again. "They said I was coo-coo, but they'll know now, won't they, Bradley boy?" He shuffled over to Brad and clapped him on the shoulder. "*You* know, don'tcha? That's why *you're* out *here*, and them other chickenshits are scootered under their beds like rats in a hole. Hell, *these* folks can't hurt 'em! Buncha dummies—they gotta come out sooner or later." Somewhere a woman screamed. "Jesus H.," Eddie said, scowling. " 'Nuff to wake the dead." When he realized what he'd said, his lined face cracked in a smile. "I knew they was here," he said, nodding his head. "I seen 'em all the time," and he moved on down the street, looking with satisfied eyes at each glowing figure as he passed it.

Brad finished crossing the street. He stood next to the green bench by Western Auto, and spoke to what was half sitting, half lying there. "Hey, Rorrie," he said. "Mind if I sit down?"

He sat.

Jim

". . . I wondered how far I should turn out
faithful to that ideal conception of one's own personality every man sets up for himself secretly."
—Joseph Conrad, "The Secret Sharer"

CHAPTER
6

When the sirens woke Jim Callendar, his first concern was for Terry. The boy hated sirens, especially in the middle of the night. "Bat-shees!" he'd called them when they went off a few nights after they'd seen *Darby O'Gill* on cable, and it had taken Jim a few minutes to realize that he was saying "banshees."

Jim was sitting up in bed before he remembered that he did not have to worry about Terry crying in the night. He had not had to worry about that for a long time now. What was it, four years? Five? But still, whenever the sirens wailed he thought of going into Terry's room to stay with him until silence returned.

He fell back in the bed and felt Beth stir beside him. "Bastards," she moaned, covering her head with the pillow. He snorted a half laugh in the dark and rolled onto his side, hoping the keening sound would soon stop and the dogs stop quickly after.

But the sirens screamed on and the dogs kept barking. Melba, their Persian cat, began to growl from somewhere under the bed, and Beth took the pillow away from her ears.

"Melba," she called softly. " 'S'okay, girl. Just sirens."
The cat meowed shrilly and spat. "What's *wrong* with her?"
Beth said. "Sirens don't bother her. . . . C'mon, girl." She
reached down and put her hand under the dust ruffle. There
was another hiss, and Beth gasped and pulled her hand up.
"She *scratched* me!" she said in surprise. "Why, that little
bitch."

"I'll turn the light on. Close your eyes." Jim flicked a
switch and the bedside light exploded into life. He had to
blink several times before opening his eyes wide enough to
see the thin red parallel lines slashed across the heel of Beth's
right hand. "Christ," he said. "She really let you have it.
I'll get something for it."

"It's all right, I'll go." She got up and left the room. Jim
lay in the bed, wondering why the sirens didn't stop. One
blast signified a fire in Merridale proper, and two a fire in
Randallsville, a village three miles away. But he couldn't
remember ever hearing those shrill ululations repeat over and
over again as they did now.

Beth came back into the room, holding a wet washcloth
against her hand, a bottle of Bactine between her fingers.
"What is going *on* out there," she said.

Jim shrugged. "What I was wondering. You think it could
be the plant?" *The plant* was what everyone called Thorn
Hill Nuclear Station, a million-kilowatt power facility ten
miles away that had been completed in 1977.

Beth shook her head. "It's not the plant. They played us a
tape of the sirens a couple of weeks ago at Hatch. Along with
the fire sirens, the nuclear-attack sirens, ambulance, *and*
police."

Jim grinned lopsidedly. "What was all *that* for?"

"American Legion's idea—the kids oughta know what
they're in for—Preparedness Day, they called it."

"More like Paranoia Day. How's the hand?"

She took the washcloth away. "Still oozing. God, she
hasn't done that since she was a kitten. *Listen* to her."

Melba was still snarling under the bed. Jim got down and
lifted the ruffle quickly, holding his hand high. The cat spat,

but did not strike. "Come on, old girl," he called calmly. "What's the matter, huh?"

Only a low throaty growl answered him. The cat would not budge.

"Just sirens, y'know?" As if on cue, the sirens finally fell away into silence, but the dogs kept barking. "All gone, see?" Jim said. "Just the doggies. C'mere."

She went for his hand as she would have gone after a feline rival, front claws wrapping around his wrist, back claws kicking and tearing the skin. He yelled once, then grasped the back of her neck with his free hand, pulling her away from his ripped flesh. With the torn hand he grabbed her legs in a huge fist, like a cowboy hog-tying a steer, and threw her into the hall, slamming the door shut as she rolled screaming on the carpet.

"*Shit!*" he howled. "That *cunt!*"

"Oh, my God," said Beth, pressing the cold washcloth to Jim's wounds, "she got you worse than she got *me!*" They both heard the cat's shrieking progress through the house, past dining room, kitchen, and finally its pattering down the basement steps. Beth leaped up and ran out of the room. In a moment Jim heard the slam of the basement door. "And *stay* there, you rotten little shit! What is *wrong* with her?" Beth asked again as she reentered the bedroom.

"Same thing that's wrong with the dogs." For the first time since the dogs and sirens started, he stepped to the window, pulled back the curtains, and looked out. "Holy shit." It was not said quickly, in surprise or fear, but slowly and thoughtfully, as though something puzzled him.

"What?" Beth moved to his side and looked.

The Sundale Road development was situated on a slight rise, so that part of the town could be seen below. "What are they?" Beth asked. "Can you make it out?"

"I don't know. They look like"—he paused for a long time, knowing how silly it must sound—"like people. Sort of."

The phone rang and both of them jumped. Jim, the first to recover, picked up the receiver, thinking of unexpected deaths, midnight disasters. "Hello?"

The voice on the other end was weak and shaking. "Jim?"

"Yes?"

"Mary Spruce, Jim. Oh, Jim, have you seen?"

"Seen what, Mary?"

"*Outside*. Did you look outside?"

"You mean those lights?"

"Lights? You don't know what they are?"

"Well, no, they're too far—"

"They're *people*. Bodies anyway. It's . . . just horrible."

"*Bodies?*" Jim said. Beth's frown deepened. She seemed ready to yank the phone away.

"Yes, I . . . Look, Jim, Reg is standing here. We're going to go. . . . May I talk to Beth?"

"Uh . . . sure." He handed the phone to his wife, shaking his head quickly to show the confusion he felt. Mary Spruce was the last person he'd expect to go off the deep end. As principal of Hatch Road Elementary, she'd always been the perfect martinet, ramrod straight, unflappable, and undeviating.

"Hello, Mary," Beth said, a note of official crispness in her voice. "What's wrong? . . . Are you serious? . . . Reg wants to *what?* . . . But I'm sure it's not the plant, Mary. It wasn't their siren. . . . All right. . . . No, I don't know what else it could be either. . . . I'll call Dr. Reed in the morning. . . . All right, then. But do you really think . . . I know, Mary. . . ."

Jim began to pace. He looked out past the curtains and saw that the blue lights were still there.

"Yes, I know. . . . No, no one up here seems to be." Jim saw the Tompkins' porch light go on. "All right, I'll take care of it. Now, please don't worry, you—" Beth looked at the phone as though it had bit her ear. "She hung up on me."

"What did she say?"

"Okay, let me . . . let me try to remember. She said that there are blue *people*, blue glowing people in the street, and that they don't move or talk. Evidently downtown is full of them."

"Oh, come on." He sat back down on the bed, turning his attention once more to his cut hand.

"That's what she *said*. And Reg thinks it's got something to do with the plant, so he and Mary are leaving, going to Mary's sister's place in Pittsburgh. She wants me to call Joe Reed and tell him she won't be in school tomorrow."

"Oh, nice. That's a good piece of shit work."

"Yeah, but she wants me to call him *now*."

Jim looked at the clock radio. "Jesus Christ, it's only four. You sure she's not just trying to knock you out of her job in two years?"

"What?"

"I mean, if *I* were the school superintendent and somebody called me at four A.M., I'm damned if I'd make them a principal."

She smiled coldly. "I didn't think you cared about that."

He could not smile back. "I care about you. I still do."

The silence was uncomfortable, and she broke it quickly. "Yeah. Well, that's not going to call Reed for me." She dialed the number while Jim got a pair of binoculars from the closet and looked out the window toward town.

"Mary was right," he said finally. "They *are* people. And they're naked."

"You're joking."

"Come here and look. Mary wasn't crazy."

"I can't. The phone's still . . . Hello? Dr. Reed? . . . This is Elizabeth Callendar. I'm sorry to call you at this hour, but—"

Reed's voice was so loud over the line that Jim could hear it, faint and tinny. ". . . can't talk now," the voice said. "Everything's insane. There will be no school at all in the district tomorrow, if that's why you called. Everything's canceled. *Everything*. Call me back tomorrow." There was a click and the line went dead.

"What the—"

"I told you," said Jim, "come here and *look*."

She went to his side and took the binoculars. "They *are* naked!"

"Uh-huh. And dead, if we can believe Mary."

"Jim, they're not moving."

"That would tend to add credence to the dead part."

75

"Stop it!" she flared, lowering the binoculars. "This isn't funny! What's happening out there?"

Jim thought for a moment. "I'll call Bill Gingrich." He dialed, but the line was busy. "That's funny," he said.

"This whole thing is funny. I'm scared."

"What do you want to do?"

"I don't know."

"We could go see what it's all about."

"No," she said. "I'm not going out there."

"We just going to shiver here till morning?"

"I know I'm not going out."

He nodded. "Okay, then. Let's go back to bed."

She looked at the rumpled bedclothes and shook her head. "I won't sleep. I think I'll make some coffee. How's your hand?"

"It stopped bleeding."

"You going to get up?"

He didn't want to. He knew that if he did, she'd talk about nothing but the hysteria that seemed to be affecting the town. Besides, it was the hour of the wolf, that dark time just before dawn that he treasured, the time when he was used to lying with his guilt next to him like a lover, reliving that moment over and over again, wearing his crown of thorns while Beth was lost in her own sleeping dreams. "No," he said. "I'm still tired."

She left the bedroom, and soon he heard the bubble of the coffeepot, smelled the spicy scent of the brew drifting through the house, remembering how Terry used to love to work the grinder, remembering Terry.

He turned off the bedside lamp and lay on his side, so that he would not see the dim frame of light surrounding the door.

Remembering Terry . . .

CHAPTER
7

"Your *great*-grandfather, Terry. . . . Can you say hello? Hello, hello?"

He held the baby out toward the old man so that they could see each other. There was no understanding in either face. The baby's was smooth and blank; eyes, nose, mouth, were all there, arranged in a cherubic perfection of scale, but it might as well have been featureless like an egg or lifeless like marble for all the reaction it showed to its ancestor.

Jim's grandfather displayed the same outward lack of enthusiasm. His eyes, so small amidst the yellowish pouches of flesh that surrounded them, glittered brightly as they always did, but whether with recognition or with merely the wet slickness of cataracts was something that only Grandpa Foster knew, for he had not spoken a word in three years. His mouth, merely a ridge in a pasty plain, had lost all ability to verbalize. All that remained was a slightly cockeyed smile that fortunately hid the absence of teeth. The mouth and tongue knew only softness, delivered by spoon with the help of patient nurses or by straw from those more hurried. Sucking, like Terry sucked at Beth's breast. Cycles, Jim thought:

four generations apart and both babies sucking for nourishment.

Though never a tall man, Jim's grandfather had once exuded strength just the same, a tight spareness of frame making him look like a little Hercules standing behind the counter of his small grocery store, or tossing the heavy cartons of canned goods out of the cellar hole. He'd been a fixture in Merridale for decades, and the sign over the store, "Foster's Red Rose (Since 1923)," was proudly repainted every few years, at least until the Acmes and the Weis Markets moved in, making the little two-aisle store as obsolete as the pickle barrel, or the soft-drink cooler on the porch where bottles of Sun-Ripe and Moxie and Ma's Root Beer sat neck-deep in water just a touch from freezing, or the ten-pound glass-lidded cans of pretzels that would be measured and sold at the customer's pleasure, bagged without benefit of rubber gloves or cellophane. It was remarkable, Jim remembered, how smiles and friendly words had made up for the lack of sterility. But in 1974, it was all sterility and few smiles. Even in Merridale there was not a "general store" to be found. Oh, other shops were still small and personable, but comestibles were in the hands of the giants, and the happy friendly grocer was a soulless shell who dribbled bloody urine into a plastic bag, while the little store was emptied, stripped, and newly stuffed with a batch of old cookware and battered furniture that was labeled "Antique" by the new sign on the window.

"I think he's tired," said Jim's mother, hovering at the bedside. "Are you tired, Dad? Would you like to sleep now? Did you like the baby, Dad? Isn't he pretty, hmm?" Jim's father made a sour face and looked up on the wall at the picture of Christ sitting in profile, the sleeping Jerusalem beneath him. Then he looked at Jim and shook his head, as if to say what he would say later in the car on the way home: "Can't hear a thing. Didn't even know we were there." Jim smiled sadly at his father, agreeing tacitly. "Do you want to go to sleep now, Dad?" his mother went on. "I think we'd better go. Dad wants to . . ."

Just then the baby gurgled and cooed, and its doll-like hands began to flail the air as if the most beautiful and exciting and colorful toy in all the world hung before its great-grandfather's face. It was the most animated it had been since coming home from the hospital three weeks before, and Jim, Beth, Jim's mother and father, all froze in surprise as baby Terry babbled his magic syllables and weaved his arcane spell.

The enchantment produced a small miracle—a tear, large and crystalline as a diamond, slid from a corner of the old man's eye and drifted over his cheek, pausing momentarily as it slipped from crevice to crevice.

"My God," whispered Jim's mother. Old Dan Foster started to shake then, and more tears dripped from his eyes, while a thick boll of mucus appeared at each nostril.

"He's crying," Jim said. "He understands. He really knows," and the craggy head nodded ever so slightly.

They talked nonstop to the old man then, telling him things they hadn't thought about before because they had been so sure that Grandpa Foster wouldn't understand them. Jim's mother told him about the antique store, lying when she said it looked nice. Jim told him about the company newsletter he was editing, lying when he told him how much he enjoyed doing it, and thinking it ironic that old people should be told so many lies, especially an old man who had just miraculously demonstrated a capacity for understanding the truth. So, while Terry bubbled and babbled, Jim told the lies. The truth was not shocking, not even atypical.

He disliked his job. It was that simple. His official title, as related in his job description, was Administrative Associate, Employee Services. It meant that he was in charge of editing (organizing, laying out, and writing ninety percent of the copy for) *The Open Eye*, an eight-page biweekly newsletter for the white-collar staff of Linden Industries, a building-equipment company that owned a hefty piece of Lansford and employed a large number of its residents. When he'd taken the job in 1967, right out of college, he'd felt as though he'd been gently blessed. It was, as Harry Oakes told him, a *great* job for a college grad with a major in journalism. "Perfect place to learn the ropes," Oakes had said. "You'd be surprised—kids don't *want* to work for business these days.

79

They'd rather starve on some dipshit small-town newspaper staff. Think they're gonna *express* themselves. What they wind up expressing is bake-sale announcements. But here you'll be your own boss, Jim. It's *your* paper. Of course, Mr. Matthews and I will want to take a look at each issue beforehand just to make sure you don't spill any beans that shouldn't be spilled, if you get me. After all, you'll have access to a lot of important information, more than any other young fellow in this company, I'll tell you *that*. But I think you'll be surprised at the free rein you'll have."

Jim *was* surprised. Not at the free rein, but at the bit that was inserted between his journalistic teeth after he put together his first issue. Too political, was Mr. Matthews's verdict. Too topical, Mr. Oakes's. Matthews's strike-outs and changes were numerous, and drafted in a rude, thick red. The line in an article about proposed housing starts for 1968; "With the expected escalation of the Vietnam Conflict, economists have predicted a small downturn in . . ." was slashed savagely, a huge *"NO!"* emblazoned over it for good measure. When Jim asked Oakes the reason, Oakes smiled uncomfortably.

"That's my comment," he said, "about being too topical. You see, Mr. Matthews really doesn't like any mentions of . . . uh . . . hard news. After all, it *is* a *company* newsletter, and should be fairly well restricted to what goes on in the company."

Jim was honestly confused. "Mr. Oakes, doesn't what directly affects the company have some bearing on what goes into it?"

"I *don't* think it's necessary to mention Vietnam."

"But if Vietnam escalates, there aren't going to be as many housing starts because a lot of prospective home buyers will be going over there."

"Would you just make the change please, Jim?"

"But don't you think—"

Oakes's face hardened. "Jim, let me clarify this. Mr. Matthews and I would prefer to see no mention of Vietnam, race problems, peace movements, hippies, the draft, Eugene McCarthy, Bobby Kennedy, communism, dope, rock and roll

80

music"—he thought for only a moment before adding—"and sex. We make building equipment. We don't make guns or placards or marijuana. Understand?"

Jim didn't answer.

"Okay?"

Finally he nodded. "Okay."

Mr. Oakes leaned forward. "You like your job, Jim?"

He made himself nod. "I like it."

"Good. Because a lot of other people would like it too. Good health coverage, insurance, nice retirement package, decent salary . . ." Oakes smiled again. "Listen, Jim, I'm sorry we had to have this little talk. I like you. You're a bright young guy and you've already added a lot to Linden. But we just have our own ways of doing things."

Jim smiled. It tasted sour. "I understand. I'm sorry about the hassle."

"That's all right then." Oakes stood up and walked Jim to the door of his office. "You know, business is a lot like being married, Jim. You're married, aren't you?"

"Yes."

"It's a partnership, you know? A bond. And there'll be ups and downs, and disagreements galore, but if both parties stick it out, you can have a long and beautiful relationship. 'Till retirement do us part,' huh?"

"Yeah. Sure."

"Well, then." Oakes made his smile even broader. "Enough said?"

Jim nodded. "Enough said. Thanks." And he walked back to his office, his stomach churning with fury, his teeth gritted together so hard he imagined he could hear the enamel crack.

"Quit?" said Beth that evening as they prepared dinner. "You just *got* the job, Jim."

"I know."

"Why in God's name would you want to quit?"

Jim made the hamburger patties and told Beth about Oakes and the *Eye* and the Vietnam line. "He threatened me," he concluded. "I didn't even *argue* with him—just disagreed— and the son of a bitch actually *threatened* me."

Beth said nothing. She kept her eyes on the soup she was stirring. Jim stopped patting the cold meat and stared at her.

"Did you hear me?"

She nodded. "I heard. So you want to quit."

"Yeah."

Beth sighed and turned to him. "Jim, we're not in school anymore."

"What's *that* mean?"

She took the burgers and lay them in the electric skillet, speaking over the hissing they made. "It means that this is the real world now. We can't just . . . walk away from things if they don't work out right away."

"You can *always* walk away from shit."

Her voice rose, angry. "Sure you can walk away, but you've got to walk *to* someplace too! What really happened? You were insulted, that's all, because Mr. Oakes wanted things done the way they've always been done. That's his *right*."

"It's not just that!" he flared back. "It's just that it's *indicative*."

"Indicative of *what?*"

"Of what I've got to look forward to there. Bullshit, repression . . ." He barked a humorless laugh. "Matthews has *already* made cracks about my beard, for Christ's sake."

"You've only been there three months," Beth said, turning off the burner. "Can't you give it more time than that?"

"Why? They're not going to change, and I'm damned if I will."

"Have you got another job, then?"

"You know I haven't."

"Let's eat," she said, putting the burgers and soup bowls on a tray and carrying them into the dining room.

"We're not done talking about this," he said, following her.

"All right," she answered, sitting down and opening her napkin. "See if this finishes it. I teach school"—she ticked off the points on her fingers one by one—"for sixty-two hundred dollars a year. You work at Linden for eleven-five. Our car payment is a hundred dollars a month, our rent is a

82

hundred and seventy-five. Our student-loan payments are a hundred and fifty.'' She paused. ''That's over five thousand a year. You quit, we live on my salary. Now, do you think we can even *eat* for a thousand dollars?''

He stared at the food on the table for a long time before answering. ''All right. I'll wait.''

''For how long?''

He looked up at her. ''Until I find something else.''

''Or until it gets better?''

''It won't get better.''

''I'm sorry,'' she said. ''I just worry.''

''Don't worry. We won't starve.''

They didn't. For the next few months Jim made a conscious effort to write only what Matthews and Oakes wanted to read, and did it very well. Oakes commented on it several times, and even Matthews dropped into Jim's cubicle to congratulate him on a job well done.

''A job well done,'' he told Beth at home, shaking his head and sipping a cold glass of white wine. ''God, I can't wait to get out of there.''

''Have you been looking?'' Beth asked, thumbing through *Newsweek*.

''I've been looking. Plenty of jobs, but they're all in business and industry. Hell, *they* could be *worse*.''

''Well, what do you want?'' She put the magazine down with a sigh.

''I was a journalism major,'' he said dryly. ''Words are my business, my business is words. It would be very nice to find a newspaper at which I could be Jim Callendar, Boy Reporter.''

''At a hundred bucks a week.''

''It's better than selling out.''

''Bullshit, selling out. Jim, Linden Industries isn't the Bank of America or Dow or Boeing. Besides, it could be worse. You could've been drafted.''

Jim grunted. ''Thank God for trick knees. Gonna have to get pretty bad before they take *me*.'' He finished his wine. ''Yeah,'' he said, ''it could be worse. I'm sort of getting used to the crap.''

"That's good."

He looked up quickly. "No! That's *bad*. I don't *want* to get used to it. Next thing you know I'll be *happy* there."

"And what's wrong with being happy?"

"Maybe 'happy' isn't the word. Maybe it's 'contented.' Or '*satisfied*.' I don't want to be satisfied with that."

Beth shrugged. "Just hang on a little longer. You've seen them at their worst. So why not take the money as long as you want and run?"

"Just so I remember how to run."

"You'll know," said Beth, "when the time comes."

The time did not come for nearly eight years. It was not that Jim did not think about alternatives, for he did. He looked into the possibilities of work in Philadelphia, New York, Boston, even Los Angeles. But the jobs that were available always had something wrong with them, real or imagined. For the truth, which Beth dimly suspected but which Jim would never admit even to himself, was that he did not want to leave Merridale. He was bound to it with long-standing chains of affection. His family had lived there always, he knew the people on the street, the stores where they bought the necessities and pleasures of life. There was a sense of eternity about the town. It was an ageless place whose outer face would change with time but whose heart would remain as it always was, and he had no desire to leave it. On occasion he would travel in his job, and he found the great cities exciting, but ultimately as cold and unfriendly as the steel and glass of their buildings. It was always a relief when the train pulled into Merridale Station and he stepped off, the smell of honeysuckle that covered the embankment strong and sweet and welcoming, Beth waiting in the Toyota to take him back to their apartment.

And later to take him back to their house on Sundale Road.

And still later, Beth waiting, not alone, but with Terry strapped securely into his car seat, muffled in bright blue blankets so that only his face was visible, red and round as a lumpy apple.

Beth had been hesitant when Jim first brought up the idea of having a baby. The school was growing to the extent that rumors were flying of an assistant principalship that would probably be created in a year or two to aid Hatch Road's principal, Mary Spruce. Beth wanted the job. She had not always yearned for an administrative position, but found that the day to day classroom grind was beginning to oppress her, because she could not detach herself from the role of surrogate parent. Her involvement with her students had become emotional as well as tutorial, and the twin giving sapped her energies. Her days were full of loving and caring and teaching, her nights full of planning. If, she felt, she could acquire an administrative job, she would be a step withdrawn from the children, and though she loved the closeness that being in the classroom provided, she retained enough self-awareness to realize that continuing as she was could ultimately prove self-destructive. So when Jim suggested the possibility of a child, her response was guarded.

"I'd like a baby," she said, "but if the job opens up when I'm pregnant, or in the first year, there's no way I'll get it."

"Why not talk to Mary?" Jim said.

"I couldn't do that."

"Why not? You're friends. Just tell her how you feel. You both know damn well you're the best teacher they've got out there. See what the chances are. Maybe they don't need an assistant for a few years."

Beth talked to Mary, and found her surprisingly open. Mary told her that it could be two, perhaps as many as three, years before the school population warranted an administrative expansion at Hatch, and Beth would certainly be considered. "The board makes the final choice, Beth," Mary said with a smile, "but I'd bet they'd go by my recommendation. And I certainly think you could handle it."

"Even if I took a leave of absence for a couple of years?"

"Why?" Mary took off her bifocals and looked at Beth from sharp, unglassed eyes.

Beth told her then about their plan to have a baby, and Mary grinned, putting her glasses back on like a happy-face mask.

"Are you pregnant now?" she asked.

"Not yet."

"Well, don't worry about a thing. I'll see you get maternity leave for as long as you want. As for leaving, it would be convenient if you could finish a year rather than leave in the middle of one."

"With a little lucky timing," Beth said, and both women laughed.

"Oh, it's time. How old are you, Beth?"

"Twenty-six."

"Well, you wouldn't want to wait much longer. Is Jim excited?"

Beth nodded. "I think he wants one more than *I* do."

"Reg was the same way. But when the twins came he changed his mind." Mary put a hand on Beth's shoulder. "You go ahead and *do* it," she said. "There'll be a job for you when you're ready, even if I have to make one." And then her sixtyish, blue-haired principal said something that amazed Beth. "And if you want to get pregnant fast, put him on the bottom and when it happens, just *sit* on it. Don't move a muscle." She grinned crookedly. "If you can help it." They both giggled like schoolgirls.

When she got home, Beth told Jim what Mary had said. They laughed about it, then they tried it.

Beth was pregnant by February. She requested maternity leave for the 1973–74 school year, and was granted it. By June she was starting to show, and the mounding of her stomach brought out all the protective instincts that Jim had never realized he'd had. He also got a job moonlighting for the *Merridale Messenger*.

Jim had known Bill Gingrich since Jim was in high school. When his eighth-grade English class had gone on a tour of the *Messenger* offices and press room, Gingrich had acted as guide. Jim had been fascinated by the workings of the small weekly, and talked to Gingrich for such a long time that he nearly missed the bus back to school. His interest in journalism grew, and in his freshman year he became a junior reporter for the *Merridale High Sentinel*, which was printed at the *Messenger*'s offices. Jim would consistently volunteer for the little-loved job of going to the offices Wednesdays after school to pick up the papers for Thursday distribution.

He'd always used the time to talk to Gingrich, who spoke gruffly but was secretly pleased to have an audience to whom he could tell his stories of working on the *Lansford Courier* in the forties.

So when Jim entered the *Messenger* offices twenty years later and told Gingrich his name, Gingrich, a little balder and a lot fatter, grinned. "Jimmy—the kid who used to make me tell all my war stories!"

Jim laughed. "Was I that big a pest?"

"Nah. Hell, I liked it. So what can I do for you?"

Jim told him that he was looking for a part-time job, explaining the situation with Beth and the expected baby. "I suppose I could stock shelves or something," he said, "but I'd rather do something that I know about and like. Frankly, Mr. Gingrich, I don't know where else you could get my experience for the money I'm willing to take."

"What kind of stuff do you want to do?" Gingrich wasn't smiling anymore.

"What do you need?" Jim shrugged. "I'll do it."

"Well, there *have* been two things that've been a pain in the ass lately. One's the advertising. I guess I'm just getting too old and fat to toddle around town trying to sell the shit."

"You mean you don't have a permanent-space agreement with any store owners?"

"Oh, a few, but most of 'em only advertise when they've got a sale or a little money to burn. Keeping them buying regularly's like pulling teeth. The other thing's the 'Around the Square' column. Lettie Parker'd been handling that for me, but her husband got transferred and I've been doing it myself. There's a lot that people call in, but never enough to fill it up, so I gotta go hunting and I got no time to hunt."

"What kind of hunting?"

"Calling churches, the Lions, Moose, the high school, asking them what the hell's going on, then writing it up. A few little gossipy things—who went to Europe on their vacation, who visited who in Florida . . ."

Jim smiled. "Sounds like Marie Snyder'd be a natural for it."

Gingrich barked a laugh. "*That* old bitch? But you're

right. She'd be a damn good source. I'd doublecheck everything from her though.''

"I will.''

"You *will?* Hold it, kid. We haven't talked money yet. I'm not a rich man, in spite of my luxurious surroundings.'' He gestured expansively around the cluttered office at the scattered papers, dented furniture, and a multitude of empty Styrofoam coffee cups.

Jim chuckled, still liking the man and his style. "Oh, I think we can come to a mutually acceptable agreement.''

"Listen to him. He even *sounds* like a journalist. You use those two-dollar words in my quarter rag, kid, and you're out of work.'' He frowned. "How's five bucks an hour for working the advertising sound? And twenty-five a week for 'Around the Square'?''

Jim thought for a minute. "How many hours a week will the ad stuff take?''

"Seven or eight. Thursday or Friday nights or Saturdays.''

Sixty-five a week. Jim thought it would help, and he'd probably enjoy it. He nodded. "Sounds good.''

"Hot damn, I got me a sucker. Wanta start next week?''

"Sure.''

"Tell you what,'' Gingrich smiled. "How about another column? Write it all by yourself, an extra fifteen bucks a week.''

"Great. What about?''

The older man shrugged. "Leave it up to you. Just connect it with the town somehow. And not too political or controversial, y'know.''

Jim nodded cynically. "I'm used to that.''

"I bet you are, working at Linden. Everybody's running scared, especially with that dumbo Nixon and this Watergate mess. It's gonna open a few eyes before it's all over, see if it doesn't.''

"Wait a minute,'' said Jim carefully. "I thought you were a Nixon man.''

"Ha! *That* stinker? Don't believe everything you read in the paper, kid, especially mine. As goes Merridale, so goes the *Messenger*. I've been a Roosevelt Democrat my whole damn life. The paper supports Republicans because it's *bought* by Republicans. Hell, you run Mussolini as a Republican, this town'd vote for him.'' He shook his head sadly. ''And I'd probably write an editorial supporting him. Welcome to yellow journalism.''

Jim liked Bill Gingrich's brand of yellow journalism. The Saturday visits to the town merchants to peddle ads were not at all unpleasant. On the contrary, he enjoyed talking to these men and women who had put their stake in Merridale, and even if he didn't come out of a store with a sale, he came away with a feeling of warmth and communication nonetheless, of his batteries being charged in the dynamo of small-town humanity, so different from the calculated heartlessness of Linden Industries. *These* businesses were manned by human beings, not automatons whose sole loyalty was to profit. And in the stores and small businesses of Merridale there were no scapegoats to blame, no gray faceless clones far down the line. In Merridale if something went wrong, it was the owner who took the blame, and if he succeeded, it was due to his own efforts. Rugged individualism still survived here—in Stephen's Drugs, Byer's Book Store, the Friendly Gift Shoppe, and dozens of other one- to five-man businesses that ran up and down and across Market and High Street like marchers in a parade.

That was the very image Jim used for his first fifteen-dollar column. It was shamelessly pro–small town and pro–small business, and he wrote it in a white-hot patriotic fervor that seemed strange to him even as he did it. ''Good stuff,'' Gingrich said after reading it. ''A little thick for my blood maybe, but everybody else'll eat it up.'' He looked at Jim a bit suspiciously from over the top of his glasses. ''You really meant what you wrote here, didn't you?''

Jim smiled.

''Don't be embarrassed,'' said Gingrich. ''Nothing to be ashamed of. I'm just a little surprised you feel this way.''

''I *like* Merridale.''

''Yeah. I do too. Only reason I've stayed here so long.'' He leaned back and propped his feet on the desk top. ''Got a lot of nice folks here. Got a lot of assholes too. Now the secret is that there are assholes everywhere you go. You can't escape them. But me, I've learned that I like the Merridale assholes better than the assholes anywhere else." He grinned. "They're Norman Rockwell assholes. I like Norman Rockwell. How about you?"

"He's okay."

"You'll weaken with time. Wait till you have your kid and he starts getting bigger. You'll *love* Norman Rockwell."

Jim wasn't sure of that, but he was sure of his love for the town. It shone through his columns and even in "Around the Square." He discovered that people were not merely willing but anxious to report on the most pedestrian doings of their lives and organizations. It amused him and delighted him as well, for in a solipsistic way they were right: Don and Rachel Martin's trip to Vermont and the St. John's Chicken Corn Soup Supper were, in the universe of Don and Rachel Martin and the ladies of the church, far more important than the talks between Henry Kissinger and the representatives of Ho Chi Minh, or all this fuss in Washington about the burglary at that Watergate place, or the earthquakes in Nicaragua. No one from Merridale had ever *been* to Nicaragua, except for Pastor Craven and his wife, and that had been a good fifteen years earlier.

Oh, yes, Jim thought and thought again, Merridale was as self-centered as a Broadway star on opening night. But was that such a flaw? After all, he was beginning to believe himself that the world revolved around the town. "All is dross that is not Merridale." When one lives their whole life in one place, doesn't that place become life itself? Life and death and birth.

And in October 1973, as was his father, Terence John Callendar was born in Lansford General Hospital and taken home to Merridale, where he was shown off to sundry relatives and loved, Jim felt, as no baby had been before. Beth was an excellent mother and spent more time with Terry than Jim had ever expected her to. "I've got him for a year, all to myself," she told him, "before I have to go back to the school. So I'm really going to make it count." Jim wished that he had more time to spend with the two of them, but

Linden stole his days, and the *Messenger* took most evenings and much of the weekend. It was far from an ideal situation in which to form a strong father-son bond, but he tried, writing after Terry had gone to sleep, and getting up early on Saturday mornings so that he could often finish his ad work by noon.

Beth's attention paid off, for Terry was a bright, lively, healthy baby whose infectious spirit proved strong enough to reactivate even Jim's grandfather. Although speech never returned to Dan Foster, they were able to work out a simple yes-no code with eye squints.

When his grandfather died peacefully in his sleep in the nursing home, Jim was in the hospital himself, about to undergo an operation. Beth, although she knew of Grandpa Foster's death, did not tell Jim. He was upset enough. He'd begun coughing in June, three months before. It was a dry phlegmless cough that refused to disappear. Finally he'd gone to Dr. Page in Merridale, who could find nothing wrong. "Give it another week," he told Jim, and gave him some antibiotics. "If it's still bad, call me."

Four days after the exam he started to cough up small gobbets of dark red blood. The next day he called Dr. Page, who reexamined him and sent him to a throat specialist at Lansford General. At the hospital, Jim went through a battery of tests that revealed a growth on his trachea. The doctor was strangely unsmiling, uncomforting. "We'll have to remove it," he said across a desk top littered with indecipherable papers.

"Do you have any idea what it is?" Jim asked, trying to keep the panic out of his voice.

"Not really. There's no way of telling until we remove it for a biopsy."

"Then it could be cancerous," he ventured.

The doctor nodded. "There's always that possibility."

"What are the chances it is?"

"I don't give chances. We're not gambling here. Some doctors would say one chance in ten, another one in five, another one in a hundred. Then if it *is* malignant, the patient

91

feels cheated. Me, the only odds I give are fifty-fifty. Either it is or it isn't."

"And"—Jim's throat felt thick, lined with heavy velvet—"and what if it is?"

"Then we treat it. But let's find out first. One step at a time."

"But do most people . . . I mean, could I survive it?"

"Every case is different. It depends on a lot of things. But it should be done quickly. The faster we find out, the better chance we've got of doing something about it. Can you come in tomorrow?"

"So soon?"

"No point in waiting. It won't go away."

Jim nodded. "All right. I guess so." Then he started to cry. It was nearly internal, a shaking of the shoulders, a trembling in the chest, the Adam's apple bobbing rhythmically. Tears trickled weakly from his eyes, but there were no audible sobs. The doctor looked down at his desk top and gave Jim instructions on what to bring and do when he entered the hospital.

When Jim got home he cried again, this time loudly, unashamed, in Beth's arms. "It's all right," she whispered. "It'll be all right. He *had* to say those things. Just in case. Just to protect himself. But it'll be all right, you'll see. They always get you ready for the worst, the very worst, that's all. You'll see."

"It's not," he sobbed, "it's not that death scares me. It's just that I don't want to *leave* you—you and Terry. I just . . . can't . . . *bear* that."

"You won't. You won't. Shh . . . shh . . ."

He kept crying, and didn't cry again when he was finished. The next afternoon he entered the hospital. The tests and preparations left him weary and shaken, and the nurse had to wake him the next morning at 6:00 A.M. to take him to the operating room. He remembered the prick of a needle, a drowsy journey down halls, through elevators, the silver metal of the operating room, and then nothing. His next sensation was that of violent peristalsis, striving to turn his head to let the vomit come up, but being strapped to a table

92

and then nothing once more, and finally slow waking and a pain in his throat as though it were raw and rubbed with salt. Beth beside him, smiling and pale. "They say it's benign," she whispered.

He tried to talk, to voice a syllable, but it was impossible.

"They won't know for sure until they do a full biopsy, but the frozen section . . . Well, they say it looks okay."

It would be all right. He would live. He was not going to die.

Jim learned of his grandfather's death two days later. He was eating soft solids and was able to speak in a whisper. "He died instead of me," he said quietly when Beth told him the news.

"Don't say that," she said. "You had nothing to do with it."

He smiled and nodded then and said she was right, that that was a silly thing for him to say. But he thought to himself over and over again, He died instead of me, and that night he whispered "Thank you" to his grandfather and to God until he only thought the words, and then until he was asleep.

While he recovered in the weeks that followed, his mind took a decidedly mystical bent, and he saw the elements of his life coalesce into an imagined whole of which he had not previously dreamed. It was his near approach to death that had caused this more superstitious view of life, and he began to see meaning where before had been only chaos. Everything was fraught with signs and portents, indications of guidance. He had *not* died and there was a reason for that, but there was also a reason why he had come so *close* to death. It was *ordained* that he should feel the brush of the dark wings. What point was there otherwise to the suffering he had gone through? What point to his grandfather's death on the very night before his operation? It was a warning, a cautionary call that life was short, too short to be wasted.

Signs and portents.

The day before he was to go back to Linden he told Beth that he was quitting.

"Quitting?" she said, only mildly surprised. "For good?"

He nodded. "You want to go back to work anyway. And the paper's going well. I'd like to work full-time on it."

"What about Terry?"

"I can do a lot of my work at home. And when I can't, there's my mom, and what about Marty Pierce? She watches the Humphreys' baby."

"Just tell me—*why* do you want to quit?"

He told her about dead ends in life, of the happiness that working on the *Messenger* had brought him, of the dropped hints by Bill Gingrich that he could use a full-time assistant.

"It'll be hard," she said. "The money."

"We can manage."

They did manage. Beth secured a job at Hatch before Jim quit. It was short notice, but Mary Spruce pushed with all her might to wedge Beth into the as yet nonexistent assistant principal's position. That enrollment was up twelve percent helped, and Beth found herself making a salary of nearly a third again as much as when she had taught. Unfortunately Jim was offered only a bit more than half of what he was earning at Linden. Nevertheless, he accepted Bill Gingrich's offer, and turned in his resignation to Mr. Oakes, who was sincerely sorry to receive it.

The editorial page of the *Messenger* contained a new addition the following week: "James Callendar, Assistant Editor."

"Just goes to show you Horatio Alger was right," Bill Gingrich said wryly when he handed Jim a copy of the paper. "A man *can* become a legend in his own time."

Once he began newspaper work full-time, Jim liked it even better than he had before. To his relief, he found that he was able to spend a large part of his time writing and doing layout at home, so he was able to care for Terry with only occasional recourse to his mother or Marty Pierce, a large-boned kindly-eyed woman who lived only a few blocks away. Although he tried at first to do his work during the day, he found that the baby kept him far busier than he had expected, so most of the work was done at night. Gingrich quietly accepted the situation, particularly since Jim was always ahead of schedule on his duties and assignments. Once or twice he would growl, "Man oughta be a bachelor to work on a newspaper," and added, "or a childless widower." But the bantering was good-natured, and the relationship between the two men grew to be almost familial. Gingrich had dinner at the Callendars' every other week, and he and Jim often stopped in at the bar at the Anchor on Wednesday evenings after the weekly edition was in the hands of the printer and Beth was home with Terry.

So the years went by calmly. Jim was happy and content with his work and his family, and he flowed with the seasons as they passed effortlessly into one another. Beth liked her administrative position as well, and seemed far more relaxed than when she had been in the classroom. The youngest member of the family, Terry, was fulfilling all expectations. He was an active child, afraid of little, self-confident without being overbearing. Jim thought the time that he had spent with the boy was in large part responsible. While other fathers might come home tired and irritable, wanting only to be left alone and finally feeling communicative when it was too late and the kids were in bed, Jim had always made it a point to stop and listen when Terry had something to say. The work would always be there, but his son would not. Before he would even realize it, Jim thought, Terry would be gone. Though it made him immeasurably sad, he thought of the old song about turning around to find your children older, and then finally grown and out the door. He thought of it often, to remind himself of what was truly important, like a Catholic bearing a crucifix with the figure of his dead Lord.

Later, after the accident, he was almost sorry they had grown so close. It only made the loss that much greater, made him say over and over again, "If only . . . if only . . ."

If only things had not happened as they had. But it was of no use to contemplate. It *had* happened, all of it, one event leading inexorably to the next.

They could have done without the money. Had he known, had he even suspected, had a voice said to him, "There is a risk factor here of a thousand to one," he never would have gotten behind the wheel. But there was no one to whisper or warn; there was only the promise of five dollars an hour to drive the school bus.

It was not a great amount for a college graduate to be paid in 1981, but 1981 was not a great year. Everyone was feeling the pinch, especially the small-town merchants whose goods were going unsold because few people had enough money to pay full retail price, and those who did also chose to conserve by buying what they could at the recently opened K-Mart, or at the Jewelcor in Lansford. Lower sales meant lower profits, and the burghers of Merridale decided independently, yet *en masse*, that advertising would be the least painful thing to let slip by the roadside. Their motivations were for the most part humanitarian, although Bill Gingrich didn't see it that way.

"Damn fools are gonna kill themselves—and *us*," he said over the first of their Wednesday evening beers. "Don't know why they can't see it. Oh, sure, they'll keep most of their people on and cut out their advertising when they need it the most. 'Do anything I can to keep from letting my clerks go,' Matt Sheller—hell, you heard him."

"You can't blame them, Bill," Jim said, nursing his beer. "Most of his people've been there for years. I remember Mike and Pete from when I was in high school."

"I'm not blaming them," Gingrich said, his temper rising. "Sheller doesn't have to fire *anybody*. If he and the other clowns in this town made their prices competitive with the chains, they'd do fine and they could *still* buy advertising."

"Can they really compete?"

"Hell, yes. Matt Sheller might have to start driving a Volkswagen instead of his yearly New Yorker, but what he'd lose at first in profit he'd make up eventually in volume."

"If it's that simple, why haven't they done it already?"

Gingrich looked at Jim and smiled slightly. "This, in case you hadn't noticed, is *Merridale*, my boy. You've been on the paper seven years, you oughta know by now. Things are done here as they've been done for two hundred years. One neither stands up in the boat nor rattles the oars, or one will find one's ass pitched overboard." He held up a finger for another beer. "Tell me, what do you think would happen to the first Merridale merchant to change his store's name to 'Discount City'?"

Jim frowned. "I'm not sure. But he'd probably do well."

"I beg to differ. In *my* scenario he would be shunned by his fellows, his wife would be ignored at Thursday morning Bible study, and his kid might get the shit kicked out of him at school. The few customers he had had would desert him, and he would go bankrupt, followed by an early death and a pauper's grave, leaving his widow and orphans to the mercies of the Reagan nonwelfare state."

"Come on, Bill." Jim laughed. "You're not serious."

"Bet me." His smile vanished. "Some outsider comes in and builds a K-Mart or a Thrift Drugs on the outskirts, and there's a little bitching and moaning, but before you know it everybody's out there snuffling up dish towels three for a dollar. But let one of our *own* turn traitor, and spiderwebs will form on his door real fast." Gingrich took a long draft of beer and stifled a belch. "Nope, they're content to go along doing what they've always done and what their daddies always did. Wouldn't know a good marketing idea if it bit 'em in the ass. And when they *need* to advertise the most— sell their small-town friendly service if they can't sell price— they don't advertise. No, *they* only advertise when they don't really need to. Dim bulbs. All of 'em. Just dim bulbs." He shook his head and gnawed his lower lip. "We're hurtin', Jim."

"That bad, huh?"

"That bad."

"Hell, Bill, I've tried to get them to buy."

"I know you have. I'm not blaming you at all. But goddammit . . ." Gingrich paused, and Jim sensed a frustration and a self-hatred that was alien to the man. When he spoke again, the words came slowly, painstakingly, an apology in each syllable. "I didn't know how I was going to tell you. I guess there's no easy way." He turned and looked Jim full in the face. "I'm not going to be able to keep you full-time anymore, Jim. I just can't afford it."

Jim Callendar felt as if he'd suddenly swallowed a lump of ice, but he said nothing.

"Maybe," Gingrich went on, "maybe if I kept you on and the economy got better real fast, I could make it. But that's a pretty big maybe." He put his hand on Jim's arm, the only time other than a handshake that they had ever touched. "It's not you, okay? I mean you've done a wonderful job, and you deserve a helluva lot better than this. But I just . . . have no choice. I've been working on the *Messenger* for forty-one years, Jim—"

"No, look, I understand." He didn't want to hear a speech, not now. He was angry, hurt, bitter, and though he was also displeased with himself for feeling that way, he could not help it. Gingrich still had his paper; Jim had nothing.

"*Forty-one years*," Gingrich pressed. "I can't risk losing that."

"You don't have to *justify* it, Bill," Jim said, snappishly enough to make Gingrich draw back. Jim added, more gently, "I understand. Really I do."

They sat in silence for a time, watching the foam dry into moist, white webs on the insides of their beer glasses.

"If you could," Gingrich finally said, "I'd like you to keep doing your own column and 'Around the Square.'"

"Look, you don't have to—"

"I didn't just think of that," said Gingrich, the old spark returning. "I'd intended to ask you all along, okay?"

Jim stared at him, then nodded. "Okay. Until I find something else." Gingrich nodded back. "How much?" Jim asked.

Gingrich pursed his lips, but his eyes relaxed, as though he were once more on familiar ground. "Fifty for the 'Square,' Thirty for yours."

Jim shrugged. "All right."

"And one more thing," Gingrich said. "As soon as I can afford to hire you back, I *want* you back."

"We'll see."

"Goddammit, I'm *sorry*." The word was so loud that even the regulars turned. Gingrich noticed and returned his tone to normal. "You are the only guy except for me who has ever

98

liked both newspaper work and this fucking blindered town enough to maybe be able to make a go of the *Messenger*. Now *someday* I am going to die—''

''Aw, come on, Bill—''

''I'm *serious*. I've got no family, nobody I can trust this rag to. . . . All I've got is Thelma for the secretary stuff and Clarence for the shit work, and they're both two years older'n dirt and not much brighter. So where does that leave me? You may not be much, kid, but you're all I've got.''

''All you *had*, you mean.''

''I can't apologize forever. You gonna let me talk? Okay, then, what I'm saying is that you stick with me and the paper's yours someday. That simple. If you want it.''

''Jesus Christ, Bill, you just fired me. Now to make up for it you're leaving me the paper?''

Gingrich looked puzzled, as if he hadn't seen it in that light. ''Yeah,'' he said. ''I guess that's what I'm doing.''

Jim shook his head. ''I'm sorry, I can't deal with this right now. You do whatever the hell you want. It's your paper. I'm going home.'' He put the money for his beer on the bar. Gingrich tried to return it to him, but he wouldn't take it. ''You'll have my columns on time,'' he said, and left.

Beth was reading *Time* and Terry was watching *The Muppet Show* when Jim came into the rec room. He dutifully kissed them both, but Beth sensed the tension inside him. ''Get it put to bed?'' she asked.

''Yeah,'' he answered. ''Did I ever.'' She looked at him, and he gestured upstairs. A minute later, at the kitchen table, he told her about losing his job. She stood, came around the table to where he sat, and embraced him from behind.

''It's okay,'' she said, stroking his hair as though he were crying. But he was nowhere near tears. The feeling was too empty for that. It was as though someone had taken a freezing metal scoop and dug pieces out of his stomach, and the places where the chunks had come out were now cauterized, not by fire, but by ice. ''We'll be all right.''

Dully, he told her about the eighty dollars a week his columns would bring, and she brightened. ''Maybe if you don't find anything right away you could get something part-time." He listened while she rattled off several possibilities, praying that she would not suggest trying to return to Linden and loving her when she did not.

It was not until much later, when they were both in bed, that she thought of it. "Buses . . ." she said, propping herself on an elbow.

"Hmmm?"

"I don't know why I didn't think of it before. Otto Floyd is retiring soon."

"Who's Otto Floyd?"

"Our garbageman. But he also drives the Hatch Road school bus. And they don't have a replacement for him."

"Me? I never drove a bus before."

"Oh, it'd be easy. It's just like a car, only bigger. Isn't it?"

He lay quietly in the darkness, thinking.

"It's a couple of hours in the morning and some in the afternoon. And you get a lot of extra time for trips and things. Five dollars an hour is what Otto's getting."

"How do you know all this?"

"I make all the bus arrangements."

"You do the hiring?"

"The board. You can't buy a pencil without the board. But I'm your *in*, right?"

"Only a hundred a week," he mused.

"Plus eighty for the columns plus whatever extra there might be for field trips and sports and such. It's almost as good as a full-time job."

"I'm not a bus driver, though."

"Otto can teach you. He likes me."

"Oh, yeah? Why?"

"He says I'm pretty."

"You're—"

"And he likes my garbage bags. Says they never split open."

He laughed, then stopped suddenly.

"What's wrong?" Beth asked.

"It's crazy," he said. "Here I am, a thirty-five-year-old

100

college graduate, and a garbageman is going to teach me a trade."

"Well," Beth said after a moment, "recessions make strange bedfellows."

They retreated then to their individual thoughts, and Jim wondered if he would be able to drive a bus, wondered if the board would think his hiring smacked of nepotism, wondered if it would all come easy.

And it did. It was so simple that he could hardly fathom it. It seemed that he, who had never driven anything larger than a Mustang, had been born to drive a bus. After Otto had shown him the basics, the big orange-yellow box became an extension of his body, going nimbly where he wanted it to, turning, twisting, stopping precisely as his hands and feet guided it. "Jesus, but you got the touch there, Mr. Callendar," Otto told him. Jim had asked him to call him by his first name, but Otto ignored the pleasantry, as if sensing a caste separation that the necessity of sharing the same duty was not enough to bridge. "Jesus Christ, you got it sure."

Jim backed the bus into the allotted space where it seemed to nest, engine purring lovingly. "I'll tell you, Otto, it handles better than a car. Hell, I can barely parallel park in my Dodge."

"Don't matter." Otto grinned through a mouthful of worn and broken teeth like a battered picket fence come to life. He pushed his Schmidt's beer cap back up on his forehead, revealing a vast expanse of mottled leathery skin. "Ain't the same thing. Now, you get your truck drivers and they think right off they can handle buses. Why shit, man, 'tain't the same thing at all. Bus is in *one* piece and a truck's in *two*. Ain't got no hitch on a bus, see what I mean. And that's why your car drivers is often a helluva lot better at buses than your truckers. 'Cause of the pieces. Leastways that's what *I* think." He wiped his nose with a dirty sleeve. "Let's take her out again."

Later, Jim thought of the bus the same way he thought of a Harlem whore. Everything is so easy until you step into that dark hallway, and *bang*. You know suddenly that all those

101

smiles and come-ons and having everything so easy was only to lure you in, to draw you to that dark place where the force comes out of the black corners and cuts you down, tears out your heart, steals everything worth having. The scene was carved into his memory, slammed with chisels and mallets into the tough granite of his mind never to fade or to be eroded by years.

It was three days away from the shortest day of the year. It was cold and grim and gray, and the clouds spat snow instead of letting it drift down. It was a cruel day, and the wind bore knives that cut through the thickness of even his down jacket. The darkness had started to close in before four o'clock, and as he guided the massive hulk of the bus down the road on the last leg of its journey, he turned the lights on full bright. The children were in the back, only five of them not yet home: Tracy Gianelli, a third grader with eyes so black and large that Jim fancied her a changeling; Bobby Miller, a sixth grader, tall, thin, aviator glasses perched on his acquiline nose like a wide-eyed bird about to take off; Jennifer Raber, short, fat, freckled, the butt of second-grade jokes because of her stuttering, jokes that Jim would not permit on his bus; Frank Meyers, loud, a troublemaker, forgivable only because he came from a broken home, an excuse that became more tiresome and less acceptable as the weeks passed.

And Terry. Terence John Callendar. Flesh of the flesh, blood of the blood. Only son and heir of the Driver, the Man Behind the Wheel, the Guardian of these five lives, sworn to protect and defend them from the tempest raging outside, pledged to give up his own life in the service of God and country and five little kids in the back of the bus, one reading a Hardy Boys book, two singing a Dolly Parton song, two talking quietly, looking out the streaked windows, watching the snow descend solidly onto the two-lane where Ginder Road met Kaylor Hollow Road.

They began themselves to descend the hill, for perhaps the seventieth time that school year and for the seven thousandth in Jim Callendar's determined memory. Nothing changed. No giant magical hand (Tracy Gianelli's sorcerous friends?)

102

scooped the bus up out of harm's way. Harm fell again, in the shape of the rusting farm truck that slipped down Kaylor Hollow Road, skidded through the stop sign, and slammed into the right rear of the school bus, swinging its huge mass over the snow-covered slope as lightly as a skater, so that the rear of the bus splintered the spindly guardrail.

The bus did not poise and hover over the edge, as in a movie or a dream. There was no millisecond of breath for God or Superman to yank it back onto the road. It simply went over, rear end first, rolling down the forty-degree bank like a mammoth Tootsietoy. Jim was aware of many things at once—his own disbelief, a sharp jolt to his shoulder, sudden cold, a rain of sparkling crystals, and cries.

The cries were wordless, mere animal noises of fright and panic. And as the bus rolled over and over again they seemed to ebb and flow, as though he were putting his hands over his ears in rhythm with the turning of the bus. Then just before it suddenly stopped rolling, he felt himself being lifted and turned once more, thrown against cracking hinges on the other side of the cab, and he was lying in the snow, his right arm and leg tangled in a thornbush that gave him up with a hiss of ripping nylon as he tore away from it, thinking for a moment he had been trapped by some beast.

But reality returned, and he remembered what had happened. The bus lay on its right side like a slaughtered behemoth, its engine still grinding away with a howl of twisted metal. Something covered by brush lit up the darkness with brightly crackling sparks, and he thought of the fire extinguisher, but realized he could not get to it. The door through which he had been hurled was now against the ground, but he did not pause to think about how closely he had come to being crushed. One thought only beat at him: *Terry Terry Terry* . . .

The children were still calling now, the end of motion allowing true words to form for at least one of them, who cried "Mama, Mama" in a voice so pinched with terror that Jim could not tell the sex of the speaker. "Terry!" he shouted, but there was no answer.

The sparks glowed brighter as he limped back to the rear

of the toppled bus. The interior lights were off, but he could detect glimpses of movement through both the broken and intact glass of the windows. "Terry!"

"Mama, Mama!" The litany droned on hysterically, mingled with the other softer sounds of pain, of not *understanding* what had happened or why. Jim kept moving, around to the back door, where he tugged at the handle. But the door had warped, buckled under the ruinous descent that had sprung the front door, and would not be moved. He battered on the bent metal. "Hey!" he yelled. "Push the door! Push it open!"

A face swam into view then, illuminated only by the reflection of the whitening sparks, like some luminous fish in a midnight aquarium. It was a thin face, made skeletal by the absence of eyes. Bobby Miller's aviator glasses had imploded into him, and Jim could see shards of glass sparkling in the gouged out hollows. The boy's mouth was a black hole smeared with red, and his thin fingers scratched at the glass of the back window like a mole digging into darkness.

Jim gasped and stumbled back, tripping and falling in the curiously wet snow. But the thought of his son drove him up again, and he scrambled apelike on hands and feet around the side of the bus to where the gaunt machinery of its underside was revealed in the white glow of the sparks. And now he could see that the sparks had set something on fire so that blue and yellow flame tinted the pure white light that the still-groaning and ratcheting engine had caused. He paused, wondering for a second, then stepped onto the inside of the right rear tire, grasped the high edge of the left tire, and so pulled himself up onto the side of the bus, thinking, A window, I can pull them out through a window.

From on top of the side, the interior of the bus seemed filled with ink, though he could see small bits of movement. "Terry!" he cried again, scuttling on his knees to a window that had been shattered by the fall. "Look out!" he called, and began to pound with his bare fist at the sectioned shards that remained, which flew apart into small sharp-edged pellets like clearer, more solid snowflakes.

"Mama! Mama!" came the cry from within, louder now without the glass to filter it.

Oh, Terry, Jim thought, *be* alive, be all right, not like the other boy, and then he called his son's name again, willing at that moment to give an arm, an eye, his life, just to hear the boy call back, even to hear him scream. He lay on his stomach and thrust an arm down through the shattered window, reaching about, feeling for flesh, a coat sleeve, the smooth rubber of galoshes. "Come here! Come to the window! Give me your hand!" There was something then that brushed his hand and slipped quickly away. He grasped frantically and small fingers touched his own. He tightened his grip then, desperately, and felt the bones of the hand he held snap like twigs beneath his maniacal hold. The fingers did not move otherwise. There was no attempt to pull back, away. But when he tried to lift up, the little hand slipped into the blackness as though it had been greased, and when he looked unbelievingly at his own empty hand, he saw that it was smeared with red.

"Nooo!" he howled, and swung his body around, putting his feet through the window and placing his weight on his arms to drop down inside the bus.

A new sound stopped him, a dull roaring *whoosh* that silenced the voice that cried for its mother, quieted the other wordless voice in the black void beneath Jim's feet, even stilled his own ragged breathing. A second later the glow from the underside of the bus grew much brighter, and Jim suddenly realized how strong the smell of gas was, and why the cold dry snow had seemed so wet.

He twisted, dragged his feet out of the hole, and slithered over to the edge. The snow beneath was blue with flame, and the now-vertical underside of the bus was a growing wall of fire at the top of which he stood. He did not feel the fire's heat or the storm's cold. There was no feeling at all except for the overwhelming sense of standing on the edge of a great abyss with death below and something worse behind. He seemed to balance there for an eternity, all thinking relinquished to the primitive urges of the viscera as he hovered between the fire and the darkness behind him while the snow fell and the monster roared beneath.

Jim turned, ran, and leaped into the night. But he did not fall.

He leaped forever, away from fire, away from shattered glass, away from the blackened, silent metal womb. He did not feel himself touch the ground, did not feel himself land in snow or brush or high grass. When he looked again, he saw a pyre rising, brightening the night sky, the falling snow making the scene appear dreamlike, subaqueous. He was standing watching it, wondering how he had jumped, what had pushed him. Had there been a blast? An explosion that had thrust him from his perch? But he had heard no explosion, and he was not singed, burned. No, there was just the fire. The bus on fire, outside and in. He could see the flames through the glass now.

And he realized that his son was dead, and that there was nothing he could do about it.

Something pulled him down onto the snow, and he sat and watched dry-eyed as the bus continued to burn, sat and watched with the sure and certain knowledge that he had done something wrong, something bad, and that his world would never be the same because of what he had done.

It was a child's thought, and they treated him like a child when they finally came, far too late, with their sirens and their flashing lights and their long hoses that made the heated metal hiss. They carried him to the ambulance because, although he could walk, he would not, and when they went to put him in the back, he broke away, half running, half falling down the slope, calling Terry's name as he went. The firemen stopped him before he could reach the smoking bus, and one of the ambulance attendants stabbed him with a needle. After that, he let them take him, and he fell asleep on the way to the hospital.

When he awoke, Beth was with him, her eyes red from tears, and he thought that it was years earlier, and he had been operated on again, and she was crying because it *was* malignant and she was afraid he was going to die. He was about to tell her that it was all right and not to worry, when he remembered the fire, and remembered jumping, but not landing, and he thought it strange that he could not remember landing.

Then he remembered Terry.

Beth gasped as he sat bolt upright, the room swimming dizzily before him so that he fell back at once. "Terry . . ." he croaked, and her face twisted with an anguish too great for him to look at, so that he closed his eyes against it. When he opened them, her face had not changed, and her body was shaking with heavy, silent sobbing.

Jim went home the next day. The house was echoingly empty. Terry's toys, books, clothes, all stood as mute reminders and accusations. All the children were dead, all burned in the fire that had resulted from the splitting of the gas tank. Dead too was Henry Martin, whose truck had struck the bus. Of all those involved in the accident only Jim survived.

"And I only am escaped alone to tell thee."

The quotation echoed and reechoed in his mind, and he was unable to banish it. Beth cushioned him from most of the harsh realities in the days that immediately followed. She identified the body and was pasty-faced for hours afterward; she made the funeral arrangements; she dealt with the insurance company that had held the $10,000 policy on Terry's life. Jim himself was physically untouched. His shoulder ached from when he'd been thrown out of the bus, but the pain vanished within days. He was sorry to lose it. It had been a symbol to him, a sign that he had somehow shared in what had taken his son. He had not yet been able to cry.

Terry was cremated, the ashes interred, and a small memorial service was held for the five children. The bereaved parents were asked to sit together in the first few pews of the Merridale United Methodist Church. Though most of them smiled wanly, forgivingly, when they saw Jim, there was one man about Jim's age who fixed him with a dull malevolence. It was not as obvious as a snarl or a sneer, but something in the eyes that seemed to glitter with silent promise. The man looked menacing to begin with, Jim thought, with his close-set eyes and rapier-straight nose nearly hidden by the dense growth of beard and hair that, even now at the service, seemed unkempt and uncombed. He wore a tired blue blazer with unfashionably wide lapels and worn elbows. Jim noticed that one of the hollow fake brass buttons was pushed in so that it resembled a dented coin. The woman he was with (his wife?) seemed to draw neither strength nor comfort from the bearded man at her side, as though they were strangers, or had been familiar once a long time ago.

When they were seated, Jim glanced to the side briefly to find that the man was watching him, head and shoulders slightly forward, out of rank. Jim sat back and did not look again, but he felt the man's gaze on him throughout the service, and it unnerved him so that he heard little of Pastor Craven's words.

After the service Jim remained seated, his eyes closed as if in silent prayer. Only he knew the hypocrisy of his position; he was not praying—he was waiting. Waiting for the bearded man with the accusing eyes to leave. At last he felt Beth's hand on his arm, heard her whisper his name over the high drone of the organ, and opened his eyes to find them alone in the pew. He sighed in relief, and together they walked down the aisle.

Bill Gingrich and some other friends were in the narthex waiting for them, feeding them empty words of comfort. The other families were there as well: the Rabers with their two surviving children; Vince and Angie Gianelli, grim-lipped, next to Father Murphy; Rodney Miller, a widower who ran Miller's Feed Mill, standing with his brother Sim and his wife, all of them talking to Pastor Craven. Jim drew Gingrich aside and asked softly, "The one with the beard. Who was he?"

Bill Gingrich frowned. "Frank Meyers's father. Brad. The woman's the mother, but they got divorced a few years back. The boy lived with her. Why?"

"He . . . I don't know. Just curious."

Gingrich shook his head. "Don't pay any attention to him. He may give you the evil eye, but he's relatively harmless."

Jim nodded, and they rejoined the small group of mourners. But when they left the church Jim saw Brad Meyers sitting alone behind the wheel of a battered green Volkswagen parked next to their Dodge. The Volks was on Beth's side of the car, and Jim went with her, opening the door and holding it as she got in, oblivious to Brad Meyers's snakelike stare. Jim closed the door behind her, his heart pounding as he knew what he would do next. He turned to the man. "I'm sorry," he said through the open window. "I'm sorry about your boy."

Meyers made no response. He only stared at Jim until he turned and got in the car next to Beth. When he backed out, Jim could swear he saw a small smile form amid the layers of beard.

"That was Bradley Meyers, wasn't it?" Beth asked when they were out in the street. Jim nodded. "I thought so," she said.

"You know him?"

"By reputation. It's no wonder Frankie Meyers was as mean as he was. You remember that time in the Anchor parking lot? It must have been at least a year ago."

"The fight?"

She nodded. "It was Brad Meyers who started it."

At last he remembered. He simply hadn't made the connection before. Bradley Meyers, Merridale's own Peck's Bad Boy. Not that he was much worse than a lot of the rowdies who hung out around the town—he was just a bit more obvious about it. Jim frowned as the brief paragraphs in the *Messenger*'s police log came back to him. Meyers must have been arrested by the town police four, maybe five, times in the past few years, twice for fighting at the Anchor, Jim recalled, a night spot unused to brawls. It was run by Leo and Emeric Jerney, Hungarian refugees. Though it had a separate bar where all classes seemed to gather, there was

109

also a fairly reputable dining room adjacent, so the Jerney brothers were always quick to clamp down on loud swearing or any signs of fighting. However, that hadn't stopped Brad Meyers from luring a nonresident trucker out to the parking lot, where he broke the man's jaw and lacerated his face on the lot's rough gravel. Leo called the police, but the trucker wouldn't press charges, although Meyers wound up spending the night in the single cell at the Merridale police station. There was a similar incident at the Anchor that got thrown out of Lansford County Court when Meyers's alleged victim never showed up to testify. There were rumors, never proven, that Meyers had persuaded the man not to show. The only other run-in that Jim remembered was the vandalism charge that had been filed by Jacob Groff, who lived in the apartment above Meyers. According to the police log, Meyers had been playing his stereo at an excessive volume, and when old Jake rapped on the floor several times, Meyers stormed up to the third floor and kicked Jake Groff's door in, then went back to his apartment. That stunt had cost Meyers a six-month suspended sentence and a hefty fine. Jake Groff had moved soon after.

"He's a prick," Beth said.

"How come you know so much about him?"

"I know a lot about all the kids at Hatch. And their parents, present or absent. Bonnie Meyers spilled her guts out to me quite a few times when we had problems with Frank."

"You never told me."

"Confidential."

"Oh, sorry. Now you're a priest, huh?"

"What's wrong with you?" she said, her voice dangerously close to losing control.

"My son's dead," he said simply. "I killed my son."

Her eyes widened. "Don't say that," she said. "Don't even think it."

"It's true."

"That's stupid. Why do you say that?"

His eyes filled with tears so that he could no longer see to drive, and he pulled the car off the street. And then he told her what he had told no one before, about trying to get the children out, and seeing the fire, and leaping from the bus. "I jumped," he said. "I don't even remember doing it, but I did. I let them go . . ."

"There was nothing you could have done."

"I don't know how long . . . I don't remember how long it was. . . . There might have been time. . . ."

"No," she said firmly. "There was no time. You couldn't have done anything." Her eyes bored into his, and for a moment he believed her. "You couldn't have saved them, Jim. No matter what you'd done. You did everything you could." She gazed at him, wanting it to be the truth. "Didn't you?"

"I—"

"You *did*."

He nodded, his mouth slack-jawed. "Yeah," he said quietly.

Each was so intent upon the other that neither one noticed the green Volkswagen slowly pass them.

The following week there was a hearing into the cause of the accident, the blame for which was placed solidly on Henry Martin, whose brakes had locked on the ice, sending him skidding into the bus. His truck had been found nearly fifty yards away from the burned bus, his nearly severed head protruding from his splintered windshield. At the hearing, Jim Callendar answered the questions put to him listlessly, automatically, until the presiding magistrate asked a question that made him blanch. "Mr. Callendar," he said, "from what you've told us and from the evidence we've seen, would you agree with me that you did everything you could to avoid the accident and save the children?"

Jim did not answer immediately, and Beth straightened in her chair, expectant, wary, fearful. The small group gathered in the room sensed her discomfort and Jim's unease, and the room became very silent.

"I couldn't have avoided it," Jim said. "There was . . . no way I could have avoided it."

"And afterward," the magistrate said. "You did all you could for the safety of the passengers, isn't that true? You said you tried to get them out, after all."

Jim sat looking at the man as though he were a stern, unforgiving father before whom he dared have no secrets. "I jumped."

The room stirred. Faces turned to one another and then back toward Jim. "You . . . *jumped?*" the magistrate asked.

"Off the bus. I saw the fire and I jumped . . . leaped off." His voice was hushed, as though he wanted only the magistrate to hear. To hear and give him absolution.

"But you . . . were in danger. Of being caught by the fire yourself. Isn't that true?"

"I . . . don't know. I don't know how long I was . . . in the air."

"I'm sorry, Mr. Callendar, I don't—"

"Don't you *see?*" Jim hissed, his eyes wide. Each word came painfully slowly now, as if explaining to a child. "If I jumped . . . and landed before the fire was . . . was *big*, then it was wrong, then I did wrong, but if when I hit, the fire was where I would have been standing, then it wouldn't be so *bad*, but I . . . don't *remember!*" His voice was shaking now, on the point of tears. "I don't . . . remember . . . *landing*. I was just *there*, and the fire was . . . it was . . . Oh, Terry . . ." He broke down in sharp staccato sobs, and Beth put an arm around him.

"He doesn't know what he's saying," she said, her own voice nearly breaking. "It's been such a shock . . . everything . . . it's been too much. . . ."

"I understand," the magistrate said kindly. "Mr. Callendar, no one blames you for anything that happened. There are occurrences that are tragic, unfortunate, but no one is really to blame, and most certainly you can't be held at fault for what happened. No one is accusing you of a thing. If the fault lay anywhere, it lay with Henry Martin, who has already paid the highest price he could. Now, my advice to you"—and he cleared his throat, as if embarrassed that Jim

112

had not ceased crying—"my advice to you is to stop holding *yourself* responsible for what happened to your son and to the other children. You could . . . It's simply not realistic," he finished weakly.

After a few formalities, the hearing was adjourned. Only three of the other parents had been present—Rodney Miller, Angie Gianelli, and Brad Meyers, who had been sitting in the back wearing a bulky fatigue jacket. Miller and Mrs. Gianelli rose and left the meeting room immediately, their faces stony. Brad Meyers sat and watched the Callendars leave with Bill Gingrich. Jim seemed unaware of his presence, but Beth noticed his gaunt face, wiped clean of any expression, and shivered as though the cold outside had crept into the overheated meeting room.

By the time they reached the car, Jim's tears had dried and Beth felt some of her self-confidence returning. "Well, Bill," she said tightly to Gingrich as they climbed inside, "did you get a story?"

"That's not fair, Beth," he replied. "That's not why I came. I came because you're my friends."

"Is that compatible with honest journalism?"

"Beth," Jim said weakly, "that's enough."

"No. I want to know if you'll print it, Bill. What Jim said."

Gingrich glared at her. "No."

"Because you're our friend?"

"Because there'd be no point. I'm concerned with the outcome, not how it was arrived at." Gingrich shook his head and looked at Jim. "Though why you ever gave that goddamn *mea culpa* is beyond me."

"I could have done something," Jim whispered.

"*Stop* it!" In the confines of the closed car Beth's cry was painfully loud. "Will you stop it! It wasn't your fault!"

Jim bit his lip and stared at his hands in his lap.

"Oh, Jesus," sighed Beth. "Jesus. Will you take us home please, Bill?"

It was late in the afternoon when Gingrich dropped them off. Beth went directly to the kitchen to make dinner, which

113

was usually Jim's job. But today he simply sat in the living room in front of the TV set and watched a talk show. They exchanged as few words as possible that evening, and went to bed early, without kisses or embraces.

That night, as on all the nights since the accident, sleep came hard to Jim, and when he could attain it, sleep was no longer a flat black, but a dark and muddy gray, like burnt charcoal, its texture not smooth, but viscous. He allowed himself to sleep only lightly, fearful that he would dream. But his dreams could have been no worse than the conscious memories that he replayed over and over. Bobby Miller's shattered hole of a face, the cries of "Mama, Mama" from the dark cave of the bus, that other mindless call, and he thought again and again, Was it Terry? Was he in there waiting for me? If I had stayed, could I have gotten him out, gotten them all out? Was there time, was there time? and he would tell himself that it was over and done and didn't matter anymore, because nothing could change it now, so go to sleep and forget.

But it *did* matter. He knew that. And beyond that he knew that it was the *only* thing that mattered. The feeling bound him with chains stronger than love or sex or hunger, and he identified it, quickly and correctly, as guilt. He had to bear it; no one could take it from him, strip it off his back like a tired, patched coat. He chose it and wore it, thought it would be his forever, and decided the best he could do was to live with it, as others went through life sightless, or on crutches, or in hospital beds. But it was his mind that was crippled, and he soon learned that any sympathy he expected to receive came hard to those who were sound of body.

The news of his admission at the hearing spread quickly through the town, and people who had been friendly to him before still smiled, but with a studied tolerance and a look of wary suspicion, as if not quite sure whether the man in front of them was really the same person they had known all these years. The fact of the accident itself did not separate him from them. That alone would have been dismissed in a year or so; it would have been remembered as a tragedy, but Jim's name would not have been as inextricably and permanently linked with it.

What made the difference was the dark doubt that he had expressed publicly about himself and his actions. If one were an adulterer or a thief or a cheat—or a coward—one kept it to oneself. It was the admission as much as the suspicion that made the people of Merridale shun him. Rumors were rampant. Bill Gingrich heard them but did not communicate them to Jim. One ran that he had never been thrown from the school bus at all, but had crawled out immediately once the bus came to rest. Another crueler one intimated that the children were found burned to death piled up against the back door of the bus, and all would have escaped alive and unharmed if Jim had not run.

Though Jim heard none of these, he could feel the tone of the community easily enough the first few days after the hearing. He could not bring himself to face anyone at first, and called Bill Gingrich to tell him that he had written neither of the columns Gingrich needed for that week's *Messenger*. Gingrich listened quietly, then said, "Can I count on you for next week?"

"No. I think we'd better just forget it for a while."

"How long?" Jim didn't answer. "Don't do this to yourself, Jim. Don't do it. You've got to get out. You can't lock yourself away."

"I've seen them. Seen their faces."

"Fuck *them!* Whoever *they* are!" There was silence on the line, and Gingrich thought Jim might have quietly hung up. "You there?"

"Yes."

"I want to talk to you. I want you to meet me—"

"Can you come here?"

"No. Out. At the Anchor."

"I can't."

"Yes, you can."

"No. I won't drive. And Beth's at school."

"I'll pick you up."

"No—"

"Be there in ten minutes." And Gingrich hung up.

At Jim's house, Jim followed Gingrich fearfully, almost blindly, into his car. It was four in the afternoon when they entered the Anchor, and only a few workers from early shifts were seated at the bar. Gingrich guided Jim to a booth at the side. The bar, already quiet, became more so as they entered, and when the conversation resumed, it was in a low hum, with frequent sidelong glances at Jim. Gingrich returned the glances with glares, but to little effect. When he looked at Jim he was surprised to find him smiling. It was a small shy smile that hinted of self-satisfaction. Jim looked at Gingrich.

"They're talking about me," he said.

Gingrich nodded. "Yeah. They probably are." He paused. "That bother you."

"No." Jim shook his head. "They should be. After what I did."

"What are . . ." Gingrich began, but the waitress was beside them, smiling at Gingrich, trying to smile at Jim. They ordered beers. "What are you talking about?" Gingrich asked when they were alone. "After what you did?"

Jim looked at him, no longer smiling. "It's simple, Bill. I'm not going to be punished for what I did. Not by the law. So *they'll* punish me."

"They? *They?* Who's this '*they*'? *These* clowns?"

"The town. Merridale."

"Jesus Holy Christ, what do you need to be punished *for?* You didn't do *anything* wrong."

"I think maybe I did."

"You don't *know.*"

"I don't *remember.* Wouldn't I be more apt to forget what I didn't *want* to remember?"

Gingrich looked at Jim for a long time. "I'm not going to be able to talk to you, am I?"

"What about?"

"The weather, what do you think?"

"Talking about what happened can't change anything."

"Talking about it could change you."

"I don't want to change. Not now." He looked expectantly at the men at the bar. Their voices were growing louder, the intonations harsh.

"You want to leave?" Gingrich asked.

"No. I want to drink my beer." They sat in silence, Gingrich refusing to leave until Jim was ready to go with him. The men kept talking, kept looking, though none of them spoke directly to Jim. When the beers were gone, Jim and Gingrich left. They did not talk to each other on the short drive back to Jim's house, and Gingrich was both confused and angered by the constant half smile, half smirk on Jim's face. He didn't call Jim again, and he received no more columns.

Jim and Beth still talked. When two people who have been so close for so long suffer a loss, it is mere romanticism for one to assume that a house becomes steeped in tragic silence. There were admittedly more times than before when no words passed, but conversation, if only out of necessity, went on. Smiles were given and accepted, and even an occasional laugh was heard. They had one serious discussion after the hearing, in which Jim told her that he would no longer drive a school bus. Not ever. She accepted it and told Mary Spruce the following day. Mary had seemed so relieved that Beth was certain she'd been about to suggest to *her* that it would be best if Jim no longer drove.

Beth didn't push him when she got home in the evenings, and later she wished she had. He was spending his days reading and watching TV, and when she asked, over the dinner he'd made, if he was working on his columns, he told her that he wanted to take some time off from them to get his head together about a few things. She nodded acceptance, understanding far more than he suspected she did.

She had thought long and hard about the course she would take with him. In a way, his reaction to the accident and her concern for him made her own grief easier to bear. She had loved her son deeply, and his loss had literally stunned her when the policeman had arrived with the news. Terry had been *their* child, enjoying the time he spent with his mother equally as much as the greater time he'd spent with Jim, and at first she had been jealous over what she interpreted as

117

Jim's refusal to share his grief with her. It was only later she realized that it was not grief he was hoarding, but guilt, and that she could not share it.

Her love for her husband forced her own grief into the background. She grieved, but inwardly, her outside energies conserved for the battle it would take to free Jim from his demons. At last she determined that her greatest contribution would be to do as little as possible. She would love him, support him, but would not force him. He was all she had left now, and she could not bear the thought of driving him away. This proscribed inactivity became the most difficult thing she had ever tried to accomplish. Beth was a doer, a mover. She could not sit still. It was difficult for her to read a long book, or watch television without a magazine in her lap. So for her to sit back and watch while her husband sorted out the bits of his life made her want to scream.

It got no better, and a week before Christmas she decided to get rid of Terry's toys. She had already boxed a good many things, but the boxes of the child's clothes and toys still sat in the now bare-walled room next to their own, and she thought it would be best to banish them for good and turn the room into something other than the vacant memorial it now seemed. But when she told Jim of her plans to give the toys and clothing to a child welfare agency in Lansford, his face soured. "Why do we have to give them away?"

Why not? she thought. He's dead. Our boy's dead. But instead she shrugged. "I thought, since it was getting to be Christmas, that maybe the agency could use them. It seems foolish to have them here when someone could be using them."

Jim's mouth straightened and his lips went white. "I don't want to give them away."

"Why not?" In spite of herself, she could feel her anger growing.

"I . . . just don't want to. They're all we have."

"We can't keep them forever. We have our memories."

His face puckered like a child's about to cry.

"We can use the room for something else," she went on, giving him no chance to respond. "A sewing room, a

118

little study . . . We could put the desk in the basement in there.''

Jim looked away from her and walked out of the room. When he did not return, she loaded the boxes into the trunk of the car and opened the windows of what had been Terry's room, as if the chilling wind could blow away the pain that still remained.

Christmas was miserable. Jim's parents came up from Florida, where they had moved two years before. Both of them wore martyred looks throughout their three-day visit, breaking the masks with the required smiles as they opened their presents. Beth got Jim some books he had expressed interest in, and some sweaters. He gave her only one present, a moderately expensive gold wristwatch he'd bought before the accident. She kissed him, put it on, and kept it on.

Finally, in mid-January, Beth began to ask Jim, as diplomatically as possible, what he intended to do with himself. "You write so well. Why don't you write something,'' she suggested. He nodded and said that maybe he would. When she got back from school the next day, he was sitting at the kitchen table, the typewriter in front of him, a four-year-old *Writer's Market* at his side. He seemed embarrassed.

"I was looking through this,'' he said, "just flipping through, and I saw this section on greeting cards.'' He laughed, and she laughed too, not sure why but glad to see him *doing* something. "And I thought, hell, I *hate* greeting cards, but it was always because I thought any idiot could write them, and *then* I thought well then why couldn't *I?*''

"So did you?''

He chuckled again, self-disparagingly. "Yeah. Nine of them.''

"Nine?''

"Uh-huh. Four birthday, two Mother's Day, three Christmas.''

"Are they good?''

"Of course not. They stink. After all, I want to sell them.''

"Well, can I hear them?''

His smile faded slowly. "You really want to?'' She nodded. "Okay, then." He picked up a sheet of yellow tablet paper, handwritten, with numerous strikeouts. "Here's . . . uh . . . a birthday one." He read it. It was a short verse, sing-song yet clever, and she was smiling when he looked back up at her.

"Pretty terrible, right?"

"No," she said quickly. "I've read a lot worse." And some better, she thought. But he seemed for the first time in weeks to be actually enjoying himself, and she would not allow herself to dampen that. "Actually, I thought it was pretty good."

"Well"—he smirked—"thanks for the compliment. But it doesn't *have* to be good—it just has to sell."

"You're going to submit it?"

"What the hell. All it costs is eighteen cents, right? And they pay up to twenty-five bucks for them. Not bad for a ten- or fifteen-minute poem."

Beth encouraged him to send them in, not worrying what would happen when they came back, as she had no doubt they would. It was enough that he had regained interest in something—*anything*—again, and she would do all she could to foster that involvement. To her surprise, however, four of the ideas sold the first time out, for a $65 total. In the meantime Jim had been writing more, spending more time on the ideas and on the verses themselves, turning out four or five a day. Tru-Line Cards began to buy nearly everything he sent them, and he began submitting what he thought were his better efforts to Hallmark and Gibson, who slowly began to accept his material, and eventually to ask for specific subjects.

So the months went by, Jim stayed at home, and soon the financial concerns that Beth had had were resolved. Jim was making close to $800 a month writing greeting cards, and some weeks his income actually exceeded her own. The next winter, when he figured it out, he found that he was able to sell four fifths of what he wrote.

But although the cards kept him busy and kept them financially secure, his reclusiveness increased. He had occasionally accompanied Beth to school functions, but he'd

120

seemed so self-conscious and the parents had been so obviously ill at ease in his presence that she no longer pressured him to come. When they *did* go out, it was to a restaurant in Lansford, where few people knew them. The only public place in Merridale that Jim was willing to frequent was the Anchor, where he would sit alone and drink two or three beers after his daily writing was done at 2:30 or 3:00. Beth didn't realize it at first, and discovered it one day when school was dismissed early, and there was no Jim to greet her at home. "Well, who do you know there?" she asked him when he told her he went there almost daily.

"Nobody. To talk to."

"You just sit and drink alone?"

"Yeah."

"Why?"

"I have to."

"I don't—"

"Some of the factories—they let out at three or so. And . . . the guys who work there, they know who I am."

"I still don't see," she said, but she was afraid she was starting to.

"They know about what happened."

"And that's why you go there?" He can't be saying this, she thought.

"Yeah."

She could feel her lip trembling. "I don't understand, Jim," she said. "I just don't understand."

"I don't really know if I do either," he said, shaking his head and smiling apologetically.

She turned and went into the kitchen, where she stood shaking. It had been too easy, she thought. The way she had changed the house, had so slowly and methodically covered the traces of Terry's existence. Every week, every day, she had made something else disappear—into the attic, the cellar, the garbage, out of the house. Only the photographs remained, the big hand-tinted 12″ by 24″ over the piano, the smaller 8″ by 10″s in the hall, the family portrait they'd had taken when Terry'd turned six. She had thought she'd been storing the memories away too, and with them the guilt.

121

But she'd been wrong. The house they lived in was haunted, and the ghost would always be there no matter what she did, what she said, because Jim wanted it there. He would remember Terry, and would remember what he thought he'd done to him his whole life. But the memory would not be as other bereaved parents remembered children they'd lost. Remembering Terry would be bitter, not sweet. Remembering Terry would mean remembering Terry's death. Remembering Terry would always mean remembering a nightmare.

Remembering Terry . . .

CHAPTER
8

Jim Callendar lay in his bed staring into darkness, reliving what he could not forget. He turned his head when he heard Beth cough from somewhere in the house, and then he sat up, listening to the dogs barking, barking incessantly. Rising, he walked to the window and pulled back the curtains once more.

A gray tinged with crimson was beginning to lighten the sky, but the blue lights were still there, shining more faintly with the approach of dawn. With the binoculars he could make them out as human figures, men and women, naked. He tried to call Bill Gingrich again.

This time he got through. Gingrich's "Hello" sounded brisk, perfunctory, as if he'd been awake for some time.

"Bill, this is Jim. Callendar."

"Jim, yeah, hi."

"I tried to call before, but your line was busy."

"Uh-huh."

"Beth and I've been wondering what's going on in town. We've seen the blue lights and—"

"Okay. I just got off the phone from talkin' to AP and UPI. Now, I've been checking this thing out for about an

123

hour, and from what I've been able to figure, this whole place is crawling with ghosts."

"Ghosts?" He heard a noise behind him. Beth had come into the room.

"Right out front with you, Jim. There are *people* all over this town. Blue people. Glowing. They don't move, they don't talk, and I'm damned if I'm gonna be the first to try touching them, so I can't say if they're solid or not. But you can sorta see through them."

"Bill, are you—"

"Shut up. You said you want to know, so I'm telling you. The weird thing is that I *recognize* some of them, and they're all *dead*. Some for years."

"But what—"

"*Jesus*, will you stop interrupting me! Maybe I *am* nuts, but if I am, so is the whole fucking town. People are going apeshit down here—scooting for the high timber. But not me—I got the story of the century!"

Jim had never heard Gingrich so excited. "Well, what . . ." he stuttered, feeling foolish. "Well, I wonder what . . . what we should do."

"Take off if you're chicken, hang around if you're not. Me, I'm getting out the Leica and shooting a few dozen rolls of film before we all wake up."

"Bill, wait. These . . . these *dead* people. I mean, *why* are they there?"

"Christ, *I* don't know. At first guess, I'd say they show up where they lived, maybe where they died. Got one accident victim I remember, spread out on the town square just like he was thirty years ago. I've still got that photo in my files. Oh, Jesus, it's incredible . . ." Gingrich's voice broke, but whether from excitement, fear, or awe Jim couldn't tell. "Hey," he added, "if you like, I could use you down here later today. The outside press'll be coming in in droves if I'm any guesser, and I could use some help to handle them. I'll talk to you later." And he hung up.

"What did he say?" Beth asked.

Jim told her everything. When he finished, they were both pale.

"What shall we do?"

"Get dressed," Jim said. "Then we'll decide." He kissed her on the cheek, went into the bathroom, and stepped into the shower, turning the nozzle so that the hot water stung his skin. Only for a second did he wonder if all that Bill Gingrich had said was true. Then he thought about what he had seen and about what Gingrich had told him. He thought about the ghosts of people appearing where they had lived in life, and where they had died.

After he dried himself, the first thing he did was to go into what had been Terry's room. He was both disappointed and relieved at finding it empty. When Beth went into the bathroom, he walked through the entire house and then outside into the yard. There were no dimly gleaming figures nearby.

He stood shivering in the cool fall air, thinking about what had happened and what would happen. He did not wonder *if*, only *when* he would go out to the place where Kaylor Hollow Road met Ginder Road to look for the children.

And to find Terry.

The Town

GHOST, *n*. The outward and visible sign of an inward fear.
>   —Ambrose Bierce, *The Devil's Dictionary*

CHAPTER
9

Nearly all of Merridale thought it was still dreaming when it had actually awakened that Friday morning. Al Dixon stood staring at Susan, his dead wife, who was sitting naked at the kitchen table, until he could stand it no longer. Then he sat down on the floor in his bathrobe, his mouth still hanging open, and was found there two days later when the National Guard did a house-to-house check.

Marjorie Longenecker had a fatal heart attack when she entered her living room and saw her mother sitting in the air where the sofa used to be. Her sister found Marjorie's body on the floor, and screamed at that, but screamed even louder when she saw her mother and Marjorie hovering together by the window.

Three-year-old Christopher Jackson was delighted when he first saw his father (whom his mother had said was dead) standing in the living room, but became disappointed when he would not tell Christopher where he had been. He grew concerned when his father did not hug him, and finally woke his mother to tell her the news. Her reaction was not what he had expected.

Practically every home near the center of the town was the scene of some like occurrence, and the older houses doubled and trebled in drama those that had seen only one or two generations pass. Mrs. Viola Stauffer, a spinster who could trace her Merridale ancestors back six generations, and who still lived in the house her great-grandfather had built, was inundated with blue unmoving shades. She walked with effort from room to room, looking at them, recognizing some, and crying all the while, frightened, but also thinking that now she would not be quite as alone.

The Martin Rest Home, just off Market Street, was the scene of pure chaos. The shrieks of the nurses could be heard for blocks, easily drowning out the alarmed squalls of the elderly who suddenly discovered that the beds in which they lay were occupied by others, sometimes as many as seven, forming a lump of blue light and churning flesh, one moving and several still faces on the same pillow, as equally hard to look at as to imagine.

Some of Merridale's residents rushed to their cars and left the town immediately. Others feared to step outside, finding the company of familiar ghosts more congenial than those who lined the streets. Still others went into empty, unhaunted rooms, turned on radios and television, and waited for the machines to tell them what to do, listening to the sounds of fenders crumpling and bumpers clashing outside as the hasty, fearful multitude fled their spirit-laden town. The telephones proved ineffective, as the lines to anyone important—police, fire department, local TV and radio stations—were all busy, and before long, all the lines became choked with people trying to call *anyone*. It was not, thought Frank Kaylor, going to be his day.

Frank Kaylor was the chief of police of the village of Merridale, charged with keeping "lawn order," as he self-deprecatingly put it, among the 8,000 inhabitants. It was fairly dull work, and he liked it that way. Anything else would have meant that he wasn't doing his job. There were four men on the force beside himself, and together they were more than enough to handle things. Merridale was a tame place. The last murder had been eight years before, when the

Kline boy had strangled little Ginny Fuller. It had been ugly—the high school whiz kid . . . seven-year-old retarded girl . . . sex-crime-then-stuffed-in-a-garbage-bag school. Kaylor had had nightmares about it for months. And two years from now Peter Kline would be up for parole. It was a shitty system, Kaylor thought. And very early this morning it looked like he might be going to get involved in it again. The phone had just woken him up, making both him and Lettie curse, and Dotty Sanders was on the other end, telling him that Marty had murdered Sheila Sommers, had just confessed it to her, and had begged her to call him. Kaylor thought they were both drunk at first, especially after what Dotty told him was in their bedroom, but she didn't really *sound* drunk, only upset to the point of hysteria. He told her to take it easy, he'd be right over, hung up, and began to dress.

"What is it?" his wife asked from the bed.

He shrugged. "A D and D. I hope." In the den he tried to get Bob Rankin, who was on graveyard shift, on the radio, but Rankin didn't reply for a moment. Just as he came on, sirens started to wail outside.

Rankin, his voice rising to a near-falsetto at times, told his chief what was happening and what had appeared in the town. "I'm not lying," he stressed over and over. "I really see them, Chief. Honest to God."

Kaylor made plans to meet Rankin at the Sanders house. By the time he got there he had seen hundreds of the shapes lining streets and sidewalks, palely visible inside houses with undrawn curtains. "You see them? You see them?" Rankin pressed when Kaylor joined him outside the Sanders house on Glenview Terrace.

"I see 'em," Kaylor replied grimly. "Jesus, Bob, what have we got here?"

"I don't know, Chief, but I hope to shit they go away soon."

Inside the house they found Martin and Dotty Sanders sitting at the kitchen table, their eyes averted from each other. Marty had come to himself enough to protest that it was all an accident, that he'd been scared Sheila would tell Dotty. Dotty was silent, her eyes wide in near-shock. While

Marty babbled on, she gestured for Kaylor and Rankin to follow her, leading them into the bedroom, where they both gasped at the sight of Sheila Sommers (or her ghost, they both thought) lying naked on the bed.

"It's not her," said Rankin in awe. "She's buried."

Kaylor leaned down and tried to touch the glowing flesh. The way his hand passed through it terrified him for a moment, but he regained his composure and nodded. "You're right. It's not her. But it's something."

While Marty Sanders moaned, "I didn't mean to, I didn't mean to," Kaylor had Rankin get the Polaroid from the car and take some shots while he contacted the state troopers. It took a while, but he got through, reported the incident, and asked for assistance.

"Chief," the voice on the other end crackled, "you're gonna get more assistance than you know what to do with. We've been getting calls for the last fifteen minutes, and trying to get you for the last ten. What in hell's going on over there?"

"Damned if I know, but if it's some kind of hallucination, then I'm seeing it too." After learning where the staters would arrive, Kaylor radioed the Merridale Fire Hall. "Kaylor here. Where the hell's the fire?" he asked whoever answered.

"No fire." The voice shook. "We just didn't know what else to do. You seen 'em?"

"I've seen 'em. Folks are probably upset enough as it is without the damned sirens. Shut 'em off." Within a minute the sirens fell into silence.

The Polaroids that Rankin gave him showed the bed, the bedside table, the lamp, but no sign of Sheila Sommers, or whatever psychic residue remained of her. "What is it, Chief?" Rankin asked. "What are any of them?"

"Let's not worry about that now. We got a man to take in." When Kaylor told Dotty that they'd have to take Marty to the station, she clutched at his arm.

"I can come with you, can't I? I mean, I can't stay here."

"Dotty, there's no place to stay down at the station. We only have the one cell. We could drop you off at a friend's if you like, or you could stay here, just not go in the bedroom."

"Could you"—her voice sounded very small—"could you take it away?" Kaylor didn't answer and Dotty shook her head. "No. No, I guess not." She looked up at him. "Shut the bedroom door. Just shut the door and I'll stay here."

She didn't say good-bye to her husband when they took him to the car, nor did he speak to her. Soon the three men were nearing the small downtown section of Merridale, and the blue forms were everywhere, like silent sentinels. There were several in both standing and sprawled positions across the roads, and once, when there was no room to go around, Kaylor told Rankin to drive slowly through one of the shapes.

There was no sense of contact, but for a moment the top of the figure's head and part of his back were visible on the floor of the police car. They all jumped, and Rankin turned the wheel spasmodically, but kept the car on the road. "Steady, Bob, steady," Kaylor said. Martin Sanders giggled.

Rankin pulled the car into one of the spaces in the town square. There were four or five cars parked nearby with their headlights on. While Rankin took Martin Sanders into the police station, Kaylor walked over to them. The cars of Tom Markley and Pastor Craven were parked side by side, so close they nearly touched. Markley's right-hand window and Craven's left were rolled down all the way, and Kaylor could hear them talking through the gap as he approached. He rapped lightly on the mayor's windshield and Markley jumped like a rabbit.

"Jesus!" he said in disgust when he saw Kaylor's face peering through the glass in the coming light of dawn. "You scared the life outa me, Frank." Then his eyes narrowed and he looked around suspiciously, as if something were creeping up on them. "You wanta come in here?"

"Why don't you come out here?" Kaylor answered.

"You think it's safe?"

"You see them moving? Besides, I have a gun."

"Don't know what good *that'll* do," the mayor grumbled, but he slid back over to the driver's side and opened the door quietly, as though he didn't want to be heard. A haze of cigarette smoke followed him as he left the car and he lit another immediately. He fixed Frank Kaylor with a bulldog stare, although he had to look up to do it, and coughed as the smoke leaked out of him. Have a stroke in another year, Kaylor thought as he stared into the lumpy, florid face. Mayor Tom Markley smoked two packs a day and was only five pounds short of being fat. Not, Kaylor had decided, a good prognosis for longevity. "Well?" Markley said.

"Well what?"

"C'mon, Pastor," Markley called softly to Craven, who was just getting out through his passenger door, and turned back to Kaylor. "Well, what have you done about all this?"

"What's to do?" He shrugged. "Staters are on their way."

"Staters!" Markley barked. "We got a town full of spooks and people scared shitless about 'em—including *me*. And you tell me the staters are coming. Frank, there are people *leaving* town—actually packing up and *going*."

Kaylor looked at Markley's eyes and read the near-panic in them. "You want me to calm folks down?" he asked.

"*Yes*. Damn right I do!"

Kaylor walked back to the police car, opened the trunk, and took out a bullhorn. Flicking it on, he aimed it down South Market Street and spoke into it. "Attention. May I have your attention, please. This is Police Chief Kaylor speaking. There is nothing to fear from the"—he paused— "the things that we are all seeing on the streets and perhaps in your homes. They can't harm you. There's no need for panic or to leave town. The mayor and Pastor Craven are here with me now and we assure you that these creatures are harmless. We don't know as yet what they are, but an investigation is under way. Please remain calm and continue with what you would normally be doing." Kaylor switched off the bullhorn and looked at Markley. "Happy?"

"What did you tell them *that* for?"

"You wanted me to calm them down."

"*We* don't know these things are harmless!"

In answer Kaylor walked over to the figure of an old woman ten yards away and swung his arm through the space she occupied. "She's not hitting back," he said grimly, returning to Markley's side.

"I think Frank is right," said Pastor Craven in his deep

baritone. "They seem too ethereal to do us any harm."

"Well, what about this investigation then?" Markley went on.

"I'm investigating," Kaylor replied, "right now."

Craven smiled. "Aren't we all?"

"What do *you* think, Pastor?" Kaylor asked. "This is more in your line than in mine."

"Tom and I have been discussing it, and from what I can make out, as crazy as it sounds, we've got a town full of ghosts here. I don't recognize them all, but I do a lot of them. And they're all dead. With some it looks like they're positioned right *where* they died—at the moment of death. With others it seems they show up where they lived, or where they spent much of their time."

"Jesus Christ," moaned Markley. "Excuse me, Pastor," he added, "but I feel like I'm still sleeping, like this can't really be happening."

"It does feel like a dream," Craven agreed, "but I'm fairly certain *I'm* awake."

"What about hallucinations?" Kaylor suggested. "*Mass* hallucinations."

Craven pointed to a blue shape visible through the window of the Bar-Kay Dress Shop. "You see that woman?" Kaylor nodded. "Describe her to me."

Kaylor did, noting the woman's bobbed, antiquated hairstyle, her thin lips, heavy frame, large pendulous breasts to which her stubby fingers were pressed.

"You've just described Grace Moyer," Craven said when Kaylor had finished. "She died of a heart attack when I was ten, years before you were born, Frank. My mother used to take me in her shop. So how could *you* hallucinate something that's in *my* memory?"

Kaylor shook his head, thinking that it *did* seem like a dream, and feeling grateful for that. If he could just keep that idea in his mind until he could accept what had happened as reality, he thought he'd be all right.

"They're really here then," said Markley. "Holy shit . . ." He gave a half-laugh. "I wonder . . ."

"What?" Kaylor asked.

"I can't help but wonder if . . . if Eddie Karl's been telling the truth all along."

Neither the minister nor the police chief made any comment, but they wondered too.

The state troopers arrived with the sun twenty minutes later. As always, they seemed cool, withdrawn, dryly professional, at least at first. Once they learned exactly what they were dealing with, many of them seemed as jumpy as Tom Markley. The mere act of filling them in did wonders for Kaylor, and he felt almost in control once more.

People were starting to come out on the street at last, most in pairs, hurrying to the comforting-looking group of living men gathered in the square. Most people, however, stayed in their houses, closing the doors of rooms where the figures, glowing softer in the light of day, were stationed.

Some were not frightened, but were touched in other ways by the reappearance of those dear to them. Joe Longsdorff sat all morning on the couch next to the apparition of his wife, Judy, who had died very quickly of leukemia three years before. Though her face was expressionless, her eyes were open, and her naked body still looked firm, youthful, appealing. As Joe told her what had happened in the years she was gone, he gradually put an arm around the space she occupied, and ultimately piled up pillows that he rested his head upon, positioned so that his cheek seemed to be lying on her breast.

On Locust Street, Thorne and Evelyn Beech sat in their cold backyard under the willow tree, where the swing set had been thirty years before. "Can I get you anything?" Thorne said. "Coffee?"

"Coffee would be nice."

"You can't stay here forever, Evelyn," he said gently.

"She has," the woman replied, never taking her eyes off the little girl who lay arms akimbo, neck cocked at an angle several degrees past awkward.

Throughout the town grown men and women became children once more in the presence of their returned parents, and trembled at the impossibility of it all. They had gone to sleep alone and had awakened in the presence of their ancestors. Mothers saw sons returned from the battlefields, snatched from flaming accidents, just as they had been at the second when death had claimed them. Widows and widowers, most finally used to their lot, now found themselves married once again.

In nearly every house with a living occupant, both radio and television were turned on. However, KMRA, Merridale's local radio station, was the only media source that as of 8:00 A.M. had mentioned what had occurred in the town. The morning DJ, Hal Drake, was playing his usual "Mellow Morning Music," but between each record he cut the commercials and instead said what Chief Kaylor had requested: "Okay, this is Hal Drake for the Drake Wake on KMRA Merridale, and if you're a Merridale resident and a bit upset by what's happening in the town, Police Chief Frank Kaylor has asked me to say that we should all stay cool, and that whatever this phenomenon is, it seems to be completely harmless. We got state police in here now, and other government agencies have been contacted, so go easy on the panic button, all right? Stay in your houses if you like, or go to work, or if you're really bugged and want to leave town and visit the folks for a bit, hey, feel free. But drive carefully, okay? And remember, there's nothing to worry about." Drake hoped to hell there wasn't—he didn't like the way the station's former owner was staring at him from where he hovered, gauntly thin, three feet above the tile floor. "Now let's get back to some music—Mr. Vic Damone singing 'Come Back to Me.' "

Fifteen miles away the news manager for WLMA, Lansford's CBS affiliate, hooted in laughter and turned off the radio. " 'Come Back to Me!' Jesus H., what a choice."

WLMA's morning news anchor grinned and puffed on a cigarette that sprinkled ash over his blue uniform blazer. "We go with it or not?"

The news manager scratched his head. "It is so fucking wacky I can't believe it. But *something's* doing up there. You got the story?"

"Right here." The anchor held up a typed sheet.

"Okay, let's do this. Don't lead with it. Rhoda started up there twenty minutes ago and we ought to hear from her any second. We'll get the dope by the first commercial, guaranteed. Then we'll know.''

Twelve minutes into the show, Rhoda called and verified the story in a trembling voice. The manager gave the anchor the high sign, and WLMA became the first TV station to report on what would become known as the Ghost Town. Before the half hour was up, the news manager had sent a two-man camera crew to join Rhoda in Merridale, and also called the CBS regional office, who said they would send their own crew as soon as possible.

By noon, when the crew arrived, Merridale was in no mood to welcome them. The square was filled with people, and Kaylor had ordered detour signs put up directing traffic up Park, across Spruce, and down Lincoln to bypass it. The square had become the kraal of the town, the place of safety from which the natives would face the dangers of their particular jungle. Although it was a Friday, most of the husbands had remained home from work in order to be with their families, and now a good majority of those families occupied the several thousand square feet that were formed by the meeting of High and Market streets. At first glance it looked almost festive, as though a town fair or *Oktoberfest* were in progress. The sun was shining, and although the day had started off chilly, it had become quite warm for late October. People sat in clusters on lawn chairs, mothers and fathers with children on their laps. But there was no trace of festivity in the faces. They were solemn, concerned, filled with a dark fear. There had been over two dozen bodies visible in the square itself, but once people started gathering there early that morning, Henry Zeller and his son Buck set cardboard partitions around the grisly figures, concocting them from the refrigerator and washer/dryer boxes in the basement of their hardware and appliance store. There were still visible apparitions up and down the streets, but the square at least was secured as well as possible. Too, daylight weakened the effect of the things. The sun seemed friendly, and although it did not diminish the forms completely, it was enough for people to feel perplexity rather than sheer terror, as they had in the dark.

So they sat and stood and crouched, heads together, some whispering, an occasional out-of-place laugh breaking the silence along with the cries of babies and the whining of children. Photographers took pictures, reporters scribbled on pads, a few looking nervously over their shoulders as if expecting the makeshift boxes to split apart or the hollow-eyed *living* people to suddenly erupt into madness. The CBS crew moved into the square warily for all their experience. They had seen the ethereal shapes on their way in, and so were prepared for the expressions on the faces of the townspeople. "They look like refugees," muttered a cameraman as they walked in front of Zeller's Hardware. "Look dead themselves." None of his colleagues disagreed.

While one reporter talked to the mayor, another walked through the crowd, which looked at him sullenly, until he spotted a face with just the right combination of tension, fear, and aggression. "Sir?" he said. "Would you mind if we talked to you for a while and taped it?"

The man was overweight, somewhat shabby, and in his early sixties. His crew-cut head was hatless, and a black-gray beard ran from ear to chin to ear without detouring for a moustache, as though it had been hurriedly painted on rather than grown. He gestured at the cameraman with a stubby finger. "We on TV now?"

"Not yet. We'll tape it now, air it later. With your permission."

The man nodded gruffly. " 'S'okay."

"Gimme a sound check."

"What's your name, sir?" the reporter asked.

"Uh . . . Fred Hibbs."

"And do you live here in Merridale?"

The man nodded.

"All right, Mr. Hibbs, you can look at the camera if you like, or at me if that's more comfortable. Ready, Kevin? Okay." The reporter's casual air dropped away and his face grew stern and tight as the red eye of the camera winked on.

"I'm talking with Mr. Fred Hibbs, a Merridale resident, just one of thousands who have been stunned by the overnight phenomenon that's taken place in this quiet Pennsylvania town. Mr. Hibbs, as we can see, the town square is just packed with people. Could you tell me why *you're* here right now?''

Hibbs licked his lips almost guiltily, glancing up and down at the camera. ''Don't wanta be alone is all.''

''You live alone, sir?''

''Yeah. Got me a little house by myself.''

''What was your first reaction to this phenomenon, Mr. Hibbs?''

Hibbs's head wagged and a crooked smile split his features. ''I . . . uh . . . I was pretty scared. I mean, I, uh . . . I seen my momma and daddy.'' His voice bubbled, cracked a bit. ''Just went into the kitchen, and I seen 'em sitting there at the table plain as day, lookin' just like they did the day they died. Only they's naked.'' Hibbs bit his lip. ''I never seen 'em naked.''

''And what did you do then?''

''I got *out*. I . . . I just ran out of the house. And I seen more of 'em outside. But then Chris Spickler come by in his pickup and seen me and told me to hop in, and I did real quick and we come up here to the square.''

''When was this?''

'' 'Bout ten or so.''

''I understand the . . . occurrences took place much earlier.''

''Guess so. I'm a pretty sound sleeper.''

''Have you considered leaving Merridale?''

Hibbs shrugged. ''I got no place to go.''

''But would you like to?''

''Yeah. Yes, sir, I would.''

''Do you have any thoughts as to what these things might be?''

''You betcha I do.'' He paused, gathering strength. ''Ghosts. That's what they are. It's that simple.''

The reporter nodded sagely. ''Do you have any thoughts as to the motive behind their appearance?'' Hibbs looked puzzled. ''The *reason* they're here,'' the reporter clarified.

'' 'Cause we fucked up!''

It wasn't Fred Hibbs that answered. When the reporter turned, he saw an elderly man with a crisply lined face.

Hibbs, who had jumped at the words, now frowned, his face turning red with anger and embarrassment. The reporter slashed a finger across his throat, the camera's red light winked out, and Eddie Karl laughed in a high-pitched cackle.

"Goddammit, Eddie," Hibbs said through gritted teeth. "We're on TV here!"

"Whoop-de-shit." Eddie Karl turned to the reporter. "What are you talkin' to Loafer for? He don't know *nothin'*."

"You mean Mr. Hibbs?" the reporter inquired with a sickly smile.

"Mr. Hibbs, hell. Loafer's the name. 'Swhat everybody else calls him, right, Loafer?"

"You old—"

"Now, you want to know what this is all about, you just ask *me*."

"You know?" the reporter asked.

"Damn right. They just don't like what the hell's goin' on here. They think we're fulla shit, and this is their way of tellin' us."

"Full of shit," the reporter repeated.

"You heard it here first, buddy."

The reporter ignored Eddie Karl, thanked Fred Hibbs, and moved away, closer to the tight group of men in the center of the square that seemed to form the command core. He stopped and listened to his colleague, who was still interviewing the mayor. "So you really have no idea of the cause?" The reporter was in her late twenties, tall, slim, attractive, her tailored wool suit in cosmopolitan counterpoint to Mayor Markley's somewhat garish double-knit blazer and wide polyester tie.

"Well, no. No. It could be due to any number of things, and I'm *certain* there's some logical explanation. Certainly no need to panic or leave town."

"But in 1980," the reporter reminded him, "a good many people left immediately after a minor incident at the Thorn Hill Nuclear Station, isn't that correct?"

Markley grimaced. "Yes, that's right. But there was no danger then, no danger at all. And there's no danger now either."

141

"Some people are already blaming the plant for the occurrence. Any comment on that?"

The mayor's face soured again. "No, no, that remains to be proven. Of course, if it turns out to be true, we will certainly demand a reckoning."

"As you did in 1980?"

"Well, that's still tied up in litigation, but we expect . . ."

Kim Bailey hurled an armful of clothes into her suitcase, a frown wrinkling her pretty face. She thought of Dave again, picking up his picture and laying it carefully between two pairs of jeans, cushioning the glass. Damn. Where was he anyway? She'd tried to call his house as soon as her father had dropped the bombshell that they were leaving Merridale, but Dave had not answered. She knew he wasn't at school—the whole district had been closed. But where then?

Just as she was sitting on her suitcase to force it shut, the phone rang, and she leaped up like some giant jack-in-the-box, her clothes spilling out over the handmade quilt. She jerked the phone from the receiver before the first ring had been completed, and said hello breathlessly.

"Kim?"

"Dave, I tried to call, but you weren't there."

"My folks and I were in the square for a while. I've been trying to get you all morning, but the phones are all screwed up."

"Listen," Kim said, "we're leaving."

"*Leaving?* Leaving Merridale?"

"Daddy's freaked out. Nobody knows what's happening. We're going to Lansford, Mike Davison, a guy Daddy knows. We're staying at his place. They have two kids in college, so they've got the room."

"How *long?*"

"I don't know. Till somebody knows something or these things disappear. You seen them?"

"Yeah. My grandma lived with us when she died. I was just a kid. Mom didn't want me to look, but I did. Just once though. I don't want to again."

"*Kimmy!*" her father called sharply from downstairs. "You ready?"

"I've gotta go, Dave."

"When will I *see* you?"

"I'll call you. Or call me. Mike Davison in Lansford. I love you."

"I love you. It'll be all right. Don't be scared."

"I won't."

Everyone was scared.

It was not the fear of the outward appearances of the dead returned so much as the fear of what had brought them back. It was the fear of the *unseen* rather than of those poor, shabby things, ethereal and real at once, that terrified.

Where did they come from?

Why are they here?

What do they mean?

They asked themselves the questions over and over, then talked of theories, possibilities. What if, suggested Hen Ebersole, the nuclear plant had put something into the air that made these things visible? What if they'd been there all the time, only invisible, and what if some nuclear dust settled on them so everyone could see them? Howard Flory held out for the ozone layer. The spray cans, he said, breaking down the ozone. You can't see them when there's ozone, but now all the ozone's going away. Jerry Earhart held that they were ghosts, just ghosts pure and simple. As to why they showed up when they did, Jerry couldn't say.

Pastor Robert Craven, moving from group to group in the square, calming, cheering, had his own explanation. "All we can know is," he said, "that the hand of God is behind it. We can't see His purpose, but He's allowed it to happen. All we can do is wait and try to do His will."

"You think it's a sign of the Revelation, Pastor?" asked Josie Betz. "The dead rising and all?"

"Only God knows that, Josie. And He's told you as much as me."

The pastor moved on to the next cluster. At most he was welcomed; at a few, only kindly tolerated. Craven was not the kind of minister who inspired faith. If his sermons and his manner had had the theatrical majesty of his physical appear-

143

ance, there might have been those who would have followed him into hellfire. He was tall, cadaverous, prophetic-looking. Though only in his early fifties, his hair was nearly pure white, combed straight back without grease so that he always appeared to be striding directly into a gale.

Yet, in spite of his prepossessing looks, his manner had far more in common with the Gentle Shepherd of the New Testament than the zealous warriors of the Old, whom he more closely resembled. His sermons were flat and unexciting, offending no one and captivating few. Still, he was liked by his congregation, who attended services out of habit and appreciation. If a church member found himself in the hospital, he also found Bob Craven at his side no later than the following morning. At funerals and viewings he would be there for just as long as the family wanted him, knowing unerringly what they wanted most to hear.

In spite of this there were those who felt Craven's qualities were best summed up by his name, due to his refusal to lend that name to anything that could be interpreted as controversial. In 1980, when Tom Markley had asked him to sign a petition demanding the closing of Thorn Hill until a full safety investigation could be launched, Craven had declined, saying that he couldn't use his position in the church to accomplish secular ends.

"Bob," Markley had pressed, "as a private citizen do you believe in this?"

"Yes."

"Well, why don't you sign it as a private citizen?"

Craven had smiled. "Does that mean I can go out and get drunk as a private citizen?"

Markley had begun to argue that it was not the same thing, but he could see that in Robert Craven's eyes it was, and he had given up, still liking Craven, but thinking less of him than he had.

The criticism had filtered back to Craven, and though it bothered him, he would not change. During his years of pastoral apprenticeship he had seen a long line of ministers who, by taking a stand on a controversial point, had pulled their churches apart. Take sides on *any* secular topic, he

144

thought—abortion, welfare, the military, even *sports* in some communities—and you ran the risk of polarization. For there is always someone sitting out there in one of those pews who is ready to disagree, sometimes violently. And then it starts. The backbiting, the innuendos, the innocent acts made to look guilty. Craven would never forget the look on Pastor Albemarle's face when his church's lay council decided that "it would be in the best interests of the church to find another head pastor."

It had been in 1952, and Craven, fresh out of seminary, had considered himself fortunate to have received the assistant pastorate, particularly at such a fine new church as St. Peter's. The congregation was upwardly mobile, as befitted a west Philadelphia suburb in the fifties, and from St. Peter's it was only an hour and half drive to his family in Merridale. But one fatal Sunday Dick Albemarle, a handsome, thirtyish bachelor, had spoken out from the pulpit against Joe McCarthy's witch hunts, knowing full well that some powerful and influential members of the church were all for "Old Joe's stickin' it to the commies." What had followed was disgusting: the discovery by the church caretaker of a half-empty jar of Vaseline beneath the couch of the pastor's study, a brazenly stained pair of men's briefs in the wastebasket, several homosexual magazines under the religious newspapers on the desk top. There were even some rubber sex aids found when the members of the church lay council, with Craven looking on, forced open the locked drawers of Albemarle's desk. Though Craven did not definitely know that the items had been planted, he suspected so, and voiced those suspicions to a member of the council whom he felt was sympathetic toward Albemarle. "I wouldn't bring that up," the man had told him, not unkindly. "You're married, and that helps, but you've got no kids yet. Don't get tarred with the same brush, Bob. You'd never get it off." Craven, young and scared, remained silent, not speaking as the council held their off-the-record meeting, confronting Albemarle with their evidence, doing it quietly so as to cause "no public scandal" and "wreck any future career you may have in the ministry." Albemarle was so shocked, so white-faced, that Craven won-

145

dered if his suspicions were incorrect, if Albemarle were homosexual after all. He did not deny the charges, but only smiled grimly once his initial reaction had passed. He said merely, "I see I'm not wanted here. You'll have my resignation tomorrow." The council president replied with a gracious thank you, and stressed that what had happened in the meeting would always remain confidential.

And well it might, thought Craven. He had spoken to Albemarle fifteen years later at a church conference in Pittsburgh, where Albemarle now preached. He was married, with three children, and told Craven that the evidence had been planted. "They couldn't have made it public," Albemarle said. "They'd have been open to slander then." When Craven apologized for not voicing his doubts, Albemarle shrugged it off. "They just would've got you too. No, it was the best thing. I learned my lesson. Politics and the pulpit don't mix."

Craven learned the lesson too, and had been noncontroversial ever since. Quietly, safely, he had wended his way from church to church, watching the politically and socially aware lose their congregations and ultimately their positions, until finally he was back where he wanted to be. Back in Merridale. Back in the church of his parents and his grandparents, of Pastor Dunson, bald, moustached, overweight Pastor Dunson who'd said, "I see the calling in you, Bobby, I can *see* it." Pastor Dunson, whose death brought Bobby Craven into the pulpit of Merridale United Methodist, from whence no sly plot or bridled congregation would ever remove him.

Chief Kaylor's voice broke into his thoughts, startling him. "Dotty Sanders on the line, Pastor. She'd like to talk to you."

"Oh, yes," Craven said absentmindedly. "I'd wanted to visit her. Forgot in all the excitement."

On the phone Dotty Sanders sounded upset and scared, as though she needed a living, calming presence. "I can't get hold of my sister, Pastor. But I don't want to go outside. I see *them* out there."

"You relax, Dotty," Craven said gently. "I'll be right over."

146

He drove apologetically through the crowd in the square, then through the streets, empty of all but the blue forms, which he avoided when he could, and closed his eyes and drove through when he couldn't. He tried not to think about the phenomenon, tried to clear his mind of it enough to decide how he could best comfort Dotty Sanders.

When he arrived, she explained what had happened, opening the bedroom door and showing him the faint shade of Sheila Sommers. He was shocked by this new sight, the product of lust and rage. But he drew on his calm facade as easily as a surplice, and, in the warm hominess of the kitchen, across cups of coffee, he spoke to Dotty Sanders of the frailties of humanity, of how King David had been tempted, of how all save Jesus had fallen short of God's trust and glory. "But love will win over all," he told her. "The love of your friends, the love of your husband"—she winced—"because I have no doubt that Martin still does love you, in spite of what you may feel right now. And most of all God's love, Dotty."

"God's love."

"Yes. Of course."

"If God loved me, how could He let this happen?"

"We can't understand His ways, but we must believe that there is a purpose."

"*Purpose?*" she snarled. "What *purpose?* What conceivable purpose could there be in Marty screwing that . . . that *whore*, and her getting her head smashed? You tell me *that!* Purpose!" she went on, flecks of spittle coating her lips. "What *purpose* that . . . that parents beat their babies, or . . . or plane wrecks kill a hundred people, good *and* bad? Why do people die of cancer? Like my mother? She was *sixty*, only sixty, and she suffered like she was in hell *before* she died. Why do killers walk free out of courtrooms? Why does the plant get to throw that *shit* into the air we breathe? Why do *we* take the chances? Why do we have a town—*right now*—full of *dead people?* Why don't you *tell me!* Tell me something that makes sense to *me*, not to God. But please, *please*, don't tell me there's a reason that we're all too stupid to see. Don't insult my intelligence anymore."

147

Her voice had slowly become less frenzied until now she sounded nearly in control, almost reasoned. It discomfited Craven. He had always been able to deal with emotion. But pure reason left him at a loss. His faith, that which he personally bore within him, would not let him spar with reason. "I'm sorry, Dotty. I don't know what else to say. Only that I believe that what I say is true."

She cried then, and apologized afterward. He left her house feeling like he had poured buckets of water into a barrel only to find there was a hole in the bottom. I believe it, I do, he thought violently, trying to avoid looking at the glowing figures that increased in number as he neared the town's center. They seemed to mock him, as if saying, "Explain us. Why are we here, Pastor? Why have we come back?"

"I don't know," he said aloud. "But God does," and he thought of the church, and turned in its direction. It was always there for him, that huge, somehow motherly building with its warm wood interior and bright stained-glass windows. When he felt troubled, worried, or simply tired, he would seek out the sanctuary and sit several pews from the front, waiting for his strength to return, listening for his faith.

There were not many ghosts near the church when he arrived. It was relatively new, built in the mid-fifties at what was then the edge of town. But now, several decades later, the town had moved outward, surrounding it with tract-home suburbs so that it rested amid young houses, young streets, young families.

Pastor Craven opened the unlocked door of his church and walked through the narthex and into the sanctuary, where Pastor Evan Dunson stood naked in the half light that penetrated the stained glass. The old man's shade was behind the right pulpit as Craven faced the altar, so that only the head and upper torso were visible. There was no expression on the pale blue face, no wry smile beneath the heavy moustache. The eyes no longer twinkled. It was a face as lifeless as an art student's statue.

Craven stood, incapable of movement. He had seen them before, by the hundreds. He had seen people he had known

148

in life, people he had called by name, had shaken by the hand on Sundays, people at whose deathbeds he had knelt in prayer, seeing the tears roll down their faces, wondering if anything he did or said could ease their terror at leaping into the great unknown.

But he had not yet seen his grandparents, or his father, or the older sister he'd loved so. He had not seen anyone he had loved until now.

Pastor Dunson had been like a second father after his dad had died when Craven was fifteen. And now he stood at his pulpit, stripped of not only clothing but of humanity as well. He was like . . . like . . .

Like a locust shell, Craven thought. The form is here, but not the soul. The thought emboldened him, and he regained the power to move. He walked toward the altar with a deliberate tread, but at a moderate speed. Had it been faster, he might have frightened the image away, though he knew that was unlikely. Any slower, and he might have stopped out of his own fear. He paused only a few feet from the pulpit, looking up at the round robust body the heart attack, unheralded, had claimed during Dunson's sleep. Craven's eyes grew wet with tears, and he held out a hand to be taken and held in return.

It did not happen. "Pastor," Craven said, his throat tight, "can't you tell me? Tell me so I can tell them?" The face did not move. Craven's nose was stuffed up; he breathed through his mouth, shallow, insubstantial breaths. "Is it so much to ask? To know?" He could not see the face now. His tears blurred his vision.

"*Why!*" he cried out before he went to his knees, pressed there by doubt, by sorrow, by fear of his own mortality, which, in spite of all his declaimed faith, had never been as strong as at this moment.

CHAPTER
10

"Doris . . . Jesus Christ, come in and listen to this."

Doris's voice, weakened by three rooms' distance: "I'm not done with the dishes."

"Screw the dishes. Hurry up."

Doris appears wearing rubber gloves and a look of irritation. "What is it?"

"*Shh*. Listen."

A newscaster, gray-haired and earnest, is speaking: ". . . in this small Pennsylvania community. Unheralded, as yet unexplained, it is mystifying scientists and parapsychologists as well. Needless to say, it is also terrifying the residents of the town, and a state of near-panic exists. *CBS Evening News* will have a full report with filmed coverage." A film of a dog turning away from a bowl of food replaces the newscaster's head.

"What was that?" Doris asks.

"This town in Pennsylvania. Merry-something. *Dead* people are starting to appear."

"What, like a mass murder?"

"No. No, like ghosts."

"Like ghosts."

"That's what they said. The whole town is full of ghosts."

"Great. Can I finish the dishes now?"

"I'm not kidding."

"You sure that wasn't a commercial? For a horror movie?"

"Nah, it was a bulletin, hell, you heard it. It's gonna be on the evening news."

"Yeah. Sure."

"Look, I gotta leave for the game now. You watch it and tell me when I come home, okay?"

"Let me finish the dishes first."

Doris in Boston didn't watch the *CBS Evening News*. Walter Peschke in Manhattan didn't either, but he watched it later that evening on his VCR when he got home from his job at Mr. Steak. After he saw the Merridale story, heard the interviews, watched Dan Rather disappear immediately afterward, and cursed his timer once more, he called Alice Meadows, hoping she would be home. She was.

"Alice, Walter," he said when she answered. "Didn't know if you'd be home so soon."

"Oh, yeah," she said. "Ever since Freeland's been conducting, the tempos are faster by a good twenty percent. Show wraps at ten-fifteen now." Alice Meadows had been performing in an Equity Library Theatre production of *Anyone Can Whistle* for the past two weeks. Walter still hadn't seen it. Walter didn't like musicals.

"Friday night—I thought you might be out," Walter said.

"No. Not tonight." It was a noncommittal answer. Typical of Alice, Walter thought. Always noncommittal. "What's up?"

"I just heard something on the news about your old hometown."

"Merridale?" The name came slowly, as though she were hesitant to speak it aloud.

"Yeah. Listen. I'll play it. But it's pretty strange." He held the receiver to the speaker and pushed the play button.

Alice Meadows listened to Dan Rather, listened to reporters interviewing Tom Markley, Frank Kaylor, Pastor Craven, even Fred Hibbs, whom she did not remember. As she listened, she slowly grew chilled, in spite of the steam radiator that had driven the apartment to a cloying seventy-eight degrees, and by the time the voices had stopped and Walter was back on the line, she had already realized the possibilities.

"You hear it okay? Alice?"

She tried to answer, but had to clear her throat first. "Yes. Fine, Walter."

"Bizarre, huh? Your folks aren't there now, are they?"

"No. No, they're not." Alice's father had worked in a civilian function for the Air Force. He had been stationed at the now-defunct Fort Harris base, twenty miles from Merridale, where he had had his longest span of service—six years, from the time Alice was fourteen through her twentieth birthday. They were in Colorado now.

"You still keep in touch with anyone back there?"

"Not really. Walter, listen, I'm kind of busy right now. I'll talk to you later, all right?"

"Yeah, sure. But listen, what about that Vivaldi concert next week? You said you'd let me know this weekend."

"Thanks, but I don't think so. I'll be out of town next week."

"Out of town? What about your show?"

"I'll work something out."

"But where are you going? What's—"

"Talk to you later, Walter. Thanks for giving me the news." And she hung up.

"Shit," Walter mumbled into the dead receiver, trying to remember what he'd ever done to piss her off. Their first dates had been great, even if his taste in shows had been a little heavier than hers. Sex had logically followed, and it had been very good for both of them. What's more, they related well—even Alice had admitted that. She'd gotten under his skin all right, and he was damned if he could get her out. But when he had suggested living together, he was suddenly talking to a different person. She seemed offended, as though he'd asked her to go down on him in the Plymouth lobby at intermission. "I can't commit to a relationship like that," was all she said, and when he pressed her for a reason, she withdrew, not only from the conversation, but from him as well. A week ago they'd created a small monsoon on his waterbed, and now he couldn't get a luncheon date. Walter Peschke cursed the perversity of women and shuddered at the thought of hauling his VCR down to Crazy Eddie's in the morning.

In her apartment, Alice Meadows shuddered too. I wonder if he's there, she thought. Oh, Jesus, is he there?

She opened a kitchen cabinet and looked in at half-empty bottles of Irish Mist, Sabra, and a nearly full fifth of Smirnoff Vodka. The sweetness of the first two at that moment repelled her, and the thought of the flavorless raw vodka was equally odious. She needed something that would hit her directly, that she could taste.

In the desk drawer she found the small stash of grass that Walter had left there a few weeks before. She had intended to return it to him, but now she rolled a joint with unpracticed fingers, lit it, and sucked in the harsh smoke. She didn't like grass, but tonight its immediacy of effect seemed more appealing than the slow-working alcohol in the kitchen. I hope it doesn't wreck my throat, she thought, and then realized it didn't matter, that Sharlaine would be more than anxious to do the role, and that Cal, the director, wouldn't mind either. He and Sharlaine had been getting it on since the second week of rehearsals, and it would be a good chance for each of them to score points with the other. The show had opened, the reviews had been good, and it was damned near sold out already. She didn't feel guilty.

When she called Penn Station she was put on hold for five minutes, but finally heard a well-modulated voice say, "Hello, thank you for calling Amtrak. May I help you?"

"Yes. I'd like to know when trains leave for Merridale, Pennsylvania."

"Oh, my God, miss." The voice slipped, and she heard the unmistakable tones of street black. "You don't really want to go there now, do you?"

Alice was surprised at first, and she almost laughed before annoyance took her. "Yes, I do. Now when do the trains leave?"

"Honey, I seen the news tonight. You really don't—"

"Listen! I want a ticket, all right? Not a lecture."

"I'm sorry, miss." There was an indecisive pause and when the woman spoke again, the voice had returned to its buttery flow, telling Alice that she would have to go to Philadelphia first, "but there will be no trains out of Philadelphia after eleven-thirty P.M. for Merridale."

The morning then, Alice thought, and jotted down the time of the New York train and the connection on the Philadelphia-Harrisburg run. Then she hung up and began to pack, planning to call Cal in the morning.

By late Friday evening, when Alice Meadows was hearing the news, the population of Merridale had increased by over 200. The majority were newsmen, but others had begun to arrive as well—out-of-town relatives, several close friends of residents, and even the first few curiosity seekers, as well as a group of four spiritualists from Philadelphia who had come to investigate for their psychic research society, which consisted of the four of them plus one other who had to work the next day. Unknown to Alice Meadows, ABC and CBS each did a half-hour special at 10:30 that evening about the situation in Merridale, one of which nearly every Merridale resident watched.

Seeing their town, their people, themselves, on prime-time television filled them with a strange mixture of dismay and delight, and most of them agreed that the treatment was fair, that the town looked good, if a bit upset, but that was only natural under the circumstances, wasn't it?

The figures themselves did not photograph well at all, and at best only faint outlines showed up on videotape and film. The townspeople were relieved by that. It was bad enough that the on-the-spot strangers could view their naked dead, let alone the whole world. ABC used artists' sketches to depict several of the less grisly specimens. CBS stuck with the unsatisfactory live footage. In Merridale's two motels, filled before dinnertime, cameramen worked late into the night trying to figure out ways to push their film into capturing the evanescent images, but even at night the best any of them got

155

was a man-shaped blue blur, without any details or further evidences of humanity.

By that evening more residents had made up their minds to leave the town, intimidated by the media attention, but most of all by the ghosts that hovered unsmiling near them. The majority, however, decided to remain, the stubbornness of their German forebears (now clearly visible) keeping some in their homes. Others were held by something less easily defined. Had they been able to phrase it dramatically, they might have termed it a sense of destiny, of a grim and unaccountable certainty that their town, their particular spot on earth, had been chosen above all others as a great question mark at the end of life's most baffling riddle.

But instead of this motive, which would have struck them as wearily pretentious, they might have responded instead as Sim Dupes had when asked by a reporter why he was staying. "It's my home. Don't know what they are, but they ain't hurt me yet. And it's my home."

And because it was home, people remained. They put up curtains, shut up rooms, moved high bookcases and china cupboards in front of their dead. They slept in the guest rooms or on the living-room sofas if their bedrooms were already occupied. Frightened children slept with frightened parents; frightened widows and widowers moved in with others of their kind so that few were alone in that dismal blueness of night. Even Evelyn Beech left her daughter's side to finally go inside with her husband. "She'll be here in the morning," Thorne told her, and she knew he was right. A few blocks away, Joe Longsdorff slept peacefully with his head cushioned on pillows in his wife's lap, dreaming that they were really together once more. And Mrs. Viola Stauffer had long since stopped walking in awe from room to room of her giant house. She sat asleep in the wing chair next to her father, her mother, and her sister, Buddie, who was as young and lovely as on that sad day more than sixty years before when the influenza struck.

In his apartment, Brad Meyers sat drinking a beer. His chair was pushed back against the wall so that he could face the television set and the apparition of the old man, both of which emanated a glow that made the room bright enough to read in. A kung fu movie was on the late show, and Brad grinned at the overdone grunts and groans that accompanied each motion of the fighters.

"Brad?" Christine called from the bedroom.

"Heh?" Brad replied gutturally, giving his voice the brash, husky quality of the film's overdubbers. "What you want, eh woman?" he mimicked.

"Will you *please* turn that down?"

"Heh? Why for?"

"It's keeping me awake. And Wally." The two of them were sleeping together, both scared as much by Brad's disregard for the ghosts as by the ghosts themselves.

"Shit," Brad mumbled, and then called, "So turn it down yourself!" She did not answer. "What's the matter? You want it turned down, come turn it down." Still there was no sound. "You scared?" he said. "Scared of Old Black Joe here? He won't bite. C'mon." Then he heard the bedroom door close. He shrugged, watched for another minute, then stood up and turned the volume to half of what it had been. On his way back to the chair he stopped in front of the dead man. "Joe," he said. "Your name Joe? You like that name? Okay, Joe. Joe you are."

He sat down, watched the end of the movie with Joe, then went to sleep on Wally's single bed.

At 8:30 the next morning, *boing, spwang, thwack, thrubba-dubba-dubba*, and *clang* were the first sounds to pierce his consciousness. He staggered into the hall in his underwear, but instead of the noise coming from the TV in the living room, its source was his and Christine's room right across the hall from Wally's. He kicked the door open.

Christine and Wally were sitting on the bed eating cereal and milk, watching the TV on the dressing table. "Oh, what the hell is *this?*" Brad yelled. "What's the TV doing in *here?*"

"I brought it in," Christine answered, her mouth full of Cheerios.

"*Why?*"

"He is *not* going to watch TV with that *thing* right beside

157

him. It took all the guts I had just to bring the goddamn TV in here, so just don't start!''

Wally, one eye on the TV, one eye on his mother, trembled imperceptibly.

''Oh, shit, all right. Just turn it down is all. I turned it down for you guys last night, remember?'' He twisted the knob so that the Roadrunner's sharp beep was barely heard, and walked back into Wally's room, throwing himself on the bed.

''I'm not through,'' Christine added, following him into the tiny room and closing the door behind her.

''Oh, Christ, let me sleep.''

''Sleep my ass. You think *I* slept last night?''

''Why not?''

''Jesus, what is *wrong* with you, Brad? You act like you *like* all this.''

''Maybe I do. Old Joe's a pretty good guy.''

''Well, we're leaving.''

''Who's *we?*''

''Wally and me. You too, if you—''

''Bullshit you are.''

''What do you—''

''You're not leaving, so shut up.''

''You can't *keep* us here.''

''No, but I can come after you. And you won't like it when I catch you.''

She was quiet then, her jaw shaking the more she tried to hold it still. ''Please,'' she finally said. ''Please let's go.''

''Please,'' he repeated, the anger gone from his tone. ''That's more like it. More polite. That's what you should've done in the first place. Can't catch flies with vinegar, Christine. Am I right?''

''Yes.''

''What do you use instead?''

''Honey.'' It was almost a whisper.

''Got to be *nice* to me, don't you. You gonna be nice?''

She nodded. ''I'll be nice.''

He lifted his hips and tugged off his underwear. ''You

show me how nice you can be and then maybe I'll be nice too, huh?''

Lacing his hands behind his head, he watched her as she shuffled to the door and opened it an inch. "Wally," she called feebly, "don't come in here for a while. . . . Wally?"

" 'Kay," he muttered, lost in the antics of Elmer Fudd, who had just shot Daffy Duck for the fourth time in two minutes.

Christine closed the door and started to unzip her jeans. "Uh-unh," said Brad. "Don't need to do that. Sing to me, bright bird. Make your throat warble. Understand?"

She did, and did as he wished. Afterward, she sat on the floor, her back resting against the bed. "Now can we leave?"

"*Please?*"

"Please."

Brad looked up at the ceiling, sighed, and smiled. "Evacuation of one's home is a pretty high price to pay for a blow-job."

"Brad—"

"And a second-rate blow-job at that."

"Come *on*, you said that—"

"You look at it one way, though, and there's no such thing as a second-rate blow-job."

"*Stop it!*" Christine's voice choked with rage. "You're a *bastard!*"

"You knew that when you moved in with me."

"I am *leaving!*" She began to get to her feet, but Brad reached out, grasped her arm, and pulled her across his body until her face was only inches from his own.

"And go *where?*" he snarled in a low voice. "Do *what?* You gonna be a model in New York, Chris? Or an actress in Hollywood? You gonna find yourself some rich asshole who comes twice a year and be his mistress?"

"Let go of my arm—"

"Or maybe you're too chubby for that. Maybe you could find a job as a receptionist, huh? Oh, but for that you have to be well spoken. What about a waitress, then, or a salesclerk? But for that you've got to be friendly and be able to add, and you're not so hot at either of those. What about a shoe

159

factory, then? You know, I think you'd be *perfect* for that. Loading boxes in a shoe factory. And it so happens that there's a job like that. For you. Right here in Merridale.''

"Stop it." She was crying now. He had made her cry.

"A job for Christine Grimes."

"I *work* there, I *work* there, that's where I work," she babbled.

"For Christine Grimes *Meyers*."

She stopped dead, but the tears kept gliding down her cheeks. "What?"

"I have to spell it out for you? M-e-y-e-r-s, Meyers."

"You . . . want me to *marry* you?" Her eyes narrowed distrustfully.

"What's wrong? Wasn't it tender enough?" He touched her hair, let his finger run down the curve of her cheek to rest on her lips. "I give you a pretty rough time, don't I?" He asked gently, and she nodded.

"Do you . . . you really want to marry me?"

He fell back onto the bed, pulling the sheet over himself. "I don't know what I want. I just don't want you to leave, that's all. Maybe I want you to marry me."

"Now it's '*maybe*.' " Her tone grew sharp again.

"Remember what we said when you came here," he cautioned, "No promises."

"Sure." She stood up and walked to the door.

"You're staying. Right?"

She opened the door and walked across the hall into their bedroom, where the Smurfs were working their way to the next commercial. He followed, and through the door saw her sit on the bed and pick up a bowl of soggy cereal. It was answer enough.

Then Brad walked into the living room. Joe was there. "Waiting for me, huh?" he said. He walked over to the figure and raised his hand so that his finger seemed to touch the grizzled cheek. "Don't worry, old-timer. I won't desert you."

CHAPTER
11

"Business as usual," Beth said, hanging up the phone. "They'll have classes Monday, though Reed isn't sure if any kids'll show up or not."

"They'll be there. The ones who didn't leave." Jim Callendar sipped at his second cup of coffee. "Everybody wants to get back to normal. Did he say what the school was like?"

Beth nodded. "He and Doug Bryant and Harv Kimball visited each school in the district. Nothing in the buildings, but a few of those . . . *things* on the grounds." She laughed uncomfortably. "Indians, he said they looked like. You believe that? Indians."

He shook his head. "Incredible. The town *is* close to the old Conewago Trail. But think how many years ago that must have been."

"I can't believe any of this," Beth said, sitting across from him. "I keep thinking I'll wake up soon."

"It's no dream. Yesterday was no dream." The two of them had driven downtown around noon. It had been like something out of a Bosch landscape. Bodies littered the streets and sidewalks, only half visible in the bright sunlight. The town square had been an island of comfort in comparison, despite the worried concern etched on all the faces. Beth had talked to her acquaintances, Jim standing beside her, but the withdrawn, alien attitude that he had previously felt in the presence of the townspeople had ebbed, as though an emotion stronger than the distaste they felt toward him now somehow made them brothers. He saw Bill Gingrich across the square, talking with a group of people, all of whom carried either cameras, tape recorders, or notepads. When Gingrich noticed him, he beckoned, but Jim only waved, ignoring the summons. They had stayed in the square for nearly an hour until Beth, white-faced, returned to his side.

"Let's go," she had said. "I just want to go home."

They had spent the rest of Friday in their house, the sheer curtains in the windows admitting light but nothing else. They played cribbage, watched television (even the network interruptions that grew more frequent as the day faded), and read. Jim tried to work on some card verses, but was unable to concentrate. His thoughts were implacably on his son, and they remained there through Friday night into Saturday morning, hung poised over the strong black coffee, seemed to fill not only his mind, but the world. He *had* to go out to where the accident had occurred, down in the brushy hollow past which he had never driven since that day. He had to see if Terry was there. And to see how he looked.

"I'd like to drive around a bit today," he told Beth, rinsing his coffee cup in the sink.

She frowned. "Why?"

"History's being made," he answered glibly. "I'd like to see the town, see how far this thing extends."

"They've got roadblocks up now. To keep out the curiosity seekers."

"They know me," he answered, with a trace of that warped pride that she hated so. "Besides, I have identification." His mouth curled. "Want to come?"

"No."

"You can't stay shut up forever." His urging was half-hearted, perfunctory.

162

"That's good, coming from you." She bit her lip. "I'm sorry."

"No, you're right."

"When are you going?"

He shrugged. "Now," he said, and picked up the car keys.

Christ, thought Thornton, what the hell am I getting into? He looked out the window and down at the mottled patchwork of field and forest, and sighed. Clyde Thornton, Ghost Breaker. It was pretty funny at that. Of all the people in the Federal Disaster Management Agency, he gets stuck with this Merridale mess. When he'd been appointed Director for Region I he'd been delighted. Floods, hurricanes, tornadoes, sinkholes, mud slides—they were the problems of the boys in the South, the Midwest, California . . . Hell, *nothing* happened in the Northeast except an occasional snowstorm. Of course, there were nuclear plants, but they were everywhere, and the NRC boys could take care of anything in that department except for maybe a meltdown.

Or a bunch of ghosts.

"You're our troubleshooter, Clyde," Weinberg had told him yesterday. "I know you've been a little down because you haven't had all that much to do [Thornton had almost laughed at that], but this Merridale thing should keep you busy." Thornton had then been briefed on the phenomenon and its possible causes. There was the Thorn Hill Nuclear Station a few miles away, the management of which swore up and down and left and right that there had been *no* incident, no near-miss or unannounced bit of sloppiness that could have released any additional radiation into Merridale's air. Norton Chemical was another possible industry source. Though thirty miles northwest of Merridale, it did some controlled dumping into the Susquehanna River, which ran four miles west of the town.

"Wait a minute," Thornton had said halfway through the briefing. "It's really a consideration that *industry's* at fault here?"

The wiry little scientist who'd been interrupted gazed back

163

deprecatingly. "Would you suggest a supernatural cause, Dr. Thornton? We don't deal with witches' curses and zombies here. No matter how this phenomenon has manifested itself, it must have a natural explanation. Now, perhaps that explanation will change the way we view certain data, but it *will* be *natural*. If the reports from Merridale are true—and that is what you and your team will be sent to find out—then apparently some form of energy exists after what we think of as life has fled the body. If this is the case, then there is a natural reason for why this energy has become visible, and a reason for why at this particular place."

"It's just another investigation, Clyde," Weinberg added. "Discover the source, define the needs, relay what relief is necessary to the people of the region, and that's it."

"Good enough on the needs and relief." Thornton sighed. "The source is what's got me bugged."

"That's what the rest of the team is for. Jackson and Pruett are the best we've got. You merely reinterpret their data into a social scenario."

"Terrific," Thornton said softly. And less than six hours later, barely enough time to pack and grab a little sleep, he was landing at Harrisburg International Airport, preparatory to his two-hour drive to Merridale.

When he saw the white, sleeping cooling towers of Three Mile Island, he smiled, remembering the NRC's Harold Denton a few years back, during the crisis. Denton, an unknown, faceless bureaucrat, had become an instant hero in those first few days of near-panic. Maybe if he were lucky, he could do the same. Think of it—Clyde Thornton on the cover of *Newsweek*. He grinned and pulled his seat belt snugly over his paunchy waist. Behind him, Jackson and Pruett extinguished their cigarettes and went on theorizing in guarded tones until the Lear touched down.

Walking down the dingy yellow hallway of the terminal, Thornton was worrying about finding the car-rental station when, rounding a corner, he saw ahead no less than twenty newsmen and photographers. At first he looked behind him to see who was following who would be worthy of such a welcome. But there were only Jackson and Pruett, plodding

164

along behind with their cases of instruments they had not trusted to the small luggage bay.

"Dr. Thornton?" one of the reporters called above the raucous blur of sound.

Thornton nodded, confused, and immediately several lights shot on, momentarily blinding him. A dozen voices started to ask questions at once, and on millions of TV sets viewers saw a nondescript, slightly overweight man blink tired-looking eyes as if to exercise the dark patches beneath. Before he could say a word, droplets of sweat seemed to leap out from his skin and hang on his brown bushy moustache and unfashionably long sideburns, as though they were suddenly exhausted from their futile effort to mimic youth. Then the eyes looked about fearfully and the man relaxed somewhat, discovering himself flanked by the flat-faced Jackson and Pruett. Such was the national television debut of Clyde Thornton, FDMA.

"Please," he croaked, cleared his throat, and tried again. "Please! One at a time."

"Dr. Thornton," said a middle-aged woman with a piercing voice, "Myra Santel, *Newsday*." Thornton squinted, then realized it was an introduction. "What do you expect to find here?"

"A rental car," he replied, surprised by the sincere chuckles that echoed off the concrete walls.

Even Myra Santel smiled. "Seriously though."

"Uh, just looking for some answers, that's all."

"Think you'll find them?" someone cried from the back.

"We intend to try."

"Any theories so far, Dr. Thornton?"

"A lot of theories, but nothing positive."

The questions started to come all at once, and Thornton smiled and held up a hand for silence, which fell slowly. He nodded to a well-dressed man at the side, who asked the next question, which he skillfully and calmly answered. His lucidity and imperturbability were remarkable, considering that Clyde Thornton had never before in his life been interviewed. In fact, not once had anyone paid the slightest bit of attention to Clyde Thornton, Ph.D.

But now they were, and Clyde Thornton liked it. He liked it very much indeed.

If Thornton's arrival at the Harrisburg Airport was warm and friendly, Alice Meadows's immediate reception at the Merridale train station was entirely the opposite. It wasn't as though she hadn't been warned. When she'd boarded the connecting train in Philadelphia, the conductor had said, "All those with Merridale tickets, may I have your attention please. Unless you live in Merridale or have some sort of business there, local authorities will not permit you to leave the train at that station. If that is the case, Amtrak will have to charge you the additional fee to Pennbrook, the following stop on the line, plus an additional three-dollar on-board sale service charge." He had repeated the message, and by the time he was finished, several passengers had sourly gotten off the train. Nearly all had cameras, and one carried a portable tape recorder. When the conductor punched her ticket, he asked her if she had heard what he'd said.

She nodded. "I have friends there."

The trip from Philly took two and a half hours. She tried to read a Dick Francis mystery, but found she could not keep her attention on the book's surprising twists, so she put it in her handbag and watched the scenery change from warehouses and factories to smooth flat farmland, all tinted a dusty yellow by the car's less than immaculate windows. She drank several cups of coffee, but even so the motion of the train rocked her to sleep.

When the conductor called, "Merridale," she awoke with her heart in her throat, as if the sudden awakening had also made her aware of why she had come back, what she was looking for. She scuttled for her coat, her purse, her bags, but stopped when the conductor went on. "Just stay in your seats, please. Local officers will talk to Merridale passengers before permitting you to get off the train."

Bob Rankin had been two years behind her in high school, but she recognized him anyway. His police badge gleamed as if he had shined it for this particular occasion, and she thought involuntarily what a handsome man that skinny kid who had had a crush on her had become. Rankin talked to two other passengers before getting to Alice. One he let off after a brief conversation, but the other, a young man, he would not permit to leave the car. Their words grew louder until she could hear from where she sat. ". . . all this way for nothing?"

"I'm sorry, sir, but unless you have some sort of written evidence, I can't let you off."

"Look, I got *relatives* here."

"Names?"

"Uh . . . Smith. Name's Smith."

A thick sheaf of papers materialized in the air in front of Rankin. "First name?"

While the man tried to guess what conceivable first name the Smiths of Merridale might bear, Alice's attention was distracted by the low hum of voices that had slowly filled the car.

" . . . see them?"

"I think so . . ."

"Yes, yes, yes, *look*—"

"Oh, my God . . ."

She noticed what her concentration on Bob Rankin had not let her see before: nearly all the other passengers' faces were pressed to the windows, staring out at the town slightly below. Their eyes were wide, their expressions slack-jawed, awed murmurs coming from every mouth. She looked herself then, and saw, far away and very faint in the bright sunlight, patches of pale blue like transparent, oblong bubbles. Fascinated, she stared at the unmoving things, realizing for the first time that it was true. She had not come for nothing after all.

Then, in the brush a few yards from the track, she noticed a much closer human shape. It was prone, and the upper part of its torso was covered by weeds, but the part from the sternum down was visible. The abdomen was split in two like a ripe fruit, and milky loops of intestine were floating in the pool of blood the chalice of the body cavity had formed. *Blue blood*, Alice thought with a chill, and looked away, swallowing heavily and hoping there would not be many that looked like that.

Farther up in the coach, the false Smith had finally surrendered to the inevitable and sat back defeated, while Bob Rankin moved down the aisle toward Alice. She held up her hand and smiled. "Bob?"

He didn't recognize her, and could not hide his surprise that she knew his name. "I'm sorry, miss . . ."

"Alice Meadows," she said. "Been a long time."

His eyes lit up. "*Alice!*" he said. "I'll be darned. Good to see you."

"Thanks, Bob." She cocked her head coquettishly. "You going to let me off?"

"Oh, sure, sure. Uh . . . where you staying?"

"I wasn't sure. Merridale Inn maybe."

"Uh-unh." He shook his head. "Filled up. Reporters, scientists—you name it."

"So soon?"

"Look, why don't you go wait for me on the platform. We'll figure something out." She did as he asked, and in a short time he reappeared, preceded by an older man, who started to cry as he walked down the station steps, and a heavyset younger woman, whose speed belied her weight. "Miriam Eberhart," Rankin told Alice when the woman had disappeared. "Came back to be with her mother. Her mother's alive," he added uncomfortably. "I don't remember the old fella, but he has some proof he lived here years back. On Cherry Street. Came back to see if his wife was still here."

"Is she alive?"

"I don't know. Suppose not." He looked at her. "And what about you, Alice? What are you back for?"

"Would you believe . . . to study reactions of people? For roles?" He frowned. "I didn't think so."

"Tim?" he asked quietly.

"I'm not sure," she said, but the way her face went pale told Rankin the truth.

"Well, at any rate we have to find you a place to stay. Both motels are booked solid, but I was thinking what about with Kay and me?"

"Oh, Bob, I couldn't—"

"Sure you could. We've got an extra room with its own bath, and Kay would love to see you again."

"No, she must think I'm awful. I haven't written for a couple of years, and—"

"It'll be all right, really."

Alice thought for a moment. She and Kay Weaver had been best friends in high school, even though Kay had been a year younger. They had met when both acted in *Oklahoma!* in Alice's junior year, Alice as Laurey and Kay as Ado Annie. When Alice had moved to New York, they'd remained in touch, and Kay had stayed at Alice's apartment several times, though Bob, whom Kay married a few years after graduation, never came along. "He's still got a crush on you, Alice," Kay would say, laughing, "but he *hates* cities." Kay always cheered up Alice on her visits, and for Kay it was like being recharged: an annual jolt of New York City rhythm to enable her to get through another year of Merridale. But five or six years back Kay had missed one of her yearly trips, then another, and another. And finally the letters and phone calls slowed and died. Even so, Alice had thought of Kay often, and it was not until today that she knew how much she had missed her.

"Okay," she told Bob. "If you're sure it's not too much trouble."

"No trouble at all," he said, beckoning to the police car and picking up her two pieces of luggage. "I hope you don't mind if we don't go to the house right away. Frank Kaylor wants me to check a few of the roadblocks first." He put the suitcases in the backseat and joined her in the front.

"Roadblocks?"

"Yeah." Rankin spoke loudly enough to be heard over the engine. "Got eight roadblocks up all around the town."

"People are trying to get in?"

"Sure. Just like that guy on the train. Curiosity seekers, free-lance writers, photographers. It's amazing. It's barely been a *day*, Alice, and already the ghouls are descending. I figure by tomorrow someone'll be selling T-shirts and souvenir beer mugs." They drove in silence for a while. Rankin checked the roadblocks and found that the volunteers manning them were doing a satisfactory job. "Glad this happened on a weekend," Rankin said as he finally turned the car toward his house. "Lots of people to help." He told Alice then about the schools and stores and factories closing the day before, the way people had gathered in the square, about Marty Sanders (Alice didn't remember him), and by that time they were home. It was a neat little bungalow on Poplar Street, and Bob honked the horn lightly. Alice shivered as she looked at the pale shapes scattered here and there like transparent leaf bags on some nearby lawns. "There aren't any inside our house," Bob said, sensing her discomfort. "Kay's getting braver," he added. "Got some shades up."

When they were halfway up the walk the front door opened, and Kay, older and heavier by ten pounds, stared at them both. "Alice?" she said hesitantly.

Alice nodded, and Kay ran down the steps and threw her arms around Alice, weeping and laughing at once, and Alice began to cry too without knowing precisely why. Bob gave the embracing pair a gentle push toward the house and went to fetch the luggage.

"It is so *good* to see you," gushed Kay, unwilling to relinquish the hold on Alice's shoulders. "I *never* thought you would come back, and not now especially, but, my *God*, I can't think of anyone else I'd rather see. This place has gone *crazy*, Alice. You can't talk to anyone around here now; all they want to talk about is this terrible thing that's happened, and . . ." She paused for a breath. "Oh, I'm just so glad you're here."

"You look good, Kay."

"Pooh!" Kay laughed. "A dumpy old housewife next to you. And you're *older* than me too. You have a portrait in your attic? How about some coffee?"

"I could use it," Alice said, sitting thankfully in a kitchen chair while Kay pulled a jar of instant from a cupboard. "I got up at five-thirty."

Bob stuck his head in the door. "I asked Alice to stay with us, Kay. All right?"

"I wouldn't *think* of her being anywhere else. Honestly,

Alice, you're like a godsend. I just want you to tell me *all* the things you've been doing, and tell me about the shows. I mean I haven't seen a show for *years*, except for the road companies when I can talk Bob into going. And what about that guy you were dating when I was up last? I could *swear* that I saw him in a soap a while back, and—"

"Kay," said Alice with a weak chuckle, "*please* slow down. My brain's so dopey right now I can barely follow you."

"Oh," Kay said, her face falling. "Was I talking too fast?" She tried to smile again, but faltered and took a deep breath instead. "Sorry." She turned her attention to the coffee.

"*I'm* sorry," Alice replied. "You don't have to stop entirely, you know."

"No, it's my fault. I'm not myself." Her hand shook as she set down Alice's coffee, sending the liquid over the cup's rim into the saucer.

Bob's head reappeared. "Gotta go out again. Your bags are in the guest room, Alice."

"Again?" cried Kay. "Bob, you haven't slept since—"

"I will tonight," he said, smiling. "I'll be home for dinner." And he was gone.

"He's been . . . busy," Kay added.

"I can imagine." Alice started to lift her cup, but froze as she noticed something stirring at the edge of her vision. *A ghost,* she thought blindly, but could not stop herself from turning to look. "Oh, God," she said in relief, "Vivo."

"What?"

"I thought she was a ghost . . . good old Vivo." Alice knelt beside the basket and scratched the pale brown head of the dachshund that was only now just finishing the lengthy yawn that had drawn Alice's attention. "Nice to see you, girl. You're looking a little worse for wear."

"Arthritis," smiled Kay. "You believe it? The one eye's gone for good, and her sight's real bad in the other."

Alice nodded. It was obvious. The one eye had atrophied and was wrinkled like a raisin. The other was as cloudy as an old marble. Nevertheless the dog's personality shone through

171

the grizzled face. As always, she seemed to be smiling. "Is she in pain?"

"Sometimes. Bob thinks we ought to have her put to sleep. But I think as long as she can still enjoy things . . . Besides, she's probably the last dog in Merridale."

"What do you mean?"

"When this . . . this thing started," Kay explained, "the dogs just went crazy. Barking and barking and barking. Even when they were taken out of sight they still kept it up. As if they *sensed* them. So early this morning they had a roundup. Put all the dogs in cages and on some trucks and took them down to the SPCA kennels in Lansford."

"My God, there must have been hundreds of them."

"Try nearly a thousand. Bob said it was a nightmare." She smirked. "As if anything could be a nightmare after all this."

"It hasn't bothered Vivo?"

"No, her eyes are gone, she barely hears anymore. Maybe whatever senses the younger dogs have Vivo's said good-bye to long ago." Kay knelt beside Alice and rubbed the old dog's ears. "I'm glad. She'd never survive a stay in the kennels. Maybe a day or two she'd be all right. But who knows how long this is going to last?"

Who knows indeed? Alice thought, and bit back what she had been about to tell Kay, swallowed down her reason for returning to Merridale. But Kay knew just the same, although she didn't bring up the subject of Tim Reardon until late that evening.

CHAPTER
12

The years had not changed the place. Jim didn't know what he'd expected to find—certainly no man-made response to the accident, no new sign saying, "Dangerous Curve for School Buses," no granite memorial by the roadside as they had every few yards at Gettysburg, where he and Beth and Terry had gone every summer. There was only the rough gray road, the hill, the curve, the high trees now nearly stripped of brown and dying leaves.

He pulled his car as far off the road as he could and got out. At first he listened, but heard nothing but the empty branches clicking together in the wind. He looked around to see if anyone else was there, but saw only a battered car parked several hundred yards down the road. Hunters, he thought. Taking a deep breath, he walked to the edge of the embankment.

Ice settled deep in his throat as he saw them, only dim shapes in the late-morning sun. He stood for a long time before moving down the slope toward the bare patch where even the weeds had not grown again. Ten yards away from the nearest shape he stopped.

It was several inches above the ground, the thickness, he tried to reason with detachment, of the side of the bus. Though it glowed with a weak blue light, the texture of its skin (could *skin* be so wrinkled, so puckered and deeply fissured?) made it look black. They burned, he told himself, and then remembered that he knew they had burned, that the *bus* had burned and they were inside. But he had come back today to learn something else, hadn't he? To learn *how* they had died. To learn how Terry had died.

Now he knew. Not in the accident, not in the rolling and battering descent down the hill, but in the fire. They had died in the fire. Their pitiable images were like photographs taken at the moment of death. If the flesh would have been smooth and untouched save by the kinder cruelties of jagged glass and sharp metal, Jim Callendar could have walked away. But the sad little ghost before him had been touched with flame, blackened by the fire before death came.

There must have been screams. Why can't I remember the screams?

And he thought that perhaps he had been in the air all that time that the children had been screaming, locked in the middle of that leap from which he was not certain he had as yet descended.

He closed the ten-yard gap then, walking dreamlike to the banquet table to gorge himself on the physical evidence of his guilt. The guilt opened now, like a bloom fully mature, its five blue petals gleaming in the sun: Bobby Miller, his hair charred to a pale ashy fluff, as easy to blow away as a dandelion gone to seed, his eyes hollow, abraded, the blood from the cavities frozen in tiny bubbles on his blackened cheeks, as though about to boil. . . .

Tracy Gianelli, her burned hands out in front of her as if warding off more flame, her black changeling eyes ruptured by the heat, mouth wrenched open in a silent scream. . . .

Jennifer Raber, in a more peaceful position than the others, lying fetally curled, her flesh only darkened, not burned, as though she had died more quickly than the rest. Perhaps, then, Terry had not suffered for long either. . . .

Frank Meyers, his fingers like burned sticks clutched to his

174

throat, trying to rip out the searing pain that had lined his nose, mouth, windpipe, lungs, his body blackened and wrinkled far more than the others, proof that he had taken far longer to die. . . .

Finally he saw Terry, apart from the others. He was lying as Jim had seen him lie a million times, facedown, arms bent so that his hands were next to his face, his head turned to the left. His naked skin was clear and untouched by the fire. His eyes were partly open, his mouth a small "O" of surprise.

He didn't burn. The crash killed him. He didn't burn.

At that second guilt dropped from him to let the wide expanse of relief flow in, not for himself, not from any sense of vindication, but solely from the knowledge that his boy had not suffered too much. Jim Callendar cried in that relief, and lay on the cold bare ground next to Terry's still shade, his face only inches from the boy's, as he had years before, sharing the closeness of father and son, grabbing the moment in a wish that it would stay forever and the boy would never go away.

But the hollow, he learned quickly, was no cozy bed; the vision beside him, no living son whose breath puffed in and out with a reassuring metronomic precision. This was his dead boy, now truly ash, just the impression in sand of a seashell whose inhabitant is long dissolved in the waters. He took one more look at the small face and stood up, again aware of the other blue forms nearby, again allowing the guilt to settle on him with crushing weight. Then he heard the voice: "This must be visiting day."

Jim whirled, staggered, righted himself, looked twenty yards up the slope to where a man was standing. He was of medium height, stocky, in an old fatigue jacket. Long hair and a beard nearly hid his face. At first Jim didn't recognize him.

"Startled you? I'm sorry." The man walked down the slope toward Jim with a feline grace. As he came closer Jim remembered the close-set eyes, the straight white teeth in the wide mouth that now grinned at him without humor.

"Meyers? Bradley Meyers?"

"Brad's fine. For my friends. And we ought to be friends.

After all, we've got a lot in common, huh?'' He jerked his head at the tableau of dead children. ''Each lost a son, right?''

Jim nodded.

''What's that?''

''Yes.''

''Ah.'' Brad looked around with slight interest, as though he were in a singles bar checking what was available. ''So. This is your first time?''

''What?''

''Out here. First time you came out here? Since the bang-up, I mean.''

''Yes.''

''Really something, isn't it? You know, if it hadn't been for this weird thing that's happened, why, we really wouldn't've known *how* our kids died. I mean *really* died, not just what the coroner says.'' He shook his head back and forth. ''I think there's a *reason* why things like this happen—oh, not the accident, but these, uh, *ghosts*. What do you think?''

''I don't know.'' Jim felt sick, but unable to walk away from Brad Meyers.

''Do you believe in God?''

Jim nodded.

''Sorry, I didn't get that.''

''Yes. I do.''

''That's good. I do too. Maybe not, uh, *God* exactly, but in *something*. That divinity that shapes our ends. I think there's a reason for everything. Even the smallest thing that happens. The way the leaves fall off the trees. Where they land. It all affects other things.'' Brad crouched, resting his buttocks on his heels. ''Haven't you ever thought that when some things happen, they happen just for you?''

''I guess so.''

''You guess so. You think that maybe what happened here in Merridale, these ghoulies and ghosties, that maybe *that* happened just for you?'' Jim didn't answer. ''Well?''

''I don't really know.'' If Brad Meyers had sounded stupid, if he'd slurred his words, Jim wouldn't have felt as uncomfortable as he did. But Brad's words were slow, stud-

176

ied, his delivery, if not the ideas themselves, smooth and intelligent.

"I think it did. For you. And maybe for me too. For *us*, Jim. May I call you Jim?" Jim nodded again. "That's good. And I'm Brad, Jim. Jim and Brad. Brad and Jim." Brad's face didn't change as he went on. The thin smile stayed in place. "Do you know you killed my son?"

Jim didn't, couldn't, answer. His throat was thick with sickness.

"That's all right. You don't have to say anything. I'm certain you've been feeling pretty badly about it ever since it happened. That's why I never did anything about it, never said anything to you. That, and also the fact that I didn't know what the truth was. My guess is that you didn't either. Not until today." He straightened up and took a deep breath of the cool fall air. "But now, well, seeing what I can see and remembering what you said at the hearing, I think I can figure out what happened. Postulate a bit.

"When the bus caught on fire, I mean *really* caught so that the underside was in flames, you jumped, just like you said. No big deal. I might've done the same thing. Something like that happens, and self-preservation takes over. Understandable.

"But now, and here's where the problem comes in, I don't think that fire could've killed those kids right away. In fact, I think that maybe, just maybe, there would've been time to get them out. And the reason I think that is that if there *hadn't* been time, you would've remembered. The reason you forgot, the reason your story is so fuzzy, is that you blotted it out, because you did something that you *had* to blot it out. Am I making sense, Jim? Or am I full of shit?"

After what seemed like minutes, Jim made himself answer. "It . . . it makes sense. Yes."

"Good. Thank you. Now would you like to know what you blotted out? What you did while the fire spread? I think you did nothing. I think you sat where you landed, maybe even got farther away, and then you watched. I think you heard the kids screaming, I think you saw the fire engulf the bus, I think maybe you even saw my son go up in flames. And I think you didn't do anything, and when it was too late . . . then . . . then you remembered."

177

"Then I landed," whispered Jim.

"What?"

"Nothing. Nothing."

Brad Meyers sucked his lower lip and looked at Jim appraisingly. "You notice I preface everything I said with 'I think.' Conjectures only. No certainties. But with some things we have to react as though our conjectures are true. We have to trust our feelings, do you agree?"

"Yes."

"Good." He turned in the direction of the road. "Will you come with me a minute? I'd like you to see something. Oh, don't worry, they'll still be here when you come back. I think they'll always be here. For us anyway." He started walking, but Jim did not follow. Brad turned back. "Ahab beckons. Are you afraid to come with me?" Jim followed, his eyes on Brad Meyers's bootheels as they crushed down the dying weeds.

They walked up the slope to the road, then turned left and went to the curve where Henry Martin's truck had wrecked. Brad climbed over a cable barrier and started to disappear from view. "Come on, Jim," he called, and Jim followed obediently, digging the sides of his shoes into the loose dirt that covered the steep grade.

"Here we are," Brad said, pointing to another dim blue shade half covered by very high weeds. He pushed the weeds back so that Jim could see what was left of Henry Martin. The gaunt bony frame was savagely twisted, the head attached by only a scrap of flesh. "Meet Henry Martin, Jim, whose carelessness in mechanical details has condemned him—or his shade—to hover here for . . . eternity?" Brad released the weeds, which closed over most of Henry Martin's revenant. "There's your son's killer, Jim. I can tell from seeing your boy that he bought it in the crash, not the fire. You know that, don't you?"

"Yes."

"Then you know too about the others. You saw *my* boy." Brad jammed his hands into his deep pockets, the smile gone from his face. He sighed deeply. "If Henry Martin were here right now—I don't mean *that*, I mean Henry Martin alive, healthy, untouched—what do you think you'd do?"

"I . . . don't know, I—"

"Come on. It's all right. You can tell me. Just you and him. The man who killed your son. Nobody else. What would you do? *To* him."

Jim's jaw clenched. "Nothing."

"I should have known. You're good at that. Doing nothing."

"What do *you* think I should do? Kill him?"

"He caused your boy's death."

"It was an *accident!*"

"*Ah!*" Brad's right hand leaped from his pocket, his index finger pointed upward. "Precisely. An *accident*. Something unavoidable. And you're right. In that case I should do nothing either. As I have not to *my* son's killer." The smile returned. "That's *you*," he said gently. "Not him. *You.*" It was a whisper. "And it wasn't the *accident* that killed Frank. It was an error of omission. A sin, if you will. A betrayal of duty. Cowardice. *Those* are the things that turned my boy into ashes, that sent fire through him while he was still alive."

Brad turned his back to Jim, as though he were unable to look at him any longer. When he spoke again, his voice was even quieter. "There are worse things than that. There are worse ways to die . . . and worse things than death." He stood, looking up toward the higher ground.

Jim was shivering, even though the air was only cool. He didn't know what Brad Meyers intended doing. He didn't care. If he would kill him then and there, maybe the pain would stop. His head felt filled to bursting, his stomach crawled as though furies inhabited it. He wished either to die or to go home to the warmth of his bed, where sleep would blind him to what he felt and what he was. "I'm going to leave now," he said, but did not move.

Brad turned around, his smile becoming nearly jovial. "All right. We'll see each other again, I'm sure." He held out his hand, and Jim took it. "It wasn't a coincidence, our meeting out here. It was the hand of fate, don't you think?"

179

Jim didn't answer. "And fate will bring us together again, Jim."

Brad relaxed the gentle grip with which he'd been holding Jim's hand. Then he climbed back up the slope, got in his car, and drove away.

CHAPTER
13

"George? . . . Hi, Bob Craven here. I just wanted to call and invite you and Gladys to attend service tomorrow. . . . Oh, sure, I thought you'd come, George, but I'm calling everyone today. I think it's pretty important that the congregation sticks together in the face of something like this. . . . Well, I hope to. I don't quite know what I'm going to say about it yet. . . . All right, George, see you tomorrow."

Craven hung up the phone, looked at the church directory, and sighed. George Langdon. Only at the L's, and it was nearly four o'clock. But he would keep calling, all the way through to Michael Zerphey.

"Bob?" Joan opened his study door. "Would you like some coffee?"

"Thanks, that'd be nice."

She smiled and disappeared, and Craven turned back to the directory. Nearly a third of those he called did not answer, having left the town, or gathered at the square, or perhaps visiting relatives or friends so as not to feel so alone. Those that *were* home were predictably obliging, as if they were anxious to meet once again in a large group, believing there was sanity in numbers.

It was up to Pastor Craven to supply that sanity. All was chaos in Merridale. The dead should not appear on the earth, yet they had. Why? He had asked himself a hundred times since speaking with Dotty Sanders, since seeing Pastor Dunson behind the pulpit he had preached from in life. And still the only answer he could give was the tired, old, crusty "God's will."

All right, then. If that was the only answer he could come up with, then that was the answer he would give, and give with all the force he could summon. He was not used to preaching with power. The Jim Bakkers and Jerry Falwells embarrassed him as much by their studied theatrics as by any political or social stands they took. But he could not deny that the style worked, gathered believers, harvested converts. To everything there is a season, he thought to himself, and smiled when he realized it was the old Byrds song and not the biblical verse itself that he heard in his mind. Nevertheless it was applicable. Maybe it was time to change the way he approached his congregation, time to get . . . ballsy? The word would do as well as any. If ever the town needed to be led, it was now, and if he felt worry, concern, a crumbling in the wall of faith he had built around himself over the years, he would keep it to himself.

"Here we go," Joan said, reentering the room with a steaming mug of coffee. He sipped it thankfully and put an arm around his wife.

"You're a good lady."

"How's it coming?"

"To the L's."

She picked up the directory. "Let me do it. You can work on your sermon."

He shook his head. "I'd rather the calls came from me."

"You'll never get it written."

"I can do just an outline."

Joan frowned. "Bob, you *hate* outlines. You *always* work from a full text."

"This one's different," he answered. "I want to try to get a feeling of . . . of spontaneity tomorrow. Like I'm really talking to each one of them, and not just reading a sermon."

"Honey, no one can ever tell you're reading—"

"Joan," Craven interrupted. "This goes beyond good eye contact, you see? Tomorrow morning I'm going to have four, maybe five, hundred frightened people in that church, and if I can't touch them, can't *calm* them somehow, then I might as well give up." He took her hand. "Don't you see? The only thing that can get people through something like this is faith. They've got to believe me and believe *in* me."

"All right," she said, cradling his head against her. "I *do* understand. But let me know if you need anything."

"I will," he said, and she left him alone, needing things that she could not give. He dialed the next number.

Bob Rankin was sleeping at last, exhausted after what seemed days without rest. Kay and Alice sat in the living room finishing the remainder of the coffee. Their conversation, never ceasing except between four and five, when Alice took a short nap, had been only of surface things. There had been no probing and no confessing. They had simply told each other what had happened in their lives since they'd last met. Alice's narrative had predictably been more eventful than Kay's. The Broadway tryout the previous spring (the show closed in previews), the four-month stint on the soap, the two small film roles, the off-Broadway review that had run for a year (she'd sent Kay the cast album) . . . Kay nodded, smiled, asked the expected questions, and felt inexplicably sad, though whether *for* Alice or *because of* her she could not say. She told Alice then of her life, her church bazaar, her volunteer work at Lansford General Hospital, the little side business she had selling Tupperware. She didn't mention the abortion until the coffee was long gone and the town was dark.

"We just couldn't afford a baby," she said. "I wanted it, but it scared me. The money. Bob does all right, but we're only *comfortable*, you know? Just comfortable. And with a baby, well . . ."

"I understand. Really, Kay."

"I thought you would. You're the only one I thought would understand."

183

"When was this?"

"Six years ago. And I haven't told anybody about it. Just Bob and I know, that's all. How could the people here understand something like that?"

"Six years," said Alice. "That's when you stopped coming to New York, isn't it?"

Kay nodded. "Maybe I wanted to punish myself, I don't know." Her mouth twisted in an attempted smile. "I've been punished anyway."

"What do you mean?"

"About two years ago Bob and I thought the time and the money were right. For a baby. And we couldn't." She laughed hollowly. "*Can't*, I guess I should say. It's not Bob's fault, it's mine. I can't seem to get pregnant." She sighed heavily.

Alice took her hand. "Ain't life a kick in the ass," she said.

Kay gave a sharp, little laugh. "My God, I haven't heard that for—"

"For a dozen years? I was the only girl in our class low enough to say it."

"*Worldly* enough, you mean. Besides, once you set it loose, *everyone* was saying it. 'Ain't life a kick in the ass?' " she repeated. "You remember when my mom heard me say that?"

Alice laughed. "I remember. She went red. I was surprised she didn't wash out your mouth with soap."

They laughed again, then sat back, looking at the ceiling, their heads resting on the sofa's high back. Finally Kay spoke. "What made you come back, Alice?"

Alice didn't answer.

"Is it what I think?"

"Tim," she whispered. "Is that what you thought?"

"Yes." A moment passed. "But why?"

"I . . . did wrong," Alice answered, her eyes still on the ceiling. "I haven't been able to forget what I did."

"You were young."

"I shouldn't have."

"It wouldn't have made any difference."

"Yes, it would. He wouldn't have died alone."

"He didn't. He had his parents."

"He didn't want them. He wanted me. And I ran."

"Nobody blamed you."

"I don't believe that. Besides, it doesn't matter what anybody else thought, or who they blamed, or didn't blame. They weren't in New York. *I* was. *I* knew who to blame. I didn't need them to tell me."

Kay didn't know what to say. From the moment she'd seen Alice step out of the police car, she knew why she'd come back, and it amazed her and dismayed her at the same time. It should not have stayed with Alice for so long. Twelve years had passed since Tim Reardon, or what was left of him, had returned from Vietnam. Alice and Tim had dated steadily ever since their sophomore year in high school, and the Army had gotten him as soon as he graduated. Nine months later he came back without legs, with only one arm, and with plastic tubes doing what his own inner organs were no longer able to accomplish. Kay recalled that Alice had gone to see him in his parents' home and had not gone back again. When she asked her what had happened, Alice told her it was not Tim, but someone else. She would not talk further about it, did not return to the Reardons', and a month later left for New York City. Kay stayed in touch through Alice's parents, who seemed confused but supportive of their daughter's decision to plunge into theater, and Alice, in a tremendous brush of luck, got a role in an industrial her first month. That led to an agent audition, and the agent took Alice on, finding her freshness a highly marketable commodity. The agent, a fiftyish gay, guided Alice to the right teachers and the right auditions, her parents footing the bills and paying for her room and board at an Upper East Side hotel for young women.

Six months later Tim Reardon died (of natural causes, the *Messenger* reported), and Kay sent the clipping in a letter to Alice. Alice responded as always, though she made no mention of Tim's death, and neither of them had spoken of it in all the years since.

"So what are you going to do?" Kay asked.

"Go to his house. See him. Talk to him."

"He won't hear you."

"Maybe he will."

"Why, Alice?"

"I've got to make up for it."

Kay turned to face her friend. "There's nothing to make up for. And even if there were, it's too late. Alice, it was a long time ago. I'm surprised that it's still . . . bothering you enough for you to come all this way."

"I had to."

Kay grimaced. "This isn't a play, Alice."

"I know that." Alice seemed confused, so that the tragic mask dropped for a moment.

"I don't think you do."

"You think I've been in a play that I wrote myself for the last twelve years?"

Kay looked away. "I'm sorry. I don't know what you've gone through."

Alice grabbed Kay's hand. "Kay, I know it must seem crazy. And maybe it is. But it's something that's been bottled up inside me for too long. Maybe seeing . . . Tim won't matter, won't change anything. But maybe it will. Maybe I'll be free of it then. I just felt that . . . when I heard it on television last night . . . I thought I had another chance." She laughed self-consciously. "That sounds stupid, doesn't it? All this just to give me a chance to get loose."

"It doesn't sound stupid."

"Self-centered, then. But I wonder how many other people think the same thing. One more chance to see a mother again, or a husband or wife, to tell them what you never told them in life, either because you were too shy, or because you didn't *know* what you know now. Some of those people who got off the train today looked as anxious as . . . as pilgrims heading for Lourdes." She picked up her cup, found it empty, and set it back down.

"That reminds me," Kay said. "Do you want to go to church with us tomorrow morning? Our pastor called this afternoon. He's after everybody to show."

"I don't know, I—"

"Why don't you, Alice? You'll see a lot of people you haven't seen for a long time."

"I'm pretty tired."

"The service isn't until ten-thirty."

"Maybe. I'll see how I feel in the morning."

That night Alice and Kay went to bed at 11:30. Jim Callendar went to bed at 11:45, but didn't sleep for a long time. Clyde Thornton watched himself on the 11:00 news, and was so buoyed by the experience that he kept taking hits from his bottle of scotch until 12:30, when he fell asleep on his solid motel-room bed. Brad Meyers joined a sleeping Christine at 1:30, after *Nightowl Theater* was over, and Robert Craven entered his bed at 2:00 in the morning, still not quite sure of what he would say the following day.

The church was full. Though there was no need to put up extra chairs, the pews, both on the main level and in the balcony, were packed shoulder to shoulder. The congregation whispered and murmured in unease when they saw the red curtain erected around the right-hand pulpit, but for the most part they felt comfortable there with their fellows. The hymns were sung, the offering taken up, and then it was time for the sermon.

Pastor Craven stepped up to the pulpit on the left, and as he looked out over the people, it seemed to them that he had changed in some way. The lines of his face were no longer softened with piety and quiet devotion, but instead seemed edged with determination, even with anger. He grasped the front of the pulpit with white-knuckled fingers, as though trying to break it, and spoke more loudly than he ever had before.

" 'Since we are justified by *faith*,' " he boomed out, " 'we rejoice in our sufferings, knowing that suffering produces endurance, and endurance produces character, and character produces hope. And hope does not disappoint us, because God's love has been poured into our hearts through the Holy Spirit which has been given to us.' So said Paul to the Romans.

187

"Suffering. Tribulation. All suffering is not of the body. The suffering and tribulation that every one of God's men, women, and children in this town is feeling is not of the body, but of the mind. Even the soul. What we have seen in the past few days has been hard. We've seen the people we loved returning in their bodily forms as they were at the moment of death. Terrible? Frightening? Awesome? Of course. And as yet, no one has been able to tell us *why*, to give us a logical, physical reason for it. And that *terrifies* us. What we cannot understand, we fear.

"There are those who would give us explanations. But up to this point it has been mostly our nation's religious leaders. You've heard them interviewed on television, read what they have to say in last night's or this morning's paper. One television minister said that it heralds the end of the world. Others said it gives definite proof of life after death. Still others are more cautious, saying that it could be a scientific phenomenon, but that since it's occurred, it might be taken as proof of *some* sort of further survival after death.

"They're wrong. It proves nothing. Because *God doesn't give us proof*. God gives us only *faith* and *love*. What's the condition? How does suffering make us rejoice? 'Since we are justified by *faith*,' says Paul.

"Oh, I know what you're thinking. Take it on faith, take it on faith, we always have to take it on faith. *Yes you do*. Because what else have you got? God isn't a lawyer, or a scientist. He doesn't give us evidence, he doesn't offer data. Because if he did, then faith would not be necessary. And without faith, we have nothing.

"So what am I saying, then? Just this, and in as simple terms as I know how: This is a tribulation. This is a testing. For some reason that we do not and cannot know, God has caused this to be. So accept it and trust Him to do His will.

"Right here, right now in this church is an example of this thing that God has done. You've all seen the draperies, all talked about them, now look behind them."

Craven crossed the space between the two pulpits and tugged at the curtains, pulling them back until the form of Pastor Dunson was revealed. A loud gasp came from the congregation, and Craven had to raise his voice to be heard over their continuous, shocked remarks.

"Many of you recognize this man. This was Pastor Dunson, pastor here before I came. He was among the best and finest men I ever knew. But *this* is not him. At the least this is not his soul. His soul is with God. This is only some empty shell that God has chosen to put here.

"But why? Why? Why? I don't have an answer. I can only guess. But my guess is that he is here to teach us something, perhaps the relative brevity of our lives, perhaps that life is only the preparation for death, and the time of our being with God. Perhaps there are as many lessons as there are people on the earth.

"Merridale is not cursed. On the contrary, it has been touched by God's hand. This town and what has happened here is a manifestation of his purpose. Remember that. *Remember* it. And if you doubt or fear or worry, call me, come see me, and talk to me. We are one in Christ.

" 'Who shall separate us from the love of Christ? Shall tribulation, or distress, or persecution, or famine, or nakedness, or peril, or sword? . . . No, in all these things we are more than conquerors through him who loved us. For I am sure that neither death, nor life, nor angels, nor principalities, nor things present, nor things to come, nor powers, nor height, nor depths, nor anything else in all creation, will be able to separate us from the love of God in Christ Jesus our Lord.' "

He raised his hand in blessing. " 'May the Lord watch between me and thee, while we are absent, one from the other.' "

Pastor Craven turned from the pulpit and sat in the high-backed chair with the cross carved in its center. Forgive me, he thought, his eyes locked on the deep redness of the carpet at his feet.

Forgive me, God. Forgive me.

Advent

It looked as if a night of dark intent
Was coming, and not only a night, an age.
—Robert Frost, "Once by the Pacific"

CHAPTER
14

For a time, the events in Merridale were all that were talked about in the western hemisphere, Europe, and much of Asia. The Soviet bloc countries paid little attention to the phenomenon publicly, but privately sent a team of four scientists to study it. The American government, finding their own people could not quickly solve the riddle, graciously allowed the Russians in. They learned, as did the other chemists, physicists, and biologists who had arrived that first weekend, that there was nothing to study but optics, and the findings in that discipline were useless. The wavelengths of the blue light were all between 4,000 and 7,000 angstroms. The president was uncommonly taciturn on the subject as the weeks passed, saying only that he hoped a solution to the mystery would soon be found.

Both European and American antinuclear groups were quick to take advantage of the near proximity of Merridale to the Thorn Hill Nuclear Station, and portrayed on placards and celebrated in chants what they felt to be the newest horror of rampant radiation. Both power and chemical executives (who were also catching flak from environmentalists) sent their own representatives to Merridale in an effort to discover the true cause and clear themselves, or, if the fault *were* theirs, find some way to reverse the phenomenon and/or cover up their involvement in it.

The media, entranced at first, slowly began to retreat from Merridale coverage as the weeks passed. In those first few weeks, however, it got its money's worth out of the situation. Every network ran a special the first week, ABC and CBS had fifteen-minute updates at 11:00 every evening, and even *60 Minutes* did a surprisingly tame and inconclusive segment investigating the Thorn Hill tie-in. Merridale and its residents made the covers of *Newsweek, People,* and *Time,* the last in a surrealistic painting that drew an angry letter from Mayor Markley, carping about insensitivity of the media. He received no apology.

But the problem with the media's coverage of the Ghost Town was that nothing happened. There were no hostages to be freed as in the Iranian crisis, no blame to be placed as there was at Three Mile Island, no threats to health as in Centralia or Love Canal. There were only scientists unsure of what they were searching for, apparitions whose purposes were unknown and unguessed, and residents, to whom the apparitions and scientists alike were becoming more commonplace every day.

There had been a fair amount of drama at first—the small number of heart attacks and strokes and cases of hysteria brought on by the first sight of the manifestations, the promises that the finding of an answer was momentary (this from Clyde Thornton, who quickly learned that the longer he stayed in Merridale the better), and the interviews with those who fled and those who remained. Hundreds of people in the town were interviewed, and even Eddie Karl was to be the subject of a five minute feature, after a reporter from NBC heard more than one person mention his purported foreknowledge of the spectres. But the reporter found him "so weird, creepy, and unable to say two sentences without saying *shit*," as she told her superiors, that the segment was scratched even before it was edited.

Still, all these events made for flashy journalism and highly entertaining television. But after a while nothing happened. The town, now set up as a fortified camp, strictly barring those who had no business there, held only the grim reality of the corpses, now guardedly accepted. The president's visit was over; so too were the visits of the senators, the congressmen, Billy Graham, Oral Roberts, the PBS documentary crew. Only the scientists from eight different countries remained, with less to say each day.

Finally ABC brought its people out, and relieved NBC and CBS brass soon followed suit. They would report any changes or related stories, but an unanswered riddle of mortality was considered too grim for the audience to handle every night. The news was already grim enough.

Bradley Meyers sitting on the floor, hearing the whirring sound inside again, battering his muscles with short, downward jerks of his neck, trying to pull his head into his shell, and Old Black Joe watching the wall behind him.

Bradley Meyers, face to face with Old Black Joe, eyes inches from rheumy blue-yellow eyes, you found me, you found me, over and over again.

Bradley Meyers, sunk crotch-deep in a thick beer-dream of remembrance, white eyes, dark skin gleaming in fire glow, and redness dripping from a half-seen chin, eat it, eat it, it's the only way yes, eat the dink's heart.

Bradley Meyers, taking the knife and tossing it, flying away like a metal whirlwind into the vines, black and red and black soaring away, chopper blades of God flying out, leaving him alone, all alone.

Bradley Meyers together with them, one of them one of them now *I have tasted the flesh I have drunk the blood and it is life and life is all is everything Home Don't think about Home Don't think Stop Taste the Life.*

Old Joe Old Joe that's why you're here, so I wouldn't forget couldn't forgive But I had to had to, had to live, had to come Home, no don't think of Home, no Home now, don't deserve Home, but you give and you give and you want Home, and you'll do anything for Home, even that, even all that you will do to come Home, even taste the flesh, drink the blood.

For Home.

Brad Meyers's eyes opened. He was lying on the couch, the TV screen just so much white fuzz. Joe stood in his usual place, his blue light dim in contrast to the strings of bulbs that hugged the Christmas tree in the corner.

Brad looked at his watch. It was 1:30. Standing up, he walked toward the bedroom, shaking his head to toss away the images that still remained. At least he didn't have to go to work in the morning, even though it was Friday. Thank God, he thought, for Christmas vacation.

"Chris?" he said softly as he entered the bedroom. "Christine?"

There was no answer. The bed was empty. What had she said? "I'm going out with some of the girls."

"Who?"

"Oh, Barb and Pat, maybe Ronnie."

"Where?"

"Oh, they talked about going out drinking, but we'll probably just stay at Barb's."

"When you coming back?"

"I won't be late. Don't wait up for me if you're tired, though."

Sure. "Don't wait up." This was the third time this month she'd told him that. And each time she had come home at three or so in the morning. He hadn't pushed her, hadn't asked why she'd stayed out so late. He really didn't care that much. But tonight was different. He felt strange tonight. Mean. He wanted to catch her in a lie.

He got Barb Kelso's number from Christine's phone directory and dialed it. After nine rings there was an answer, a woman's voice, thick with sleep. Brad hung up without speaking. Then he opened the door to Wally's room. "Hey," he called until the boy stirred and finally answered.

"Your mommy's a whore."

"What, Uncle Brad?"

"Your mommy's a whore. You can ask her what it means

196

in the morning. Just make sure you remember. Whore. Now go back to sleep."

Then he went back into the living room, pulled the plug on the tree lights, changed the channel to an old William Gargan movie, and waited for Chris to come home.

At that moment, coming home was the farthest thing from Christine Grimes's mind. She was trying with all her might to bring forth a sexual climax from the partly flaccid organ that was doing its best to penetrate her. The heavyset trucker on top of her was one drink away from drunkenness and two away from unconsciousness.

She had not been happy with the match-up, but she felt as if she would do anything to sleep again in a town unhaunted by specters. So, since a twenty-dollar motel bill would be noticed by Brad's penurious budgeting system, she had driven ten miles to Needham Springs, gone into a roadhouse across from a motel, and had succeeded in picking up the man who now gave a sharp yap, as if his puny orgasm had hurt him, and collapsed loosely on top of her.

"How was't?" he asked, nuzzling her neck with his whiskery mouth.

"Fine, just fine," she lied, putting her arms around him, feeling her own orgasm drift away untouched into the night, thinking that at least she could sleep now. Perhaps he hadn't been so bad at that. He cared enough to ask, after all, which was more than her first partner had done, although she *had* come with him. The second she preferred to forget, a cruel man, tall and thin, who had wanted some of the more disgusting things that Brad sometimes made her do. But she had done them, had thought she'd have done anything, just to have a night away from Merridale.

Sometime later she awoke and looked at her watch: 4:00. What she should do, she thought, was get up, get dressed, and go home. But the thought of driving through those dark streets deserted by all but those grim sentinels frightened her more than the image of Brad waiting for her when she returned. *Fuck him*, she thought savagely as she burrowed closer to the man sleeping beside her, who now seemed not nearly as fat and as sour-smelling as she had first imagined.

But even though the nearest specter was a good ten miles away, she found that she could not go back to sleep.

"A whore," Brad told Wally again the next morning. He stood in front of the TV screen, blocking the boy's view of Mighty Mouse. They were both in the living room. Wally, with a child's casual acceptance, had grown used to the sight of Old Joe, and had even gotten to the point where he could not understand his mother's constant revulsion. It was like a poster, that was all. Like the Mickey Mouse poster Uncle Brad had bought for him last Christmas.

"W-h-o-r-e," Brad spelled out. "But you don't know your letters anyway, do you?"

Wally shook his head no. He *did* know his letters, had learned them from *Sesame Street*, and numbers too. But no one had ever asked him if he knew them or tried to help him read or count. Mommy used to, but that was just a game. He didn't really *learn* from that, like he did from TV. But he wouldn't tell Uncle Brad he knew them, especially since that would have meant telling Uncle Brad he was wrong. So he shook his head no.

"Now, you tell her when she gets home, won't you?"

"Yeah." Wally twisted his head to the right, trying to see past Brad.

"You listening to me?"

"Yeah."

"Okay, then," Brad said, not moving. "If Mommy's a whore, then what does that make *you?*"

"I dunno."

"It's simple. A *son* of a whore. Right?"

"Yeah."

Brad moved away from the TV then, his rage toward Christine escaping just enough that he cuffed the boy roughly on the side of the head.

Wally gasped, and his own temper broke suicidally. "I didn't do nothing!" he cried.

"Sometimes being born's enough, sweetmeat," Brad said softly. *Frankie didn't do anything. I didn't do anything.* "Sometimes you just get whomped for the hell of it."

The door opened. They both turned and saw Christine standing there, her black hair hanging long and only partially combed. Her makeup seemed cemented on, and her coat was hanging open, so that the tight sweater beneath seemed to Brad like nothing more than a walking come-on. He felt both angry and aroused.

"Well, look who's back." He smiled, then chuckled as her eyes darted nervously to Old Joe and back again to him. "And where have you been, my pretty one?"

"Spent the night at Barb's."

"Why for?"

"I drank too much."

"At the bar?"

"Yeah, and . . . back at her place afterward."

"Wrong. I called Barb last night, talked to her," he half lied. "She said you weren't with her. She didn't know *where* you were. So from that information Wally and I could draw only one conclusion. What *is* your mommy, Wally?"

The boy whispered it. "A whore."

"Louder."

"A whore."

Christine whitened, staring with wide eyes at her son. Then she turned to Brad. "You taught him that!"

"Only the word. His mommy has taught him the concept." Brad dropped the bantering tone. "What were you doing last night?"

"Wally, go to your room."

"Were you getting fucked?"

"Wally!" The boy ran down the hall.

"Huh? A little on the side? Is that what you were doing the other times?"

"No, I—"

"Don't lie to me. That's the worst. The lying is the worst. What I want is the truth. I want to know why."

"I just—"

"Why?"

"I just want to get away from here!" she flared. "I can't *stand* this anymore. All these *things!* I just wanted to get *away* for a night. That's all!"

"You mean you . . . picked somebody up so you wouldn't have to spend the night here in town?"

"*Yes.*"

"But"—he shook his head, his cold anger replaced by genuine puzzlement—"you can't see anything in our bedroom."

"I *know* they're there," she answered, her voice breaking in frustration. "I can *feel* them. Please, Brad, we've got to go. We've just *got* to." She had come to his side, her fear of him nothing in comparison to the fears that had sent her into a stranger's bed.

He put his arms on her shoulders, almost tenderly. "Chris, I *can't* go."

"Why not? You're strong, you're smart, you could do better than the shoe factory. Why do you want to stay here?"

His mouth quivered, and for an instant she saw the face of the man she had loved enough to move in with without benefit of marriage. His face had suddenly changed so that it looked like a little boy's, full of a trusting vulnerability that melted her. It was as though a mask had dropped away, as if a statue had become flesh. "I don't know myself," he said, the unexpected wetness in his eyes making them look larger, entranced. "I just know that I have to, that there's a reason. That there's something I have to . . . make up for. And I can't do it without you. I mean I can't bear to be alone now. Not now, when it's coming."

"What's coming?" she asked, clinging to him.

"Judgment," he said. "I think judgment."

"I don't know what you mean."

"No. I didn't expect you to."

Her face fell. "You always thought I was dumb."

The moment was over. The seconds of warmth, of communication that they had shared was gone, and Brad's eyes narrowed with a hint of their former cynicism. He tried to hold on nonetheless.

"That's not what I meant."

She turned away. "You told Wally to call me a whore."

He remembered then, and he smirked. "I didn't tell him to call you a *dumb* whore."

"Don't teach my son words like that!" She whirled, snarling.

"He ought to know them."

"He's *four*, for crissake!"

"Was he good?"

"Who?"

"Your friend. The one who traded you half an out-of-town bed for your little pussy. Was he good?" Some of the tightness went out of her jaw. He had her on the defensive now. "Well? Was he?" She didn't answer. "You know, Chris, in all the time we've been together, I have not once slept with another woman. Did you know that? And we're not even married, so it wasn't fear of God or the loss of reputation. You want to know what it was? Come on. Can I have a response here?" She nodded stiffly. "It was honor." He took his time with the word, so that it seemed to ease itself off his tongue. "Honor. You know, people don't talk about honor today. People have forgotten what the hell it is. Well, I haven't. Maybe I did once or twice before in my life. And maybe that's why it's been so important since. But I'm not forgetting now. I'm living with you, so I don't fuck anybody else, not even if they beg me, which no one's been doing anyway. And maybe I'm foolish enough to expect the same thing in return from you. Do you think that's unreasonable?"

She breathed deeply before she answered. "I think . . . that staying *here* is unreasonable."

"That's not the *point!*" he roared. "Not the goddamn point! The point here is *cunt*, and the fact that you've been spreading yours for a night at the Rammit Inn and a cup of in-room instant in the morning and I don't *like* that. It pisses me off." He backhanded her lightly on the left cheek, as casually as if he were brushing away a gnat. She gasped and drew back, but swerved as soon as she realized she was stumbling blindly toward Old Joe. "Uh-unh," Brad said, smacking her, this time with his open palm, on her right cheek so that she moved back onto her previous route. "You're not a very honorable lady, Chris," Brad said viciously, striking her again and again, sharp blows that stung her face, left, right, left, right, pressing her backward toward the old black man silently watching the room.

Finally she flailed at Brad with her fists, but he caught them and whirled her around so that she faced the phantom. "Nooo!" she cried, bringing up her knees and trying to kick him, but he evaded most of her blows, and those that connected he ignored.

"Scared of Joe?" he grunted, forcing her closer. "Huh? Scared of Joe? Why? He's a man, see? Maybe he'll give you a room for the night if you fuck him, huh?" Now he held her less than a foot away from the blue-yellow eyes. "Why don'tcha show him the merchandise, Chris? Huh? Come on, let's show him!"

He had her coat off and her sweater pushed up over her breasts before her terror allowed her to cry out. It was a slow, choking wail of despair that Wally heard in his bedroom, but he did not open his door. He only sat on his bed, hands in his lap, hoping that whatever the man was doing to his mother would satisfy him. He listened to the first cry, then to the high keening, and finally to the primitive, almost rhythmic grunts of pain that followed. The silence lasted then, and he thought perhaps that, for this time, it was over; he was safe.

One other person heard Christine's cries. The ears were old, yet still sharp enough to catch the sounds through the closed windows and above the purr of Saturday morning Market Street traffic. Eddie Karl frowned and spat, looking up toward the second-floor window from which the cries had come. "Mean shit," he muttered, shaking his head and shuffling through the melting snow. "Turned into a mean little shit." Eddie stepped to the curb and crossed the street. He passed the Western Auto store, glancing briefly at the makeshift plywood box that stood where the bench had been. "Mornin', Rorrie," he said as he passed it and made his way to the Hitching Post.

It was a typical small-town restaurant—six booths, a counter with red leather stools, tired-looking pies under dull plastic shells. There were greasy menus and greasier food, and a waitress called Jake who handled the whole with aplomb. When Eddie entered, only a few people were having a late breakfast, and he sat on the empty stool between Fred Hibbs and Tom Markley. "Howdy, Jake," he called to the chubby waitress. "Coffee 'n a doughnut, please. And how's Mr. Mayor today?" he asked Markley, who didn't look up from his coffee cup.

"Okay, Eddie," he said, taking a deep drag on his Camel.

"How's the store doin'?"

"It . . . could be better."

"Yeah, I bet. Hell, a lot fewer customers these days. And I'm bettin' they don't feel much like Christmas, am I right?"

"You're right."

Eddie shook his head. "Just a coupla days away, and everybody's walkin' around with Good Friday faces. Don't know what they're so scared of."

"They're scared of what they don't understand."

"Maybe so. Thanks, Jake." Eddie dunked the doughnut in his cup and took a large, wet bite. "This Thornton guy finding out anything yet?"

Markley snorted, the smoke rushing from his nostrils in twin torrents. "*Thornton*. Biggest waste of taxpayers' money I've ever seen. Him and his fucking scientists have been here almost three months now, and *nothing*. Got the power companies and the chemical firms kissing his ass every day too."

"You think he's a crook?"

"Don't know what to think, but he sure as hell doesn't give a damn about Merridale. I had to fight like hell to get us declared a disaster area. Son of a bitch didn't wanta do *that*. You believe it? People running out of town, businesses gone to hell, being shut off like we're in quarantine." Markley's voice fell. "You know what would've saved our asses? *Tourists*."

Eddie grinned crookedly. "Tourists?"

"Sure!" Markley seemed obsessed with the idea. "Why, people *want* to come in here. What do you think the roadblocks are for? Personally, I think they're sickos, but they *want* to see these things. So why shouldn't the town make some money off of it. You could do plates, T-shirts, even religious stuff."

"Some people'd say that's just as sick as wantin' to look."

Markley stubbed out his cigarette. "It's just an idea. There's no harm in ideas."

"I ain't so sure of that," said Eddie Karl. "That Hitler had ideas."

Markley stood up and threw two singles on the counter, then turned back, pocketed one bill, replaced it with three quarters, and walked out without another word.

"Testy, ain't he?" Eddie said, turning with a friendly smile to Fred Hibbs. "Just 'cause I didn't agree with turning Merridale into Disneyland. Might not be too bad at that." He dunked, chewed, and swallowed. "Deadland. And we could have like a Dracula mascot—the Count of Merridale. You know, like they got Mickey Mouse at Disneyland? Sure. Buttons and T-shirts and beer mugs and pennants for the kids. Maybe we could even use some old '39 World's Fair stuff. You know, 'I have seen the future.' "

Jake laughed in spite of herself. "You're awful, Eddie!"

"Just thinking of ways to make a buck, Jakie. Just like our mayor."

"It ain't funny," Fred Hibbs said. "You shouldn't make fun."

"Well, I'm goddamn sorry, Loafer, but when I see some greedy tweedly-pom like Tom Markley all bent out of shape because his business is gone to shit, damned if it don't make me chuckle a little."

Jake refilled Eddie's coffee cup, grimacing at the multitude of crumbs that bubbled up as she poured. "Mr. Markley's not all that bad. We had worse mayors."

" 'Sides," added Fred, "it ain't just *his* store, it's the whole town. Whole town's dead." He blanched. "I didn't mean that."

Eddie sent up a whoop of laughter. "Maybe not, but you're right as rain anyway. Yep. Deadest place I ever saw."

Fred Hibbs stared down at his soiled plate. "Jeez, I hate it here."

"Why don't ya go?"

"Go where? Got no relatives. All I got's my daddy's house."

"Sell it."

Hibbs grunted. "I can see you ain't been talking to no realtors lately. Nobody's sold a house here since this's all started."

"Been renting some," Jake said.

"Oh, sure, to them scientists and such. But now most of *them* are pullin' out. I talked to Melva Dupes about sellin' my place, and she told me no way. Said Merridale's just another—what'd she call it—Love Channel or something."

"Love *Canal*," said Jake. "Where they dumped those chemicals."

"Yeah. Love *Channel's* a pussy." Eddie raised an eyebrow. "Sorry, Jakie."

Jake blushed pleasantly, said, "You're a dirty old man, Eddie," and disappeared into the kitchen with Fred Hibbs's empty plate.

The two men sat for a while without speaking, and then Eddie said, "You still seeing your parents?"

Hibbs shook his head. "I put . . . like sheets of cardboard around 'em. But I know they're there."

"Really bothers you, huh?"

"Wouldn't it you?"

Eddie shrugged. "My folks weren't from around here. Never got married, nor nobody ever lived with me. Folks lived there before moved away." He sighed. "I got *nobody* in *my* house. Lotsa old friends though. All around town. I can see *them* a whole lot better now, if only people didn't keep tryin' to hide them."

"You're crazy, Eddie, you know that?"

"Crazy, huh? You just remember who seen 'em first, son. You remember *that*." He dropped the final piece of doughnut into the coffee and wolfed it down, licking a crumb from his wrinkled lips before bending them in a smile.

"I may be crazy, but I ain't scared."

While Eddie Karl was finishing his breakfast, Tom Markley was pushing open the door of his sporting-goods store on High Street, noticing as he did that it was empty as usual. Max Douglas, his only remaining salesman, sat behind the counter reading a paperback Executioner novel, which he tried to hide when he saw Markley enter. Markley pretended not to notice. He was past caring. "Anything?"

"Cy Holland was in, bought a headband. He and his family's going skiing for two weeks over Christmas. I think they just want to—" He stopped as Markley held up his hand.

"Take an early lunch, huh?" Markley said. "Be back around noon or so."

"Sure, Tom. Whatever." Max bundled up and left the store.

Alone, Markley looked at the single bill of sale registered that morning. A headband. A four-fucking-ninety-five head-band. The Friday before Christmas, and a total of five bucks. It was enough to make a body sick.

Markley ripped off his bifocals and looked around his empty store. Empty? Not quite. In one way it was full—full of merchandise that sat and sat and sat waiting for someone to come in and buy it. He kicked the side of the counter savagely, doing more harm to his foot than to the sturdy wood, but it helped nonetheless.

God*damn* Clyde Thornton, he thought. It was Thornton who was responsible, Thornton up there in Ted Bashore's big house, rented for a pittance because rich old Ted couldn't bear to *sell* it, oh, no, not even if he could have found a buyer, but he could afford to *run*, couldn't he? Off to god-damn *Florida* for a few months until this unpleasantness clears up. Sure, that's what *everybody* with money does—runs away. Doesn't matter if their town goes down the toilet, that there's no money left to keep the merchants in business.

Why doesn't Thornton find something? That's what he's here for! Markley was starting to think maybe Thornton really didn't *want* to. Maybe he liked being the big man too much. Markley shook his head and jammed a Camel in his mouth. Not only was his business shit, he was barely even mayor anymore. At the town meetings everyone deferred to *Thornton;* everyone asked *Thornton* questions. And Thornton would smile and be gracious, while never saying a goddamn thing, and would refer to Markley as "Mr. Mayor," while wearing a smirk broad enough to tell the whole town that

"Mr. Mayor" meant absolutely nothing in his scheme of things.

That thinly veiled contempt had begun to spread, touching the rest of the town, so that when before people had smiled, had helloed, had stopped to chat with the mayor, now they only nodded and walked on, the ends of their mouths twitching skyward in a vague memory of warmth toward this man who was now an impotent fool, who could only say, "I don't know," when they asked their questions. Thornton would *never* say that. Instead it was always, "We've thought of that possibility and are looking into it at this time. We'll inform you as soon as we learn anything definite." Or maybe, "Our investigations have so far not disproved those possibilities, but we can't make a positive statement yet." Or, "No, radioactivity cannot be ruled out as a possible source for the phenomenon, although it seems highly doubtful," and, "Chemicals, combined with the precise amount of wind or underground stream activity, are a somewhat remote possible source, but we're not ruling anything out yet."

Tom Markley would sit there fuming, wanting to stand up and yell at Thornton to cut the bullshit and confess that he didn't know any more than anybody else. But he didn't. He was afraid to, afraid that the people of Merridale would interpret his outbreak as jealousy and think even less of him than they already did. God, but it was a lot of crap to put up with for a token $500 a year.

What was happening with Mim didn't make it any easier. Of all the things he did not understand, Tom Markley understood that least of all. Miriam, his wife of thirty—what was it?—thirty-six years, and rock-steady all through them. When he was in Korea and she had to have Katy on her own, when he quit his job at Shaub's in Lansford to go into business for himself, when he had his operation and she had to handle the store and the books for a month and a half because he didn't trust his clerks to, she'd been as strong and supportive as he'd ever hoped a woman would be. But lately, in just the past few weeks, she'd been strangely aloof, only half listening to what he was saying. Last weekend, too, they hadn't made love.

It was that which hurt him the most. Rejection did not come easy to him, nor did failure. And he knew somehow that he *had* failed with Merridale, and with Mim. Their relationship, like the town itself, was deteriorating, small pieces of it being eaten away. He wished that none of this had ever happened, that the ghosts and the TV crews and Clyde Thornton had never set foot in Merridale.

Clyde Thornton, on the other hand, was delighted with his lot. From his first fearful doubts about what he would do and find in the town, he had fallen comfortably into his role of media hero, guru, and surrogate mayor. People finally realized who he was, knew what he did, even if, up to this point, he had done nothing but stonewall. But hell, people were used to that, used to getting no answers, only verbal disguises that reassured while they confused.

There were side benefits too. The recognition was damn nice—the sense of being someone important, someone looked up to. It was *him* the people listened to at the town meetings, not the mayor or the police chief. It was *him* the TV cameras were on, him the reporters wanted to talk to. Maybe there weren't as many now as when it started, but there were enough. Besides, fewer reporters meant fewer eyes to see things that shouldn't necessarily be seen.

Ted Bashore's house had been a godsend for purposes of secrecy. Bashore had practically forced it on Thornton. It was a huge, three-story colonial with two large wings, one of which Thornton occupied, and the other of which was shared by Jackson and Pruett, who had turned the large recreation room in the basement into a laboratory, where they continued to poke and probe, checking water, air, and soil samples until Thornton wondered if they were really humans or just cleverly disguised androids. The agency was happy to pay Ted Bashore's account $300 a month rather than the $700 they'd been paying the Lansford Holiday Inn, and Thornton was happy to finally have a residence private enough to entertain some of the women who'd been yapping at his heels.

The first one he'd taken back had been a thin, wiry blonde in her late thirties whom he'd met in a cocktail lounge. Her first words to him were, "Hey, you're a lot better looking in person than you are on TV." He'd bought her a drink, unable to keep his eyes off the spots on her leotard top where her nipples pushed out the fabric like rounded buttons. He could have sworn that they were growing larger as he watched, and she proved later that their propensity for rapid change was no illusion.

She'd balled him silly, worn him out fast, and if she hadn't come, he hadn't been aware of it. To his delight and slight embarrassment, she seemed to be in a constant orgasmic state from the time they got in his rented Fairmont to when he drove her home just before sunrise. It was as though just being with him excited her, and he realized later that it wasn't he who thrilled her, not his kisses, or his fingers, or his cock, but rather his *image*, the one on the TV screens and magazine covers, that she'd been fucking. And he thought, quite rightly, that there must be other women like this.

He found them readily enough. They'd been there all along, smiling and teasing, but before the blonde he'd made no reprisals owing to the simple fact that even if they were serious, he was too recognizable to be seen leading a woman to a motel room that opened directly on a crowded and well-lit parking lot. But Ted Bashore's house changed things. There was no one to see him drive the women off the main road and down the tree-lined private lane, no one to watch as they got out of the car and went inside, and no one to watch what followed. Oh, one or two of the girls had run into Jackson or Pruett the next morning in the kitchen, but the scientists were circumspect.

The big benefit of this whole trip however, the *crème de la crème* of benefits, far above media exposure or free and eager sex, was the financial arrangements he'd made. Not that *he* had gone to any great effort to make them; rather they had fallen into his lap like ripe plums, dark and juicy with promise. The man had not given Thornton his name when he called. It had been late at night and Thornton had been alone in the house.

"Dr. Clyde Thornton?"

"Yes?"

"Dr. Thornton, I believe I have a proposition that might interest you."

"Yes?"

"I represent a coalition of people who call themselves Friends of TriCounty Power."

"Never heard of it."

"It's a very exclusive group. Private."

"So what can I do for you?"

"A great deal. A man with your influence could be very helpful to us."

"Look, I don't know what you're driving at, but—"

"There's no tap."

"What?"

"I just wanted to let you know that there is no tap on the phone, so we can speak freely."

"Hey. If you're talking about what I think you're—"

"I'll tell you what I'm talking about, Dr. Thornton. I'm talking about your trading your help for our money. That's it in a nutshell. We wouldn't ask you to withhold any information that posed a real threat to the public . . . not a *real* threat. But we *would* hope to be informed first. We would simply like a bit of heat taken off of us and perhaps put elsewhere."

"I'm not interested! Who are you, anyway?"

"I *could* be the best friend you ever had."

"I said I'm not interested."

"All right. Just think about it. Think about more money than you ever dreamed of having. More than the six hundred and four dollars and seventy-three cents the government pays you every week and takes back two hundred before you get it. Think about the house you're in now and what it would be like to live in a house like that all the time. And think of the women that money would buy. Think of safety and secrecy and cash and just bending the rules a little. We'll be in touch."

Clyde Thornton *did* think about it, and the more he thought, the more harmless his participation seemed. Take some heat off, that's all, and it would be easy enough. So far no one, not the Russians or the French or the independents or Jackson and Pruett, had found a damn thing linking the Merridale phenomenon to Thorn Hill. Nor had they found proof of a link to any other source, natural or man-made. It must be the uncertainty, Thornton thought, that was driving the power people crazy. In the eyes of the public, nuclear power was already at fault; a *Newsweek* poll had found that sixty-two percent of those questioned felt that the nearby nuclear facility was somehow responsible for what had happened. Thornton didn't blame them for their fears. He knew damn well that N-plants weren't as safe as they could be, but he also knew that the easily panicked public would blame nearly *any* mysterious happening on a nuke if there were one within a hundred miles. Odds were that Thorn Hill was in no way responsible, so where would the harm be if he made that implication public?

The next day he had grilled Jackson and Pruett on the problem, but they were reluctant to fully clear low-level radiation as a cause. "But you see no link," Thornton pressed, and the scientists confessed they didn't. In that case, Thornton told them, perhaps the time had come to clear the air just a little.

The man called the next day. Thornton told him that he would talk to him, but not over the phone, and they agreed to meet on a back road several miles outside Merridale. The man was there when Thornton arrived, his tan BMW parked with its rear to the trees so that Thornton could not see the license plate. He stood beside it, the impeccable tailoring of his topcoat giving his massive body an intimidating V shape that made Thornton doubly aware of his own predilection to flabbiness. The man, clean-shaven, hair close-cropped, grasped Thornton's hand firmly. "Glad you came," he said.

Everything went smoothly. Deals with the devil usually do, Thornton thought later. He agreed to do what he could to clear Thorn Hill in the eyes of the public, to inform his contact (who unimaginatively asked to be addressed as Mr. Smith) in advance of any detrimental findings, and to withhold any of those findings from the public for as long as reasonable. "We're not asking you to endanger the public," Smith assured him. "Merely to give us time to work out a viable response." Thornton's stomach tightened. "Viable response" was one of those corporate buzzwords that meant everything and nothing at the same time. Though he used it, he disliked it when others did.

"Now," said Smith, pulling two thick packets from his pocket. "Two hundred and fifty twenty-dollar bills in each of these. That's ten thousand all together. An advance honorarium as a symbol of our good faith. Do a good job for us and you'll receive an additional five thousand per week. If this thing is resolved with no blame being put on the facility, you'll receive fifty thousand dollars. As a bonus, we'll say."

"That's not enough." That Thornton protested surprised him even more than it did Smith.

"Not enough?" Smith asked, his jaw suddenly tense.

"A hundred thousand would seem more equitable. TriCounty Power can afford it."

"Perhaps. But I represent *Friends* of TriCounty Power."

"I can't believe that TriCounty Power wouldn't have wealthy friends."

"Dr. Thornton, I'll be frank. I'm authorized to offer only up to seventy thousand."

"A hundred. Otherwise you're just another potential public hazard."

"I don't think—"

"A hundred." The man irritated Thornton. His good looks, his sturdy build, his unflappable air of self-assurance—all contributed to a scenario of a rich man buying a poor one. All right, then. If Thornton was to be bought, it would be for a damn healthy sum. "A hundred maximum is the price. That includes this ten and the weekly fives. If we're here another two months and you're clean when we leave, you owe me"—he paused to figure—"fifty. A hundred total. If you have to check with your boss first, you know my number." It tore at him to hand the ten thousand back, but he did it and turned toward his car.

"All right, Dr. Thornton," Smith called just as Thornton was about to close the door. "That should be acceptable."

They agreed to meet every Saturday morning at the cleared spot they now occupied just off the infrequently used back road. Thornton would report whatever was necessary, and Smith would hand over the five thousand in twenties.

It had not been difficult to take the heat off the utility. Thornton did it subtly, carefully, so that there should be no suspicion of any connection, and Smith was well pleased. Only this Saturday morning something was different. When Smith handed Thornton the money, Thornton noticed that instead of the plain white envelopes he'd always received before, these bore the printed return address of TriCounty Power.

"Coming out of the closet?" Thornton asked.

Smith smiled coolly. "Things were in a rush this week. Let's just say that TriCounty contributes stationery to us because of the fine volunteer work we do for them."

Thornton put the money in an inside pocket snug against his wallet, and the men exchanged a few words, then drove away separately. As he felt the healthy heft of cash against his chest, Thornton smiled. That made twenty-five thousand so far. Not a fortune, but in only four weeks he had more than he'd made from take-home in a whole year of working for Uncle Sam. He turned left on Coleton Road and, whistling, headed toward Merridale.

Passing through the roadblocks with ease, he drove into and parked in the square, calling friendly hellos to the people he knew and nodding sagely at those he did not. The newsstand was his first stop. It was empty except for Marie Snyder, who looked up sharply from her magazine and smiled, her glasses dropping obediently, dangling from the chain around her neck.

"Good morning, Dr. Thornton, or should I say"—she glanced at the RC Cola clock—"good afternoon. My, isn't this weather something though? Coldest Christmas we've had in years, I think. Guess you're not so used to winters like this, being from Florida originally and all."

Florida? Thornton thought. How did she know I'm from Florida? Then he relaxed, remembering that it was in the *People* article. She must have read it there. Still, she gave him the creeps, always seeming to know more than everyone else *about* everyone else in town. "How's business, Mrs.

Snyder?" he asked, stepping around the jury-rigged affair of canvas and poles that hid Marie Snyder's late husband, Lloyd, from view of the customers.

"Oh, it could be better. Lots of customers who used to come in early in the morning don't bother anymore. But I still open at five-thirty just the same. Have for thirty years, and I'm not changing now. Everything's fallen off around town, you know. Tom Markley's not doing well at all, and I'm afraid it's getting to Mim. 'Course, Bob Craven's been a wonder at keeping people's spirits up. He's even giving a guest sermon at St. Luke's tomorrow before the one at his own church. Weren't for him, most of the people'd be gone instead of just some. Frank Kaylor told me it was about thirty percent, isn't that something though? I just thank God people still buy newspapers, and my magazine and paperback sales are all right. Escape reading mostly, and who can blame them? If this situation isn't something to escape from, well I don't know what is."

Thornton put a stack of magazines on the counter and Marie Snyder flipped through them, adding the prices in her head. "*Newsweek, Time, U.S. News, TV Guide, Scientific American, Playboy* . . ." She sniffed. "Don't think much of this one myself," she said, peering snakelike at Thornton, "but I sell it 'cause so many want it."

"There's an article," Thornton explained, angry at himself for doing so, "about Merridale. They interviewed me for it."

"Oh," Marie said, as though that were barely enough of a reason to buy filth. "And *Food and Wine*. That's fourteen-fifty. I didn't know you cooked. Do you cook?" Her eyes were wide, as if ready to *see* an answer, to gather in one more unnecessary smidgen of information to jam into her already overrich trove.

"Not me. Dr. Pruett." Thornton reached roughly into his coat for his wallet. "He likes to cook. And with that huge kitchen over at Bashore's, well, he's . . ."

The wallet came out, followed by one of the envelopes whose flap had hooked onto the card case that protruded slightly above the rest of the wallet. The envelope fell onto the counter with a dull slap, faceup, so that Marie Snyder could easily see the TriCounty Power logo and name in the return-address space. Her hand shot out and clutched the envelope, lifted it, and returned it to the suddenly pale Thornton, while her thin, blue-veined fingers pressed and prodded the unmistakable sponginess of stacked currency within.

"Yes?" Marie Snyder said.

Thornton had the envelope now and stuffed it awkwardly into his pocket. His lip quivered, and he knew he must look as guilty as he felt. "What?"

"The kitchen?" she replied, smiling more sweetly than before. "At Ted Bashore's house?"

"Yes," Thornton said. "Dr. Pruett likes the kitchen."

"I see." Marie took the magazines and slid them with practiced fingers into a brown bag. "That was fourteen-fifty dollars?"

"Ah!" Thornton picked up his forgotten wallet that lay on a pile of *Messengers* and paid her.

"Thank you. I hope you enjoy them."

He looked at her, uncertain whether or not to read complexity into her simple words, then walked quickly out the door.

Marie Snyder watched him go, thinking how open people were, how they wore their secrets on their sleeves for those wise enough and experienced enough to know where to look.

Through the years little had escaped Marie's birdlike eyes. Infidelities, dishonesties, lies, cheats—all had been obvious to her. But of all the thousands of secrets that their owners had unconsciously revealed, she channeled only a small number into the town's network of rumor, and those with discretion. Oh, of course there were those stories that were too good to keep to oneself—stuffy old Grant Evans, the banker, bringing back a case of gonorrhea from one of his banking conventions, or Ed Kravitz finding Thelma in bed with his brother. These were filtered out to selected individuals who would tell only a small circle of people. Such items were never picked up for "Around the Square," so where was the harm? Marie also had a way of getting intimate details of events that everyone knew about—the way Emeline Barnes cursed her daughter from her deathbed, not only *what* she called her but *why*—and the *reason* that Josh Foley's daughter went to visit an aunt in Philadelphia for a few months.

There were some stories, though, she would not spread. Although she was fairly certain that Bob Rankin's wife had had an abortion, she kept her suspicions to herself. The Rankin girl was nice, and though affairs and teenaged pregnancies could be forgiven and forgotten over a number of years, murder was something different. So in this case, and in others, Marie Snyder remained silent out of good will. She had never, in her sixty-four years, thought about keeping a secret for any other reason. She had never thought of remaining quiet for money. Not until today, when that fat packet of bills landed like a windfall on her counter.

She had spotted Clyde Thornton's guilt as easily as if he'd been wearing a wanted poster. And when she did, she was overwhelmed by an epiphany nearly stunning in its clarity. For years and years and years she had sat behind this counter collecting nickels and dimes and quarters, while the Clyde Thorntons of the world passed through, gracing her with their temporary beneficence, buying two-dollar magazines instead of quarter papers. She had always known that guile lay behind the facades, but now she was confronted with rank criminality, a seeping cancer that touched *her*, and took from *her*. The money that she paid (and it went up every month) to the electric company was in Clyde Thornton's pocket, she was sure of it.

Bastard, she thought, hearing in her mind a word she never spoke. It was the Clyde Thorntons, she realized with sudden bitterness, who kept her here in this town of the dead collecting her dimes, counting profits in increments of pennies, the Clyde Thorntons who had caused the pressures that had finally killed her husband, Lloyd, who now lay mute under his shroud of green canvas, lay right where the stroke had killed him in 1964.

Well, maybe now was the time to get some of her own back. Just enough to go somewhere where no dead people glowed blue, somewhere where life wasn't so damn dull that she had to pry into other people's lives in order to make her own exciting enough to be livable. Maybe Atlantic City. Or Arizona. She had friends in Arizona.

She waited a half hour, and then called the number of Ted Bashore's big, expensive house.

CHAPTER
15

Beth Callendar finished stacking the dishes in the dishwasher, then walked back into the dining room, where Jim sat gazing at the far wall.

"It is not easy for me to do this.

"If you had done something, *anything*, to show me that you care, that you'd just *try* to change. Not even *try*, but just *want* to try . . . if you'd only *want* to. But you don't. You don't at all, do you?"

Jim shook his head as though it weighed a hundred pounds. "I can't," he said. "It's not a matter of wanting or trying. It's a matter of being. 'I am what I am.' "

"God*damn* it!" she flared. "Don't quote the Bible to me! The Bible, the Koran, the fucking Upanishads, you name it—every moral system in the world would call you . . . *sick*! You are . . . are . . . *sick*! You've got an obsession, Jim. I tried. I have done everything I could. I babied you, I listened to you, I shared your guilt, and when that didn't work, I bullied you, threatened you . . . but none of it's worked. None of it." She sat wearily in the chair across from him. "Don't you love me?"

"I love you. Very much."

"I've still got to go."

"I know."

"You can still come with me."

"No, I can't."

"Jim"—she leaned toward him intently—"my car is packed. I've got everything I need out there. It's *today*. I'm *ready*. And once I go, I'm gone."

"You could come back. When this is over—"

"What? When what's over? The bodies? The manifestations? They could disappear now and I'd *still* go. It's not *these* ghosts that haunt you."

He swallowed deeply. "Maybe someday . . . I'll be over it. I can . . . can come to where you'll be."

"I don't know if I'll want you then."

His lip quivered and a large, wet tear rolled down to rest on his cheek like a tiny glass globe. It was not too difficult for her to keep from circling the table and holding him. She'd been ready for his tears, and to her surprise and relief found herself barely moved by them.

It had been less than six weeks before that she'd begun looking for another job. Even if Jim had been as normal as anyone could be in Merridale, she still would have wanted to leave. The night haunts that Jim nurtured were grim complements to the voiceless, incorporeal terrors that stalked many of the children who still attended Hatch Road. Although most had come to a wary acceptance of the still and harmless figures, there was a dull fear in many of the young eyes, a lack of interest in classes until midmorning, when the bus rides to school were finally forgotten, a nervous foreboding that began to creep over them around 2:00, when they realized that soon they must go outside again to be driven past and through the grisly residue of fled lives.

The sentiments were contagious, and she soon found that the intense curiosity that had followed her own first feelings of awed terror had been in time replaced by a violent loathing of the revenants. She was at the point now where she could not bear to look at one.

Yet in a deeper sense it was not the phantoms themselves

but the lack of meaning for their existence that bothered her. She found the phenomenon irrational, and irrationality was one of the few things with which Elizabeth Callendar could not cope. It shook her prescribed ideas about life, made her edgy and irritable. If there had been an explanation, she might have been able to accept it, but no one was offering any.

She hated too what the phenomenon had done to Jim. He had, she thought, been getting better, had not seemed as withdrawn and private as before, even though she could see that he was still partially and perhaps eternally haunted by the memory of the accident. But the visitations had changed everything. She had suspected from the start that he would go out to the crash scene, and when he had returned, she'd asked him about it. He'd admitted it freely enough, but did not say what he'd seen. As for herself, she had no desire to see the embankment, especially after seeing how pale and shaken Jim looked after his visit.

"When are you going to go?" he asked in a choked voice.

Beth looked up. "Now, I think."

"I don't want you to."

"I've done what you wanted for too long. Now I've got to do what's right for me."

The opening had been a godsend. A pregnant teacher quitting right after Christmas, her former replacement deciding not to take the position at the last minute, and Beth's résumé right on the principal's desk top when the news came. An interview had followed, and Beth was in, starting January 3. Leaving now gave her a week to find an apartment, get settled, and prepare her head for being in the classroom once again. Jim had refused pointblank to go. If he would have argued or gotten angry, it would have been easier for her. But he only sat stoically, as he did now, looking and speaking for all the world like a suffering pseudo-Christ who would tearfully accept whatever blows were thrown at him.

It sickened her, and it was with relief that she left the driveway, left the town, drove past the final blue form, and passed through the roadblock. And all the way to Pittsburgh she did not once weep or feel any sorrow at leaving Merridale.

221

CHAPTER
16

His fingers were so fine, so beautiful. They were long and thin, like those of a violinist. It was strange, she thought, that those lovely fingers of the right hand should have remained untouched. Such fragile things, always dangling freely at arm's end, unprotected by thick pads of muscle, layers of fat. Only pencil-thin bones, small strands of ligament holding them to the palm. She examined the back of the hand again and saw how the veins stood out against the skin, blue on blue like blade channels on a frozen lake in moonlight. She remembered again how warm and soft that hand was, holding her own, resting lightly on her shoulder, and moving down her back, under her blouse with the clumsy craft of youth, then up to cup her breast through the thick cotton sponginess of her brassiere, and reaching behind her to undo the glowering lock of hook and eye, freeing her to the grateful touch of that warm hand, a touch that gave her grace, bestowed on her something beyond girlhood.

And here was that hand still, unsullied, pure as that first night, nails lovingly pared, scrubbed immaculately clean so as not to offend death when he came to the bedside and took it in his own.

It seemed like only moments before. So much time had passed, yet it was as though all of it had been compressed in Alice Meadows's consciousness, like that time she had smoked that bit of opium at a party. Tim's life, Tim's death, her return to him, were all stuffed into a tiny pill, a true time capsule she had swallowed effortlessly.

She was in Merridale a week before she gathered the courage to call the Reardon home, but when she did, there was no answer. She borrowed the Rankins' Volkswagen then, and drove to the house.

It was a large house, a long and wide two and a half stories painted a somber dark green. Thick-boled maples shaded it from the sun and separated it from the other houses on Park Street. It was precisely as she remembered it, down to the wide wooden swing dangling from the hooks screwed into the porch ceiling. The autumn leaves, however, were unraked, and weeds swelled Mrs. Reardon's gardens, covering whatever blooms might still remain in October. Blinds were drawn over all the windows, and a sign proclaiming "For Sale or Rent—Brouther Realty" stood slightly lopsided in the yard.

Despite all the evidence of vacancy, Alice walked up the cracking cement path and up the steps to the porch. Knowing she would receive no answer, she knocked. The wooden door was thick, so that no reverberations returned from within, and she waited half a minute, then knocked again. At last she left the porch and circled the house. The doors of the garage were closed, and she looked through the dusty glass panes to find it empty of cars. Garden tools were standing neatly inside, and three rusting bicycles, 1960 vintage, huddled together in a corner, their tires so low the rims touched the dirt floor.

How could they have gone? How so quickly?

She drove downtown then, parking the car in the square. There were still people there, by the dozens now, rather than the hundreds who had gathered when the visions first struck. There were still newspeople, some wandering idly from group to group, most waiting near or sitting inside their mobile offices parked in a row in front of the newsstand.

The realty office was unpleasantly hot, but the heavyset woman within beamed with a rosiness that showed she flourished in heat, like an orchid. She smiled heartily, with a trace of cynicism. "Hello," she said. "Are you going to make me guess?"

"I beg your pardon?"

"Whether you're a newswoman, a seller, or a buyer."

Alice laughed uncomfortably. "I . . . a buyer maybe . . . or a renter."

The cynicism vanished, but the smile remained. "I'm sorry. It's just that I haven't had anyone in here but reporters and sellers for the past week. Everybody wants out, it seems." The woman frowned slightly. "You really want to rent a place?"

"Yes. Maybe. The house on Park Street. The one with your sign."

The woman's face became blank, unreadable. "A green house? Big?"

Alice nodded. "110."

"Yes. That's the Reardons'. Just went up this week." The woman snorted what might have been a laugh. "Most of what I have went up this week."

"So it's available?"

"Yes. It's available. Would you like to see it?"

Would you like to, Alice? See it?

"If it's no trouble."

"Not at all. Oh, sorry to be rude. I'm Ellen Brouther." She stuck out a thick hand.

"Alice Meadows."

"Meadows . . . Say, didn't you used to do shows at the high school?"

Alice said she had, and they chatted about past shows as they walked to Ellen's Chrysler. They talked the whole way to Park Street, and when Ellen pulled up in front of the Reardons', she turned to Alice. "I just want to warn you. There's one of these . . . these weirdies in the house."

"That's all right."

225

"It doesn't bother you?" Alice shook her head. "This one," Ellen went on, "is . . . well, bad. One of the worst I've seen."

Then he's here, then he's here . . .

"In fact, I think that's why the Reardons left. They've got a summer home up in Clinton County they went to. Now, it's in an upstairs room, and you wouldn't have to see it at all—just keep the door shut."

"It's okay. I'd just like to see the house."

Ellen Brouther babbled about the house's good qualities as they crunched through the autumn leaves on the sidewalk. Inside, the house was chilly, the furnace off, and though the furniture was still in place, all the books and knickknacks that enlivened a home were gone. Only an unfaded patch of wallpaper remained to mark the family portrait that Alice remembered hanging over the fireplace.

"Everything's still hooked up," Ellen said. "Electricity, water, even the phone. And the furnace is full of oil."

"It's very nice," Alice said, and her words, despite the carpet and draperies and overstuffed furniture, still echoed as though the house were empty.

"This was the parlor, just a sitting room really. The living room's a little bigger, right through here, and then back into the dining room, and of course the kitchen, nice big kitchen. The cellar's unfinished, but there's a washer and dryer down there. Would you like to see?"

Alice shook her head. "That's all right. I'd just like to see the upstairs."

At the top of the stairway a hall ran the length of the house, with two doors opening off each side and another at the end. Ellen showed Alice a large bedroom done in a soothing green, a smaller daisy-yellow one with twin beds that was obviously a guest room, another room with only a few chairs remaining ("They used it as a den," Ellen told her), and a fair-sized bath with an old, claw-footed tub.

Alice waited until Ellen was moving toward the stairs before she asked about the room at the end of the hall.

Ellen licked her lips nervously. "That's the room where the apparition is. The one I told you about."

226

"I'd like to see it."

"Are you sure? I mean, you could just leave it closed. You'd never even have to look at it."

"No. If it's here in the house, I have to know what it is."

Ellen Brouther sighed. "It's not pretty," she said, moving slowly toward the door. "It's the son of the people who lived here. He was . . . hurt badly in Vietnam." She put her hand on the knob and looked at Alice.

Last chance, Alice thought. Last chance. Do you want to? Do you want it? And something made her nod, and Ellen Brouther opened the last door.

It was worse than she had imagined, yet her response to it was not one of revulsion, horror, nausea. She saw *Tim* on the bed, his body honestly laid before her, with no tubes or prosthetics that over a dozen years before had drawn a film over her recognition of him, so that she had gone away certain that this was not, could not be, Tim Reardon. Youth and pride and insensitivity to the fact that this heap of stumpy flesh was still human had blinded her to other things as well, and she had laughed, laughed at the terrible joke someone had tried to play on her. And then she had started to cry as the twisted face puckered in an emotion she couldn't read, and weeping, she had told the Reardons to let her know when Tim came home, and had walked out of the room under their shocked stares.

I was wrong. You've waited all this time because you knew I'd realize it someday. That I'd come back. Her lips curved upward in a slight smile as she saw him as he was all those years before, whole and strong.

But Ellen Brouther had no memory of that. She saw only a flagrant obscenity. Only a torso, head, and right arm remained of what must at one time have been a strong, young man. Both legs ended near the tops of the thighs. Where the genitals should have been was only a folded-over flap of skin that accentuated the incised pockets that further wrinkled the parchmentlike abdomen. The pockets gaped roundly, as though invisible hoses were still there to suck away ghostly wastes. The chest was thin, the ribs visible, the skin sallow and sickly; the face was a rag doll's, torn and sewn up without

227

skill, so that the seams showed whitely. "Why make him pretty?" Ellen imagined the surgeons saying. "Who will want him like this?" All this she saw in seconds, before turning away to look at her client, to see how *she* responded.

"Miss," she said, not at all surprised at how hushed and weak her voice seemed. Alice did not turn. "Miss Meadows?"

The girl looked at her then, and Ellen Brouther shivered. There was a beatific smile on the young woman's face, and her red hair framed that placid mask like a halo, glimmering in the light, so that Ellen felt she beheld a Madonna, but a scarlet one, with secrets deeper than motherhood.

"All . . . all right?" Ellen said. "Have you seen enough?"

Alice nodded and they left the room, Alice closing the door softly, as one secures the door of a room holding a dearly loved collection. "I'll take the house," she said when they had returned downstairs.

"You will?" Ellen could not hide her surprise. "But . . . we haven't talked about the price."

"How much, then? To rent it."

"Well, it'll rent furnished. Actually, the Reardons *preferred* to rent. They had wanted two-fifty a month."

"That's fine." Alice's three-room apartment in the city was twice that.

"How long are you planning to stay in Merridale?"

"I'm not really sure."

"Well, the lease has a condition that the Reardons can move back in on thirty days' notice."

"That's all right," Alice replied. "One thing though—is there any way that you can avoid telling the Reardons my name?"

Ellen's eyes narrowed. "Why?"

"I knew the family when I lived in Merridale. I wouldn't want them to . . . be embarrassed."

"You knew the Reardons?"

"Yes. Slightly."

"Miss Meadows, is there something you're not telling me?"

"No. I like the house, and I've no problems with the boy upstairs. I'll just keep the door closed, that's all." Alice

Meadows was a consummate actress, and Ellen Brouther believed her, allowing her to sign the lease under the name of Dorean Oates. Alice could imagine what might happen if the Reardons learned who their tenant really was. They'd storm down from upstate and evict her personally.

After she left the realty office, she bought cooking utensils at the hardware store and groceries at the Acme, then drove back to the Rankins'. Bob was on duty, and Kay was just finishing the lunch dishes. "I found a place, Kay. Moving in today."

"What?" Kay turned from the sink, tea towel and glass in hand. "What do you mean you found a place?"

"I just can't mooch off you and Bob anymore. I don't know how long I'll be here, and—"

"Alice, are you crazy? You can't stay here in Merridale—not indefinitely. What about New York, your career?"

"I can pick it up again. That's no problem."

Kay set down the towel and glass, and stood directly in front of Alice. "What house did you rent?"

"There's no point in lying. The Reardons'."

"Oh, my God," Kay said quietly. "Did you see him?"

"Yes."

"Oh, Jesus. Alice, how can you . . . I mean, you shouldn't do this."

"We already talked about it, Kay. I've already done it."

"All right!" she cried. "You've seen him! Now isn't that enough? Alice, you are my friend and I *love* you. But I don't understand this."

"I don't either. But I will."

She didn't.

Ultimately she experienced, but she did not understand, not to the point where she could put it into words, or even conscious thoughts. The ease of it all astounded her. From the first evening when she walked into his room and sat there beside his bed and looked at him until his grotesqueness seemed natural, commonplace, it had been easy. She sat and watched and wept for the lost time, wept for his loss, wept for herself for going away when it would have been easier to stay.

229

She floated on her own tears and they bore her up so lovingly and with such kindness that she thought how foolish she'd been to live all those years trying to banish the memory when it would have been so simple to accept it, to return and drink it in.

She looked most often at his hand. Although his torso and face did not repel her, they were far from beautiful, while the hand was truly lovely. She wished that she could touch it, but when she tried, she felt nothing. Still, she frequently placed her hand under his, so that it looked as if they were holding hands once more.

Alice Meadows then drifted into an existence that bore traces of both vampirism and necrophilia. She was the necrophiliac, but it was Tim Reardon's pale, inconsequential wraith that drank the life blood from her. She seldom left his side, only to sleep a few hours each night and to buy food and cook it. She'd started out eating three meals a day, but a short time later that had shrunk to two, and finally to one, a small repast of a sandwich and perhaps a bowl of soup taken in the afternoon.

Alice, unlike Eddie Karl, did not talk to her dead lover. She only sat at his side, looking at his hand. She sat there for seven weeks, eating little, bathing seldom, answering the phone when Kay called to see how she was, and hanging up almost immediately. To those in Merridale who knew of her tenancy at the Reardons', she was an enigma, though most believed she remained inside for fear of coming out. No one knew she was Alice Meadows; no one had recognized her on her infrequent trips in and out of the house.

It was the nearing of Christmas that broke the spell that bound her. Pastor Craven had organized a hayride and carol sing for the Friday evening before Christmas. There had been a heavy snow the week before that the poorly manned Merridale street crews had not been able to thoroughly expunge from the roads, so the sound of horses' hooves and heavy wooden wheels outside was as soft and delicate as the new snow that had started only an hour before. It was a new, unaccustomed sound, and Alice turned from Tim's hand and listened.

On Christmas Night all Christians sing
To hear the news the angels bring—

> News of great joy, news of great mirth,
> News of our merciful King's birth.

She stood and walked to the window, pushing back the curtain.

> Then why should men on earth be so sad,
> Since our Redeemer made us glad?
> When from our sin He set us free,
> All for to gain our liberty.

It was a moment with a dark magic in it; not a magic of the childhood religion she had learned and long ago dismissed, but a magic of time and place, certain words and sounds that lifted a thick veil from her face. It was a magic of snow and dark and candlelight, young voices pure as crystal, clean as the flakes that drifted onto the glass, melting in ecstasy at the touch of warmth.

> All out of darkness we have light,
> Which made the angels sing this night;
> "Glory to God and peace to men,
> Now and forevermore. Amen."

She peered through the pane, and when the carolers were gone, the horses' hooves silent, she saw herself in the glass and gasped, wondering for an instant who the gaunt, pale, hollow-eyed woman was who was hovering outside. Her next awareness was of her own smell, and she choked at the rank pungency. She had a sense of schizophrenia then, of knowing what she had been doing, but feeling that it had not been her at all. When she looked again at the shape on the bed, it did not repel her, but neither did it draw her as it had before.

She left the room, stripped, and took a nearly scalding shower, staying under the spray until the bathroom was heavy with mist, as though she were trying to sweat out the poisons that had filled her the past few weeks.

Weeks? The past twelve years, she thought, lifting her face to the spray. I'm leaving this town. I have done everything I could for him, and I've been able to do nothing. What did I expect?

What did I expect?

She had hoped for, and expected, forgiveness, redemption. Instead, she had found only self-flagellation. Ultimately there had been no purpose for her return, and knowing that, she could go back to New York. She had done what she could. What more could be expected of her, even from herself? A snatch of melody from her childhood, inspired by the caroling, ran through her mind:

Come home, come home,
Ye who are weary, come home.

She toweled herself dry, fixed her hair, and put on makeup for the first time in weeks. Then she stood naked in front of the full-length mirror in the Reardons' bedroom. She wondered if she had ever been this thin before. Most of her ribs were visible, and her stomach was perfectly flat, having lost the womanly rondure she disliked, but which her infrequent lovers had treasured. Even her breasts looked smaller, as if fat had dropped from them as well. Her hands came up to her face and framed it.

So gaunt. So pale. I could play Camille.

The only bit of pleasure she found from her weight loss was the fact that her cheekbones were now starkly prominent, like a *Vogue* model's, but the hollowness of her cheeks and lankiness of her neck made the total effect cadaverous.

She rubbed some of the lighter makeup from her cheeks, and fixed her hair so that it framed her face more, easing the harshness of bone. Then she dressed in a medium-green pantsuit, which lovingly complemented the lush redness of her hair.

I'm going to the Anchor, she thought. I'm going to have a few drinks and eat a huge dinner with lots of appetizers and a dessert, and then I am going to a motel and sleep, and tomorrow I am going home.

The thought made her smile as she stepped into the hall, and she kept smiling even when she saw that she had left

232

Tim's door slightly ajar. She walked to it and closed it without looking in, thinking, I loved you, I loved you, but that's over now. That's dead.

She had rented a small car to go back and forth to the supermarket, and turned its key gleefully. As she drove over the packed snow that crunched beneath the Ford's weight, she sang carols to herself until she reached the Anchor. Colored lights were strung just under the single-story roofline, and on the porch, a plastic, illuminated Santa stood six feet tall, his red hat melting the falling snowflakes the instant they touched him, so that he gleamed wetly.

Shouldn't he be blue? Alice thought with grim humor. Stop it. Not tonight. No ghosts tonight.

She entered through the bar, which was filled except for a few stools at one end next to a large packing case that was nailed to the floor. Three steps brought her down into the restaurant area, where a chubby girl in her twenties showed Alice to a small corner table next to the coffee station. Alice drank a Manhattan on the rocks, and scanned the menu ravenously, ordering oysters on the half shell, clam chowder, and a medium-rare filet with a side of spaghetti. She had had far better meals at least twice a week in the city, but thought that it was the most delicious she'd ever tasted. When she'd finished, she was delighted to find that the bar stocked Dry Sack, and ordered a glass, feeling at peace with herself, with Tim Reardon, with Merridale and the world in general.

The sherry was almost gone, warming her stomach with its gentle fire, when she heard the voice raised through the fisherman's netting that separated the dining room from the bar.

CHAPTER
17

They were both, they felt, men betrayed: by themselves, a long time before; by their women, only recently. It was sorrow and anger and self-pity and self-disgust that drove them to the Anchor bar, to find in liquor and a thick, smoky atmosphere what they could not find in their own homes.

Jim Callendar was the first of the pair to arrive. After Beth had driven away, he had roamed the house like a caged animal, feeling the house's emptiness the same way he had in the first week after his son had died. Only then Beth had been there. Now there was no one, and he thought he might go mad. His life had shattered like a mirror when the bus had wrecked, and one by one the pieces had fallen away until even Beth was gone, and only one sharp-edged shard remained, small enough to reflect back only his own tired, sad face and nothing, no one else.

Around five o'clock it had begun to snow, slow, heavy lumps of cold that seemed to explode as they landed, like bubbles of tar under hot sun. He wanted a drink, wanted many drinks, wanted to drink and drink until he was insensible, incapable of remembering. But he was also afraid, because if liquor could *not* push him into oblivion, he did not know what else he could do. At last he decided to try it, but by that time being alone was unbearable, so he got into the '72 Mustang Beth had left, and drove to the Anchor through the dark December evening.

There were only a few seats at the bar, and he took one near the door, where the chill wind swept past him from the entryway whenever a patron came in or left. He ordered scotches neat with a water chaser, and drank, and nibbled peanuts, and once got up to go to the bathroom. No one spoke to him but the bartender, but on the other hand no one paid him the kind of negative attention he had come to expect before the specters had appeared. It seemed there were weightier concerns in Merridale than a several-year-old accident.

Jim Callendar drank, and drank more, looking about edgily at times, so that the bartender wondered if he was meeting someone he didn't particularly look forward to seeing. Expected or not, the man soon came.

Brad Meyers took a more circuitous route to the Anchor than did Jim Callendar. The first thing he did when he had finished with Christine was to get in his car and drive to the town park. He took the basketball that he always carried in his trunk, walked through the foot-deep snow to the outdoor courts, and began shooting baskets. It was something he did from time to time during better weather, though he wasn't very good at it, sinking only one out of three shots. But he enjoyed it, playing alone, declining any suggestions to go one on one. He had never played in the snow before, but Chris had never cheated on him before.

The nets were down, but the hoops remained, and the ball stayed where it fell, lodged in white pockets. He could not dribble, only shoot, and he did so over and over again until his shoes were filled with snow and the legs of his jeans were soaked through to the skin. Passing cars slowed, including one police car, which Brad gave only a fleeting glance. Playing basketball in the snow was not illegal.

Finally he stopped, panting for breath. Despite the cold, he could feel wet warmth under his arms as the perspiration sank through his T-shirt into his wool sweater. He plodded back to the car and drove the fifteen miles to Lansford, where he ate at a McDonald's and went to see movies in a mall with five minitheaters. It made no difference to him what they were. He simply paid, sat down, watched one to its close, and moved on to the next.

By the time he left the third film, it was dark, and the snow had begun. He stood for a long time under the mercury-vapor lights in the mall's parking lot, letting the wet flakes fall on his forehead as if they could ease the pain he felt. He thought about Christine, about himself, about Vietnam, about promises, about honor.

It *was* about honor, he thought, all about honor. Doing the right thing, the ethical thing. He had tried to live with that thought foremost in his mind his whole life, and he had failed at times. But everyone fails, he knew that. Everyone cheats or lies or even worse, and they accept it and live with it. But Brad had within him the soul of a time in which you didn't lie, in which you tried to ferret out lies and show them for what they were, and in his eyes his sins loomed far greater than they might have to others, and the sins of others were magnified as well.

Truth still lived in him. *Honor* rode his back, spurred his ribs, reminding him, always reminding him that he had sold his soul for life in a thick, wet jungle, had spilled blood and worse to keep his own blood in his veins. He had yielded his manhood in order to be a man.

I didn't have to eat the heart. . . .

The thought came unbidden, and he pressed it back, tears forming. It came seldom, but when it did, it was lightning fast and deadly, like a snake coiled in his brain. Twice only had he put it into words, once many years ago to Bonnie, who had not heard him.

The second time was after Frankie died in the accident. He had thought that he might go insane then. He had loved the boy deeply, despite the sudden flarings of cruelty that he could not seem to control. He didn't take full advantage of his visitation rights because it hurt too much when the boy left to go back to his mother. When the accident occurred, he was devastated. This initial grief was followed by a hot anger toward Jim Callendar, which was intensified by Callendar's behavior at the hearing. Brad had quite simply wanted to kill Jim Callendar, and one night sat in his car outside the Callendars' house watching as lights and shadows moved behind the curtains and the house finally went dark, figuring where the bedroom was, thinking that since he didn't care if they caught him, he could let the wife live.

The next day he called the Veterans Administration and asked to be referred to a psychiatrist, something that Bonnie had often urged him to do, but which he had always angrily dismissed. This time was different. He had never wanted to kill anyone before, and it frightened him. The psychiatrist he was assigned was stationed at Fort Susquehanna, a cluster of yellow frame buildings that over the years had housed horse cavalry, World War II enlistees, Cuban refugees, and National Guardsmen.

Dr. Danvers was tall and fortyish, with a boyish face aged only slightly by a bushy moustache. "What bunch were you with?" was the first thing he said when the office door closed.

"Pardon?"

"In 'Nam, right?" Brad nodded. "What division?"

"Ninth Infantry."

"No kidding. Me too. Cobra Gunship. You want to sit down?"

"No couch?"

"That's for the movies and Park Avenue. What brings you here?"

Brad sat in a cushioned chair next to Danvers's desk. "I've been worried about myself lately."

"Worried."

"Yeah, I, uh"—Brad gave a half laugh—"I think I'm in danger of becoming a cliché." Danvers said nothing, so Brad went on. "I mean, I look at myself in the mirror and I see this character from central casting. Your typical whacked-out

Vietnam vet. You know . . . uh . . . long hair, beard, old fatigue jacket.''

Danvers smiled. "Do you have a jacket that says, 'When I die I'm going to heaven 'cause I spent my time in hell'?''

"I'm not that far gone yet.''

"Have any other Hollywood symptoms?''

"Kind of. I've been feeling . . . inclined to violence lately.''

"How so?''

"I get angry fast. My temper's been pretty shitty ever since I got back from 'Nam.''

"Outbursts?''

"Sometimes.''

"Ever feel like carving people up?''

Brad laughed uncomfortably. "I get pretty mad.''

"Any run-ins with the law?''

"A few.''

"You enjoy it? Having hassles with the cops?''

"Are you asking if I hate authority?''

"I asked what I asked, that's all. You don't have to read anything into it.''

"No, I don't enjoy it.''

Danvers sat quietly for a moment before he spoke again. "So you're afraid of becoming a TV-movie villain, then.'' Brad didn't respond. "Is that right?''

"I guess so.''

"What specifically brought you in here? The last straw that made you pick up the phone.''

Brad told Danvers about the accident, Frankie's death, waiting outside Jim Callendar's house. "I wanted to kill him,'' he said. "Maybe he's not at fault at all, but I wanted to kill him just the same.''

"That's not unnatural. You feel he's responsible for your son's death.''

"He *is* responsible! If you'd seen him . . . *you'd* have known. He had guilt written all over him! And I know about guilt,'' he rattled on. "I know *all* about guilt.''

"Maybe so,'' said Danvers quietly. "Listen, Brad. That cliché . . . about the wild-eyed Vietnam vet taking potshots at people. A cliché is all it is, just like Archie Bunker is a cliché of the working class, or Sanford and Son were clichés of American blacks. Sure, there are people like that, but most Vietnam vets are good guys. They've gotten back into the mainstream of American life, they've got jobs and families they don't beat, they pay their taxes and vote and go to church, and not one in a million skewers babies on bayonets."

"Then why the hell don't they show *that* in the movies?"

"Because that wouldn't sell tickets. Look, I admit, Vietnam was not pleasant for anybody, and for a lot of us it was goddamn ugly, and I can't pretend that there haven't been some guys who *did* go off the deep end—over a third have been arrested for one thing or another, and that's much higher than the general population. But that means that there are *two* thirds who've lived exemplary lives. And so can you. You don't have to live a worn-out image of what nonvets expect of you." Danvers sat back, tapped his desk top with a pen. "I think there's a lot of rage bottled up in you, but if you want me to, I think I can help you get rid of it. I'm sure that there's nothing that you brought back from 'Nam that you can't escape from."

"That's what you think, is it?" Brad's voice was cold, reptilian, and Danvers tensed slightly, as though expecting an attack.

"Yes. Don't you?"

"There are some things you do," Brad said, "that you *can't* forget. Not ever."

"Maybe you can't forget them, but you can come to terms with them."

"Accept them? No. Maybe somebody else could. Not me. Maybe if you don't know any better, maybe then. But I knew better. I'd been to college. I'd read the wise men. I knew wrong from right. Maybe the others didn't—but that's an excuse I can't use."

"You want to tell me about it?"

"No."

"Why did you come, then?"

"It wouldn't do any good."

"It's not for me to judge, Brad. I'm a doctor. You can

240

afford to ignore this uniform. I don't care what you did ten, twelve, years ago. If you fragged your CO, barbecued a village of civilians, it doesn't leave this room."

Brad looked steadily at Danvers. "You swear?"

"Absolutely. I've heard things from counselees that strain the bounds of credulity, but I've never told a living soul. Don't worry. You can't tell me anything worse than what I've already heard."

"I don't know if I can. I don't know how to start."

"Close your eyes. Pretend I'm not even here, that you're talking to yourself."

Brad closed his eyes, let his head fall.

"Now, just remember it. Talk about it. As slow as you like. Start when you were drafted, in training, when you saw your first combat, any place that's easy to slip into."

Danvers's voice was slow, soothing, hypnotic, and Brad began to relax under its ministrations, began to let the pictures come into his head. "I . . . didn't like the Army," he began tentatively. "Hated basic. I really didn't get along too well with anybody. More my own fault than anyone else's, I guess. I was scared, so I put a chip on my shoulder, without really daring anyone to knock it off. But I got through it, got sent to 'Nam. We saw lots of action in the Ninth, but I never killed anyone that I know of. We fought Cong. I never saw a woman or kid get killed, just those little guys in their black pajamas. No . . . atrocities, not yet. But still, I hated it. I was scared of being killed, ending up on those damn pongee stakes, or stepping on a mine, or half a hundred other ways to catch it. And I was a loner. Didn't see any point in making friends with guys who might be dead the next day.

"Well, one time on stand-down our company was called together. Some looey told us that there was an opening in an interrogation team and asked for volunteers. Nobody stepped forward. Nobody. Not one in a hundred and fifty guys who knew they were gonna have to go back into the jungle in two days and play peek-a-boo with the monkeys again. And I thought, shit, interrogation, how tough can that be, and I stepped forward.

"It was like stepping off a fucking cliff, though I didn't

know it at the time. I mean, I wasn't *thinking*. At least that's what I try and tell myself. I just wanted to get out of combat. But because I really didn't *talk* to my buddies, I just didn't realize.

"They asked me questions, whether I had any experience, and I just bullshit—said I thought it sounded interesting and all. I didn't think they'd take me, but they did. My squad leader probably told them I was sullen, a loner, maybe a crazy, and that's what they needed, all right.

"Christ, instead of getting *out* of the jungle, I just got deeper *into* it. Later, I could've kicked myself. In comparison, we were fighting a clean war. Your typical NCO was Audie Murphy compared to Kriger.

"That was his name, Lieutenant Kriger. He was in charge of the team. Tall guy. Barely thirty, but he'd lost a lot of his hair. Face like a hawk. The others' names I hardly remember. It doesn't matter. Kriger was all of them anyway. There were five all told, six with me. The guy I replaced had suicided, I learned later. The others adapted, but he couldn't. Maybe he was the lucky one.

"We lived in a cave. It was tunneled into a cliff face, went back for about ten feet and turned, and there was a big room there, maybe thirty feet square. The way the thing was set up, you could have light back in there and nobody by the entrance would see it, not even at night. Hell, the brush was so thick that the odds of finding the entrance at all were slim. Even the Special Forces guys who took me back had trouble remembering the way.

"The cave was perfect, though. Aesthetically right, like a modern Sawney Beane. Kriger and his men came out to meet me, and I thought right away I was in for it. They looked like animals—dirty, ragged clothes, scraggly beards, looked like they hadn't washed in months and smelled awful. All except for Kriger. He was as neat and clean as if he was expecting a visit from Westmoreland. 'Don't worry,' he said first thing. 'The animals here are for show. Scares the shit right out of the Cong.' And filthy or not, they all seemed friendly enough, and their teeth smiled nice and white at me.

"I think Kriger was crazy even before he came to Vietnam. 'Nam was just . . . sort of a proving ground for his ideas, his theories. He explained them to me real fast. 'We get secrets,' he said. 'When nobody else can get the little bastards to talk, *we* can. We do it by being mean and being a little bit crazy. Nobody cares what we do back here.' I asked him how his squad got started, and he said it was his own idea, that he volunteered to try it on the condition that nobody messed with him, looked into his methods. And nobody had. Then he smiled at me and said, out of the clear blue sky, 'You ever eat steak tartare?' I said no, and he said that they ate their meat uncooked because they couldn't risk lighting too many fires. He asked if I thought I could handle that, and I said I thought I could. So one of the guys brought me a chunk of pinkish gray meat, raw, like they'd said. It smelled okay, pretty fresh, and I asked what it was. Beef, they said, and I cut off a small piece and put it in my mouth. I wanted to gag, but I wouldn't let myself. So I chewed and chewed and chewed and finally got it down. They all smiled at each other, and I kind of laughed and asked if they didn't ever get any k rations. 'We like this better,' Kriger said, and they all laughed. Then we went into the back chamber of the cave."

Brad stopped talking.

"Yes?" Danvers said. "Go on."

"I saw . . . I saw a body hanging upside down. There was a metal stake jammed through its ankles. It was naked, and parts of it were missing. And they all grinned and Kriger said, 'They grow good beef in this jungle.'

"I fell down and vomited, and then I just lay there, wanting to die. Kriger knelt down next to me and pushed my hair back, wiped my forehead with a handkerchief like my mother would have done. 'It's all right,' he said. 'You've done it. You're one of us now.' Then I cried. But he told me that they all had acted like that at the beginning, and each one of them nodded. But it had to be done, he said. There had to be some way to get the information from the Cong. 'You'll see,' he told me. 'It works. In a few days you'll see.'

"The next days were nightmares. They cut pieces off the

243

body and ate them raw. I couldn't. I ate canned fruits and vegetables. They didn't try to force me to eat the meat. They seemed to know that it would take time for me to become what they were.

"The third night I was there, Kriger had a long talk with me. 'Anthropophagi,' he said, and sounded proud. He told me it was all in what society approves, nothing more. Then he talked about tribes in Australia where devouring dead relatives was thought to be the most respectful way to treat their bodies, and about tribes in Africa, South America, New Guinea, you name it, who ate the bodies of their enemies, as much for ceremonial purposes as for any food value.

" 'But we're *Americans*,' I said, and he just smiled at me. 'So were the Hametzen,' he said, but he didn't tell me who they were. Not then. I told him I didn't know if I could do it. He said that no one would force me, but he wanted me to play the role. When I asked what that meant, he told me he wanted me to look like the rest, to pretend to be as savage as I could. 'We're brothers,' he said. 'Will you swear to be our brother?' I didn't answer right away, and he said, 'It's either us or them,' and he gestured to the jungle. So I said I'd be their brother.

"He gathered them all together then, and they each cut the heel of their hand and let a few drops of blood fall into a tin cup. I cut mine too, and then Kriger told me to drink it. I must have looked as sick as I felt, so he said, 'It's only a few drops.' And I drank it.

"Two days later four Special Forces guys brought two Cong. One was maybe in his thirties, the other much younger, thirteen or fourteen. Their faces were set like stone, even though they were bruised and cut up pretty badly. The Berets took Kriger off to talk while the four others and I watched the Cong. I think I was more scared than the prisoners, but I tried to look as mean as the others. It was tough to do. What they did went beyond playing a role. They lived it. The Cong looked a little worried, but still sullen, secretive.

"The Special Forces left then, and Kriger spoke to us in English, told us they were father and son. Both knew a lot, but the father knew more. He went up to the father and spoke to him in Vietnamese. I couldn't tell what he said, but the Cong barked something back, and then spat on Kriger's shirt. Kriger just smiled and said, 'Take them back. You know what to do.' We dragged the two into the back chamber. The body was gone, but the spikes were still there. Kriger drew me aside. 'Just watch,' he whispered.

"I watched. There was no warning, no preparation at all. They bound the feet of both Cong, then grabbed the boy and stabbed him through the ankles with one of the stakes, right in front of the Achilles tendon. Then they lifted him up, swinging and screaming, and set the stake in the wooden framework so that he hung upside down. A long knife slit his throat, and a basin caught the blood. It all took only seconds. When I tore my eyes away, I saw the father staring at his dead son. It seemed like it took forever, but finally the basin was filled and a soldier handed it to Kriger. He drank some of the blood—there must have been two quarts of it—and then passed it to the others. They all drank, and set it down empty. Then Kriger knelt and asked the Cong something. He shook his head no. Kriger just smiled, and he nodded to one of the others. The guy took a long knife and made a bunch of slashes in the boy's chest and pulled something out. I didn't see what it was at first—just something small and dark. It wasn't until he held it out to the father that I saw it was a heart. Then he ate it.

"The father screamed then, and tried to get away, but he was tied so tight he could only thrash around. When he quieted down, Kriger talked to him again, but again the man said no. 'He's tough,' Kriger said to us in English. 'But he'll break. Five days, boys. Five days.'

"He explained it to me later. Aborigines did it, he said, and it was the worst thing he could think of. They let the boy hang where he was and put a tub beneath him. When bodies decay, they . . . well, parts liquify. And it drips down . . .'' Brad stopped, his mouth hanging open as if he was incapable of making it form any more words.

"That's enough," said Danvers. "You don't have to say any more."

"But there *is* more."

"Not for today. Later maybe. That's enough for today."

Brad opened his eyes and looked at Danvers. "We got the information," he said. "The Cong talked."

Danvers gave him a cup of coffee and told him that what had happened to him was unique, out of the ordinary. He said it was no wonder that it had affected him the way it had. But it was something that could be dealt with, and wouldn't he please consider meeting with him once a week?

Brad made an appointment for the following week, but when the day came, he knew that he couldn't say any more than he'd already said. He stayed home. Danvers called him, but Brad told him he wasn't interested anymore and hung up. True to his word, Danvers never did anything else about it.

Maybe he should have gone back, Brad thought as the snow fell all around him. Maybe if he had, he'd be someone else now, with different dreams and memories. Maybe he'd have *adapted*. War. Just war. War's not real, so the things you do in war aren't real either.

Bullshit.

He got into his car and drove to Merridale. He hadn't intended to stop at the Anchor, but when he thought how good a drink would feel without the presence of Christine or Wally, he parked and went inside.

The bar at the Anchor was shaped like a racetrack, with the patrons seated all around, and the bartender and his supplies in the middle. The music was loud, people were talking, and Bry, the bartender, raised a cautiously welcoming hand as Brad entered. It felt good to be there, homelike, and Brad smiled as he shrugged off his coat and hung it up. He sat, ordered a Miller draft, and reached for the peanuts. Then he saw Jim Callendar sitting directly across the bar from him.

For a second it seemed as if he looked into a mirror. The eyes were haunted, the face pale. The effect of being *followed* was there, tormentingly, and for the first time he felt pity for Callendar, knowing that their sins were shared, their guilts were equal, their honor had been spat upon and dragged through sewage.

But just as he pitied Callendar, so did he hate him, out of a well of strength that only self-hatred can fill. And for the first time too he knew the truth of that.

"Mr. Wilson," he said.

Jim looked up, saw Brad, but his face remained immobile.

"Mr. *William* Wilson," Brad clarified.

Recognition came into Jim's eyes, and his expression sharpened. " 'In me,' " he quoted in response, " 'see how clearly thou hast murdered thyself.' " He nodded. "Mr. Meyers."

"We meet again."

"We do. Buy you a drink?"

"Thank you, no. I've got one."

"You think we're doppelgangers?"

"Why?"

"Why call me William Wilson? I know my Poe."

"Fitting we should be." Brad sipped his beer. "Have you thought any more about what we talked of the last time?"

"Specifically?"

"Reasons. Reasons for what happened here. In town."

"Wait. I can't hear you." Jim came around the bar, thinking, It all comes together, everything comes together, and sat next to Brad.

"Why this has all happened," Brad said.

"You mean for us? For you and me? I've thought about it. And I think you're right. Idiotically, irrationally, selfishly, it has happened for *me*. No, wait," he said quickly, "I mean that my . . . fate is bound up in it." Jim's words were fuzzed. The drinking was evident. "Maybe not just for me, maybe for other people too, but goddammit, there's gotta be a reason, doesn't there?" He looked narrowly at Brad. "But why for you, eh? Why for you?"

Brad smiled grimly. "What's yours is mine. We are linked."

"We are?"

He nodded. "In ways you could not imagine. Linked . . . in life and death." Bry brought another beer at Brad's gesture. "What do you think about death, Jim? In light of what we have experienced in the past few months."

Jim smiled in spite of himself. It seemed years since he had had a decent half-drunken barroom discussion over abstractions, and he warmed to the man by his side, who seemed so enigmatic and threatening, yet somehow understanding, even sympathetic. "I don't know," he said, trying to sound more sober than he really was. "I suppose I think that death is death. Final. Forever. Complete and total oblivion. And these . . . boogeymen haven't changed my mind one way or another about that. They have no consciousness, I don't believe that. But what they've done is to change something in us—maybe our *awareness* of death. I mean, I'm *afraid* of it—death—because as shitty as life is, it's all we've got, you know? I don't want to lose it. I'd do *anything* not to lose it."

He stopped, remembering suddenly what he *had* done, or had not done, and took a quick drink. "I think everybody thinks about death a lot," he went on, looking away from Brad, "but now we think about it more. We're *reminded* of it constantly, of our own mortality, of the fact that someday *we'll* be blue spooks in the parlor. It's like living in a cemetery. Only it's more—I don't know what—more spiritual maybe?"

"It's like Ash Wednesday," Brad said calmly.

"Ash—"

"When the Catholic kids would come to school with ashes smeared on their foreheads. To remind them one day a year of their own deaths, that they were mortal and would have to suffer death to be with God." He sipped lightly from his glass. "It's as if every day is Ash Wednesday."

"Do you believe in that? That there's something after?"

"I believe more than you. It isn't final. Whatever happens, it isn't final. Death is too kind for that."

"Kind? Death kind?"

"I told you once before that there are worse things than death. And there are."

"Nothing's worse than death."

"What do you know?" Brad said sharply. "How much do *you* know? You go through one thing in your life that tests you and you fuck up and that makes you an expert? You gutless *shit!*"

248

"Hey, hey," Bry said from a few yards away, "take it easy now."

"Fuck off!"

"I mean it, Brad. No fights in here."

"I'm not fighting, I'm *talking!*"

"Well, talk softer or take it outside!"

"Who's gonna make me do *that?* You, Brian?"

Bry pushed a button underneath the bar, and Emeric Jerney appeared from the kitchen as if by magic. "What's the problem?" he asked.

"Brad's gettin' loud," Bry told him.

"I'm just *talking*, for crissake!"

Jerney squinted, his broad face becoming broader. "Why you hasslin' in here again? You been okay for a long time. Now you wanta start more trouble?"

"I'm not starting any goddamn trouble!"

"And you watch your mouth! I got diners in here."

"Fuck your diners! And the horsemeat you serve 'em!"

The Hungarian reddened. "Okay. Okay, that's it. Out. Right now. Out! Pay up and out!"

Brad threw a five-dollar bill on the bar. "You want a tip, Bry? Huh? You want a tip? Here's a tip—watch your ass. That's my tip to you, fuckface." He looked hard at Jim Callendar. "How about you? We gonna finish our conversation?" Then he turned and walked out, snatching his coat from the rack and rattling the hangers. Jim paid, and followed him.

When he got outside, Brad was standing at the bottom of the ramp that the Jerneys had installed a few years ago for the nursing-home residents who banqueted there once a month. "Now, whose fault was all that, I wonder," Brad said, his left leg shaking nervously. "What do you think? No, don't bother, I know, my fault. Always my fault. Always the fault of the half-nuts Vietnam vet, right? The coiled killer on the edge of sanity?" He shook his head. "You have no idea of what it's like to be a figure out of legend. In another ten years mamas'll be scaring their children with stories of people like me. And you know the crazy thing about it? It's *not* a bum rap. Oh, for most maybe. But not for me." He stepped closer to Jim. "*You* know, don't you? You know that there are a lot of things inside me . . . but the greatest of these is rage. Because you have it inside you too."

He put out a hand and touched Jim's face tenderly. "We're two of a kind, Jim. You just don't realize it yet."

Jim stood, oblivious to Brad's touch. "No. I don't . . . have anger in me."

"Of course you do." He tapped Jim's cheek lightly, barely enough to sting. "It's just that you don't know. You just haven't been pushed to the edge yet. But you will be." He struck Jim's face again, harder, so that Jim's head jerked aside, but snapped back immediately, as if he were a soldier at attention. "I bet you've never even been in a fight, have you? Never had anybody hit you for real, huh?" Brad made a loose fist, and backhanded Jim so that he staggered slightly. "Do you think that *I* could make you angry?" he said, and threw a left uppercut into Jim's middle that left Jim breathless.

Brad straightened up. "Come on," he said. "Come away from the light."

Jim followed him, pausing only long enough to let his aching stomach eject the several hours worth of drinks he had poured into it.

They were in the shadows now, and Brad went about his work slowly, methodically, with the careful placement of a sculptor seeking the correct balance between flesh and stone. The blows were not meant to disfigure, maim, or draw blood, although they did all three. Their purpose was pain, and in that they were most highly effective, although Jim Callendar seldom cried out. His grunts and squeals were bound with the iron of his own fulfillment, so that they seemed to be the calls of long pent-up and suddenly released passions.

Soon Brad Meyers was moaning as well, grunting with each blow like a butcher killing sheep. At last he stopped, panting, sweating despite the cold and the falling snow, watching Jim Callendar as he lay on the wet whiteness, no longer able to rise to be struck once again. "We'll hear no more of this night, will we?'' he said, and then knelt and repeated his words.

"No." Jim's reply was a red, bubbling whisper, and Brad turned away, walked to his car. Jim lay there for a long time, until the cold started to feel warm.

CHAPTER
18

Alice Meadows frowned. She didn't like fights, and the harsh voices filtering from the bar through the decorative fishnet promised a real brawl. But soon they faded, and were replaced by clinking glasses and tableware, music, other more peaceful voices. She finished her sherry leisurely, paid her bill, and left the Anchor.

The sound reached her just as she was about to open her car door, a thin, unmanly sound of quiet intensity. At first she thought it might be a dog or cat hit by a car, but there was a human depth to it, so she moved toward it and found Jim Callendar, lying against a slatted wooden fence that hid garbage cans.

"Oh, my God!" she cried, watching him from a few feet away. "I . . . I'll get help."

"No," he croaked, raising a snowy head. "No."

"But an ambulance—"

"No," he said again. "No one . . . You, *you* help me?"

She swallowed stiffly and knelt beside him. Small cuts scored his face, but the cold had made the blood run slowly, so that he looked painted, aboriginal. His lip was puffy and split in several places. His eyes were swollen, the left one nearly closed. The nose, though bleeding, was unbroken. He held his stomach oddly, as though trying to make the pain captive so that it would not leave him. "What shall I do?" she asked.

"You have a car?" She nodded. "Take me to your car."

She got an arm under him and heaved. Had he been completely helpless, she could not have begun to move him, but he used her as a lever, rising to his feet of his own volition, gagging as he swayed erect. They staggered together to her car, where he fell into the passenger seat, his teeth suddenly chattering like ratchets. She got behind the wheel, started the engine, turned the heat to maximum. "Look, I'm going to take you to a hospital."

"*No!* Please . . . I don't . . . I don't want questions. I'll be all right. If you'll just take me home."

"You could be very badly hurt."

"I'm not. Please, *please* take me home."

He told her where he lived and she took him there, helped him out of the car, unlocked the door, and guided him onto the living-room couch. Then she stood, uncertain of what to do next. "Do you . . . have any antiseptic? Bandages?"

He nodded. "The bathroom. Through there."

She scanned the cabinets, noticing the touches of femininity in towels and accessories. She noticed too that large sections of the bathroom cabinets were empty, as if denuded of what they had formerly held. There were no women's products at all. At last she found Sea Breeze, cotton balls, some gauze and adhesive tape, which she clutched under her arm while she soaked a washcloth in warm water.

Rejoining him, she wiped the caked blood from his face and moistened the cotton with Sea Breeze, which she daubed on the open cuts. She was surprised when he did not flinch as the alcohol seared the raw tissues, but thought that perhaps some other pain of which she was not aware was greater. Then she put gauze on the still-oozing cuts, and secured them lightly with tape. "I hope that's all right," she said. "I've never done this before."

"It's fine," he said from a corner of his mouth. "I must

254

look like a mummy." The corner turned up, just a little, in a vain try at a smile. "Thank you."

"Sure. I just hope you'll see a doctor." She looked at his hands, still locked over his middle. "How's your stomach?"

"Not so hot. Could use some coffee."

"Warm milk would probably be better," she said. "You have milk?"

"In the fridge. But look, you've done enough already."

"Don't be silly. I won't be a minute."

The kitchen bore the same male-female dichotomy as the bathroom had, and she wondered where the woman could be. She heated a cup of milk and made herself some instant coffee, then put the drinks on a tray and took them into the living room.

"Here we are," she said. "This should help." He thanked her and took the cup, sipping from it as though the act hurt him. She drank the coffee, watching. Finally she asked it. "Where's your wife?"

His mouth wrinkled, and he didn't answer immediately. "That's why I was drinking tonight."

"She . . . left?"

He nodded, grimacing. "Yes. Today."

"I'm sorry."

He tried to shrug. "It wasn't like she didn't warn me." After a moment he added, "I shouldn't have let her go."

"Sometimes you *have* to let people go."

"You sound like you know."

She shook her head. "Just an observation."

"No. You know." He sipped more milk. "Do you want to know why she left me?"

"No. I'd rather know how you got like *that*."

"Basically the same reasons," he said with a grin. "Who I am and what I've done."

"That's a broad reason," she said, smiling back. "Who we are and what we do are all the reasons any of us have for what happens to us."

"Do you want me to pour out my life story, then? It's not wholesome, or even particularly entertaining."

"The not wholesome part I can believe—but not entertaining? From a man who gets abandoned and beat up on the same day? Now *that* has the stuff of tragedy in it."

"No. Melodrama at best."

"I like a good melodrama."

"I really don't think I'm up to it just now."

She got to her feet nervously, remembering his injuries. "I'm sorry. You must be exhausted."

"Yeah. I'm tired." He set down the milk and tried to rise, but slumped back into the sofa.

"Let me help," she said, slipping an arm around him. Together they got to the bedroom, and Jim collapsed across the quilted spread. She started to tug off his wet shoes when he stopped her.

"Listen," he said sleepily, "unless you're a nurse, I can undress myself, okay?"

She didn't believe him. He seemed incapable of fluffing up a pillow. "I *am* a nurse," she lied.

"Come on . . ."

"No, really, at Lansford General. I was visiting relatives today in Merridale."

She wasn't sure if he believed her, but after a moment he said, "All right, all right, I can use the help. . . . Will you bill me?"

"The coffee's payment enough."

With her help, he stripped to his underwear, and she pulled the covers over him. He looked like a little boy with only his head sticking out from beneath the sheet, and she could not help touching his forehead, pushing his fair hair back gently.

"Thanks," he murmured, almost asleep. She stepped to the door and turned out the light. "You're not a nurse," his voice said from the darkness. "When you patched me up, you said you'd never done it before."

"Oh . . . I . . ."

"Never mind. You may be a liar, but you're a beautiful one." With the next words his voice drifted into silence. "I'm glad you were there." Only soft breathing followed.

She closed the door and walked back into the living room, sat, finished her coffee. When it was gone, she did not leave.

She was there when he woke up in the morning.

CHAPTER
19

"Hello?"

"Hi, Kim."

"Dave!"

"Surprised to hear from me?"

"Why haven't you called me?"

"I did. You're never in."

"Jesus, I'm *always* in."

"That's not what Mr. and Mrs. Davison say when I call."

"Those bastards! I'm in *all* the time."

"Why didn't *you* call *me?*"

"Dad doesn't want me to. He's crazy about this Merridale thing. He doesn't want anything to do with the town, and he doesn't want me seeing anybody who lives there."

"Holy shit."

"He's closing on a house in Lansford next week."

"Kim, I'm not gonna let you go like this. I *love* you."

"And I love you. So what are we gonna do?"

"Hello, Thornton here."

"Mr. Thornton, this is Marie Snyder."

"Yes. Hello."

"Mr. Thornton, I was thinking that we should have a little chat."

"A chat . . ."

"Yes. You know, I have a bit of a reputation for being gossipy. I don't know if you realize that."

"No, I didn't."

"I'm afraid you're just being polite. . . . Are you all right? I can hardly hear you."

"I'm fine."

"Oh, that's better. I guess you just weren't speaking up. Anyways, I put two and two together out of something that happened today, and I was just wondering if maybe you'd like to know how I got four?"

"You think you can really do it, Kim?"

"Well, if *you* won't . . ."

"I *can't*. He watches the odometer like a hawk. Forty thousand miles on the damn thing and he still figures his mileage."

"Mom could put thirty miles on it as easy as anything. He'd never know."

"But without them hearing you?"

"I'll let it drift out onto the road."

"That's an interesting theory, Mrs. Snyder."

"I just thought you might like to hear it, Mr. Thornton."

"Yes. Well."

"I was thinking that since I found it so interesting, other folks might find it interesting too."

"Uh . . . I don't know if they would. Maybe you could keep it a secret."

"Some secrets are valuable, Mr. Thornton. How valuable do you think this one is?"

"Oh, sure, I can sneak out okay."

"I'll meet you on the corner of Park and Spruce, then. Around twelve-thirty."

"That's good, good. I love you, Kim."

"I love you, Dave."

"Look, that's just *unreasonable*. I mean, there may be nothing to this."

"Maybe not, Mr. Thornton. Only you know for sure. And only you know what it's worth to you."

"It's too *much*, dammit!"

"All right, then—I'll have to hang up. I have some other calls to make. Big calls. Important ones."

"Wait! Do you know who you're dealing with here?"

"You don't frighten me, Mr. Thornton."

"Not *me*, not *me* . . . *bigger* interests."

"I'm not scared of them either. Besides, I don't think you'd want them to know that you were so stupid as to let a nosy old woman know what was going on, now would you?"

"I . . . no . . ."

"Then why don't you come to the newsstand Sunday afternoon. I close at one, so come after that. That gives you until tomorrow to find the money. All right?"

"I'll see you Saturday night."

"I'll see you Sunday afternoon."

CHAPTER
20

The rage had not left him.

If only, he thought, Callendar had responded in some other way, gotten angry and tried to fight back, or had tried to get away, crawling and staggering on hands and knees. But he had gotten to his feet, over and over again, like the Lamb of God ready to taste death as many times as was necessary to take away the sins of . . .

Whose sins? Surely not the world's. His own, then? And Brad's too? But Brad would not let him. If he was not capable of paying for his own sins, then he would bear them alone as well, even if it brought the agony he now felt. Had Callendar done it on purpose? Had he let him hit him repeatedly because he knew that only in that way would Brad find no release in the beating?

He suspected, but he didn't know. All he knew was that the rage was still there, eating inside him, not with the slow stealth of a cancer, but with the rapid, careless ravening of a weasel gnawing at his entrails, or the constant alimentary torment that drives on the shark to his incessant feeding until only death gives him rest.

Shivering from the cold, he looked through the windshield at the sky. The snow had stopped, and the stars shone crisply out of the stark blackness. He turned on the ignition and ran the heater once more until the car was warm.

Three o'clock. Three o'clock on a Saturday morning in the town of the dead. He gripped the steering wheel and pulled out into the street, headed for the Anchor. Threw him out. They threw him out like a dog, and for what? A little noise. Well, he'd give them *more* noise, and maybe after that, maybe he could rest.

Getting inside was easy. There were no alarms, no watchdogs, and even the lights around the outside were dim. After all, there were no burglaries in Merridale, were there? He broke a pane of glass with a gloved fist, reached through, and opened the door.

The lighted Budweiser sign gave the bar its only illumination, but it was enough for Brad, who moved slowly and leisurely, trying to decide what to do first. One by one, he took the bottles from the bar, unscrewed the caps and poured the contents over the bar, on the floor, around the padded seats. Cutty Sark, Drambuie, anisette, lime vodka, Beefeater, each and every one mixed in an ultimate cocktail that flowed into every corner, while hundreds of drips and trickles made the room sound like some rain forest, thick with verdant moisture. It was a quiet, gentle sound, which, combined with the heady odor that suffused the air, made Brad feel magically, dreamily intoxicated.

He eyed the empty bottles he had left on the bar, but dismissed the thought of breaking them. He was now in too tranquil a mood for that. So he turned to the beer taps, connected them, and one at a time drained them. The bubbling froth added a new, jubilant tone to the sea of alcohol that had turned the bar and its stools into islands, and the mixture began to cascade over the few steps to the restaurant below.

"Lovely," Brad whispered, smiling, "lovely."

He stepped to the Seeburg jukebox in the corner, plugged it in, and, his gloves still on, clumsily dug a quarter from his pocket. He pushed it into the slot, and the machine illuminatingly offered him three selections. "Something old," he said, pushing D5, "Amazing Grace." "Something new." Q7, Kim Carnes's "Dying for a Living." "Borrowed and blue." It took a while, but at last he found A4 "Shake," performed by the Blues Brothers.

The machine engaged, gears ran, there was a soft pop, and the music started, but so low as to be nearly inaudible, Brad heard, barely,

> Amazing grace,
> How sweet the sound . . .

The words were intelligible only because he knew them from long ago, and he frowned, looking at the back of the machine for a volume control.

> . . . that saved a wretch like me.
> I once was lost . . .

"Shit," he said softly, running his fingers over the back of the jukebox.

> But now am found . . .

"*Dam*mit!" Only smooth metal, then ridges, rents . . .

> Was blind but now I see . . .

"*SHEE-YIT!*" Pounding now on the back, drowning out the whispering rivulets of booze, the tiny, tinny guitar riff somewhere deep inside the yard-wide grille.

"You fuck fuck, *fuck, fucker!*" he brayed as he hugged the top of the machine and heaved outward, toppling it onto the floor with a wet, metallic *smack*. Something hissed and crackled, and the lights went out on the jukebox, in the Budweiser sign on the wall, pressing blackness on the room.

Brad froze, stunned into inaction. Then a primal fury at being blinded took over, and he swung about, fists smashing into whatever would yield—bottles, stools, tables that rocked and toppled, sending ashtrays, salt shakers, sugar bowls, skittering onto the booze-wet floor. A gurgling scream began to force itself from his throat, and he blundered through the room, the fishnet tangling in his outstretched fingers, falling from the pegs that held it to bind him for a terrifying minute before he struggled from beneath it. Then over and across the bar, bruising his thighs as the beer taps snapped from their stems; legs tangled in stools as he came off the other side, falling and landing on a box, feeling its rough wood, something to kick, to hit, to splinter, and he did, and suddenly, as the wood broke, there was no longer darkness.

There was light. Bright, radiant, blue light.

He had fallen onto and destroyed the packing case that had been nailed to the Anchor bar floor, the packing case that Emeric Jerney had told everyone hid an old man who had died so long ago that no one even remembered who he was. But Emeric Jerney had lied. It was not an old man.

It was a woman, young and not unattractive despite the deep patina of death that coated her features. She was on her back, legs spread wider than Brad would have believed possible, and he felt certain that whatever bound legs to hips in her was broken. Her vagina gaped roundly, as though some unseen cylinder dilated it, and her pelvis jutted upward, supported invisibly from beneath. There were scratches on her neck and large breasts, one of which seemed compressed, smaller than its companion, and as Brad looked closely he could see five round marks in the fatty tissue, and wondered if that were the hand of her killer, or of someone holding her down, or of someone who'd already had a dip and just wanted a quick feel to remember before he slunk home.

Because her face was peaceful, he thought at first that she hadn't been forced. But the idea that she'd been willing didn't fit the broken bones, the thin scratches. Passed out, then. Oh, yes, passed out near to closing, and the good bartender and the upright burghers of Merridale unable to pass up a pass-out, and who would know? But somebody got a little rough, and somebody got a little rougher, and before they knew it the good burghers were not only rapists, but killers.

Where did she lie now? he wondered. The bottom of the river? In some unknown grave in all the acres and acres of woods? It could have happened years ago; those who had done it might all be dead.

And anyway, what did it matter now?

The question was unanswerable, and he looked at the still, sad, closed eyes and stood up. "Love ya to death," he said with an angry smile. "They loved ya to death."

He looked around in the blue light at the ruin he had made of the Anchor, and decided to leave the woman exposed for them to find in the morning. He wondered how quick Emeric and Leo would be to call the police if they had to show them *that*. He left by the door he had come in, closing it gently behind him. A feeling of peace swept through him as he drove home, as though the shark were fed and happy at last. Yet it had not been perfect. The woman had made it bittersweet, for she had made him remember more than he had wished to.

It was 4:00 A.M. when Brad arrived back at his apartment. A light was on in the living room, but when he went into his and Christine's bedroom, she was not there. The bed was made. Her purse was gone.

He opened the door of Wally's room. The boy was, as usual, buried beneath the covers, looking not so much like a sleeping child as a pile of laundry before sorting. "Hey," Brad said, but the boy did not stir. "Hey, Wally," he called louder, and a muffled response came from beneath the blankets. Brad crossed to the bed and flipped back the covers.

The boy gave a startled gasp, and his eyes blinked open, though he remained curled fetally.

"Where's your mother?"

"I . . . dunno," he said sleepily.

"What do you mean you don't know? You mean she just went out and left you alone?"

"I guess so."

The boy looked fragile, vulnerable, and Brad felt a sudden surge of tenderness toward this child who was not his own. He pulled the covers up to Wally's shoulders and sat on the bed next to him. "Did she say where she was going?"

265

"No."

"When did she leave?"

"After supper."

"She didn't put you to bed?"

"She said I go to bed when I'm sleepy. So I did." He looked at Brad with a fearful resignation. "You mad?"

Brad sighed. "Not at you." He put a hand on the boy's head. "I don't know if I've *ever* been mad at you."

"You hit me. Sometimes."

"Yeah. I know."

"You mad at me then?"

"I'm mad, Wally. But not at you."

"At Mommy?"

"Sometimes. Sometimes at myself."

The boy frowned as though the concept was too foreign for comprehension.

"Sometimes," Brad tried to explain, "big people get mad at themselves for things they do that they shouldn't have, or maybe for things they didn't do that they *should* have. But when you get mad at yourself, there isn't much you can *do*. You can't hurt *yourself*, so sometimes you hurt other people. Sometimes even people you love."

"Do you love me?"

Brad stared expressionless at the boy. "As much," he answered finally, "as anyone."

Wally half smiled, not fully understanding, but content just the same.

"You go back to sleep now. I'm sorry I woke you up."

" 'S'okay. G'night."

"Good-night." He closed the door and lay down in his own bedroom. Maybe he could do something with Wally tomorrow. Sledding perhaps. They could go to the five-and-ten and buy a sled, maybe one of those saucer ones. He wondered if they still made sleds like they did when he was a kid—Flexible Flyers, Snow Kings, how fast they went down Cherry Street, best street in town for sledding. A boy needed a sled.

A boy needed a father too.

He had never felt like a father to Wally. Even if he and

Christine got married, which seemed more and more un-likely, he wondered if he could show the warmth toward the boy that he often felt but hardly ever expressed. Was it because Wally was not his own son, or did it go deeper than that? Had he, he mused, lost the capacity for love?

He glanced at the bedside clock, then closed his eyes. It was too late for questions.

CHAPTER
21

Pastor Craven's sermon, delivered that Sunday morning two days before Christmas, was not one of his best. Christmas, to him, was a gentle time of birth and love, and try as he would, he could not relate that theme to the brooding reminders of death that littered the town. So he preached as though nothing out of the ordinary had ever happened in Merridale, of the promise of Christ's birth and what it meant to man. The majority of the crowded congregation found it moving and refreshing in its utter ignorance of the phenomenon. But there were those who heard nothing, whose thoughts were purely and impurely of themselves, what they had seen, had done, and would still do.

Dave Boyer sat striving to keep his eyes open, remembering the night before and how Kim had clung to him, had done things to him she had not done before. He smiled. The backseat had seemed so long, so wide. He had never before enjoyed it in a car, but last night was different, and he played the scenario back pornographically, feeling himself harden despite the stained-glass Christs beaming down.

Tom Markley thought about Christmas, and of how it was

not going to be nearly as splashy as in previous years. No swimming pool, like last year; no car for Mim, like the year before. No, this Christmas was perfume and one nice piece of jewelry and some clothes, and even those had put him further into debt than he felt comfortable being. He wondered what he would do if the business didn't pick up, and he thought about running away and starting life somewhere else (no—too old, too fat), thought about embezzling funds from the city treasury (no—I'd get caught, and even if I got away with it, it'd be shit), thought about other ways to change things. To end things.

Clyde Thornton sat tall and upright, the visiting pillar of this or any other community that needed his services. Within, however, he had gone jellyfish, bottomed up and boned out, the most frightened of all the frightened people in the town. He could *not* pay that woman, he *could* not—it would take away all that he had worked for, had *jeopardized* himself for. Bluff her, that was all. He could just *bluff* her. But what if she called his bluff? *She* had nothing to lose, while *he*—he had everything. But there must be some way, some way . . .

Five rows behind Clyde Thornton, Marie Snyder sat with a Christmas smile on her face, blandly ignoring the homilies the pastor recited. She was thinking of money, of getting her own back, of freedom at long last, of a visit from a certain distinguished gentleman that very afternoon. . . .

So they sat, their faces giving no clues as to what truly lurked inside—envy, avarice, hatred, lust—but the greatest of the sinners in his own eyes was the blasphemer who stood behind the pulpit, preaching the words, reading the book, mouthing the hymns, making the great, arcane, sweeping gestures in the air while intoning, "May the Lord watch between me and thee," and of it all believing nothing, nothing, nothing, and unable to even weep inwardly for his disbelief. He was a captain of a ship of faith on a sea whose waters were rising, pulling the vessel down. Believe and we will float! he called to his shipmates, who trusted him, did what he said. But he knew the ship would sink, even if it did float a moment longer, even if by some . . . *miracle* that he

270

no longer believed in the waves closed a trifle more slowly, the waves would still come.

He blessed them and smiled and sent them out onto the wet decks.

Marie Snyder had left on her church dress when she went back to the newsstand. She had time to change, but she was anxious to return so that John Grubb could leave. He charged her $3 an hour to watch the shop when she was out, and there were plenty of times when she didn't make $3 an hour to pay him. Money from my pocket, she thought as she scurried none too carefully along the icy sidewalks. She slipped once and almost fell, then slowed down, remembering that she didn't have to hustle for quarters, not anymore.

She had caught Clyde Thornton's eye when they all stood up to leave after the benediction, and had been amused at his reaction. He had gone positively white, had tried to smile but failed, and for a moment she felt almost sorry for him.

John Grubb was behind the counter selling newspapers when she entered the shop. She made her way through the small crowd of men, stopped between church and Sunday dinner for their *Times*, their *Inquirer*, their *Courier*, their *Press*, and joined Grubb, a gravel-voiced, elderly man in a plaid wool shirt. "You're later'n usual," Grubb said. "I gotta get paid through eleven-thirty."

Marie nodded agreeably and took $6 from the register. Grubb's eyes widened at the lack of argument, but he pocketed the bills and left. She sold papers steadily for the next half hour, along with cigarettes and half a dozen other items that could be purchased no where else on a Merridale Sunday. By 12:45 there were only a few stragglers, and at 1:00 she closed and locked the doors, pulled down the dark green shade with "Closed" stenciled on it, and counted the money in the register.

At 1:30 a soft knock sounded at the side door. She pulled back the shade a hair to see Clyde Thornton standing hatless in a bulky coat, his head twitching back and forth like a spastic pendulum as if in fear of being seen. When she opened the door, he practically ran in. "In a hurry?" she asked.

271

"I don't need anybody to see me coming in here," Clyde Thornton said. She noticed he was trembling.

"They'd just think you got tied up and wanted your paper," she said.

He clutched at the idea. "That's good! I'll . . . I'll take one with me when I leave."

"Then we'd better make this fast." Marie took off her glasses and let them dangle on their chain. "Did you bring something for me?"

"Some."

"Some?"

"Look"—he had his hands out to her, pleading—"what you asked for . . . it's too much. I mean, I haven't taken anywhere *near* that—"

"Dr. Thornton," she interrupted, "I think you're not telling me the truth. But even if it *is* true, that's what I want. You'll just have to make up the difference from your own pocket."

"But—"

"Ten thousand dollars, Dr. Thornton."

"It's not *fair*—"

"You lie down with dogs, you get up with fleas. I don't think it's too high a price when you consider the alternative."

The sound of Thornton's breathing filled the room. It was the heavy, labored wheezing of a man whose body is barely able to accept the charges the mind has put on it.

"Would you like to sit down, Dr. Thornton?"

He waved a loose hand in the air. "No . . . no." Reaching into his pocket, he pulled out a thick, white envelope, gazed at it lovingly, then handed it slowly to Marie Snyder. "It's . . . all there."

"You won't mind if I count it, I hope."

He stood waiting while she counted to five one hundred times and put the bills back in the envelope. "I hope you won't be careless with that," he said. "You flash all that around, people'll wonder."

"Oh, we can't have people wondering, Dr. Thornton, and we won't. I intend to be very careful with this, don't you worry."

"All right, then, all right. Now this means you keep your mouth shut, right?"

"That seems only fair."

"And you don't bother me again."

"That shouldn't be necessary, should it?" Marie Snyder smiled, and to Clyde Thornton it was the smile of a hunter who'd just bagged a deer but wanted with all his heart to gun down a second one.

Unseen by anyone, he left the newsstand and went back to the house, where he sat and brooded, wondering when he could expect to hear from the old woman again, wondering how much she would want next time.

Before the sun was down, he made his decision.

Marie Snyder opened her store as usual at 5:30 on Monday morning. She'd been toying with the idea of opening later, but the habit was long-standing and hard to break. Besides, she awoke early, the excitement of the previous afternoon's transaction still with her. So she dressed and lit the lights and opened the shade and sat behind the counter with a confessions magazine and a cup of instant.

In less than a minute the side doorbell tinkled, and a man walked in, his hat pulled down low, a muffler covering his chin and mouth. The hat went up, the scarf unwound, and she found herself looking at Clyde Thornton. She dropped her glasses and said nothing.

"I forgot to tell you something," Thornton said breathlessly. " 'S'important." He walked up to the counter, rubbing his red cheeks with his gloved hands. "You wouldn't have another cup of that, would you?"

She gave him a patronizing smile and turned toward the jar of instant and the hot plate on the shelf behind her. Without a moment's hesitation, Clyde Thornton leaped over the counter, grasped her thin neck with his right arm, and pulled her backward so that her back was on the counter, her legs in the air. His left hand grabbed her glasses, pulled them around, and twisted them, so that the slim, strong chain bit into her neck. She made no sound but a high-pitched hissing that expelled the small amount of air she still had in her nose and

273

throat. Thornton's right arm held her securely while his left hand continued to twist.

Marie Snyder's eyes seemed to grow bigger, and Thornton laughed shrilly. "No customers this early," he said through gritted teeth, hoping that she could still hear him. "I remembered. You *cunt*. You old *bitch!* The only way . . . You woulda called me again, in a week, a month, you'd've fucked with me forever . . . but not now, not anymore, oh, no. *No!*"

He twisted one final, impossible time so that the chain disappeared completely into the white flesh. The old woman suddenly relaxed, and bowel and bladder surrendered at once so that the air became rich with sourness. Thornton held on a moment longer, just to make sure, and when he opened his eyes that he had closed in fury, it was as though he had suddenly acquired X-ray vision, that Marie Snyder's gaunt, wasted body was visible through her blue dress.

Blue? She was wearing white when I . . .

He let go, leaped back, let the body slide off behind the counter so that it disappeared, yet remained, an obscene, unclothed, permanent record of murder, eyes wide, mouth stretched in an agonized grin. The thin dark line across the neck, tucking the flesh into itself, made head and torso look like two separate sections, one screwed into the other.

Clyde Thornton shivered at the results of his handiwork. He wanted to run, but then he remembered the other thing he had come for—the money. If only I'd killed her yesterday, he thought savagely. Then I'd still have it.

But he had *not* taken the opportunity when it had first been offered. He had been afraid—afraid that someone would see him entering or leaving the newsstand on a bright Sunday afternoon—and he had put it from his mind until last night, when the fear of what Marie Snyder could keep doing to him was greater than his fear of killing her.

Well, now he *had* killed her, and ghost or not, she was dead and couldn't do a thing to him anymore. That thin pale mouth, despite its gaping appearance on the counter, was shut for good.

He bit his lip, pulled his gaze away from the apparition,

and started to look for the money, knowing that it was futile, that he had only fifteen minutes at the most. The packet was not in the cash register or in Marie Snyder's purse. Thornton began to look on the shelves behind the merchandise, but gave that up quickly. Then he walked behind a curtain into the small storeroom and passed through that into Marie's apartment.

It was small—a bedroom, bath, kitchen, and living room, all in somber shades of brown or dark yellow wallpaper—and he rattled through it quickly, opening and closing drawers and closets as fast as he could. He found nothing but what one would expect to find in the rooms of an old lady in Merridale. The last door he opened led to the cellar, and he ran down the stairs, sweating heavily in his warm coat, hat, and gloves.

The cellar was empty but for an old, rusted wheelbarrow, some straw baskets, a water heater, a nearly full coal bin, and a furnace, whose air of antiquity and many branching pipes put Thornton in mind of some archetypal spider-monster crouching in wait. He turned back toward the stairs and froze.

From above, a high tinkling sound clamored, followed by footsteps. At first the insane thought hit him that Marie Snyder was not dead, followed by the even more insane one that she was, but that her revenant had taken on form and weight and motive, and was even now moving through the storeroom, into the apartment, and that in a second he would see her framed in the box of light at the stair top and she would soar down upon him, wiry and naked, bearing him to the dirt floor with arms like thin cables, her mouth split in a deadly grin.

But the truth hit him, terrifying him so that he staggered in fear. Someone had come into the newsstand, had seen the blue lich on the counter before Thornton could get out. The footsteps paused, and in the sudden silence Clyde Thornton damned his greed that had made him stay and look for the money, that had made him take it in the first place. "Jesus, oh, Jesus," he muttered, looking about for an escape route.

There was none. There was only the coal chute, a foot

wide, and that nearly buried by the piled-up coal. The windows were small and recessed, impossible to squeeze through.

The footsteps upstairs began again, much faster than before. He heard the pealing of the bell and the door slam shut. They've run, he thought, run for help or because they're scared. His only chance now was to run himself. Though there was a possibility now that he'd be seen when he left, he was trapped if he stayed, and that gave him no chance at all. He climbed the stairs quickly and stealthily, ran through the apartment into the storeroom, and peered around the heavy curtain. Except for the two Marie Snyders, the newsstand was empty.

Thornton tugged his hat down low over his forehead, wrapped the scarf to cover his nose and chin, and walked doggedly to the side door. Seeing no one, he left the shop and ran back to the alley where his car was parked.

"You shoulda seen her," Fred Hibbs said, shaking his head. "It was just awful."

Eddie Karl dunked and gulped a piece of doughnut. "I guess I can see her yet. She ain't goin' anywhere, is she now?"

"Really strangled?" Jake said, her hands trembling. "I mean, it wasn't just a heart attack or something?"

Hibbs nodded assertively. "Strangled. Frank Kaylor said so. And hell, I *seen* her neck . . . or, well, her . . . her *ghost's* neck. And it was all tucked in like."

"It gives me the creeps," Jake said. "Who on earth coulda done it?"

"Dunno why the cops didn't hold *you*, Loafer."

"Me?" Hibbs bridled. "I didn't do *nothin'!* I just *found* her!"

"So you say." Eddie smiled slyly. "But if you done it, sayin' you found her's a good way to throw suspicion offa yourself."

"Goddammit, you're looney! I had no reason to—"

"He's kiddin', Fred. He's just kiddin', aren't you, Eddie?"

" 'Course I'm kiddin'. Honest to Jeez, Loafer, if your skin got any thinner, your guts'd pop out and dance a hula.

Besides, everybody knows you wouldn'ta strangled Marie Snyder." Eddie paused a beat, took a sip of coffee. "You'da just *raped* her."

"God*dam*mit!" Fred Hibbs shouted over Eddie's cackling laughter and Jake's involuntary giggle. His next words were quieter as he saw two clerks from Sam Hershey's store come into the Hitching Post. "It ain't funny! Marie Snyder's dead, and here you are laughin' about it."

"We're all gonna be dead sooner or later," Eddie said. "Maybe it ain't funny, but it ain't no great tragedy neither." Jake went to wait on the clerks, leaving the two men alone. "What were you doin' out so early anyway?" Eddie asked Hibbs. "Sun wasn't even up before six."

"I couldn't sleep."

"Now I've heard everything. You sick or somethin'?"

"No. I just . . . haven't been sleeping good."

Eddie took another bite. His voice lost all trace of cynicism. "Your mother and father."

Fred Hibbs nodded, swallowed deeply. "I can never forget they're there. I wake up in the middle of the night thinking about them sitting down at the kitchen table, and I can't get back to sleep."

"Y'know they can't hurt you."

"I know that. Hell, they never hurt me when they was alive. But I get scared just the same. It . . . it makes me think about dying."

The two sat for a while, Eddie dunking and sipping, Fred Hibbs slowly stirring his spoon in his coffee and staring at the brightly colored cereal packs in their plastic display. Finally Eddie spoke softly. "Fred, I'm gonna give you a Christmas present."

Hibbs looked up, suspicious. "What Christmas present?"

"Peace of mind. A good night's sleep."

"And how are you gonna do that?"

"I'm gonna let you move in with me."

"What?"

"What's the matter? I wash." He put a friendly arm on Hibbs's shoulder. "Look, I like you, buddy. That's why I josh ya so much. You're one of the few people in this town that'll say more to me than 'How's it goin', Eddie.' Now I just rattle around in that house of mine, and like I said before, there ain't a spook to be seen. Y'can have your own room, get up when you want, sleep when you want, and we'll just split the food 'n' the beer. Whaddya think?"

"I . . . I don't know."

"Well, you better make up your mind quick. This ain't no long-standin' offer."

"What about your friends?"

"My friends?"

"You know. The folks you talk to all the time. The dead folks."

Eddie shook his head and smiled. "They don't come to visit me very often. And when they do, I'll keep 'em downstairs."

Fred Hibbs looked hard at Eddie Karl, then knitted his fingers and stared down at the nearly empty coffee cup in front of him. "Y'know," he said, "*I'm* not too damn easy to live with."

Eddie shrugged. "I'll take my chances. And I wouldn't mind the company. Besides"—he frowned—"I can't do things like I used to . . . lifting things around the house and such. You may not be the goddamn most industrious bastard in this town, but you're strong. You'd earn your keep."

Hibbs nodded. "All right, Eddie. It sounds all right. Just one thing though. Don't call me Loafer no more. Okay?"

"Sure, Fred." And for the first time in their lives, Fred Hibbs and Eddie Karl smiled at each other.

278

CHAPTER
22

"Hello."

"Brad, this is Bonnie."

"Yeah."

"Bonnie."

"I know who you are. I'm listening."

"All right, then. I'm leaving town. With Linda. We're going to my aunt's in Allentown and I'm going to stay with her until I can find a job up there."

"Okay. You called to tell me that?"

"Not just that. There's more. I can't sell the house."

"Big surprise."

"Will you just *listen*. There's no point in it just sitting empty. So I thought that since you're really the one who paid for it, you might like to use it, move in with that girl you're living with."

"Christine. Her name's Christine."

"All right. With Christine. And her little boy."

"Why the sudden generosity? It's yours. The courts gave it to you."

"It just seems silly not to have it used. It was your house too."

"How long will you be gone?"

"For good. I'm not coming back. If this freaky thing ever ends and I can sell it, maybe we could work something out. Or maybe you'd like to buy it yourself eventually if you don't leave."

"I'm not leaving. And I have no intention of buying a house I already bought once."

"Well, I'm not worried about it. Do you want it?"

"No cost."

"No."

"I suppose I'd be stupid not to take it."

"That's up to you."

"All right. I accept."

They discussed arrangements then, and when Brad hung up, he walked into the kitchen where Christine was finishing the dinner dishes. "We're leaving here," he said.

She straightened up and looked at him doubtfully. "When?"

"Friday. Next Friday."

Something in his tone told her it was not a lie, and she ran to him and embraced him with wet, soapy hands. "Where are we going?" she crooned. "Oh, where are we going?"

"Sundale Road," he said. "1765 Sundale Road."

He felt her stiffen in his arms, but it was not until she pulled back and away from him that he saw the terror mold itself anew to her features, and he thought for the first time that he could see madness in them as well.

Jim Callendar told Alice about himself as they lay naked in bed under the warm blankets that were pulled up to their chins. Their hands each rested lightly on the other's flank, their heads turned on the pillows so that they faced each other only partially, as if there were still something that each did not want the other to see.

He talked about it all, nevertheless, and as he did, there was the sense of a burden not so much dropping from him as being shared, but not in the way that he felt Beth had tried to share it, that detached way that accepted it only clinically, taking in facts and motivations while trying to keep emotion at bay. Alice *absorbed* the emotion, understanding not the detail, but the *sense* of it, soaking up his pain like a rich humus absorbs bitter rain. For the first time he felt understood, and with the understanding came something that he was desperate to grasp as love.

She had been there a few mornings before when he'd stumbled groggily and unclothed past the living room on the way to the kitchen for his morning coffee. He hadn't noticed her, and remembered her only dimly from the drunken and bruising night before, so that when she walked into the kitchen, the shrill blast of the teakettle having awakened her, he was standing with his bare ass to her and not a cover-up within reach.

"Oh," she'd said nonchalantly, "sorry," then turned and walked back into the living room while he stood pouring hot water over the edge of his cup. He set down the cup and scooted as quickly as his aching legs could carry him back into the bedroom for a robe. Then he made coffee for them both while she scrambled some eggs. When she asked about the night before, he didn't tell her much. Her questions were phrased delicately so that he got the impression her interest stemmed from something other than mere curiosity. He told her that there was bad blood between him and the man who had beaten him, but did not elaborate. As he talked, however, he found himself wanting more and more to tell her everything—the accident, the guilt, the way it had transformed him into someone only barely approachable by others. And one by one pieces slipped out, until he stopped himself, pulled back from touching her with more than mild interest.

Although he did not realize it, he had already touched her with far more, or she would not have stayed the night. Alice Meadows was fascinated by Jim Callendar. In him she saw the burdens and pains of guilt as plainly as she saw the sun in the sky. He knows, she had thought. He knows what I know. So she kept the morning's conversation flowing smoothly, effortlessly, and when the eggs were gone, the coffee drained, she did not want to go. But having slept in her clothes, she felt soiled and unattractive, and said that she should go back to her place and change, but that she'd enjoyed the talk, and couldn't they get together that evening to chat some more.

He had seemed surprised by her boldness, but also strangely pleased, and they agreed to meet for dinner. Alice drove back to the Reardons', called the Holiday Inn off of 283, and reserved a room. She packed, called Ellen Brouther to tell her she was leaving, and drove to the motel, gently berating herself for changing her plans and not returning immediately to New York.

But there was something about this man (and she realized that she did not even know his name, nor did he know hers) that held her. In the back of her mind lurked the thought that all those years of what she had suffered could not have been futile, even if her return to Tim Reardon's side *had* been. Perhaps she had returned for a different reason. Tim had been beyond her help, her compassion coming years too late, so perhaps her return had been for someone else, for some purpose she did not as yet understand. Like the ship *Rachel*, searching for her own lost children, had found instead only Ishmael, so perhaps she had come to repay Tim Reardon, but would instead reclaim the sad and lonely man she had rescued the night before.

They made further arrangements over the phone, and that evening he picked her up and drove her to a restaurant in Lansford. It was, she thought, like a first date should be— tentative, shy, probing, and fun for all that. At the bar of the Holiday they had a nightcap, and decided to see each other the next day as well, Jim offering to cook dinner. Alice agreed on the condition that she buy the food.

She came to his house the next afternoon with porterhouse steaks, two dozen fresh oysters, and an assortment of vegetables. They cooked, laughed, ate, and afterward drank just a little more than they needed to. Then she told him why she had come back to Merridale, told him about Tim Reardon and staying at the house, told him that she had been mentally on her way back to New York when she had met Jim and, because of him, had decided to stay for a while.

The teasing manner that had come on him with the drinking had slowly disappeared, and his face grew sober, almost stern. "Did you stay," he asked, "because you pity me?"

"No," she answered. "I don't pity you. I just think that we're very much alike."

"Why?"

She struggled to put it into words. "I lost someone. And because of that I felt bad, for too long a time, I guess. I think you've lost someone too, and I don't think it's your wife."

His jaw started to tremble, and he took his drink and drained it.

"If it's true," she went on, "if I'm right, that can't help."

"Then what can?" he whispered harshly.

"I can . . ."

"I don't need pity."

" . . . and you can help me."

"How?"

"I'm not home yet by a long shot. I've been . . . caged up too long to get free right away. Last Friday night I thought I could, but I'm scared to go cold turkey. I thought I could because at that very moment everything was right and I felt free. But those times don't last, and every moment *isn't* perfect." She touched his cheek. "But I feel good with you, like I know what you're feeling and you know how *I* feel. There aren't many people who understand, who you can even talk to."

He smiled weakly. "You make us sound like a couple of emotional junkies."

"Maybe." She shook her head. "But we don't have to be."

They drifted into each other's arms as gently and easily as if a tide pushed them. Later neither remembered moving to the bedroom, undressing, and in the morning when they awoke, it all seemed right and natural, and the one's arms were the most comforting and peaceful haven the other had ever known.

And now they were together, and he had told her what he had not thought he would tell, and she kissed him, not saying a word, not having to, for he knew she understood. They lay pressed together for a long time, and made love once again before rising and remembering that it was Christmas Day.

Later Alice Meadows drove back to the Holiday Inn, packed, checked out, and drove home.

To Merridale.

The Town II

This is the time of tension between dying and birth . . .
> —T. S. Eliot, "Ash-Wednesday"

CHAPTER
23

Christmas came and went in Merridale much as it did every year. There were perhaps fewer trees put up, not as many strings of lights stretched across eaves and around porch posts, but there was caroling and gift giving and candlelight services in the churches. Cards were signed and sent, and turkeys were carved with nearly as much flair as in years before. For most, the initial horror had fled, and although they did not seek the revenants' presences, neither did they go as far out of their way to avoid them. The face of death, if not death itself, was slowly becoming a commonplace in Merridale.

The rest of the country looked at Merridale as relatives would at a terminally ill old uncle—too obvious to ignore, too frightening to think about for too long a time. *Newsweek*'s end-of-year issue heralded Merridale as the year's top news story, calling it a puzzle that might never be solved, and running pictures of the town and one of Clyde Thornton. But most of the other magazines and nearly all other media ignored it. The attempted influx of sightseers had slowed to the point where several of the roadblocks were taken off of the rural roads.

Merridale did, however, become immortal in the lexicon of sick humor. Ads in the back pages of *National Lampoon* offered T-shirts with the legends "Jacques Brel Is Alive and Well and Glowing in Merridale" and "Merridale Is for Lovers (who just lay there)." Merridale jokes had a brief life-span, demonstrating none of the staying power of Polish or elephant jokes. The problem seemed to be that what was happening in Merridale was too chillingly inexplicable for the world to laugh at or to even think about for long.

So Merridale was, in essence, expunged from the mass mind of the world. Had the world not so ignored it, humanity might have been better prepared for what ultimately came. But it was easier to look away.

"Good morning."
"Good morning."

Jim kissed Alice on the cheek, and they got up and dressed and had breakfast. For over a month his mornings had begun in this way, and they had not yet lost their freshness, their novelty, and he doubted they would. He wasn't sure, even now, why she had stayed. All he knew was that he was glad she had. She'd brought something new to his life, something that he hadn't missed simply because he'd never had it before. He was writing again, and better than ever. His editors were glad to see his work, and asked to see other ideas as quickly as he could turn them out. Not one mentioned his infamous return address.

Alice was writing too, working on a play she'd been promising herself to try for several years, a light, romantic comedy set in a small town in the thirties. She spent much of her time in the Merridale and Lansford public libraries researching for period color, and the rest of her time working on a draft of the first act.

She had called her agent a week after moving in with Jim, and had learned that a Pond's commercial she had appeared in had gone national. Residual checks totaling over $26,000 were being held for her. When he asked when she was

288

returning to New York, she told him that she'd been having some long-standing personal problems that could only be dealt with by coming back to her old hometown, adding that they'd been nearly solved, but the experience had been traumatic enough that she needed a little more time to wind down. He tried to talk her into coming back immediately, but she gently refused. After she hung up, she realized that the money meant little to her. It would allow her to keep the rent paid on her New York apartment for as long as she chose to stay in Merridale and it assured her that she would not have to start sponging off of Jim. From the first day she was in his house on Sundale Road, she made it clear that she would share all expenses—mortgage payments, food, utilities, the works—and when Jim balked, she threatened to leave. That had made him agree quickly enough, and even a week later he grew pale at the thought of her leaving, when she told him of her agent's attempt to lure her back.

But now over a month had passed, and she was still with him. The time had been good, though naturally there were a few uncomfortable moments, coming mostly when other people invaded the island of two they had become. The first began when Alice ran into Kay Rankin in the Weis Market. Kay, who had thought that Alice had left town, was amazed to find her still there and would not let her go until she had the whole story, after which she invited Alice and Jim to dinner. Alice started to decline automatically, but paused, thinking, as had her predecessor, Beth, that it might be a good idea to get Jim into some company other than her own. Even as she accepted, she knew that it could be a mistake.

It was. Jim went solely to please her, and hardly opened his mouth the entire evening. Occasionally he would glance up at Bob Rankin with a rabbity fear in his eyes, and then look quickly down at his plate. Kay's yammering conversation was incessant and one-sided, as though trying to make up for the lack of it in her guests. Bob was as taciturn as Jim, and several times Alice caught him looking at Jim strangely.

"What was wrong?" she asked on the drive home.

Jim gave a breathy laugh and shook his head. "I don't think they liked me very much."

"You didn't give them much of a chance."

"They didn't give *me* much of one either. Did you see how Rankin looked at me when we walked in?"

"*You* looked like a kid who'd just broken the cookie jar."

"What do you mean?"

She sighed. "Sometimes you don't just walk. You slink."

"I can't help that."

"I know you can't."

"You can't . . . free me from what I am."

"I know that too. Only you can do that."

"Then why do you stay?"

"To see if I can help you free yourself." He started to interrupt, but she went on. "Because if you can, I think I would love you."

They drove silently for a moment. "You know I already love you," Jim said.

"Yes. I think you do."

"But I still can't leave. Not even for you."

"I didn't ask you to. I don't expect you to." She reached over and put her hand on his knee. "I don't *want* you to. Not until you're ready."

As she said that, Jim felt a soft peace steal over him, and knew without doubt that she did understand him, and that all she had said and all he had felt was true.

Another bad time had come when Beth wrote to him from Pittsburgh. The letter brought back a nostalgic affection that surprised him. Alice filled so much of the gap that Beth had left that when he received the envelope he thought he might feel only a vague regret on reading what was inside. But instead he heard her voice clearly, and the look of her, the sweet smell of her, her very presence all touched him so that he would have wept had Alice not been in the next room.

Dear Jim,
    I've been here for several weeks now, and am slowly getting used to living alone. My apartment is nice—a town house, really, with two floors—and

290

the neighbors are friendly. The school is large, although my class has only about twenty in it, which isn't too bad. So far everything's going all right, and I'm not as freaked out being back in the classroom as I was afraid I'd be. In fact, I'm kind of enjoying it. I guess I forgot what it was like to be around kids.

I hope you're doing well and writing again. I'm sorry we parted on such a bad note. It's kind of funny. I was always the one who told you to stick to things, that you were too much of a dilettante. But you stuck to this, didn't you? And I was the one who couldn't stick it out with you. I left you, the house, the town, the marriage. Speaking of which, do you want to do anything further right now? For me, I'm content to just let things be as they are for a while. No divorce, or legal separation, at least not yet. We may have a problem with the tax people, since April 15 is only a few months away, but if we do, I'll give you a call. I've got no problem with money right now, and I hope that you're okay in that department. If not, give me a call, and we'll see what we can work out. Number is 412-555-9377.

I won't pretend that I don't miss you, but I've been missing you now for a long, long time. I hope you decide to leave it all behind someday. If you do, let me know. I'm still your wife.

Love,
Beth

Jim Callendar licked his dry lips, feeling sordid and cheap. He wondered if Beth had slept with anyone since she left and decided quickly that she hadn't; it wouldn't be like her. But then he thought, *What am I feeling guilty for? She's the one who left, not me.*

Still, he could not help himself. Guilt had been his primary component for so long that to add the small guilt of adultery to the main was as easy as a drunk taking one more short one for the road. He wrote back to her immediately. It was a hair shirt of a letter, purgative and confessional.

Dear Beth,

I received your letter today and am glad to hear that things are going so well for you. I *am* writing again, and doing rather well at it. I'm even toying with the idea of trying some fiction, or maybe something about what's happened here in town. I'm starting to feel better about myself too, though not to the point where I'm ready to leave. That may take a while. But I have changed, and I have to tell you that the main reason for it is a woman I've met. I didn't really *try* to meet her; it was one of those things that just happen. But she's staying with me now, and we're helping each other. I hope you're not hurt by my telling you, but I've never had any secrets from you, and I wanted you to hear it from me before it got to you from any of your friends back here.

I really don't have much more to tell you than that, and I hope it won't upset you. What you mention about leaving things as they are is all right with me, unless you change your mind in light of what I've told you. I'll understand.

Love,
Jim

P.S. Money is holding out fine.

He decided not to show either letter to Alice, and put Beth's in the back of the desk drawer, while he addressed his own to her. The next day when he took it out to his mailbox along with several bills to be paid, he saw a lonely figure across the street several houses down, just at the point where Sundale Road bent and became lost to sight. Even from a distance he recognized Brad Meyers, standing in the front yard of his ex-wife's house. He had seen him there before, had figured out that he must have moved back in, although he didn't know the circumstances, and felt strangely non-

292

plussed at having the man he regarded as his nemesis living so close. It seemed to Jim that the two of them were still somehow linked, so why should they not be physically close as well?

Brad Meyers turned, saw Jim Callendar at his mailbox, and turned away, thinking that it was over between the two of them. They had had their confrontation, and it had left him empty, given him no satisfaction, only a soreness in his soul that still ached. Ironic that they now lived so close to each other, he thought, since what had bound them was severed that night, for him at least. He would, he had decided, have no more to do with Callendar. The score was settled, the transaction completed. Besides, there were other things to think about: the reasons for it all, for what had happened in Merridale.

Judgment, he had thought at first, some sort of judgment passed by the fates, by God, by whatever was up there, on him. But as the months had passed, he had come to think that it wasn't on him alone, but on everyone, everyone in the town, and maybe in the world as well. Merridale was, as all small towns are, a microcosm of humanity, and he felt that it was not his destiny alone that was being affected, but multiple destinies in an intricate framework whose structure one could not hope to comprehend much less begin to actually work out. There are powers at work here, he thought. Oh, yes, powers.

"Uncle Brad!"

He looked up and saw Wally come around the back of the house, Fluffy hot on his trail. Brad had bought the puppy for the boy just a week before, despite Christine's outspoken disapproval. "We don't need a goddamn dog!" she'd said when he brought it home after Wally was in bed.

"A dog's good for a kid," he'd answered. "Besides, we can keep it outside when it's bigger. We're not in an apartment anymore."

"It'll *howl*. It'll *bark*. Remember? Remember those *things* outside?"

"It didn't when I brought it in. And it isn't now."

"It *will!*"

"No. It's different. It's young. It can get used to these things, adapt. It doesn't know that they're not natural."

"Bullshit. How do you know?"

"We're keeping it. If it howls, we'll get rid of it. But I don't think it will."

Brad was right. The pup didn't howl, not at all. Wally had named it, choosing the ill-fitting sobriquet of Fluffy. The dog did not look like a Fluffy. It was short-haired, a cross, Brad theorized, between a Weimaraner and a pointer, a little, unblessed doggy bastard some embarrassed purebred lover had probably been delighted to get rid of at the pet shop in Lansford where Brad had found it.

Bastard or not, it was one hell of a cute mutt, eyes button-black, tongue always lolling in the middle of a permanent, sappy grin. He guessed that it was two months old, just past the roly-poly stage, but retaining enough puppy cuteness to form an endearing link between boy and dog and man, all of whom now came together in a breathless blur, Brad grabbing the boy and whirling him into the cold air, the pup leaping at his ankles. Wally laughed at his sudden freedom from gravity, staggering as Brad lowered him to the ground. "What's up, kiddo?" Brad asked.

"Will you push me and Fluffy on the swing?"

"Sure. C'mon." The three of them jogged around the back of the house to the swing set, the ground yielding wetly under their feet. The snow had disappeared completely in the last week, melting away a day at a time until not a trace was left. Even the dirty piles mixed with cinders and ash had vanished, soaking into the ground or running down storm drains, dampening finished basements and flooding unfinished ones. It was as if the winter had spent all its fury in the incessant snows of December and was now attempting to make up for its cruelty with an early spring, knowing that the town had already endured more cruelty than it should rightly bear.

Brad slipped off his jacket and hung it over the monkey bar. It felt good to be outside in shirtsleeves. He could not remember it ever being this warm at the beginning of February. Wally climbed up on the wide swing, and the dog leaped into his lap, spotting his jeans with wet earth. Brad started to protest, but stopped, remembering his own dog as a boy, a big dopey foxhound against whom it was futile to struggle on a wet spring day. Jeans would wash. Dirt would not last. But boys and dogs and memories would.

He pushed them higher and higher, so that he had to step farther back with every sweep of the swing. "Keep your feet up," he cautioned the boy. "Don't let 'em drag or you'll slow down."

"Higher!" the boy yelled, and the man complied. He smiled and thought that for the first time in so long he was happy, nearly at peace with himself. It was not a feeling that would last, he knew, but while he possessed it, he intended to enjoy it and remember it, so that he might reclaim it more often. It stemmed in part, he thought, from being in the old house again, the house he had shared with Bonnie and Frank and Linda. When he closed his eyes and heard Wally laugh, he could pretend that time had moved backward, that it was Frankie he pushed on the swing, and that his mind had not yet started its inexorable breakdown into the rage that had held him for so many years. If only, he thought dreamily, time would move even further back—back to when he was still in school, to the day he was to report for his preinduction physical, to the day he volunteered to work with Kriger.

But time *didn't* turn back. Ever. And even if it had, would it have made any difference? What had happened was over and done with, and nothing could change it, could make it *not* have happened. " 'The *moo*-ving *fing*-er *writes*, ' " he chanted softly to the rhythm of the swing, " ' and *hav*-ing *writ* moves *on*.' "

"Whazzat, Uncle Brad?" Wally asked between gulps of air, holding fast to the swing chain with one hand, to Fluffy with the other.

"Just a poem, kiddo. Just a little poem."

"Like rhyming words . . . 'silly' . . . 'billy' . . ."

"Right," Brad laughed. " 'Catty'. . ."

" 'Hatty'!"

" 'Fiddle'. . ."

" 'Diddle'!"

They played rhyming words and Brad pushed Wally on the swing and Christine watched them from inside the house, gazing hollow-eyed through the bedroom window. At that moment she hated them both, hated whatever it was inside them that let them forget what lay all around. "Bastards," she whispered, turning from the window and lying down on the bed. She looked down the length of it at her body and marked how much weight she had lost the past few months. Her breasts were still large, but her waist and hips had slimmed considerably. If she had intended it, she would have felt proud, but it had been an involuntary loss, stemming purely from her diminished appetite. She seemed to eat less each day, only pecking at her dinner while Brad and Wally wolfed down whatever was on their plates. Over and over again she wondered, How can they eat like that? when all around were those things, and then she wondered if she would ever change, ever grow used to them like so many of her friends at the plant did.

Friends? Only acquaintances now. She had lost her friends. They had slipped away, adapting, getting used to what had happened in the town: "There's no point in staying upset. They're here and that's that. There's no harm done." They were right, she told herself, and then she'd ask, What is wrong with me?

No, not *me*. What is wrong with *them*? And she would know with certainty that she was the only sane one, the only one to react and keep reacting like a normal person would to something so hideous and so unnatural. It was the others who were crazy. The whole town was crazy.

And Brad was crazy too. He was the craziest one of all, and he was making Wally crazy too. Still, she couldn't leave him. She had nowhere to go outside Merridale, and living with him was better than living alone. She didn't know what she would do if she had to live alone. She thought maybe she really *would* go crazy then. In fact, she was afraid of his leaving her, so much so that she had stopped her prowling for men, her trading of sex for a night away from Merridale. Being on Sundale Road rather than downtown was definitely an improvement, and she slept better at night knowing that there was no blue phantom inside the house itself, no Old Black Joe in the living room.

But still, all she had to do to start the nightmare was to look out a front window at the dead man in the yard, or peer out back across the narrow patch of field toward the older section of town to see the glow, shining solidly in the distance.

The back door slammed and her body jerked in sudden shock. Damn!

"Chris?" It was Brad's voice. "Where are you?" He stood framed in the doorway, half smiling. "We're going to a movie. *Bambi*'s around again. You want to come?"

"Where?"

"Lansford. Not here." His lip curled as if in disgust at her cowardice.

"All right. I'll come."

"I don't want you to come just to get out of the house for a few hours," Brad said, his face grim. "I want you to come because you want to see *Bambi* with your kid."

"All *right!*" she said. "I want to see the fucking movie, okay?"

Brad gave her a long look. "Then you'd better get ready."

They went to the movie. Brad and Wally laughed at Thumper. Christine didn't. When Bambi's mother was shot, Wally leaned over to his mother. "Where's his mommy?" he whispered.

"She's dead," she replied, not in a whisper, but in a low voice that was audible several rows away. Somewhere a little girl started to cry.

That night, as on all the others she'd spent in Merridale since the phenomenon had begun, she remained awake until exhaustion finally drew her down to sleep. Just before she drifted off, she felt a touch of exasperation at a noise that barely parted her consciousness. It was the sound of a car coming closer and then idling for some time before it stopped. It was a sound she had heard before, late, on other nights, and she thought dimly that it must be a neighbor.

It wasn't. The car belonged to Carl Bailey, and Dave Boyer was behind the wheel, Mr. Bailey's daughter, Kim, next to him, her hand riding high on his thigh. "Here? Again?" she whispered.

"Why not? It was fine last week."

"I don't know. I'd feel better out farther."

"Honey, this is the suburbs. There are cars all over, and nobody's walking. It's perfect."

"But what if somebody sees us?"

"Nobody'll see us. We'll be in the backseat with our heads down . . . won't we?" He let his finger trail the curve of her ear.

"What's wrong with farther out?" she pressed. "What about Schwanger Road? There are those dirt roads off of it."

"Uh-uh. Cops could see us from the road. And what if some creeps pull up behind us—we'd be stuck. This is fine. Safest of all."

"Well, turn on the heater, then."

"Who needs a heater?" He chuckled, but he started the ignition and let hot air flow into the Pontiac until they were uncomfortable in their jackets. "Enough?"

She nodded, and they crawled over to the backseat, fearing to open the doors because of the courtesy light. For a few minutes, as on the previous Saturday night, she was nervous and apprehensive, tensing at every infrequent sweep of early-morning headlights. But slowly Dave made her relax, and when she finally came she had nearly driven from her mind the image of Police Chief Kaylor's stern, puritanical face gazing through the back window.

She needn't have worried. Frank Kaylor's mind was as far from the thought of two teenagers making love in a car on Sundale Road as it was from the Charlie Chan movie he was supposedly watching on television. Barry, his thirteen-year-old, was lying on the floor in front of the set, entranced by each pseudo-Oriental *bon mot* that dripped so easily from Warner Oland's smiling mouth. *Everything* dripped easily for Charlie Chan. Kaylor wondered how the hell easily Chan would solve the Marie Snyder killing. Get everybody in town together in a big room, maybe.

Shit, it *could* be that easy. After all, Merridale was still a

298

town in self-imposed quarantine, so you didn't have drifters. Great. So that left, what, only 8,000 suspects? And the way Marie Snyder gossiped, there were any number of people with possible motives. The venomous old bitch had spread rumors true or false about half the people in town over the years. Maybe, he'd supposed at first, somebody finally had had enough. It was one way to close that thin-lipped, hard-lined mouth.

But the killer hadn't closed it, had he (or she)? That mouth was opened for good now, hanging over the edge of the counter where she'd counted what must have been millions of coins in change over the decades. He confessed to himself that he wasn't sorry to see her go, but he was damned if that was going to let him turn a blind eye toward this investigation. This was his town, and he loved it, and he owed it something, just like it owed him his fifteen hundred a month.

So he sat and watched Charlie Chan bump into his Number One Son in the shadows and thought some more about that day when Fred Hibbs had nearly battered down the door of the police station.

Kaylor hadn't arrived yet, and Del Franklin, who'd been stuck with night duty that week, had called him. When Kaylor arrived at the newsstand, Fred Hibbs was standing outside on the sidewalk, afraid to go back in. Kaylor left him there and went in to talk to Del, who, to Kaylor's indignation, hadn't searched the place. They went through it together, hands on holstered guns, but found no one. Del proudly pointed out that it looked as if someone had gone through the apartment opening and closing drawers, a situation Kaylor had noticed right away. While they waited for the state police to arrive, Del mentioned how cold the shop was. "Go down and put some coal on," Kaylor said. "I don't think *she'll* care one way or the other."

Del Franklin made his way to the cellar, grabbed the coal shovel, and began to toss the coal into the wheezy old furnace. When the coals were burning well, Del continued to add more. Gonna be here a long time, he thought. The coal bin was dark, so he didn't see the envelope, now blackened with coal dust, until he flung the shovelful of coal that held it into the furnace's mouth.

He heard it hit before he saw it, then watched as it ignited far more quickly than the coal, burning with a bright, yellow flame in brilliant contrast to the tamely glowing red lumps. What the hell? Del thought. What was that? Something, apparently, that didn't belong in a coal bin. He frowned, wondering if he should say anything to Chief Kaylor, but decided not to. Just piss him off that I wasn't more careful, he told himself. Besides, what's done's done. He couldn't reach in and snatch out whatever it was, and who could tell now what it ever *had* been? Probably, he thought, just some paper the old lady kept handy to start the fire when it died out.

So he shut the furnace door, and left Marie Snyder's perfect hiding place, going upstairs to share in the warmth of ten thousand burning dollars.

The investigation proved to be a dead end. There were no Charlie Chan–type clues, no telltale cigarette butts, or buttons torn off the killer's coat by the victim, or crumpled slips of paper with the murderer's handwriting. Even the forensic specialists found nothing. Hairs, pieces of thread, tiny bits of flesh under the victim's nails—all were absent. "I thought you guys were supposed to be able to tell *something* about the killer," Kaylor told a forensics man later over the phone. "After all, they got that guy in Atlanta with pieces of fiber, didn't they?"

"It wasn't just that," the man, a clerkish type named Rogers, replied. "They couldn't have got him on that alone. Besides, they had all the money and equipment they needed. We don't."

"So it's what? A question of economics?"

"All the money in the world won't buy clues that aren't there, Chief." The "chief" was slurred deprecatingly.

"So you got nothing."

"That's the size of it."

"Where the hell's Craig Kennedy when you need him?"

"What?"

"Nothing. Thinking out loud."

300

Kaylor began to think silently as well. He questioned dozens of people who had known Marie Snyder, and those who only frequented her store. "Did you notice anything different about her lately?" "Had she mentioned anything or anybody in a peculiar manner?" "Did she do anything peculiar?" He'd spent over an hour talking with John Grubb, the tight-fisted pensioner who occasionally tended the newsstand and helped Marie with the heavy work. He denied noticing any recent changes in her, except for one small thing.

"She always argues with me when I got split time—I mean, like if I got a spare five or ten or twenty minutes. I always got a full half hour out of her for it—that was the deal—but she always groused about it. The Sunday before she died, though, she didn't. I thought that was queer."

Kaylor thought it was queer too. It might have been an indication that she'd gotten some extra money from someone somewhere, which might make robbery the motive. But it also might have been only an indication that she was full of Pastor Craven's Christmas spirit sermon. Even if it *was* a clue, there was nothing to support it. Marie Snyder's bank account showed no deviation from the norm, and no secret caches of cash, gold coins, or green stamps were discovered when the apartment was searched.

So the police, to Frank Kaylor's extreme dismay, remained ignorant, Marie Snyder remained dead, and the killer remained undiscovered, for it would be incorrect to say that he was unknown, since Clyde Thornton was still easily the most conspicuous man in Merridale.

The first week after Marie Snyder's killing was torturous for Thornton. Not a minute passed in which he did not listen for the sound of a police car growling up the driveway. Every phone call was, in his imagination, from Chief Kaylor asking him if he wouldn't mind coming down to the station to answer a few questions. Thornton did his minimal work, filled out his reports, wrote up the required psychosocial profiles, but every second he expected to feel a steely hand close on his shoulder, to hear the rough click of a handcuff at his wrist.

The Wednesday evening town meeting was the worst. There he sat at the head table, Tom Markley on one side,

Frank Kaylor on the other, Pastor Craven two chairs down. The first topic of discussion, of course, had been Marie Snyder's murder. No, Kaylor had answered, there were no leads at this point and he couldn't say when they might have a suspect, and Markley had said that he felt confident that between the facilities of the state police and the inside information that their own town force was gleaning there would be an arrest before too long, and Craven had added that it was terribly, terribly tragic that in a place where death was at everyone's right hand, someone should add even more death. If this person, he went on, would like to come forth and turn himself in, or if he wanted to contact Craven anonymously, Craven would be more than willing to give whatever help he could. We are all God's children, he said, and he will comfort us no matter what our transgressions.

Thornton had actually shifted in his chair then, preparatory to rising, but he caught himself in time. It was the fear and apprehension that tormented him more than any guilt that he felt, and Craven's words of comfort, his soft, deep, soothing voice, the promise of rest, had almost brought Thornton to his feet in a public confession, like some tired sinner brought to Jesus under a canvas roof and over a sawdust floor, lured by promises of peace and a ripe ambience of agape. But a face in the mass of townspeople had shifted to his own face at that second, and the eyes of a woman he did not know by name looked into his. It was, for all he knew, one of those random movements of the head, nothing more, but his fancy saw coldness in it, the hardness of a town toward a man who takes one of their own, and the look stopped him, saved him from his own confession, and he held his fear within.

But as the days lengthened into weeks, the fear receded. In its place there grew a quiet triumph, a sense that he had done it all correctly and would not be discovered. Time, place, method—nothing had been linked to him. He remembered reading that most arrests were made within forty-eight hours of the crime. After that, the perpetrator's odds were better and better that he'd get away with whatever it was he'd done. And now, at the beginning of February, the killing was almost six weeks behind him. He no longer flinched when the phone rang, and had not peered backward over his shoulder for quite a while.

He would not, however, have entered the newsstand under any circumstance, and did not even drive past it, taking side streets and alleyways rather than pass by its green-blinded windows. He bought his papers and magazines, as did nearly all of Marie Snyder's former patrons, at the Turkey Hill Mini-Mart on Oak Street. The selection was minimal, but at least the clerks were living.

In time, Clyde Thornton forgot the fear that Marie Snyder and her knowledge had caused him. It was almost natural that Thornton, all his life nothing but an unheralded petty bureaucrat in a faceless bureau, should come to think of his now-meteoric course as inspired by something beyond his understanding. Everything that had happened here had been for the best—at least *his* best. He was known nationwide, he was receiving large amounts of money for doing next to nothing (and that was only the beginning—after all this was over he could make a mint on the speaker circuit, he was sure of it), and the only thing that had stood in his way was gone, gotten rid of forever.

And *he* had gotten rid of it, neatly, tidily, the only evidence a blue half ghost that could say nothing. And though Clyde Thornton had not believed in a God since his tenth birthday, he was now beginning to believe very strongly in a destiny of his own making, and to slowly see himself as something more than one of the poor, blind fools who walked the streets of sad, chilly Merridale.

I am meant for something more, Clyde Thornton thought as he carefully took his money and even more carefully disposed of it. I am meant for greatness, he thought as in the cocktail lounges he took his pick of the lonely ladies who were so hungry to fuck fame.

And how much more? he wondered. He was what, forty-two? Not too old to do big things, was it? He was known, he had charisma, he had trust, and soon he would have money as well. Politics? He had already proven he could lead. The people in Merridale thought he could walk on water. He had their trust and their respect. It still amazed him how quickly

303

they'd turned to him, leaving their own mayor in the lurch.

He grinned as he remembered Tom Markley's wife after the town meeting just a week ago, the two of them suddenly alone in the lobby. She had made it damn plain what she wanted, and he'd almost been ready to take her up on it when he thought it might be getting a little too close to home. Divorcées and single women (and all right, maybe an occasional married one, very discreetly) were one thing, but the mayor's wife was another. Besides, she was older, nearly fifty, he guessed (though a damn *solid* fifty), and he could do better. But if Markley became any more of a prick than he already was, well, maybe he'd still consider it. Hell, Clyde Thornton could have whatever he wanted.

"Whatever he wants, y'know? Livin' out there in that big house. I bet your ass he's got orgies out there." Fred Hibbs popped the tab on a can of Rolling Rock and took a swig. The top of the can reeked of cigarette smoke that had accumulated from weeks of sitting in the Anchor's cooler, but Fred didn't seem to mind.

Eddie Karl did, and he poured his beer into a glass with "America—200 Years of Glory 1776–1976" etched crudely on the side, leaned his chair back, and propped his shoes on the edge of his kitchen table. "He don't have no orgies," he said.

"How do *you* know?"

"Nobody's never had no orgies in Merridale. It's in the town code. If you have an orgy, you get hit by lightning."

"Bull*shit*," said Fred Hibbs.

"You ever read the town code?"

"Well, maybe he don't have orgies, but I bet he fucks a lot of women."

"Nothin' about *that* in the town code," Eddie said.

"I even heard he's fuckin' Mim Markley."

"Now *that's* bullshit."

"Why? You think she wouldn't?"

"No, I think maybe she would. Women're damn funny when it comes to doin' it and who they'll do it with." Eddie

304

stuck out his lower lip and balanced the salt shaker on top of the pepper shaker. "I don't think *he'd* do it."

"Thornton?"

"Uh-huh. Besides, I got spies. They'd tell me if Mim was screwin' around."

"What spies?"

"Ned Phillips for one. He's right near Markley's."

Fred screwed up his face and pushed his chair back from the table. "I'm gonna watch TV."

"Ned'd know."

"News is on." Fred stood up and moved toward the living room.

Eddie looked at Fred's retreating form. "You don't think Ned would know, do ya?"

"Ned is *dead*, goddammit!" Fred shouted, twisting around. "He's *dead!* Now how the hell is he gonna tell you *anything?*"

"Well, you *could* humor me," said Eddie, standing up. "You're supposed to humor us loonies, y'know?"

"I *tried* to humor you, you old fart, but you kept *at* me! Now can we just forget it and go in and watch the dumbass news?"

"Can't tonight."

"Why not?"

"I got a date."

"What in hell are you talkin' about?"

"I'm takin' Harriet Viner to the movies, if it's any of your business."

"Aw, shit." Fred shook his head in frustration. Harriet Viner had died in a rest home ten years before, and the town's sole movie theater had closed its doors for good in 1974. "I'm gonna watch the news." He walked into the dimly lit living room, turned the switch on the old Emerson, and committed his bulk to the tired cushions of the high-backed davenport.

"Ain'tcha gonna wish me a good time?" asked Eddie, standing in the doorway.

"Have a good time."

"Goin' to the Anchor after the movie. If I ain't home

tonight, you'll know I got lucky. Or maybe I'll bring her back here.''

Fred Hibbs swallowed heavily, closed his eyes, and kept them closed until he heard the front door open and shut. When he looked, Eddie was gone.

It's nice here, Fred thought. It is nice here. There were no ghosts—nowhere in the house and none in the small back-yard. There, garages encroached upon the property, hiding any distant blue forms from view, so that when you stood outside the back door, it was as though you were in Merridale before the phenomenon had taken place. From the front of the house, which looked out onto the street, the forms were visible, but they kept the front shades drawn. Fred Hibbs spent nearly all his time in the house, going out only to cash his Social Security check, or to have breakfast at the Hitching Post, or to help Eddie with the grocery shopping. It was not an unpleasant prison. The house, though small from the outside, used its space wisely. It was a frame two-story building built at the turn of the century. Though its front door was less than six feet from the sidewalk on Market Street, it was in the southern, less busy section of town, where the residential atmosphere was broken only occasionally by a convenience store or gas station. The rooms, devoid of a woman's touch for decades, were nonetheless cozy and com-fortable, the walls dark, the furniture old and friendly. Fred had been amazed by the great quantity of books that, jammed into homemade bookcases of every conceivable size and shape, filled each corner of each room. Hardcovers from the twenties shared shelf space with eighties paperbacks, the smaller books stuffed above and beside the hardbacks as though used for packing. One cellar room held a profusion of magazines, from a stack of 1932 *Argosy*, to fifties' *Popular Mechanics*, to last year's *Susquehanna*.

"Jesus, Eddie," said Fred when he first saw them. "I didn't know you read so much."

"Gotta do somethin' when you're a single man. Whatta *you* do with your time?"

Fred had shrugged. "Watch TV a lot, I guess."

"Well, I got one. Don't watch much myself, though I

306

liked that *Charlie's Angels* show. And Milton Berle. Not much worth watching now.''

''How come you keep all these?''

''The books? I keep 'em long enough I forget I read 'em, so it's like readin' a new book. But don't worry, there ain't too many of 'em in your room.'' And there weren't—just one small bookcase by the bed, filled mostly with Executioner and Nick Carter—Killmaster novels. Fred tried to read one, but the word-by-word effort he had to put forth was not worth it, and he put it aside after three chapters, thankful that the television worked.

To Fred's surprise, he had gotten along well with Eddie for the first few weeks. They cooked and ate together, watched TV (Eddie discovered that he liked the *Star Trek* reruns Fred tuned in), played cards (gin was the favorite, Eddie winning most of the time), and drank on Saturday nights. They'd start with a few beers at Ted's Place, a small neighborhood bar a few blocks away, and then wend their way back to Eddie's, where they would split a six-pack of Rolling Rock. Fred Hibbs was a Schmidt's drinker, but Eddie protested that Schmidt's made him fart.

Five beers each over a two-hour period never made either of them drunk, but it did slip them into a garrulous camaraderie, the ease of which later extended into their comparatively sober moments. At such times, Eddie seemed to forget his half promise not to be cozy with the dead when Fred was around. Lounging with his feet up on the shabby elephant-foot ottoman, Eddie would launch into a narrative of whom he had run into that day, both dead and alive. Fred would feel his stomach churn the way it did when he'd had to go into the kitchen of his own house, and he'd try to change the subject. But Eddie would be nonplussed, rambling on about Clete Wilkins or Rouamie Hack, and how goddamn *good* they looked for their age, until Fred would finally get mad and call Eddie a loony and Eddie would laugh and tell Fred to sit down, sit down, and then start to talk about something else.

It had been getting worse, though, in the last week or two. It was bad enough when Fred walked the streets with Eddie, and Eddie would call out a greeting to a dim, blue shape or, even more absurdly, stop and chat with empty air. But lately Eddie had taken to talking to the dead in his own house (*their* house, Fred thought). As yet he had not done it in front of Fred, but Fred had heard him from another room and, at first thinking there was someone in the house, had gone to see who was there. But it was only Eddie, Eddie alone, who snapped his mouth shut in midword and glared at Fred as though irked at having been interrupted.

Late that same night Fred had lain awake in his bed, listening to Eddie's voice droning in his own bedroom. The words were soft, and Fred was unsuccessful at interpreting any complete sentences. But the few words he was able to understand told him that Eddie Karl was talking to a woman, telling her how lovely she was as he ran his hand over her body, or the memory of her body.

Fred got out of bed, pulled his flannel bathrobe tightly around his pajama-clad body, and stepped quietly into the short, upstairs hall. Keeping against the wall so the floorboards would creak as little as possible, he shuffled the few steps to Eddie's door, from under which poured a puddle of dim, yellow light. What Fred *wanted* to do was to throw the door open and shout, "Shut up, shut up, you crazy old fart," but there was something about the singsong voice, an intensity, an *edge*, that prevented him.

In truth, Fred Hibbs was afraid of what he would see if he opened that door. At the least it would repulse him; at the worst, horrify him. Turning and walking away would leave him with the idea (*illusion?*) that he was the guest of only a harmless old coot with cobwebs where some of his brains used to be, and not a truly fucked-up, whacked-out pervert weirdo madman who really *had* seen the dead people before anybody else. So he turned slowly, hesitating for a moment as he noticed the keyhole and thought about how easy it would be to peek through it.

But the fear drew him away, back to his own room, where he lay listening, and where comfort finally conquered fear so that he thought, pullin' his pud . . . pullin' his old wrinkled pud to Playboy or somethin', that's all, and he rolled over and made himself sleep as the words in the next room grew softer and more infrequent, passing at length into silence.

But there were no grounds for Fred Hibbs's suspicions. Eddie Karl had not masturbated, nor had he been able to, for eight years. He only lay on his bed naked, keeping his eyes from his own withered body, watching instead how the warm glow of the Bakelite reading lamp illuminated the soft, rosy flesh of a young woman who had lain there beside him forty years before, letting his shaking hand trail down the length of her body as she lay on her side facing him, from the hillock of her hip down the slope of her waist and up again to where her breast met her side, and then down to touch that smooth breast, and Eddie always telling her, telling her how absolutely beautiful she was, how he'd never seen a woman more beautiful, no not even in the movies or in the magazines, and now she was reaching for him again, and when she did, the memory faded, because he could not remember what had happened next. Always, when it came to that, he just could not remember.

He was tired now, too tired to bring her back again, so he switched off the lamp, whispered good-night to the darkness, and went to sleep, his arm over the place where she would be when he wanted to see her again.

The next morning over breakfast Fred Hibbs had looked at him oddly. "You talk in your sleep?"

"Why?" Eddie asked. "You hear me?"

"I heard you talkin'."

"I had comp'ny. Couldn't be rude, could I?"

"What kinda company?"

"I wanted you to know, I'd tell ya."

"You're not goin' screwy on me, are you?"

"I had *comp'ny*, Fred."

"Somebody *dead*, wasn't it?"

Eddie looked down at his dirty plate, stood up, and put it into the sink. "No," he said softly. "She ain't dead. She'll never be dead."

"Who?"

Eddie sighed. "A woman. A woman I knew once."

Fred Hibbs frowned, confused. "There ain't no ghosts in

this house, so how can you be talkin' to someone here?"

"I can talk to her everywhere," Eddie replied with a crooked smile, "until I find her somewhere."

"What the hell are you talking about?"

"The love of my life, my boy. Everybody oughta have a love of his life."

"But who was she?"

"Her name wouldn't mean nothin' to you. I was mighty young, so you woulda been just a little boy at the time. But Jesus Christ she was beautiful, and how I did love her." He sat back down at the table with a third cup of coffee. "She was married, but her husband was an asshole. He didn't know what he had." Eddie's face wrinkled in bitter memory. "Or maybe he did at that. Anyways, he made it pretty miserable for her. So she started to drink. That's how I met her—over a drink." He looked up at Fred Hibbs. "Am I borin' you?"

Fred shook his head shortly. "No."

"Well, let me know if I do. We old guys do go on, y'know." He slipped back into his story as though he had never stopped. "She kept on drinkin'. I couldn't get her to stop that. But I did get her to stop fuckin' around with guys that were no good for her. Got her to fuck around with *me* instead." He chuckled, but his face immediately softened, the lines vanishing as if by magic. "Oh, God, but she was so beautiful. We had good times together, good times. Right in this house, with all the shades drawn down. And she loved me too, I *know* she did. Women can fake lotsa stuff, but she didn't fake that. Time and again I told her to leave that sonuvabitch and come live with me, *marry* me, but it scared her, the thought of divorcin' him, and him gettin' mad, and well, not too many people got divorced back then, 'specially in a place like Merridale. And 'cause she was scared, she drank more, and I finally scared her away for good." Eddie stopped talking and shook his head.

"Whatcha mean, 'for good'?"

"She left me. Left her husband. Left town. I never heard from her again. Just scared off, I guess. If I hadn't pushed her, we mighta been able to go on like we had. But I loved her too much." Eddie Karl shook his head, then looked up.

"Now ain't that a sad story though? Don't it just tug at your heartstrings and make you barf?"

"And you never found out what happened to her?"

"Nope. Probably wound up turnin' tricks in Philly. But I been carryin' the torch for her ever since. Now you tell *me* about *your* biggest heartbreak."

"Never had one. Never had much time for women."

"I never had much time for nothin' else." Eddie's eyes narrowed. "You ain't queer, are ya, Fred?"

"*Shit!*" Fred spat out. "You *are* loony."

"Not that I mind if you are," Eddie went on, "but I'll just have to remember to lock my bedroom door at night."

Goddamn, thought Fred Hibbs, half remembering, half watching the news. He didn't know if he could handle it much longer, not if Eddie kept acting so crazy. But at least his mother and father weren't there. There was that at least. *The movies. With Harriet Viner. Jumpin' Jesus, what's next?* He wouldn't have been too surprised if Eddie started digging up the cemetery to actually see his old friends and lovers once again. *As long as he don't bring them home.*

At eight o'clock *Francis Joins the Navy* was on a Philadelphia UHF station, and he watched that for a while, but Eddie's antenna was weak, diluting the antics of Donald O'Connor and the talking mule with snow to a point where it became not only unfunny, but unwatchable. Too weary to get up and change channels, Fred Hibbs closed his eyes for a quick nap. When he woke up it was long after midnight, and his back hurt. Damn couch. He turned off the TV and went upstairs, where he brushed his teeth and went to bed.

Sometime after two o'clock he awoke, wondering what was shaking him so. When it reached his sleep-dulled mind that something was indeed acting on his body, and that it was not a dream, he gasped, stiffened, and blinked in fear at the sudden light.

"Wake up," called a cracked voice that he knew to be Eddie's. But something was different in it, changed. There was none of the playfulness that had always been there, even when he had told Fred about that woman long ago. "Wake *up*, Fred. Wake up, dammit."

"Whazzit," Fred grunted. "Whassamatter?"

"Get up, get dressed," Eddie barked. "You gotta come with me."

"Come where?"

"Just get dressed!" Eddie whirled around and left the room.

Fred Hibbs, confused, frantic, obedient, pulled on his pants, drew on his shirt, thinking, What the hell, what the hell? But his mind was too befuddled to protest, and Eddie had never asked him to do anything that wasn't important. He might've been loony, but he'd never taken Fred on a fool's errand. Fire? he thought as he laced his shoes. Accident? He clattered down the steps and found Eddie waiting for him at the front door.

"Come on," Eddie said, opening it.

"*Where?*"

"Just come, goddammit, I need your help!" He was out on the front sidewalk already, and Fred ran to catch up, slamming the door behind him.

"Eddie, if this is some fuckin' half-assed idea of yours, I'm really gonna be *pissed!*"

"No. No, boy, nothin' loony this time. This is *real*, boy, *real*." They kept walking north up Market, through the square and beyond, where the houses thinned out and the streetlights ended.

Fred grabbed Eddie's arm to slow him. The older man's energy seemed to come from some bottomless well of determination, and though Fred was panting, Eddie looked as fresh as if he had just left his house. His eyes burned in frustrated rage as he turned to Fred. "No farther," Fred said, wheezing, "not till . . . you tell me . . . where—"

"The Anchor," Eddie snarled, and tore his arm away, moving purposefully into the night.

"The Anchor?" cried Fred, scuttling to keep up. "The Anchor's *closed!* It's after two—they're *closed*. There's nothing *there*." He didn't hear Eddie reply, just saw his craggy head shake in disagreement as he walked on, wielding his

312

cane like a swagger stick. "Aw, shit," mumbled Fred, stopping and looking back toward town. "Aw, *shit*," he said again, running to keep up with Eddie.

When they arrived a short time later at the Anchor, Eddie went right up to the front door and rattled the knob. It was a makeshift door of hollow pine. The Jerney brothers had not yet received the steel one they'd ordered to replace the old glass-paned panel that the unidentified vandal had ruined. Eddie shook it again, then looked at Fred. "It's shit," he said. "Hollow. Bust it in."

"Bust it . . . *what?*"

"That's what you're here for, why I wanted you to come. I'm not strong enough; you are. Well, don't just stand there *gawkin'* at me, bust it *in!*"

"Christ, Eddie, you're talkin' about . . . uh . . . breaking and entering!"

"There's worse things than that, boy. Now you either bust that door in for me, or you go home to your own house tonight. I mean it."

"But why?"

"You'll *see* why! Now come *on!*" Eddie threw himself against the door, which tossed him back as though it were made of rubber. The resulting thud was loud.

"Quiet!" hissed Fred Hibbs. "You'll wake up the whole damn town!"

"Then *help* me."

"All right, all right, oh Jesus we're gonna get in a shitload of trouble for this, damn you, Eddie . . ."

Fred stepped up to the door, lifted his foot, and kicked with all his strength at the spot next to the gold-painted knob. Something crunched, but the door did not open. He kicked again. The casing splintered, and the door swung in with a bang that made Fred's heart pound even more quickly.

Pushing Fred aside, Eddie strode into the bar, his cane carried loosely at his side as though his determination alone gave strength to his thin legs. He walked directly to the heavy wooden box nailed to the floor of the room, knelt beside it, and started to rock it back and forth so that the nails loosened protestingly, filling the room with harsh screeching.

313

"I looked," Eddie grunted as he worked. "I closed the fucking place tonight, just me and Leo tending the bar. . . . He was talkin' about the break-in, how they busted up everything, and I was . . . sittin' next to this box, and I said how about the box, and he got this funny look and said no, not the box. . . . I knew he was lyin', and when he went to take a leak I got down and I got my knife in and pried back a slat and I looked. . . . Didn't see much, no not much, but enough. . . . Just her hair, and that was enough. . . . I didn't forget."

Fred Hibbs stood watching in horror as the box came farther and farther from the floor, knowing that there was something dead beneath, and slowly beginning to understand who, impossible as it seemed. Finally the nails, with a scream of release, left the floorboards completely, and the box fell over, revealing the form of the raped and murdered woman that Brad Meyers had uncovered a month before. Fred bit the inside of his mouth.

Eddie Karl knelt beside her, his shoulders slumping, his head down, the furies departed. "It *is* you," he said, looking at the face, then at the rest of the body. "What did they do? What did they do to you?"

Fred was unable to come closer. "Is it . . . is it her? Who you told me about?"

Eddie nodded. "It's her." He lifted a hand and held it to the woman's face, and for a second Fred Hibbs could have sworn that he saw a contact, a slight yielding of the flesh where Eddie's hand met it. "All these years. So long, and she's still beautiful. But my God, look what they did to you."

"But . . . ." Fred Hibbs felt as though he stood gazing into the face of an awesome tragedy, dwarfed by the magnitude of the old man's grief. Unable to deal with the emotion of it, he sought instead for logic. "But you seen 'em before, Eddie . . . you said you seen 'em all before. You been here, been here *lots*. But you never seen her? *Never?*"

The old man gave a sigh like corn husks brushing together. "I never seen nobody," he whispered, never taking his eyes from the woman's face. "I seen what I wanted to see, that's all. I'm a liar, Fred. Some folk's killers, some's liars. I'd rather be a liar. I'd rather be a liar than the ones that did this. How could they? Just look at her. Look at her and tell me how they could."

"Eddie . . ." Fred's voice was pinched, too tight to be audible. He cleared his throat. "Eddie, come on. . . . We gotta go." Fred Hibbs's soul was filled with terror. He wanted to run out, but he could not bear to be alone, not in a town that was full of such things, full of ghosts and death and thick, choking fear. "Eddie . . ." he pleaded.

Eddie stood up and shuffled over to where Fred stood shivering. He put an arm around the younger man and smiled guilelessly. "We can't go yet. Not till I introduce you."

"Eddie, goddammit, now don't—"

"You can see, see for yourself how beautiful she was," and he tugged at Fred Hibbs, drawing him closer to the beloved obscenity. Fred tried to pull away, but Eddie's voracious strength had returned, and Fred felt himself drifting helplessly toward the woman on the floor, feeling awe at how strong Eddie had become.

The strength of madness.

"Come on, come on, you gotta meet her . . ." The humor was starting to creep into Eddie's voice again, but now it was a cackling humor, the humor of a man whose sanity has been shocked away. And Fred Hibbs felt something like madness stir in him also, so that the next time he pulled back he made Eddie stagger along with him. "No, no," Eddie admonished, his thin fingers digging more deeply into the flesh of Fred's upper arm. "You gotta meet her. . . . If you don't, you won't believe me. . . . I gotta show you, show you I'm not loony."

It was then that Fred Hibbs struck Eddie Karl, pulling back his free right arm and driving his fist full into the old man's face. Eddie neither flinched nor blinked. Indeed, he seemed to not even see the thick-knuckled hand moving toward him. It met his nose and mouth with a loud crack that shattered bone, and he fell, a dead weight, to the floor.

It took a moment for Fred Hibbs to realize that he was free, for his arm still ached as though Eddie's claw retained its grasp. Even then, he could not immediately move. Instead, he stood rooted, gazing down at Eddie Karl, hearing his bubbling breathing, watching the blood trickle out of his nose and mouth, half expecting to see Eddie turn, *change* into something naked and blue and gleaming.

But there was no change, and slowly Fred felt his muscles begin to respond, so that he was able to turn his body, to walk sluggishly through the semidarkness toward the door. But instead of the blackness he had expected to see through the upright panel, there was a red light, blinking off and on, off and on, and in that light he could see a dark, framed shape crouching, holding something metallic out in front of itself.

"Hold it," the shape said in a pinched tenor. "Police." The voice shook, as if the speaker were even more frightened than Fred Hibbs.

"Jus' lemme come out," Fred said weakly. "Outside . . ."

"Come on, then, but no quick moves." Fred recognized the voice now. Mike Gifford, the youngest of Merridale's police force. Gifford backed up, never moving his revolver from Fred's direction, while Fred slowly shuffled after him. Finally Fred was through the doorway, into the stinging coldness of night, the red flasher of the patrol car illuminating his pale face at regular intervals. "Fred Hibbs," said Gifford with a trace of surprise. "Is that you?" Fred nodded blankly. "Who's . . . who's in there with you?"

"Eddie Karl." Fred had to say it twice before Gifford heard.

"He okay?"

"He's . . . hurt. I hit him."

"Okay, Mr. Hibbs," Gifford said, his voice trembling more than before. He opened the back door of his car. "Just climb in there real slow, okay?"

Fred did as he asked and Gifford closed the door behind him, then opened the front door and fiddled with something on the dash. There was a loud click, and Fred Hibbs knew he was locked in. The wire mesh between him and the front seat reminded him of a taxicab he'd ridden in once in New York City, long, long ago. Or had that been him at all? Had he

316

ever been to New York City? He tried, but he couldn't remember.

An ambulance came a short time later, and took Eddie Karl to the Northern County Health Center. Eddie was just starting to regain consciousness when they lifted him onto the stretcher. His face felt numb, like no face at all, but a mask made from ice, pressed over and stuck to his own features. He thought about the pain, about the woman, and about Fred Hibbs hitting him. "Serves me right," he muttered.

The orderly with him heard only a wet whisper. "Just take it easy there. Don't try to talk."

"Serves me right for makin' friends with a dummy," Eddie went on, but the orderly could not understand. Stick to old friends, Eddie thought. That's the ticket.

He saw several at the Health Center. The Center was an emergency drop for a large number of patients—those not banged up enough to warrant a trip to Lansford General, or those too damaged to survive the additional fifteen miles. Eddie was one of those in-betweeners, serious enough for a hospital check-in, but needing immediate attention and minimal movement because of his age and fragility. They carried him in and took him to the tiny ward. There were eight beds, and every one of them had been filled. Had been, that is, until the doctors had ordered them moved, shifted a few feet one way or the other so that the blue forms no longer lay directly on them, but instead floated at the spots where they had died. Several occupied the same space, like some protoplasmic jumble of flesh.

"Sorry about the view, old-timer," said an orderly, settling Eddie on one of the beds. "Can't cover 'em up, we've gotta get around," and so saying, he walked through one of the ghostly assortment.

Eddie painfully swiveled his dripping head to look around. The first blue, slack-jawed face he saw was one he recognized. It had belonged to a man with whom Eddie had played poker years before. "Sam," he said. "Howya doin', Sam?"

Eddie Karl closed his eyes, the pain fading. He was thinking how good it was to be around old friends. When the darkness took him again, he was happy.

Fred Hibbs minded the spraying worst of all. What did they think he was? One of those niggers or PR's from the ward? Hell, he didn't have any goddamn lice, and he'd told them so. But that cop had just grinned at him and said, "We just like to make sure. Strip."

He wished he could've stayed in the holding cell at the Merridale Police Station. They wouldn't have sprayed him there. But the only things that would've kept him there were minor infractions, and assault and battery wasn't minor, and neither was breaking and entering. So the staters had come and taken him to Lansford, where he'd stripped, been sprayed, showered, and dressed in a drab, gray uniform that looked like a hundred other guys had worn it first. Now, finally, they had taken him to a cell with a bed and a sink and a toilet in it, and there he sat, scared as hell of what they were going to do to him next. Oh, Christ, he hoped Eddie Karl didn't die, that he wasn't hurt bad. He hoped they'd believe him when he told them that Eddie'd driven him to it, had *made* him bust open the door, had *made* him lay him out. But what if he was dead? Oh, shit, what then?

Fred sat on the edge of the bed, unable to sleep, so that he was awake when the guard came back to tell him that Eddie Karl was still alive. He'd blacked out a few times, but kept coming back. They wouldn't know for sure until they ran the brain scans, but for now, the prognosis was good.

Thank God, Fred thought. Thank God. Now I won't burn. Now they can't kill me. But the relief left quickly as the grim reality of his situation returned to him. Jail. Maybe for a long time. Years and years.

And then it hit him. Even though he still felt afraid, it was a different kind of fear, a natural, more sensible fear. Something else, that *other* fear, was gone. He listened with all his senses, and after a moment's meditation he knew he was safe. Oh, maybe not from other convicts, but why would they bother him? He was big and friendly and pretty strong, and too damn old and ugly for anyone to want to rape.

318

What he was safe from were the ghosts.

There weren't any here. Not a one. No blue forms to haunt his sleep, to creep into his mind even without his seeing them. They were all back there in Merridale. They could not touch him now.

Suddenly jail felt safe and warm and comfortable, and the next day when they told him his bail had been set at $10,000, a sum that he could have easily raised by mortgaging his parents' house, he told them he wasn't interested. Out of his parents' house, out of Eddie Karl's, Fred Hibbs had found a home.

CHAPTER
24

They would never go away.

They would be here forever, would outlive him by centuries. Even worse, he would become one of them, become what had killed him.

Tom Markley, Merridale's mayor, looked in the bathroom mirror at his own pale face, held his fingers to his neck. He could feel the artery pulsing with his blood. Sweat wetted his skin as he tried to feel a regular rhythm, tried to beat out *bump-bump-bump-bump-bump*. But although he heard the strict, solid, disciplined drumbeat in his head, he did not feel it with his fingers.

Bump.

Then a pause.

Bump-bump.

Then another, so long that he wondered if he would die then and there. But no.

Bump.

(So light, how can that keep me alive?)

BUMP-bump.

A hiccup, he thought. His heart had the hiccups, that was

all. Maybe if he cut himself open and put a bag over it, or i
he yelled boo to his chest in the mirror, maybe it would stop

And maybe what had started it hiccupping would go away
Sure. Sure.

He'd noticed it a week or so ago, a slight irregularit
somewhere within him. He'd sensed it as he lay awake in be
in the black hours before dawn, that bad time when he wa
most alone with his thoughts, when it was just him an
Merridale and Mim, and Clyde Thornton and the ghoulie
taking it all away. At first he thought it was his stomac
growling, but quickly discovered that it was not. Somethin
inside. Something inside.

His heart.

He touched it, and found the source of the odd sensation
He shook the shoulder of his sleeping wife.

"What?" she said sleepily, irritated.

"Feel this," he said. "Put your hand here." Taking he
hand and placing it on his chest, he found himself prayin
that she wouldn't feel it, would notice nothing irregular, tha
it was only temporary, or his imagination.

"It's not steady," she said after only a few seconds
forever shattering his feeble rationalization.

"My heart."

"Mmm." She felt for a while longer, then moved her han
to his wrist. "Maybe a muscle spasm. In your chest. . . .

"No," she said after a moment. "I feel it in your wris
too, I think."

"Should I . . . should I go to the hospital?"

"Does your chest hurt at all?"

"No."

"Are you numb? In your arm or anywhere?"

He flexed the muscles in his left arm, then his right
"No."

"You could go now," she said, "or maybe wait. I don'
know."

"I'll go in the morning." He *felt* all right, dammit—it wa
just that damn heartbeat, out of cadence. Mim went back t
sleep in a few minutes, but Tom Markley stayed awake unt
dawn, when he got up and made coffee.

It's killing me, he thought. Sons of bitches are killing me.

He had never before had any trouble with his heart. Then, just after Christmas he'd had a checkup and found his blood pressure elevated—160 over 100. Under a lot of pressure, he'd told Doc Barnes, who had smiled gently, given him some expensive medication, and told him to try to relax. And now this.

He didn't go to the doctor's the next morning. Part of him wanted to, knew that he should, but a greater part didn't care. Maybe his body was wiser than he was. Maybe it knew that it was time for him to die. Besides, it might be too expensive. He wasn't old enough for Medicare, and he'd let his hospitalization lapse a month before. He simply couldn't afford it.

When he arrived home that evening, he told Mim that he had seen the doctor and had received a clean bill of health. Just an irregularity, nothing to worry about.

She only nodded and smiled briefly, the kind of smile she gave when he told her that the shower faucet just needed a new washer, or the wiring in the hutch was fine, and it was just the bulb that had burned out. She didn't say, "Oh, thank God, I was so worried," or "I'm going to have to start taking better care of you," or "It's no wonder—you've been worrying too much. We'll be just fine as long as we're together," or half a hundred other things that she could have said. And because she had said none of those things, he knew for certain that she no longer loved him, and the heartbeat grew more erratic, having less reason to keep the man alive.

Now he stood in front of the mirror, sensing his heart's tripping patterns while Mim watched TV in the rec room. I'm going to die, he thought for the thousandth time since it had begun. I am going to die. He was as certain of it as he was sure of the loss of Mim's love, the lack of the town's respect, the stark glare of red with which this month's accounts had been written.

And when I die, I'll stay here forever. And she'll see me dead, and her lovers will see me too, and they'll laugh at me, laugh at me naked and lying there, and maybe, I don't know,

323

but maybe I'll know about it because maybe these things d[o] know and can see and can think.

He frowned at his image in the glass, and grew angry a[t] the tear he saw in one eye's corner.

I don't want to know. I don't want to see it.

There was one logical, inescapable answer, and he ac[]cepted it. On the way out, he stopped in the doorway to th[e] rec room. "I'm going out, hon," he said.

"Oh. All right. When'll you be back?"

"I'm not sure." He paused, then said, "I love you, Mim."

"I love you too." She didn't look at him as she said it, b[u]t kept her gaze fixed on the TV screen. At that moment [a] glance from her would have saved him.

He drove out of Merridale, northeast on a rough two-lan[e] that wove past farmers' fields, through state game land[s]. Miles beyond the phenomenon's sphere of influence he stoppe[d] and walked several hundred yards back on a trail he'd used t[o] hike with his father, and, when he'd been still younger, hi[s] grandfather. At last he stopped and chambered a cartridg[e] into the ancient P.38 he'd brought home from the war. Afrai[d] that if he held the weapon to his head for too long a time h[e] might weaken, he brought it up and pulled the trigger in on[e] motion.

Flame exploded, a roar cut through the forest's stillness and the birds leaped shrieking from the trees. The echoe[s] died away, the birds resumed their perches, and the tree[s] grew silent again. The flare from the pistol had faded, an[d] everything was dark. There was not a patch of light, not [a] glimmer, not a spark.

By the next weekend the rain had washed away the bloo[d] and the birds had finished what bits of tissue remained afte[r] Tom Markley had been lifted and placed into the ambulance. Bob Craven's three children ran far ahead, the way the[y] always did on walks, leaving him and Joan behind, hand i[n] hand.

"It must have been right around here," Craven said.

"I'm surprised the children aren't looking for the exa[ct] spot." Joan shook her head. "Poor Tom."

324

"I wish he would have talked to me. I gave him the chance. I could tell something was wrong." Craven kicked at stone and sent it rolling into the brush.

"I wish *you'd* talk to *me*," Joan said quietly, her eyes on the dirt path before them.

"What?"

"Something's wrong with *you*. Something's *been* wrong, ever since this all started."

He laughed self-consciously. "It's . . . the situation," he said with a sad smile. "None of us can be expected to be perfectly normal, not even after—what is it now?—four months?"

"I'm not talking about normality. I'm thinking of something else. Something that makes you who you are." She stopped, ignoring the shouts of the children far up the trail. "When did you lose it, Bob? Your faith."

"What do you mean? Faith in what?" He could feel himself start to sweat under the down vest.

"In what you believe in." She shook her head. "You know I've never been a . . . a holy roller. I mean, I believe in God, but I've never been a fanatic about it. Sometimes, when I think back on it, I think I married you *in spite* of what you are, not because of it, and though I do believe, it's just never been all that . . . 'important' isn't the word . . . compulsive.' " She smiled and nodded. "I've never been compulsive or obsessive about it."

"And I have?"

"In a way. I mean, doing what you do, you have to be demonstrative, don't you? But lately I get the feeling that it's just been . . . all show, like you're playing a role." He turned away from her and looked into the woods, not wanting her to see the truth. "Am I right?" she asked.

"I don't know. I really don't know."

"You don't really believe what you're telling everyone, do you."

"What *am* I telling everyone?"

"That there's a purpose behind what's happened. That God's behind it."

"I . . . I don't—"

325

"What?"

"I don't know *why*."

She laughed, not unkindly. "Who does?"

"No! I mean what's it all accomplished? We've got a tow[n]
full of scared and crazy people, Joan. Marie Snyder ge[ts]
murdered, Fred Hibbs nearly kills Eddie Karl, Tom blow[s]
his brains out! Nobody's *learning* anything."

"What are they supposed to learn?"

"How to *live*, damn it!" Craven slammed his right fi[st]
into his left palm. "I thought, when this all started, I thoug[ht]
that we'd *learn* more, that we were *lucky*, we were *chose[n]*
that by, by staring death in the face so openly, we'd learn [to]
live better. *Knowing*, you see, *knowing* that death's waitin[g]
would make us value living so much more that we'd b[e]
better, be kinder to each other. But we *weren't*. And [I]
wanted to say that, to make them see that, to tell them not [to]
be scared, to love each other."

"But you *have*," Joan said. "You've calmed them, hel[d]
them together."

"I haven't done a thing," he said grimly. "I haven't don[e]
a thing except stop believing myself."

"*I* haven't, Bob." There was a challenge in her tone. '[I]
never thought I had as strong a faith as yours, but maybe [I]
have. Maybe because yours came so easily to you and I ha[d]
to work at it."

"I don't want to argue about—"

"It isn't something you get and keep forever, you know[.]
It's something you *do* have to work at."

His words were pinched, angry. "Well, maybe I could b[e]
born again."

"Born again, bullshit! You're not just born once or twice—
you've got to be born over and over again every day of you[r]
life."

"Not in Merridale! Every day is a new *death* around her[e]
not a new birth!"

"So it depends on where you are? I can just hear Jesu[s]
now—'Sorry, folks, I'm not myself today. Must be th[e]
Jerusalem blues.' "

"Don't talk like that."

"What do *you* care? I thought you'd lost it."

"Look! What's wrong with me is what's wrong with everybody in town. We *don't* feel blessed, we feel *cursed!*"

"*Why?*"

"*Because we're the only ones!*" His face changed as he cried out, and she recoiled from him, not in fear, but in sudden awe of the understanding that seemed to have overtaken him.

"We're the only ones," he repeated quietly. "You said . . you said it depends on where you are. And maybe you're right."

"I don't understand."

"Anyone, any single one of us would have had the Jerusalem blues. Even Jesus did—'Let this cup pass from me,' remember? Because he was alone. And Merridale's alone too. We're a freak—our town's a freak, and we're part of it. But if it were—I don't know—more widespread maybe, then . . then we'd be blessed. Because we were the first, because we had a chance to get ready."

" 'Prepare ye the way of the Lord,' " Joan quoted, and Craven's face brightened.

"Exactly," he said. "Then it would make some sense. But to have this happen just to our town—*that's* what's so confusing, so damn frightening. We're too busy feeling like lepers to grasp the significance of what's happened to us."

"Wait, wait. You think . . . there'll be more of this?"

"I don't know!" His face glowed like a child's at Christmas. "But if there *is*, then we'll *know*."

"Know what?"

"Know *why.* Then the whole world will know."

She hugged her husband. "Do you know you sound half crazy?"

He laughed. "I can believe that."

"But what if it stays the same?"

"I don't know that either. But I hope it won't." He pursed his lips and corrected himself. "I pray it won't."

Far ahead their children were calling to them. They walked faster, turning their backs on the darkness that was stealing over the trees from the east.

327

Brad and Jim

Watchman, what of the night? Watchman, what of
  the night?
The watchman said, The morning cometh, and also
  the night.

—Isaiah 21:11–12

CHAPTER
25

"Ted Knotts asked me over for poker tonight."

Christine looked up. Her face was little more than a gaunt mask stretched over bone. Brad had finally made her go to the doctor, who could find no physical problem. He'd given her the card of a psychiatric therapist in Lansford, which she tossed into the gutter upon leaving the doctor's office.

"Did you hear me?" Brad asked. "I said I might play poker tonight."

"So what? Are you asking for permission or something?"

"Not really. I just thought you'd want to know."

"Well, I don't. Don't care."

His lips formed a thin line. "Fine. Then you won't miss me."

"No way." She didn't care anymore. Let him hit her, let him see how much good it would do. She was past fearing him now, having no room left for him. There was no fear left in her for anyone human. But there was hate.

She, who had once loved him mindlessly, possessively, had begun to hate him with an overwhelming intensity. He had kept her there in Merridale until inertia had claimed her.

She knew that she could not leave now, not ever, that she was there until she died. He had made her this way. It was his fault, his and the boy's. They had done other things to her too. To her body. Her hand went up to the wasted pits of her cheeks and above, to her eyes that had grown wide and large and luminous, her tangled hair, the pale temples where the muscles stiffened in constant tension, borne by the perpetual set of her jaw.

And her body, oh, her poor, poor body . . . gone beyond slenderness now to a wretched thinness, ribs easily visible, diaphragm slowly eroding into a hollow cave. Only the breasts remained in all their former fullness, absurdly huge on the withered body, as if refusing to surrender the last bastion of femininity, of motherhood.

It was a futile gesture on the body's part, for both sexuality and the maternal instinct had fled before the onslaught of mounting death-fear. She loathed her lover, hated her natural son. In her fantasies, she had gone a step beyond Medea.

"I'll probably be back around midnight," he said. Receiving no answer, he went down the hall into Wally's room. The boy was trying to teach Fluffy to sit up. Fluffy was uncooperative. "Hi, kiddo."

"Hi, Uncle Brad."

"Listen, I'm going out tonight, so I won't be able to tuck you in."

Wally's face fell. "Okay."

"Mommy can do it, can't she?"

"Sure. I guess."

Brad sat on the bed next to the boy. "Listen, kiddo," he said, "I know Mommy isn't . . . as much fun as she used to be. But I think she will be in time."

"She's just scared," Wally said. "She's still scared of all the dead people."

"Yeah, pal. I know she is."

"I'm not. Not anymore. Fluffy isn't either."

"I know you're not. You're a brave boy. But not everybody's as brave as you."

"*You* are."

"Well . . . I don't know."

332

"You think she really will?"

"Will what?"

"Get used to it?"

Brad sucked his lower lip. "Yeah. I think so."

"I don't. I don't think she ever will. She doesn't know any better."

"Yeah, Well, maybe she'll learn." He rubbed the little dog's ears. "Fluffy learned, right?"

"Right. Will you be back late?"

"Probably." The child's face contracted, as though he'd just tasted vinegar. "What's the matter?"

"Are you coming back?"

Brad's stomach tightened for a moment, as he realized the depth of affection that he had reached with the boy. "Of course. Sure I'm coming back. Did you think I wasn't?"

Wally spoke with the honesty of innocence. "If *I* went away, I don't think I'd come back. Not to Mommy. Not if I was you. And, and before, if I was *Mommy* I woulda gone away and not come back to *you*." The boy frowned. "Is that funny?"

"That's . . . kind of funny, yeah."

"It's like you and Mommy traded being nice. I wish you could both be nice at the same time."

He patted the boy's head, smoothing down the spot where an antenna of hair stuck up. "Well, maybe someday we will, huh? Give me a hug."

They had their usual Saturday night supper—a frozen pizza and canned fruit salad, a Coke for Wally, water for Chris, a beer for Brad. Christine served as though gauging the strength of the table, and did not speak throughout the meal. Afterward, when Wally was playing in his room, Brad and Christine cleaned up together.

"Look," he said, "do you want me not to go out tonight?"

"Since when has what I wanted ever stopped you?"

"I just asked. If you want me to stay home, I will."

She gave a short laugh. "It's too late, Brad. It's too late for little . . . uh . . . whaddyacallems, *gestures* on your part. You don't love me, you never *did* love me, so do me a favor and don't start to fuck with my head now, okay? I don't *care*

333

if you go out, I really don't. I don't care if you lose money, I don't care if you get laid, I don't care—''

"About a damn thing," he broke in. "You don't care about me or your son or even yourself anymore, do you?"

"You could've stopped it. You could've helped me—"

"By what, running away? I don't run anymore, Chris, even if I can afford to. I'm too *old* to run away. This is my town, my hometown, and I'm not leaving because of blue goblins."

"It would've been *better* someplace else, dammit!"

"No! It *wouldn't* have been! If there aren't any ghosts, you make your own!" He hurled the tea towel onto the counter with a wet slap. "Everywhere has ghosts. The only difference is we can *see* ours, and I'm not so sure that that's not good."

"*Good?* You think it's *good?*"

"*Yes.* Damn right I do. 'Thou art dust, and unto dust thou shalt return,' ever hear that? Well, sometimes we forget it. But if we *can't,* if we're not *allowed* to forget, then maybe we act differently, we live differently."

"I don't want to hear this." But as she turned he grasped her arm firmly and swung her around.

"But you will. Look at me. It took me a while, but it's finally started to sink in. I thought about it more and more until I asked myself, What do you leave? What will you leave behind? And I left nothing, *nothing.* So I decided to leave Wally."

Her face twisted. "*Wally?*"

"He's a bright kid, a nice kid, and the way I was treating him he was going to grow up to be a shit. So I stopped, for him and for me and for you, too. But when I stopped, by the time I came to my senses, you'd lost yours."

"You think I'm crazy?"

"I think you're confused—confused and scared."

"Scared, yeah. Oh, *hell* yeah! But not confused . . . and I haven't lost my fucking senses either. *You're* the crazy one!"

"Chris . . ." His hand went out to her in compassion, but she jerked away as though she'd seen violence in it.

"No! Just don't touch me!" she cried, and she ran to the

basement door, her shoes pounding down the steps to the rec room.

Brad gazed at the door, thinking that although it looked open, it had in truth been closed for a long time. He went into the living room then, where Wally was watching the Muppets, his puppy resting beside him, chin on paws. Leaning down, he kissed the boy's hair, then watched him watching television for a second before he turned and left the room, hearing a softly spoken something that might have been "Bye."

He drove to the poker game through the warmth of an early spring.

Alone in the basement, Christine's thoughts gnawed at her like a rat at an ear of corn:

Sonuvabitch. Sonuvabitch. He should talk, he should talk about Wally, he should talk after all he's said and done, calling me a whore, making my boy call me a whore, and hitting him, I know, I could see it, I could tell, and now he acts like I'm shit, like I'm nothing, like I'm a rotten fucking mother (MOTHERFUCKER!) because now he's nice, he's so goddamn nice, isn't he, buying the kid a fucking dog, a dog for crissake. Who needs a dog? Who the hell needs a goddamn dog?

She needed no drugs to feed her rage, no alcohol to muddy her mind or dull her edge of sanity. That edge was sharp, honed razor-thin by the powerful whetstone of fear. Her thoughts felt bright and crystalline, sane as sunlight, sensible as earth, clear as seawater. Sanity in a world of madness, that was her. Was it crazy to harm what was harming you? Was it lunacy to want to survive? Was it madness to even *kill* to keep from dying yourself?

He wants to hurt me. He wants to kill me. I'm dying now, falling away, and he still won't let me go. I'll hurt him. Yes. I'll hurt him.

It all seemed very logical. So she thought and thought about how to do it, and thought some more, sitting on the hard-cushioned couch in the half darkness, until her son called to her from the top of the stairs. "Mom?"

335

Wally.

"Mommy? The Muppets is over."

Leave Wally.

"Mommy?"

He wanted to leave Wally, that was what he said, wasn't it? Not leave, not go away, but leave him behind, leave him after, leave him to the world. Silly stupid thought, leave a little boy. Nothing else, he'd said, he would leave nothing else.

Only Wally. Only the boy.

"Mom, are you going to put me to bed?"

Oh, yes. Oh, yes. I'll put you to bed. To sleep. That'll hurt him. Then he'll have nothing to leave. He didn't want to leave, so he won't. Never leave. Never leave anything.

"Are you?"

Are you, Mom? "Yes," she answered, a hollow voice coming from a hollow under the house, "I'll put you to bed."

When she climbed the stairs to the kitchen, they did not seem as long and as steep as they had before, and when she reached their top, she was smiling.

CHAPTER
26

Hours later, midnight came. It was a new day, Quinquagesima, the last Sunday after Epiphany, the Sunday before Lent. It arrived in darkness, under an early March sky in which moon and stars were smothered by clouds, clouds that soon disgorged a cold, sheathing rain.

Just a few minutes after twelve, Brad Meyers left the poker game. He had won $9 by playing cautiously, getting out of seven-card with less than a pair or three-flush on the first three, and bluffing once or twice to keep himself unpredictable. He had had a good time, and was somewhat surprised by that fact, and relieved as well, relieved that he still *could* have a good time, that he remembered how to laugh. He thought that Wally had been partly responsible for that. The boy had helped to save him as well, Brad thought. *Had helped.* He still had had to do most of it himself. *You've got to want things. When you're sick, you've got to want yourself to get well.*

He hadn't wanted that for such a long time. He'd been content to be ill, festering in the jungle of sickness his mind had become. The confrontation with Jim Callendar had been the beginning. It hadn't been instantaneous, no miraculous epiphanic moment of truth like in the movies, but it had been the starting point, until now, a few months later, he felt cleansed at last, as if he'd thrown off something he'd been carrying for years. When he thought about what had happened to it, he felt that perhaps Callendar had picked it up, taken it on.

Brad shook his head, thinking about the man. They were two sides of the same coin, fighting their own demons in outwardly different but inwardly similar ways, bound up in each other and in that vast impenetrable webwork of destiny that included not only them, but Merridale, the living and the dead, Chris, Wally, Rorrie, Kriger, the world.

That was behind him now—if not his involvement in it, then at least his obsession with it. Let the Fates spin as they would. He wasn't going to second-guess them again. All he was going to do now was try to live without looking over his shoulder or counting his heartbeats. Maybe in time he could even love Christine and make her love him.

When he pulled off of Sundale Road into his driveway, he noticed the blue Pontiac parked across the street. He'd seen the car before, but only late at night, never during the day. Wondering to whom it belonged, he stepped a few feet closer to it until he heard the low hum of its engine. Then he smiled as the cold raindrops pattered on his hair.

Jesus Christ. Parkers. It was not the only answer, but it was the logical one, and he was tickled to think that kids still parked, even in chilly weather. He silently wished them luck, then turned back toward the house, thinking how the shadow that the latticed kitchen window made on the driveway looked like the web of a large spider. He stepped into the web, and opened the back door.

The kitchen light was on, the cellar door was closed. He heard no sound but the refrigerator rumbling in the corner, making an unseen dish, slightly unbalanced on its pile, rattle in response to the low vibration that the machine sent through the room. He went into the living room, where a low light was burning. It was empty, and he walked down the short hall into his and Christine's bedroom.

338

"Hey," he whispered. There was no answer. In the dark he approached the bed, feeling blindly for the familiar contours of Chris's body under the covers, but instead the bed was flat and smooth.

Bitch. Gone out. He could not help it. It was the first thing he could think of. In a way, he was angrier at the thought of her leaving Wally in the house alone than he was at the thought of her infidelity. He considered searching the rest of the house for her—after all, it was easier to imagine, wasn't it, that she had fallen asleep on the basement sofa than that she was out once more picking up men for a night away from Merridale's ghosts. But first he would check on Wally.

The door to the boy's room was ajar as always, the interior palely lit by the Mickey Mouse night-light. Brad edged the door open far enough to slip through, and walked softly over to the bed. Wally was there, his eyes closed, his mouth open a crack. His dark hair was plastered wetly to his forehead, and Brad thought it odd that he should be sweating with the house so cool. He pulled back the top quilt, hoping the boy didn't have a fever. Then a slight, high-pitched whine sounded in Brad's ears, and he thought it was Wally stirring in his sleep. He put a hand to the boy's head, pushed back the moist hairs, whispered, "G'night, kiddo," and went to the door. It was then that he saw the source of the whining.

Fluffy's head protruded through the doorway, his big dark eyes looking up at Brad for a moment in supplication before he came limping into the room, holding up a shattered left forepaw. "Jesus . . ." Brad knelt by the dog. "Jesus Christ, what happened, fella?" The paw, though not bleeding, was mangled and twisted into a flattened lump of fur, flesh, and bone. When Brad gingerly touched it, the dog yelped and jerked away. "There, there," he said, "it's okay, boy, it's okay," and he patted the animal to soothe it.

As his fingers ran the length of the dog's shivering body, they deposited something on its coat, dark streaks in sharp contrast to the fawn-brown hair.

It's bleeding. I didn't see it was bleeding.

He examined its head closely, but found no wound. Then he glanced at his right hand, and saw the red darkness.

339

Eat the flesh. Drink the blood.

Faces smeared crimson in firelight . . . the young boy torn from his father . . . too young for this. Oh, Christ, was anyone old enough for this? . . . *Drink it, you little bastard, drink it! . . . Talk, shit! Too late for talk!*

When was the last time he had had blood on his hands?

Ram his face in it! Now bite, bite on it, eat it, goddamn you, eat them! Chew it, make him chew it, now swallow, swallow, you bastard, and don't you puke it up, don't you puke it up or you'll eat that too!

He didn't understand. He didn't even understand what we were saying.

(then the boy's face came up, but instead of slanting eyes, the eyes were round, occidental, the face bore no scars, no blood coated the chin and mouth, and he was younger, years younger, and the only blood was the blood that hung wetly on his hair from some cut that the hair hid, some deep, horrible cut, and why wasn't his boy *breathing*, why was the only sound the dog's whining and his own lungs fluttering faster and faster and his cry that he had carried for all those years, all the way from that hot wet jungle to this cool dark bedroom, a cry of "Wally! Wally!" and that laugh, high and shrill, that laugh beneath him, under his feet, as though from hell itself, why all those sounds and no sound of his boy breathing?)

Bradley Meyers grabbed himself, left hand on right arm, right hand on left, and realized that he had lost his second son. He stood trembling for a minute, while the laughter under his feet came and went, as though joke after joke were being told silently in the basement. He knelt beside the bed then, and pulled back the sheet.

Wally lay there in his pajamas. Smears of blood obliterated the cartoon baseball players that decorated the pajama top, and a small but deep stain was on the pillow. The boy was on his side, his arms and legs positioned so that it looked as though he were sleeping. But when Brad lifted the limbs, they were unnaturally heavy, slightly stiff, with only a trace of warmth on the flesh. He moved his fingers to the neck to feel, beyond hope, for a pulse, but his motion made the head rock back with such pathetic fragility that a sob escaped him. He felt as if the stem of the loveliest rose in his garden had been snapped, the blossom tossed onto an ash heap. He had barely had time to nourish it, and it could have grown so beautifully, lived so long.

The laugh bubbled up again from below, and he pulled back the tears, his features broadening with the effort. He turned, still kneeling, and picked up the pup. Its whining ceased as he held it to him, warming it against his down-filled Army jacket. Its dead paw dangled helplessly, tapping his coat like some fleshy pendulum as he rose and walked into the kitchen, opened the basement door, looked down the stairs at the two lights, the white and the blue.

Now the laughter was louder, more mocking, nearly drowning out the sound of the rain that had begun without his noticing, and he could see Christine's feet and ankles, crossed jauntily on the hard, tile floor. From their position he knew that she was sitting on the couch. The white light from the lamp defined the outlines of her feet, the blue light gave them tone, atmosphere, the blue light of Wally's ghost, Wally's corpse-candle, the bright cerulean beam of Wally Grimes's raw evidence of mortality.

Brad moaned low, and the dog twisted in his arms, but he patted its head and it grew still. He descended the stairs, and let more and more of Christine's body come into view. Wally's form had been visible all along from the stair top—thin, stark, twisted, a blue, porcelain statue shattered from a fall . . .

Did I do it?

He banished the thought. He would not feel guilt now, he would not. Omission or commission (or *co*-commission, he thought dimly) he could deal with later. Not now. He held the dog tighter, and took the last step into the basement.

"Welcome home, Daddy," Christine giggled. "Welcome home." She gestured merrily to Wally's fallen figure. "Do you know that this is the first one of these fuckers I haven't been scared of?"

"What happened?" He had wanted his voice to sound stronger.

341

"He fell. Down the cellar stairs. *Rumpety-pumpety-pum!*"
She giggled again.

"Did you . . . push him?"

"Wouldn't you like to know?"

"I *have* to know. Did you?"

She leaned forward, elbows on knees, and looked at him intently. "So you'll know what to do?" she said slowly, sneeringly. "I'm not scared of you, you asshole bastard. Yes. I pushed him. I pushed him right down the old stairs, and then I came down them myself and watched him *leave*. You wanted to *leave* him? Well, *he's* the one who left. And it took him a long time too. I'd just finished tucking him in when you got here, when you pulled up from your night out with the boys." She grinned. "Have a good time? Win a dog? Win another little son of a bitch?" She cocked her head and shook it. "Mutt was harder than the kid. One good tramp and he was off. Couldn't find him anywhere. Didn't look hard. Watching *him* was easier." She gestured at the revenant. "It was just like a One Step photo—you know?—just . . . showed up. And he was dead." Her expression softened for a moment, her lower lip drooped, her jaw dropped slowly, as she looked at the residue of her son.

"The dog's crippled," Brad said. He took the dog and held it out for her to see. As she looked, her face was empty of emotion. It did not change until Brad grasped the animal's neck, let it hang unsupported, and twisted his arm once. With a furious snap, the neck broke, the animal voided itself, and Brad let it fall, silent and unmoving, to the tile floor, where its corporeal body occupied the same space as its master's less physical one.

"Some cripples can't be helped," Brad said, the strength in his voice returning in direct proportion to the look of shocked horror and sudden understanding on Christine's face. "It makes no sense for them to live."

Then he killed her.

He killed her out of rage and in fury and in sorrow. He killed her because he did not want her to see him cry. And when he had finished with the killing and the weeping and sat on the sofa feeling his tears dry and pass into the air, he

342

new that he had not been able to escape. But he could not weep for that, not for himself. Why weep for what had always been?

It had stayed within him, a cancer of the mind gone into only temporary remission, and now, with her act, with her pitiful, childish, helpless act of breaking the toy he loved most, it had returned, stronger than ever, to make him kill her. Even now he tried not to think about it, knowing that thoughts would do no good. It was down to actions now, following the scenario that had been so precisely laid out for him ten, twenty, thirty, years before, or earlier, when his head touched lamplight, gleaming from his mother's womb. *I tried. Oh, Jesus, I did try.*

Alternatives quickly dashed by. Tell the truth, the truth. But it was only *his* truth, and against it was balanced the truth of a dead woman and a dead child and a dead dog and a veteran of an insane war. And that veteran had a history of violent tendencies and was known in the past to have hit his wife and abused her son, and there had been drinking and who would believe it was any other way than what it looked? Who could persuade them? Would poor, blue Wally point an ethereal finger at the pale fragment of his mother positioned awkwardly half on, half off the couch? No. The dead come back, but not to speak, not to accuse.

Not specifically, anyway, he thought.

Escape? Impossible. He couldn't escape from himself, let alone a statewide search. Turn himself in? Give himself up? Why? They would only put him in a prison or a hospital, and the prison would not rehabilitate him, the hospital would not cure him.

Some cripples can't be helped. It makes no sense for them to live.

Death, then?

He paused. Unlike most men, he had seen enough death so that in a general sense it held no terror for him. But when he regarded the specifics of his own death, he hesitated. It was not the painful drifting away of life that he found unsettling, but rather the crossing over into another state of being. Had it not been for where he lived, he should have supposed that death was only the entryway to oblivion, but while the rest of the world had shown him death's face, Merridale had shown him that death also had a soul.

He shook his head, searching for an answer, finding it by remembering that it was not his choice, that he could only play out the remainder of the act, not write it.

So the options were closed. He could only toss the dice, spin the wheel, see what had been decided. The only thing he could not bear to do was wait. The *most* he could hope to do was to force fate's hand.

Then he thought of the car outside, the car sitting and purring and waiting in the cold, wet March darkness, waiting for him. The people inside were waiting for him too. All their lives they had been focused to this point, this spot, this hour. Their world was a giant funnel in which, no matter where they crawled on its surface, time pulled them inexorably down until they arrived here, on Sundale Road at 12:43 A.M. the precise moment at which Brad Meyers also reached the funnel's mouth.

He went upstairs to get his pistol and do what he would do.

The rain had stopped.

The boy and girl had moved once more to the front seat, tired and satisfied, so that their defenses were down when the man with the gun yanked open the door. Dave Boyer would have tumbled out had the man not caught him by the shoulder. "Just hold it steady," the man said, brandishing the pistol so they both could see it, "and don't be heroes."

Dave's breath caught in his throat, and his stomach twisted. The barrel of the gun was a black eye staring out of blackness, blackness that could suddenly explode into light and end light forever.

"I don't want to hurt either of you."

"What *do* you want?" asked Kim, her words bolder than she felt.

"Some help. You"—he pointed at Kim—"get out of the car and come inside with me." The girl hesitated. "I'm not going to hurt you. And I'm not going to rape you either. But

344

need"—the man paused, then grinned as though what he said was absurd—"a hostage."

"Okay, look," Dave said, unable to stop his voice from shaking, "what you need is help, okay? Now, why don't you put the gun down and—"

"Kid, don't be an asshole. You have no idea what you're doing. Now you just get your car in gear and drive down to the police station and tell them to hurry over. Think you can handle that? It's that house right there, and my name is Brad Meyers."

Dave shook his head. "Why? What's all this about?"

"It's about endings. Confrontations. Peace and freedom. Life and death."

The boy turned to Kim and whispered, "He's crazy. . . . I can't leave you here."

"You've got to."

"Enough!" Brad said, rapping the barrel of the pistol against Dave's arm. "No discussions. Now *move!*"

"I'll be all right," whispered Kim.

She opened the door and got out slowly. Brad came around the car and took her by the arm. He spoke to Dave through the open door. "You can tell them that I killed the woman I'm living with . . . and her son. They'll like to hear that."

Both Kim and Dave turned pale, and the girl stumbled, her legs suddenly weak. "I'm not going to kill *you*," said Brad.

"What do you want?" Brad looked quizzically at the boy. "Demands?"

"Demands?" asked Brad.

"You said 'hostage.' What'll I tell them? What are your demands?"

Brad licked his lips. "I told you. Peace and freedom. Life and death. Confrontation. Ending."

"But—"

"*I* know what I want. You bring them. I'll get it. Now go." Brad slammed the car door and gave the side a sharp kick. With a harsh, urgent grinding, the boy engaged the gears and drove off. Brad watched the taillights until they disappeared around a bend, and started to lead the girl back into the house. "What's your name?"

"Kim. Kim Bailey." Alone with the man, Kim felt helpless, insignificant. "Why are you doing this?" she cried in pinched tones.

Brad heard the fear and hated it. He didn't want her to be scared, only to obey. "I'm doing it because I have to. Now don't be frightened. I told you you wouldn't be hurt. I'm not after *your* death, don't you see that? Just do what I tell you and you'll be all right."

They entered the house, and Brad told the girl to follow him while he locked all the doors and windows and drew the curtains. Over the large living-room window that fronted Sundale Road, he drew only the sheers, then turned on the outside lights. "Help me," he said, grabbing an arm of the sofa. Together, he and Kim swiveled it so that it faced the window. Then he turned off the living-room lights.

The room was dimly lit from the outer radiance spilling in through the sheers, but to observers on the lawn outside, the contents of the room would be in darkness. The lawn was well illuminated, and anyone approaching the house from the front would be hazily visible to Brad and Kim. They sat in silence, Brad watching the window casually, the gun held loosely in his lap. Kim was far more nervous, glancing into the many shadows the half-darkened room held.

Finally she had to ask. "Where . . . are they?"

He turned toward her. "Not here. The boy is in his room; my . . . the woman's downstairs in the basement."

"Is that where—"

"They both died downstairs. *Those* are downstairs." He sighed. "I guess I should be down there too. Finish it down there with them. One big happy family." His voice broke, and he cleared his throat angrily. "No more questions, all right? I've got a few things to think about right now."

He had nothing to think about. He was beyond thinking.

CHAPTER
27

The morning was going well for Clyde Thornton. He had left the Lansford Holiday Inn East bar with June Sibley, an out-of-town vocalist who had recognized him and accepted his offer of a drink. When he invited her on a tour of Merridale, she agreed with a mixture of excitement and fear he had seen before in a dozen other bars, on a dozen other pretty faces. I want to see, it said. Show me. Take me to the funhouse, into the dark where the boogeymen jump out and go boo and scare me. And then you can hold me tight. Hold me very tight.

Show me the dead men so I can feel alive.

The drive through Merridale worked as Thornton had wished, a classic aphrodisiac, and it was not long before he was licking drops of Drambuie off her pale nipples as she giggled and moaned on the floor of Ted Bashore's den. They moved their activities to the king-sized Beautyrest in Thornton's bedroom, and afterward he lay exhausted, his head on the smooth flatness of her stomach. A short time later he was demonstrating Ted Bashore's in-bed sound system to the girl, turning on, among other things, the Bearcat Scanner. Then, at 1:05 in the morning, Clyde Thornton heard the bulletin on the police band.

"What's all that mean?" June Sibley asked, letting her hand trail down over Clyde Thornton's bare back.

"Shh. Wait a minute."

She gave a small, pouting frown at the rebuff, then lay back listening to the static-filled voice that she did not understand.

Thornton's face brightened as she watched. "Holy shit," he whispered.

"What?"

"Seems one of our townsfolk just kidnapped a girl and maybe killed his family to boot."

"You're joking."

"Nope. Feel like a little excitement? A little *more* excitement, that is?"

"Like what?"

"You'll see." He leaned over and kissed her right nipple. "Get dressed."

June and Thornton arrived at Sundale Road twenty minutes after they got out of bed. The girl had protested on the way. "I don't think I want to do this. I mean, what's the point?"

"Maybe I can help. Hell, everybody knows me. And everybody trusts me too." Thornton smiled smugly. It was silly, he knew. He couldn't hope to impress her any more than he already had. But what the hell, it would be something different, something on which to try out his newfound powers. He'd felt so damn confident lately, so sure of himself and his fate. If he couldn't talk this screwball into giving himself up, at least he could put on a helluva show.

Frank Kaylor and three of his officers were already there, their two police cars idling, flashers turning in offbeat red rhythms. "Hello, Frank," called Thornton. "What's the story?"

Kaylor glowered at the words. "What are you doing here, Dr. Thornton?"

"Heard the bulletin on my scanner. Thought I'd come see if I could help."

"Thanks, but I think not. State Police are on their way."

348

"Well, we'll see." Thornton gestured toward the house. "Who is it?"

"Guy named Brad Meyers."

"And?" There was no answer. "Don't tell me I'm going to have to read about this in the papers, Frank."

"Look, *Thornton*, we've got a real problem here, okay?"

"And that's why I'm here," he said firmly. "Now, what the hell's happened?" Kaylor looked away. "Don't make me remind you, Frank, that I've got jurisdiction from the government, state and federal. In other words, I outrank you."

"Not in criminal matters."

"Let's not fuck around with details, huh? Merridale is still an official disaster area, and I'm in charge. Now, what happened?"

Kaylor's shoulders slumped, and he told Thornton, not because he outranked him, but because it was easier than arguing further. "Meyers grabbed a girl. He's got her in there with a gun. Told the kid the girl was with that he killed the woman he's living with and her son, but we don't know if that's true."

"Talk to him at all?"

"Yeah."

"And?"

"And nothing. He doesn't talk back."

"Are you sure he's in there?"

"Would you like to go in and check?"

"Funny." Thornton smirked. "Where's your bullhorn?"

"Uh-unh."

"Let me have the bullhorn, Frank. You're *voted* into office, you know."

Kaylor shook his head, then reached in through his car window. "Here," he said, handing the bullhorn to Thornton. "Maybe Meyers can aim at the sound. One thing understood, though"—and he glanced around to take in his officers and June Sibley—"you're not my responsibility. You want to play, play at your own risk."

"If I play, I'll win. Don't worry about me, son." Thornton put an arm around June's shoulders. "Maybe you'd better get behind a car in case this clown starts shooting."

"Jesus," Kaylor muttered.

"What the fuck is this guy doing, Chief?" Del Franklin whispered.

"Playing cops and robbers," answered Kaylor, loud enough for Thornton to hear.

Thornton flared. "Goddammit! Don't you forget who I am!"

"*Who?*"

"I'm a social fucking psychologist, pal! I know about stresses, I know what drives people to things like this! Who the hell were you gonna let use this bullhorn, some state cop with a B.S. in fingerprinting? Or were *you* gonna try it again? Christ, you can't even find guys who kill old ladies! Now just shut up and let me work!"

Kaylor turned away fiercely, stepping behind the police car with his men. In a moment the girl joined them, her face white. Kaylor smiled a cold smile. "Old friend of yours?"

She shook her head quickly, nervously. "We just met tonight."

"Hell of a first date," said Kaylor, and his men nodded. "Knows how to show a girl a real good time."

"Yeah, a real lady-killer."

Clyde Thornton heard, and laughed inside. Then he walked away from the shelter of the cars, into the swath of light that swept the wet front lawn, and raised the bullhorn to his mouth. "Hello, Brad," he called. "This is Clyde Thornton speaking. You may know me. I'm the fella the government sent here [make it folksy, relaxed] to try to help you folks out. You know, what's been happening here has put all of us under a real strain. It's been rough for everybody. Now, some people react in different ways, and what you've done, and we're not really *sure* what you've done, is just one of those ways. Now, I *am* a trained psychologist . . ."

"He may be a psychologist," whispered Mike Gifford, "but he sure as shit don't know Brad Meyers."

". . . and I'm used to working with people and talking with people who are under the same kind of stress you're under. I'd like to talk to *you*, Brad. I hope you'd like to talk to me." He let five seconds pass. "Would you?"

350

There was no sound from the house, no movement.

"All right, Brad. I understand. Maybe you don't want to talk in front of the other people here. I can understand that. What if it was just you and me? What if I came in?"

"Aw, shit," growled Kaylor. "Thornton!"

Clyde Thornton turned, his face red. "Shut *up!* I know what I'm doing. I taught a seminar in this."

"A seminar. Sweet jumpin' Jesus."

"I saw this on TV," June Sibley said. "He'll go in there and get the guy to let the girl go and stay in himself. Oh, my God, he's so brave."

"Oh, my ass. He's so *stupid*," Del Franklin said.

They watched as Thornton moved closer to the house. "Chief, the asshole is really gonna *do* it."

"No he's *not*." Kaylor came out of his crouch and started walking into the light, toward Thornton, who heard the footsteps and turned.

"What are you *doing?*"

"You're not going in there," said Kaylor, advancing.

Thornton hesitated for only a moment, then turned back toward the house and ran. "Open the door!" he cried. "I'm coming in!"

Kaylor stopped, shocked into immobility, expecting any second to hear a burst of gunfire and see Thornton fall back stiffly. But instead he heard only Thornton's feet slapping toward the front door, the click as an unseen hand turned the knob, a hollow scraping as the door left its frame, and its final slam as it closed behind the man. As if in a dream, Kaylor's legs moved once more, taking him slowly toward that door.

"Far enough." The house amplified the voice. It was a new voice, cold, stern, Brad Meyers's voice, and hearing it made Kaylor realize how vulnerable he was. He brought his arms slowly out from his body, turned around, and walked, neither slow nor fast, back to the knot of people crouching dry-mouthed behind the cars.

"He's crazy," he said vacantly when he joined them. "They're *both* crazy."

Inside the house, Clyde Thornton stood, his back to the

351

door, wishing he could stop shaking, thinking, I showed him, I showed him, he couldn't stop me. I showed him.

Then he saw the gun that Brad Meyers, who had moved immediately to the window after opening and closing the door for Thornton, now held on him. "Take off your jacket. Slowly," Meyers said, and Thornton obeyed. "Throw it on the floor. Now lean against the wall. Put your feet apart. Okay." Brad patted him down clumsily, then turned his back on him and went back to the couch. "Sit down," he said, pointing to a chair a few feet from the couch. Thornton sat. "Why did you do that? Run in here like that?"

Thornton shrugged. "I don't know. I just did it."

"Weren't you afraid I'd shoot you?"

"No. Not then."

"Now?"

"No. Should I be?"

"Only if you try to take the gun away."

"Why don't you let the girl go?"

"No."

Thornton turned to the girl. "Are you all right?"

"Yes."

"I'm not going to hurt her."

"What's this all about, Brad?"

Brad didn't answer.

"Why did you do this?"

"Why did you run in here?"

"Did you really kill two people in here?"

Brad nodded.

"Why?" asked Thornton.

"Why did you run in here?"

"That how it's going to work? Every time I ask you a question you ask me one?"

"Is it?"

"Why did you let me in?"

Brad ignored the question.

"Let the girl go. You want a hostage, I'll stay with you."

"She stays."

"Why?"

352

"She's supposed to. That's the way it is. That's the scenario. I'm not going to hurt her."

"Will you show me the people you killed?"

"You can't help them."

"Can I help you?"

"You can't help me."

"You must want something."

"This. This is what I want."

"Will you let me go if I want to leave?"

"Yes."

"I'd rather stay here and talk to you."

"Then stay."

"This can't last forever, you know."

"I know." Brad turned his gaze from the window, looked at Thornton for a long time. "You want to see them? Chris and Wally?"

"If you want to show me."

"Sure." He nodded wearily. "We'll all go." He stood up and led the way out of the living room, looking over his shoulder to make certain they were following. He stopped at the door of Wally's room. "In there."

"I don't want to look," Kim said.

"You don't have to," Brad assured her. He gestured with his head, and Thornton entered the bedroom. In the glow of the night-light he saw the mound under the covers, the bloodstained head and face. He pulled the blankets back and felt for a pulse, but the skin was nearly cold, the joints already starting to stiffen, so he drew the sheet up over the head. "No," Brad said from the doorway. "Leave it like it was. He gets too sweaty that way."

Thornton shivered and tugged the sheet back. "What about the woman?"

"Downstairs." The three of them made their way back through the house to the kitchen, where Brad paused at the basement door and turned to Kim. "You'll have to come down with us. I can't leave you up here alone." He turned his face toward the front of the house. "They won't come in. They won't know we're down there. They don't know *where* we are." They started down the steps, Brad bringing up the rear.

Thornton, leading, was the first to see, lying in a puddle of its own urine, the dog mingled with the ghost of the little boy, like a ghoul's parody of a church calendar scene. The physical body of the woman was next. Its back was to Thornton, its face to the bottom of the couch against which it lay. And then he saw its shade still sprawled on the couch where it had come into being. First were the naked blue legs, splayed to reveal the dark pubis. As he descended farther, the flat, emaciated stomach came into view, then the large breasts, ungainly on the cadaverous frame (those breasts, where . . .), the neck a darker blue than the blue of the spirit-light, and the face, tongue puffy, eyes larger than life, the face that seemed so *familiar* that he gasped, seeing Marie Snyder's strangled countenance blending with the pouting, childlike face of the Merridale girl he had spent a night with long months ago.

(Had he said Chris? Oh, had it been Christine, her name?)

"Oh . . . Christine?"

He did not know he had said it, had only heard it inside his head. But it had escaped his lips, not so imperceptibly that Brad Meyers did not hear.

"*What?*"

Thornton turned, his face a red mask of guilt as he considered his nightmare—the husband of a woman he had fucked standing above him with a gun. All his godlike self-confidence suddenly vanished, and his bladder released a warm trickle of urine.

Brad pushed the girl roughly down the stairs into the basement, forcing Thornton across the floor, where the corpse tripped him so that he fell backward onto the couch. He yelped, and staggered to his feet. "You *know* her," Brad snarled.

"No . . . no, I don't—"

"You *recognized* her, didn't you?"

"N-no . . ."

"Recognized her—even now." Something possessed Brad Meyers. The skin was pulled tautly over his face so that the veins in the temples, throbbing rapidly, were easily visible. His eyes seemed teary, awash with moisture, and even the

354

hairs of his beard seemed to have a demonic life of their own, curling like hundreds of razor-thin worms. "Where did you meet her?"

Thornton could only moan.

"*Where?*" Brad cried, thrusting his gun at Thornton like a living extension of hate.

"The Holiday!" Thornton babbled instantly, too terrified to lie. "The Holiday Inn! She . . . she was in the bar—"

"How was she?"

"I—"

"*Tell* me."

"She . . . she . . . she was fine." Thornton was crying.

"Please . . ." It was Kim, who had started crying as well.

"You're not in this," Brad told her. "You're not in this part."

"Let me go," Thornton pleaded. "I'll . . . I'll give you money. . . . I've got lots of money."

"I'll let you go. Once you show me how you did it."

"What?"

"With Chris." He jerked his head to the apparition on the couch. "The position's right—legs spread, waiting just for you. Let me see."

Thornton coughed up bile, spat it away. "You'll let me go?"

"I'll let you go. Now show me. Show me, lover."

"I . . . I can't."

"Get on board, little children. Now."

His body racked with sobs, Clyde Thornton staggered to the couch, put one hand on its back, the other on its seat, and held himself suspended over Christine Grimes's glowing ghost. His eyes were pressed shut, but the tears ran from them.

"Closer. Get closer," said Brad, pushing Thornton's buttocks inward with his foot. Thornton grunted in pain as Brad moved to the side of the couch.

"Let me go. You said you'd let me go."

"Open your eyes. Look at her."

Thornton did, and his sobs turned into a convulsive gagging.

"*Keep* them open." Brad walked behind Thornton again, put the gun barrel an inch from the base of his skull, and pulled the trigger. The gun shrieked, Thornton's flesh parted, teeth and red debris spattered the couch. The corpse fell as though struck with a sledgehammer, yet remained where it had been, a naked man with an eternally exploding head, locked in passionless embrace with a strangled lover.

"I let you go," said Brad. "I let you go."

He wondered about the screaming until he remembered the girl. Kim was standing against the wall, her face turned away, her hands over her ears. He stuck the pistol into his belt, grasped her shoulders gently. "Hey, hey . . ."

Out of her screams came a frenzied, "Noooo . . ."

"Stop, stop, it's all right, I won't hurt you, I won't. . . . Between him and me, that's all. Be quiet, please."

Fear of him stilled her, but she kept crying. He turned her around, and she looked straight at him so that she would not have to see what he'd done.

"I'm sorry you saw that," he said. "Not sorry I did it, but that you saw."

Looking at him, she wondered how his face could be so suddenly sad, so tragically tender, like an avenging angel who, despite its destructiveness, is always and ever holy. In that second she felt safe, thinking how absurd it was to feel safe in the hands of a maniac.

"Hey! In there!" Frank Kaylor's urgent voice, amplified by the bullhorn, found them in the cellar. "Talk damn fast or we're coming in! What happened in there?"

"Come on, fast!" Brad said, drawing his gun with his right hand, taking Kim's hand in his left, and running up the stairs, through the kitchen, into the living room, where he grasped a window sash through a handful of curtains and pushed it up. "Stay where you are!" he cried, his head sheltered by the wall. "Thornton's dead! The girl's all right!"

There was a long silence from outside. "What do you want?"

Brad called back. "I'm getting what I want."

"Jesus," said Mike Gifford. "What's he doing to that girl?"

Kaylor held up the bullhorn. "We want to see the girl."

"No."

356

"We heard the shot; we can't believe she's okay otherwise. Show us or we come in."

Brad turned to Kim, who was sitting once more on the couch. "Go to the window, pull back the curtain, and wave. Make sure they see you. . . . All right. That's enough. Sit down." Leaving the window open, Brad sat next to Kim in the same position they'd held before.

Another five minutes passed before Kim gathered the courage to ask, "How much longer?"

"I'm not sure."

She paused again. "What are you waiting for?"

"I'm not sure of that either. But it'll come."

He was right. It had in fact just awakened.

CHAPTER
28

"Did you hear that?" Alice Meadows pushed herself up on one elbow and looked toward Jim in the darkness.

"Yes." Although he had been sleeping, his voice was clear, alert, as though he'd been waiting to be awakened.

"What was it?" she wondered aloud.

"A gunshot. Inside a house." He got out of the bed and looked out the window. "Up the road. There are police flashers."

"At which house?" She knew.

"Meyers. I think Meyers." Jim gave a deep sigh as he turned from the window.

I'm in a play, Alice thought. A three-act, maybe four-act, tragedy. And now it ends. Now it ends. She felt relieved, grateful, frightened of what would happen as well as of her own awareness that the time was here. "You'll go up," she said.

"Yes." He didn't move.

"Are you scared?"

"Yes. Still."

"I don't think you will be."

Jim turned the bedside lamp on and they both closed their eyes for a second against the sudden light. "How can I be sure it's him? It could have been a car backfiring, an accident."

"You know it's him. He's been a bomb waiting to explode."

Jim stood naked, his eyes slowly opening from slits as he grew used to the light.

"You'll go up." Was she acting now, playing the part she felt she should? She thought perhaps she was, but if she did not, he might come back to bed, close his eyes, and sleep through the chance that would free him, and yes, free her from him, break her last link with this town of the dead. "I'll go with you."

They got dressed, she in sweater and slacks, he in dark jeans and a black turtleneck, listening to the faraway, indistinct voice on the bullhorn that had spoken to them earlier in dreams. "Do you want to take a gun?" she asked him.

He thought of the only pistol he had, a small .22 with an opalescent grip, a ladies' gun to startle muggers, to spook burglars. It was not a weapon with which to war with nightmares. Or, he thought, with yourself. "No."

"You might need it."

"No."

They left the house, leaving all the lights off, and walked up Sundale Road. She took his hand, and though it was warm with perspiration, his tread was growing more firm as they neared the flashing lights. The small group behind the parked cars tensed when they noticed Jim and Alice, then relaxed when they saw no menace in their features, only what they read as a bland curiosity.

"Get back behind here," Kaylor told them, and they joined him.

"What's going on, Chief?" Jim asked. "We heard some noises, thought maybe there was an accident."

"No accident. And the best thing you can do is go back to your house, Mr. Callendar."

"Why?"

"It's Brad Meyers. Grabbed a girl, maybe killed his woman and her kid, and for sure killed Clyde Thornton."

"Brad Meyers . . . I know him."

360

"Doesn't matter if you do or not. I want you to go back to your house. We're just gonna sit tight until the state troopers come, and I'm not getting anyone else killed."

"Well, mightn't he escape out the back?"

"Rankin's back there. Besides, he could've escaped before. Doesn't want to."

"What *does* he want?"

"If I knew that, I'd be on my way to get it for him so I could get that girl out of there. Now go home, Mr. Callendar. Please."

"All right." Jim nodded meekly. "All right." He took Alice's hand, turned, and started walking back down the road.

"Maybe he's right," said Alice. "You'd only get killed too." But inside her chest was a feeling of deep emptiness, of chances lost.

Jim stopped and looked at her. "We're only leaving so we can go back behind the house." He moved on.

"But Bob Rankin—"

"We know Bob. Maybe he'll help us."

"What if he doesn't?"

Jim would not consider it. He and Alice walked until they reached their driveway, then crossed the road and went back the way they had come, through the silent backyards of their sleeping or departed or frightened neighbors.

They saw Bob Rankin at the edge of Brad Meyers's yard, hunkered down on the sodden, brown patch of grass and weed that was neither lawn nor field. He straightened up when he saw them and called softly, "Who's there?"

"It's Alice, Bob . . . and Jim." She brought her hand up as the flashlight's beam struck her.

"Alice . . . what are you doing here?"

"Jim . . ." She turned and looked at the man beside her. His face was grim, his expression resolute.

"I want to go in," he finished for her. "I want to stop Meyers, get the girl out."

They couldn't see Rankin's face, but there was no mistaking the disbelief in his voice. "Sure you do." He half laughed. "We *all* do, brother. But we don't want to get killed either."

361

"It doesn't matter to me. That's why I can do it where you can't."

"Uh-unh. No way. Even if you don't give a shit about yourself, what about the girl?"

"He won't kill the girl. He needs her. And if he's really crazy, he'll kill her anyway."

"I said no."

"What if I go in?" Jim said calmly. "What if I go in right now?"

"I'll stop you."

"Then stop me." He walked purposefully away from Rankin toward the darkness of the house. Neither he nor Alice spoke. The only sound was the sweep of leather against gunmetal as Rankin's police special left its holster, the sharp click of the hammer retracting, the ghostly whisper of cloth rubbing cloth as the gun came up.

But there was no blast of gunfire. There were only Jim's soft footfalls through the wet grass until he was lost to their sight in the blackness.

Rankin's arm came down, and he looked to where Alice stood. "I didn't see him. He sneaked past me."

Alice said nothing.

"I'm not going in after him."

"He doesn't expect you to. He doesn't want you to." She touched his shoulder. "Thank you, Bob."

"Does he have a gun?"

"No."

"Oh, shit." He shook his head. "I didn't see him. I didn't talk to you at all."

"Thank you."

"Get away from here, Alice. Just get the hell out."

"He has to do it, Bob."

"Yeah. Sure." And as Alice left, Rankin thought, and if that girl gets killed . . . what am I going to have to do?

Within Brad Meyers's brain something clicked, as subtle yet as certain as a rheostat. There was someone outside trying to get in. "Did you hear anything?" he asked the girl.

"No."

He sat for a moment longer until he was sure. Then he stood up. "Come with me. Stay behind me and walk quietly." They moved swiftly through the dining room into the kitchen, where Brad pulled back a curtain and saw against the night a deeper darkness that was creeping stealthily toward the back door.

"Who . . . who is it?" she whispered.

"Shh." He tiptoed to the door, unlocked it, and slipped back across the kitchen next to the refrigerator. "Stand in there," he said, pushing her gently in the direction of the dining room, listening to her move stumblingly in the black. "There. That's it. Stay behind the wall." Then he set his left hand on the refrigerator door, and held the gun in two fingers of his right hand while he blew on his right palm to dry it. A turn of the wrist, and the pistol nestled in his hand once more. He took a deep breath, let half of it out, and kept the remainder in his lungs. It steadied him, so that when the door drifted open he did not flinch or gasp or do anything to draw the attention of whoever stood on the threshold.

The intruder entered, feet pressing gingerly on the floorboards, hesitant to put his full weight on them for fear of a betraying squeal of joists. The indistinct sounds of night grew louder in Brad's ears, then died away as the door closed. Whoever it was had come inside. Now. Before he was lost in darkness. Now was the time.

Brad swung the refrigerator door open. As bottles and jars rattled against the metal and plastic of the racks, a cold light rushed out of the machine, bathing the doorway and the man who stood there in a white radiance. The gun came up, the girl inhaled sharply, the stranger's eyes widened in surprise, then hardened in expectation of the bullet.

"*You*," Brad said, sighting down the short barrel directly into Jim Callendar's face. "*You*," he repeated, his voice shaking. "Oh, no, no, this isn't right. I haven't been waiting for *you*. It was *over* between us. Finished."

"Not yet." Jim's voice trembled too, but not from fear.

"What do you want?"

"The same thing you do. You said once that we were

bound. I thought that maybe you were right. But I didn't know for sure."

"And now?"

"Now I know."

"You're wrong. *I* was wrong. Not you. Not tonight."

"It's not night." Jim smiled. "It's morning."

Brad's head was throbbing. A helmet of steel sat there, tightening, pressing his skull inward. "I'll kill you. That ends it."

"It doesn't matter if you do."

"Why? Why not?" He squinted against the pain.

"Because of how I feel. How I feel right now."

"How *do* you feel?"

"Free. Killing me won't end it."

"It will," Brad said through gritted teeth.

"No. Don't deny me. You can't deny your face in the mirror."

Brad breathed again, exhaled, held, steadied. "I can *break* the mirror," he whispered as he pointed the gun at Jim Callendar's face, a face that looked exactly like his own, and pulled the trigger.

The hammer struck the cartridge, and Brad Meyers saw the flame burst from the end of the barrel, saw the bullet spin through the air, saw it strike the hollow just beneath the nose, saw the face spring apart, leap into shreds of Jim Callendar's fair skin, Bradley Meyers's brittle bone, Bradley Callendar's blood raining in homey kitchen, James Meyers's brains mingling gray snow with red rain.

Bradley Meyers William Wilson James Callendar and in killing me see how thou hast killed thyself. . . .

CHAPTER
29

The rain and snow stopped falling.
The body lay limp on the floor.
The blue spirit hovered erect.
Moved.
Bore clothes. Hair. Flesh. And blueness departed.
Bradley Meyers James Callendar returned from the dead.
No.
James Callendar.
"Jim . . . "
Though he had seen all, he had not heard the shot.
He had not heard the shot.
He stood stupidly, holding the gun in front of him. Empty, was his first thought. Had he been less distraught, less affected by Jim Callendar's appearance in his kitchen and by his calm, sure, apostolic manner, he would have remembered that he had only fired one shot. But he did not, *could* not remember.

"You see?" Jim Callendar said. "You see?"
Empty.
The gun was already up, pointing at Jim Callendar's face.

It took Brad only a second to turn, place the gun on top of the refrigerator, and with the same hand grab one of the long kitchen knives that hung in the wall rack. Knife extended, he rushed at Jim.

And the pistol on the refrigerator fired.

The recoil threw the unheld gun backward, where it struck the wall and clattered down the cooling coils. But the bullet itself flew laser-straight into Brad Meyers's right temple, adding to his momentum so that it was with even greater force that he plunged the knife into Jim Callendar's abdomen.

The two men fell as one against the kitchen door. Jim scarcely felt Brad's weight atop him, or the pressure that weight put on the knife that pierced him. He did not hear Kim Bailey run screaming to the front door or the heavy booted footsteps only seconds afterward. All he was aware of was the bearded cheek touching his face, and the hand on his chest, a hand whose fingers twitched lightly, like thin branches in a gentle breeze. He held the hand in his own until the movement finally ceased, then closed his eyes, feeling tired, cold, happy to rest, eager to be warm again.

CHAPTER
30

Mike Gifford, Bob Rankin, and Chief Kaylor sat together in the Merridale police station drinking coffee and waiting for dawn. The other men, called from their beds, had returned to them. Gifford shook his head. "Hate to be the real-estate agent that's got to sell *that* house." Kaylor chuckled grimly. Bob Rankin forced a weak smile.

"Goddamn slaughterhouse, that's for sure," agreed Kaylor.

"You believe what that trooper said though? About hang-fire?" Gifford's young face was lined with doubt.

"From what the girl said happened, I don't know what else it could've been," Kaylor answered. "The gun behind the refrigerator supports it."

Gifford took another sip from his Penn State mug. "Never heard of that. Oh, I mean I've *heard* of it, but just never heard of it actually happening before."

"I saw it once," said Rankin quietly. "At the academy. We were slowfiring .38's on the range, and the guy on the line next to me—his gun didn't fire. So right away he starts to open the chamber and a sergeant yells at him, 'Put that gun *up!*' loud as he can. The kid does, and bam. The bullet the firing pin had struck six, seven seconds earlier finally goes off. 'That's called hangfire, asshole,' the sergeant says, 'and it happens one time in ten thousand, but that time it could've blown your fucking foot off.' Well, it made an impression on me. I've had a lot of misfires over the years, but I just hold that bitch out and count to fifteen, just like that sergeant said.''

"Sure as shit what Meyers should've done," Gifford said, then paused. "On second thought, maybe not. He got what he deserved. Couldn't believe his face. Like a fucking maniac. How'd you like to have *that* where you cook your dinner? And down in the cellar? Thornton and that Grimes woman? Jesus, he was a psycho all right. Thank God he didn't get the chance to do anything to the girl. In a way it's kind of lucky that Callendar got in."

"I should've seen him," Rankin said. "He shouldn't have gotten past me."

"No," Kaylor agreed, peering at Rankin over the edge of his cup. "He shouldn't have."

"What the hell, it worked out." Gifford smiled. "The girl's safe, and it looks like Callendar'll pull through. And Meyers is dead. That alone has got to cheer you up some."

Kaylor stood quickly. "Get this shit cleaned up. And get your feet off the desk. If anyone wants me, I'll be at home."

"Holy shit, Bob," Gifford said when Kaylor had gone. "What's with him?"

"I don't think he liked what you said. About Meyers."

"Well, Jesus H. Christ, I'm sorry, but anybody who did what that son of a bitch did doesn't deserve to live."

"Maybe not. But you don't want to get callous about it. Or worse, happy about it."

"I was only joking."

Rankin moved to the window. "Some joke, Frank," he said, staring at the blueness starting to fade at the approach of dawn. "Just look at it. It's all really some joke."

Ash Wednesday

Fred Hibbs awoke just before dawn, and he didn't know why.

He knew it was early from his watch, not from any brightening of sky through a window, for his cell had no window. He usually slept soundly until 7:00, when the bells would ring twenty minutes before breakfast, and he would rise, scratching and moaning, eventually splash some water in his face, use the toilet, throw on his drab gray clothes, and wait for them to unlock his cell, so he could march down to the mess hall for breakfast.

He lay there in the darkness wondering what they'd have today. Eggs, he hoped. Not that the eggs were all that great—they were those powdered things, and they used too much water to cook them. But along with the eggs they always had bacon, thick, greasy slices of it that crisped and hardened at the edges, so juicy it was more like ham. Fred thought maybe they got a good price on the stuff from a local farmer.

Then it struck him that there was something special about today, and he immediately wondered if there would be any improvement in the mess-hall cuisine as a result. But when he remembered he sighed. It was Ash Wednesday, that was all. Back in Merridale he probably wouldn't even have realized it. But here, with all the PR's and dagos, it was impossible to ignore. All they were talking about in the rec hall the day before was which priest would show up to put the ashes on the foreheads. Father Bill from St. Peter's was the favorite at 5–2.

Fred smiled. If he'd known what prison in Lansford had been like, he'd have beaten up Eddie Karl a long time ago. Those prison movies were just bullshit. Oh, sure, maybe if you were a good-looking nineteen-year-old you were in for some trouble, but Fred had made buddies, stayed out of the mean guys' way, and got along with the guards, who were really pretty nice if you didn't hassle them. The bed was soft enough, the food was edible and plentiful, and there were magazines to look at, TV to watch from 7:00 to lights out.

And best of all, thought Fred Hibbs, there were no ghosts. On the tail of that thought he rolled over, deciding to go back to sleep.

But at that moment, a light began to reach through the thin membrane of his eyelids, making him wonder, Guard? Guard with a flashlight? Why?

He opened his eyes and saw the shape taking form in the opposite corner of his cell, directly under the water pipe that cut through each cubicle in the cellblock. It grew slowly into existence, a foot from the floor, a steadily gleaming wraith hanging naked from an unseen rope, shedding a pale light over the staring Fred Hibbs.

The light was blue.

Fred screamed, but the vision remained, its eyes opened wide, as in watching. Fred screamed again, and again, and again.

And soon, all the others were screaming as well.

THE BEST IN HORROR

RAMSEY CAMPBELL

GRAHAM MASTERTON

THE BEST IN SUSPENSE